D0982567

JESUS on HORSEBACK

Books by John Reese

SURE SHOT SHAPIRO

THE LOOTERS

SUNBLIND RANGE

PITY US ALL

SINGALEE

HORSES, HONOR AND WOMEN

JESUS on HORSEBACK

THE MOONEY COUNTY SAGA

by

JOHN REESE

DOUBLEDAY & COMPANY, INC.
GARDEN CITY, NEW YORK
1971

All of the characters in this book are purely fictional, and any resemblance to actual persons, living or dead, is coincidental.

Library of Congress Catalog Card Number 74–157618

Printed in the United States of America
First Edition

CONTENTS

JESUS on HORSEBACK

For Pastor Paul Edward Johnson,
pastor, critic, colleague
and friend.

John Reese
Santa Maria
Sept. 1971

BOOK I

ANGEL RANGE

For Charles D. and Florence Reese

1

There was this outfit that sometimes worked as many as forty men, the Flying V, north of the Platte, and up toward Nebraska and also Wyoming, but still in Colorado and no nesters yet. That was where Rolf Ledger was heading on his sorry old bay horse. It was about where he wanted to locate for a while, and an outfit that worked a big crew was prob'ly going to be more liable than most to hire a man whose last job had been breaking rocks in the Kansas penitentiary.

Rolf had cinched his belt up to the last hole, and he was still gant and hungry, and had come down to where he was ready to coax for a job if he had to. You get as hungry as he was and you start peeling down your pride, and sometimes you find it turns out to be more shucks than nubbin.

Rolf had rode all the way up from Denver, and was still boiling. What happened, he hired out to a saloon to help build on a room, a dollar and a half a day and a place to sleep, only this fella he was working for, some way he figgered out that Rolf was an ex-convict. So after five days, he throwed him five two-bit pieces and told him to get out of Denver or he'd have him throwed in jail, and he could do it too.

So here Rolf was, looking for the Flying V, when he looked back and seen these people coming after him. He counted eight, and they sure wasn't saving their horses. So he just said to himself, Well if it's another dad-blamed posse, why to heck with them! Dad-blamed if I ain't getting fed up with the law.

A couple of them split off and headed west, like in case Rolf took a notion to hit for the brush. He knowed then that it was a posse sure enough, and it made him so sick of the whole mess of life that he started to shake, being so hungry anyway. For two cents he would of shot it out, only he knowed that shooting it out is a losing proposition, especially on a no-account horse like his'n, with its spring just about run down. So he just clumb out of the saddle to rest the horse, and slipped its bit to let it feed a little, and waited.

This fella on the big bay, he was the sheriff. They always have to have a big showy horse after they been in there a few years, and this sheriff had been in since Hector was the pup as the saying is, a real big man with quite a bit of fat, and long gray hair that he kept combed in a kind of a sweat-horse roach, and a big nose like a doorknob, and a big loud voice that could rattle your windows. But still a mighty good old man, with two pearl-handled .45 pistols, and a .30-30 carbine in a boot on his saddle, and you just knowed they wasn't for show.

He pulled up and waved his ham of a hand to stop his posse, and them two fellas that had took the west trail to cut Rolf off, they rode up too, and there Rolf was, surrounded by a sheriff and seven saddle-sore citizens that looked mighty upset at life.

The sheriff said, "Hello there, mister, is that gun loaded, I suppose?"

Rolf nodded and said, "Yes sir, Sheriff, it sure is. I always found there's nothing unhandier than an unloaded gun, when you have to shoot at something."

"Well, mister, then I want you to put both of your hands up nice and slow," the sheriff said, "and we'll just relieve you of that there loaded gun."

Rolf spread his hands out, but he didn't raise them. He said, "Sheriff, my horse hasn't got a bit in his mouth, and I might lose him if I let go."

The sheriff looked that old horse over and then said, "I reckon we could make do to run him down. Thad, take the gentleman's weapon, if you please."

Rolf let go the reins and lifted his hands, and his horse just leaned on three legs and went to sleep, purely shaming him. One of the posse got down to take Rolf's gun. He was a young fella about Rolf's age, about twenty-three, with a kind of an ignorant farmer expression, and a kind of a sheepish grin. Rolf said to him, "That's the wrong way to go at this, pardner, getting between me and your posse. If I was a mind to, I could have my gun out and use you for cover against the rest of them, only I ain't of a mind to."

The sheriff said, "Thad, you haven't got a Goddamn lick of sense," but Rolf let this kid Thad take his gun, and then the sheriff nodded for him to put his hands down if he wanted, and Rolf did.

"What's your name?" the sheriff said.

"Rolf Ledger," Rolf said. The sheriff told him how do you spell it; so he done that.

"Where'd you come from?"

"Denver last."

"Where'd you spend last night?"

"Camped on some dad-blamed creek out there amongst a bunch of dad-blamed Kincaiders and their old sore-backed horses. You could hear chickens crowing and shotes squealing until it would make you sick what's happening to the range, if you rode for a living."

"We don't speak against the homestead class in this county. We don't celebrate their coming, but so long as they keep their place, they don't have no trouble. Just remember that. What did you eat last night for supper?"

"A spring cottontail."

"Sure it wasn't somebody's chicken?"

Rolf was getting tired of all this, so he said, "It had four legs and long ears, and I never seen a chicken like that in all my born days, Sheriff. I up and shot it. It looked wild to me. It didn't have no brand on it, and I didn't have no idee it belonged to anybody."

"One little old cottontail size of a barn rat," the sheriff said. "You must not of had much appetite."

"I had plenty of appetite, but that's as close as I could get with a .45, one dad-blamed rabbit. I'm a pretty fair shot, Sheriff, but I ain't one of them gunnies you hear about that can pump three shots out and bring down three frisky young cottontails in the dusk. I often wished I was, but I ain't."

"All that is just talk," the sheriff said. "They ain't nobody can shoot that good. Thad, let's look in his bedroll. I don't see no rifle or other gun there, but let's look."

This young deputy kind of excused himself to Rolf, and untied his blanket from behind the saddle. He said, "A pair of brown wool pants and a razor strop and a wrapped-up razor in a pair of socks, is all. You want I should look in his saddlebags too?"

The sheriff said he might as well, so this Thad done it, and he said, "I'm a ringtailed son of a bitch, Abe, but will you look at what this man reads to pass the time? The Holy Bible, the Holy Rosary, the Holy Scripture, and the Book of Common Prayer."

"Are you a preacher, Ledger?" the sheriff said. "You don't look like much of a preacher to me, with a forty-five on you, and no shave and all."

"No, I ain't a preacher," Rolf said. "You won't rest easy until you know, even if it is none of your dad-blamed business. I helped the chaplain in the Kansas penitentiary, and he give me them books. And to lope ahead and cut off your next question before it gets its tail up, I got pardoned."

The sheriff said, "It beats me, how every ex-convict I run into got pardoned. None of you was ever guilty and just done your time, no sir, there's a poor old mother had faith in you, and the jury that convicted you like to died of remorse, and they got up a petition, and the governor broke his ass to pardon you. I never knowed it to fail, Mr. Ledger."

Rolf said, "Sheriff, they got a saying in the pen, the easiest way to beat your time is to die young. Well, I had better luck. The guilty party, a fella by the name of Bobby Dale, made a deathbed confession. The dirty low wheat-farming Kincaiders on the jury wouldn't of raised a hand for me, but the chaplain was on my side, and he got the warden on my side. The luck of the draw, Sheriff. I made my hand with them two cards."

The sheriff asked him what he was in for, and Rolf said murder, and the sheriff said, "Well, all I can do is turn you loose. The party we're looking for rode a real good little brown or black mare, and you'd have six hundred dollars in gold on you if you was him, and there might be some buckshot in you because this man was fired at with a shotgun. Just to be sure, Mr. Ledger, I don't reckon you'll mind taking off your clothes."

It wasn't something Rolf would of done for pleasure, but he had learned in the pen that there was times a man had to be humble, so he took off every stitch, even his socks, and proved he didn't have no buckshot in him. So the sheriff told him to get dressed. Rolf asked him what this fella they was looking for had done.

"Murder and robbery, that's what," the sheriff said. He said the victim was Colonel Pegler T. Saymill, a bachelor who lived in this county seat of Mooney, Colorado, with an old-maid sister to take care of him. He was better than seventy-five at the time of death, but he dyed his hair and had false teeth and starved himself to keep a fine limber figure. A ladies' man to the last.

Colonel Pegler T. Saymill had a lot of money loaned out, and this was what he lived on, the payments and interest, and lived mighty well. One of his loans was to Calvin Venaman, owner of the Flying V that Rolf had heard of, and the day before this, Cal had come in and made a six-hundred-dollar payment. All in gold.

Well, this morning the sister of Colonel Pegler T. Saymill was out in her garden behind her orchard, hoeing her garden, because you could bet the colonel wasn't going to raise a hand there. She didn't see anything that happened, but she knowed the six hundred dollars was in the drawer of the parlor desk.

"It was somebody Peg knowed, you can bet," the sheriff said. "There wasn't no other reason to kill him, unless he knowed Peg could testify against him in court. Peg was just cold-bloodedly shot in the chest, at arm's length, after handing over the money. It just blowed the poor old man in two, like."

The sister didn't hear that shot, but next door there was a

Dutchman by the name of Frank Mueller ran the meat market, and he also had a young orchard. He was out there chasing somebody's milk cow out of it, and he heard this shot and knowed something was wrong. He knowed the colonel didn't have no gun, because he had liked to shot himself with the last one he owned, and the sister took it away from him and give it to an Indian.

Frank run into the house and got the only weapon he had, an old Ithaca twelve. He never did get a good look at the fella, but he yelled to ask what the shooting was about, and he seen somebody leading a horse out behind the trees and vines, so he just let go with the shotgun. The robber let go with two from his pistol through the trees, and Frank run into the house, in the interests of staying alive.

"Nobody else seen him," the sheriff said, "but I can testify it was a hell of a horse he rode, because it took some fences your ordinary cayuse wouldn't tackle getting out of there. All we know about it is what Frank said, through the trees it was either brown or black. We run out of tracks soon as he hit the prairie. We seen where you had your bonfire last night, and skinned and cooked your rabbit about four miles from town."

"I don't know this country and I never been in Mooney," Rolf said, "and I'm riding the wrong horse, and let me tell you if I ever commit a murder and rob anybody of six hundred dollars, I ain't going to stop a few miles out to build a fire and cook a cottontail. I'm going to make tracks. Nothing personal meant, Sheriff, but it seems to me I've seen better police work done in my time."

"Don't get smart," the sheriff said. "I don't apologize a bit for stopping you. I run this county, and I run it my way, and any time there's a murder in it, a stranger has got to explain himself, especially if he turns out to be an ex-convict. Nothing personal meant on my part either, but you're a real ragged-ass specimen to be criticizing the law."

"Well, that's the way I am," Rolf said. "I won't fight, and I'm on the side of the law generally, but any time I feel like speaking out, I'm going to speak out."

Rolf was about five-nine high, weighing no more than one hundred and thirty-eight, and limber as a snake from being on short rations so long. He had on the blue denim pants he had wore out of the pen, and a blue hickory shirt, and a brown Texas hat he had bought in a second-hand store for six bits. He knowed he didn't cut much of a figger, and was prob'ly tetchy about it.

"You go right ahead and speak out, and if your ass lands in jail, you bet your last cent I'll have a case against you," this sheriff said. "Let's see them books of yours."

He clumb down off'n his horse, and Thad handed him the books, and he looked them over and said, "I be damned! What the hell's the difference between a Holy Bible and a Holy Scriptures, Mr. Ledger?"

"It's the Jewish Bible, is all," Rolf said.

"Is that a fact! How come they got a different Bible than every other person on earth?"

"It's a different religion."

"Is that a fact! You read a lot about the Jews in our Bible, in fact that's just about all there is in it. How does it happen to be a different religion?"

"It's too long to explain here."

"Is that a fact!" the sheriff said. "My mother claimed her mother was a Jew, but my daddy said no, she was a Spaniard. I reckon he was right. I remember the old lady myself, and she could talk Spanish. I learned my first Spanish from Grandma Rowan. Her maiden name was Lanfranco. But I remember her as Grandma Rowan."

Rolf said, "She could of been both. The chaplain said there was a strain of Jew, the Sephardic strain, that is both Jewish and Spanish."

"Is that a fact! So you think the old lady, my grandmother, could of been one of them?"

"She could, but what difference does it make?"

The sheriff said, "Mr. Ledger, it's an election year this year, and I've had my problems, one of them being this Goddamn robbery and murder of Colonel Saymill. You either run on your record of law enforcement, or you run on character and things like that. I could be the only law enforcement officer in Colorado that's part Spanish Jew. Them things take the fancy of a voter. What is this Book of Common Prayer?"

Rolf explained that it was what the Episcopalians used, and it went all the way back to Henry the Eight, and even farther.

The sheriff said, "Is that a fact! How about the Rosary, though? You can't fool me, that's Catholic, and I know enough about that sect to know that a person like you can't do nobody any good with it. You have got to be a priest in good standing, not just some old ragged-ass cowboy that happens to have the right books along."

Rolf said, "That ain't necessarily so. We had mostly Methodists and Babtists and so on in the pen, and there wasn't business enough to keep a priest on steady. One used to come around once a month to take confessions, but in the case of a dying man, anybody that was babtized a Christian could take the last confession and grant extreme unction, and it's legal."

"Now, Mr. Ledger, I just plain don't believe that!" the sheriff said. "Why, they won't even let their girls marry out of the sect! How could you do that?"

"I done it three times, as a favor to the chaplain when he wasn't around, and we had prisoners up and die on us without warning."

The sheriff scratched his jaw and said, "If we had made a mistake and strung you up, I reckon you'd of met your Maker with just about every endorsement there is. How come you to take on them chores in prison?"

"The chaplain made me his assistant."

"You ever preach a sermon?"

"No, I never was ordained. I only—"

"What's ordained?"

"Swore in as a preacher. When the chaplain was out on circuit on Sunday, I held services as a favor to him, that's all. He was always working on me to be a dad-blamed preacher, but helping him out was as fur as I was ready to go, and I done that only because time hangs so heavy on your hands in prison, and besides it got me out of my cell even more than a trusty."

"By God, if this ain't a piece of luck!" the sheriff said. "Brother Richardson, the Methodist preacher in Mooney, moved out on us several months ago. Blessed Sacrament is only a mission, and Father Lavrens only hits it to count his flock every week or so, and there wouldn't be no use asking him to bury Peg Saymill because Peg professed atheism. But somebody's got to do it, and you look like the right man to me."

"I ain't," Rolf said, "and anyway if he was an atheist, what difference does it make how he's buried?"

"It makes a difference to his sister, and anybody that had as much money as Colonel Pegler T. Saymill, it's pure blasphemy to spade him under without the proper orgies. You come on back and bury him, and I'll bet Liz Saymill will part with a five-dollar bill. No, I won't take no for an answer, Mr. Ledger, or I might say Reverend. A town without a church is a discredit, and a church without a preacher is no church at all, and it's an election year. Mount up, boy, and let's get going!"

"No thank you," Rolf said. "I only want to get to the Flying V, and get me a job if I can."

This here young deputy, Thad, said, "You can't. He'll just run you off the place with a prison record, the old son of a bitch."

"And Thad knows," the sheriff said, "because Cal has got two daughters, and Thad is sweet on one of them. If a deputy sheriff ain't fit for one of them, he sure won't take no chance on an ex-convict!"

"I was pardoned, I told you," Rolf said.

"Cal won't stand on technicalities. No sir, you come back and conduct a decent Christian funeral over this old money-grubbing son of a bitch, and then let's see what we can work out for you. You're at a crossroads in life, as the fella says, and I like to help a young man to go straight when I can," the sheriff said.

Rolf would of argued, only his knees kind of give way from pure starvation, and he had to own up how long since he had et a square meal. Them bloodthirsty public citizens on the posse had rode out with nothing to eat in their saddlebags. They had fed at a couple of ranches as they loped around looking for tracks, but all they had on them was chewing tobacco.

And as Rolf told them, he had give up chewing and smoking, as well as cursing, fighting, drinking, and other forms of public misbehavior, to hang onto his job as assistant to the chaplain. He was at their mercy, you might say. On the way back to town, they spotted some wild strawberries that had just come in, it being spring, and they all got down to help him pick, and it helped. No man can pick enough wild strawberries to fill him up, but with eight helpers it's a different proposition.

2

They had to take it slow on the way back to Mooney, on account of Rolf's sorry old horse, and the sheriff nagged at him until he got what you might call the story of his life. Rolf Ledger had made most of his own troubles, and he owned up to it. He said he knowed he was unjustly convicted and sentenced, but there wasn't no use pining, he had to make the best of it, even if there ain't much that's best in life for murder.

Rolf come from a respectable family in Smith County, only him and an older brother and sister, and his mother and father. Rolf's father was a wheat buyer. Everybody was wheat-crazy then. It was just wheat, wheat, wheat, and many a good piece of prairie was plowed up to make middling-bad wheat land.

Rolf's mother was a good sensible Swede woman, and it was her that had give him the name of Rolf, and her that run the store with the help of Rolf's brother Eddie, and kept food on the table when wheat prices went the wrong way. Them Swedes is good steady people when they're not drinking, and her family never touched it.

Eddie was good in the store, and the sister, Katie, married a good steady man, a Rock Island telegraph operator, but all Rolf ever wanted to be was a trapper or a cowboy or a train robber. He got in with the Cohelan gang before he was seventeen, while Denny Cohelan was still alive, before he got shot by a mere boy of fifteen for getting gay with his sister. In fact Rolf was at that same dance, and would be the first to tell you that Denny Cohelan stood pat when he should of drawed cards.

Rolf went up to the Black Hills with Holbrook Cohelan the next summer. Nobody around Smith County knowed what happened there, but Rolf came back that fall in a mighty ructious frame of mind, and Holbrook come back a few weeks later looking peaked from a bullet in his belly that was still healing. The gossip was that Rolf had lost all respect for Holbrook Cohelan, because they sure wasn't friends no more, and pretty soon Holbrook left town.

If Rolf earned twenty honest dollars that year, it was by mighty secret labor. Mostly he was in and out of his daddy's house, he'd leave when the old man rode him too hard about being worthless, and come back when he got lonesome or hungry, like with most kids.

The last time he come back, it was just in time to get arrested for robbery and murder of the Missouri Pacific agent in Coffeyville that paid only $76.50. Rolf was *out* of Smith Center when it happened, that was sure, and he rode back *in* with Stephen A. Douglas Latimer, and both Latimer and Holbrook Cohelan had been seen in Coffeyville at the time of the murder, and Cohelan couldn't be found nowhere afterward.

Latimer chose to shoot it out in Smith County, and was killed dead without saying a word either way about the robbery, or about anything else. Nobody knowed where Holbrook Cohelan had went to, and in fact it was the last time he was ever heard of in connection with being the head of a gang of robbers, or of anything. It was poor shakes as a robbery, and people reckoned he had give up on robbery as a life's work.

The third member of the gang was supposed to be Rolf. Nobody had got a real good look at him, but people was getting tired of his quarrelsomeness and general worthless disposition anyway, and there wasn't no tears shed outside of his family when he was found guilty by a jury. They wasn't out no more than fifteen minutes, just long enough to make sure they got fed by the county.

"You got anything to say before I pass sentence?" the judge asked Rolf.

"I don't know what good it would do," Rolf said.

"Prob'ly none," the judge said, "but that ain't the question, you got the right to speak up now or forever hold your peace. That's the law as I interpret it."

"Well then, all I can say is I didn't have nothing to do with that Goddamn ignorant robbery. The jury acts like they know a lot more of the facts than the witnesses that couldn't say they recognized me. You just look at them shifty sons of bitches, Judge, there ain't none of them man enough to look me in the eye. They know in their hearts they condemned an innocent man, if they had hearts."

"Mind your language in court," the judge said. "Is that all you have to say?"

"There's more, but what good would it do?" Rolf said.

"Don't you even want to warn the jury that when you get out, you'll come back and hunt them down and kill them if it's your last act on earth?" the judge said.

"That would be the most useless thing I could say or do, Judge," Rolf said. "Look at them! They're just a bunch of ignorant wheat farmers; how can you expect better of such miserable bastards? I reckon I brung this on myself by not trying to scratch me a living on a homestead myself, but I ain't sorry. If I was as ignorant as them, they'd take pity on me and say turn that poor boy loose, life is hard enough on him. But I tried to have some fun out of life. The wrong kind of fun you'll say, but what the hell is the right kind in this Godforsaken country, since they plowed up the grass to raise wheat and nobody can afford to hire a good cowhand?"

The judge let him get it out of his system, and he told him he had saved himself a good hanging by not harboring a spirit of vengeance against the jury, and then he sentenced him to life in prison. He said it was partly because of Rolf's attitude and partly because there wasn't no real good identification of him, only circumstantial evidence, and he didn't like to hang a man on that.

"I don't know what's to be thankful for, setting on my rump in prison the rest of my life," Rolf said. "You mean well, Judge, but Goddamn it, you don't have to do the time there, and I do."

"Well, that's true, and I know what you mean about this once being a good cow country, and I take judicial notice of it," the judge said. "I don't know if the people changed the country, or the country changed the people, or what. But I'm stirrup to stirrup with you on wheat, and another thing I detest is mules."

"You're right there, all right," Rolf said. "Mules are all right in the Army, but nowhere else."

"Right as rain! I don't mind a man raising mules to sell to the Army. But when I see these poor misguided people riding a harrow or a gang plow behind four mules, without a brood mare on the place, I wonder what this country is coming to. Where are their draft animals coming from next time? Buy them, that's all they can do!" the judge said.

"That's sure the truth! But people can only see the almighty dollar. A mule will turn out more work on less feed, yes, and that's as far as fools like these fools on the jury can think."

The judge said, "Well, look on yourself, young man, as a mule for the future, and go up there to the pen and resolve to be a good mule. You sure ain't going to procreate in no prison, and you are going to work, and if you have to be a mule, I say be a good one!"

"Well, I'll tell you how I feel about that point of view," Rolf said. "HEEEEE–HAW!" He just let out the most raucous and lifelike bray that prob'ly was ever heard in a United States courtroom. And that ended the trial. Well Rolf went to the prison, and got his head shaved, and was issued a shirt and pants and shoes but no underwear or socks, and he worked on the rock pile long enough to have a favorite sledge hammer. There wasn't really any difference, one sledge hammer was about like another sledge hammer, but convicts would stake out a claim on one, and know it by its feel, and you could get your head caved in for taking some other convict's sledge hammer.

Then this chaplain by the name of James Elroy, a Babtist by conviction but not too hardshell to sympathize with a Presbyterian or a Catholic or a Socialist, especially if he had to hang, came around and asked Rolf if there was anything he could do for Rolf. Rolf said he reckoned not, everything was going pretty smooth; making little ones out of big ones wasn't his idea of sheer fun, but he reckoned he had got himself into it even if he was innocent, by his general worthlessness. They got to be friends, and this chaplain said he thought he could get Rolf out of his cell and off'n the rock pile if he would go for being his assistant.

Rolf felt pretty sheepish about it at first, but he just dared anybody to make any remarks. He got the swing of it pretty fast, and learned to rattle off a prayer as easy as swatting flies on a cold day when they're not very spry, and mostly the job was praying with some fool that had come to his regrets too late, in prison. He never figured he'd have to take any Catholic's last confession, and forgive him his sins, or hold a funeral for somebody that jumped off and landed on his head because he couldn't stand prison no longer.

But when them jobs was dealt him, he made the best showing he could, and the other convicts got to where they stopped cursing and talking dirty around him, and in fact avoided him all they could except when they was in trouble. It got pretty lonesome, but it was still better than setting in his cell or breaking rocks.

Then this fellow Bobby Dale, who had busted out of the Arkansas pen where he was doing life for robbing an old woman and accidentally smothering her to death, he got shot in a stick-up. He kept a pillow on the woman's face to shut up her screaming, and he accidentally kept it there too long, and then after he got out and got shot, he admitted it was him and not Rolf that had been in on the Missouri Pacific robbery with Holbrook Cohelan and Stephen A. Douglas Latimer.

He told a few things about that murder that nobody could of knowed unless they was there, so it couldn't be a mistake, he done it and not Rolf. It took almost a year to ding the governor into listening, the main trouble being none of them jurymen felt like signing any petitions, not after the way Rolf had talked about them and wheat farmers in general at the trial. But finally the governor got tired of being dinged about it, so he signed a pardon and said good riddance, this fellow was more trouble in prison than he ever could be out of it.

Rolf told the sheriff about it as they ambled back to town, and it was actually a relief to him to have somebody to talk to about it, although he would ruther of been up there at the Flying V, with his feet under a good table, and a good job waiting for him as soon as he got through feeding himself. But this sheriff was something like that chaplain, he drawed a man out in spite of his best intentions, and any time you pull a gun on an ex-convict and then let him have it back and call him "mister," you've at least got him wondering.

This sheriff was Abe Whipple, a man who had been in the law-enforcement business since he helped lynch a claim jumper in the silver country at age seventeen. He was a big huge ignorant loudmouthed man, but he had proved time and again that his intentions was good, and nobody ever doubted he had the guts to go with the job.

He said, "Mr. Ledger, I always said we had the most ignorant people in the world in Mooney County, but from what you tell me, Smith County, Kansas, is afflicted with some dandies there too."

"You're right loose with your talk, ain't you, about people you have to ask to vote for you," Rolf said.

Abe said, "Oh hell, I don't ask them, I tell them. I run this county the way it should be run. What people want is peace and order, and the less cheating by merchants and saloon-keepers, the better, and anybody can pack a gun but they better not pull it in town. I don't bother to go down to the courthouse at all, unless I've got somebody in jail there. I run my job from my house, and if them county officials want to see me, they can come there. Of course you got to amuse people too, that's true. But wait till they hear I'm part Spanish Jew! That'll just charm the hell out of them. People like to think they're different from other counties, you see."

Rolf admitted that was true, even in prison. The sheriff asked how could that be, and Rolf told him. He said:

"I went into that prison real sore, I can sure tell you that, but them old hands there, they'll tell you that pining and regretting just makes it worse. Then this chaplain got me to stop cursing and chewing tobacco and losing my temper. Them's the only bad habits you can enjoy in prison, and it gives you plenty to do to break them.

"There's another thing you can do, fight. You ain't supposed to fight, but if there's no other way to settle it, you go to the captain and tell him, and he sets up a fight so nobody gets killed. I had some fights that done me a lot of good, even them I lost, before I had to swear off them too.

"How this happened, I was out on the rock pile, and the fella chained to me asked me for a chew, and I told him I was completely broke of the habit, and of cursing and fighting too. He said he never in all his life heard the like, and this was his third prison, counting one in England. He talked it around, and pretty soon about half of the convicts was swearing off cursing and chewing and fighting, just to be different.

"Well then one Sunday, the captain that run the graft where you bought thread and tobacco and a sheet of paper to write home twice a year, he called a meeting before chapel. He said, 'It looks like we got a purity movement going here, nobody is chewing any more. What do you pure sons of bitches think I'm going to do with a whole case of chewing tobacco? This foolishness has got to stop. When you line up for supper, show a plug of chewing or you lose five marks.'

"They paid you a dime a day for breaking rocks, but they charged you a penny to rent your sledge hammer, and a penny insurance so you could go to the infirmary if you broke a bone or something, and a penny for the cooks to take the pebbles out of the beans and the rat turds out of the rice, and a penny for I forget what. So all you really got was six cents, and every time they punished you by taking away five marks, there went another penny.

"That's how it was done. The captain didn't hardly make anything on the smoking tobacco. The profit was all in the plug. A lot of them convicts was just spirited enough to swear off for life when the captain said that, and I knowed I was going to have everybody in trouble.

"So I stood up and excused myself, and I told the captain I had started it for the chaplain, and my advice was just to let it run its course. And he said, 'Your advice, well I like that, I'll tell you what my advice to you is, you come out of chapel with a plug of tobacco in your hand or you go to the Hole.' I told him I had swore off due to religion, and it was against the law to make a man do what was against his religion. They couldn't make a Catholic eat the side pork in his beans on a Friday, or a Jew eat it any time, not that we ever had any problem with being fed too much meat.

"Then we had to go to chapel, and things quietened down more than somewhat, but them convicts just went plumb out of their heads afterward. I heard that when they went to mess for supper, they wouldn't show a plug of tobacco, and they banged their tin plates around and hollered and dared the screws to shoot, and they got away with it. Of course they wanted to be ornery, too, but at the start, swearing off was only being different, like you said."

Abe said, "Do tell! You say you *heard* this was what went on, where was you all this time?"

"In the Hole, solitary confinement. An old cistern with eight inches of stinking water in it, and dead rats floating in it, and nothing to set on," Rolf said.

"I couldn't stand that very long, Mr. Ledger, or I might say Reverend Ledger," Abe said.

Rolf said, "Don't call me that! I wouldn't take it from them fellas in prison, and I don't have to take it from you. Sheriff, you can stand anything when the time comes you have to. You get a man mad enough, and he has already swore off cursing and fighting and losing his temper, what has he got left but self-control? You wouldn't of knowed me, if you had knowed me before I went to prison. If I let myself go, thinking about that jury, I could of went crazy there in the Hole. So as fur as I would carry it was to wish I had some of them wheat farmers in there with me when they was worrying about a dry spell.

"Couple of times a day, the captain would lift the lid off and holler down and asked if I wanted a chew. I'd be setting there in the water, leaning back with my arms folded, with the water running down my back from that clammy old brick wall. And I'd say, 'Why God bless you for thinking of me, Captain, no I don't chew, but go in peace and remember the Commandment, Honor thy father and thy mother. That is, if you have any idee who your father was!' I still had this bitterness in me, you see."

"More bitterness than sense," Abe said. "You's in no shape to reflect on his mother's chastity, setting there in eight inches of water."

"Well, that's what too much self-control can do to you. I was in there five days and nights, and how I got out was that the chaplain come back from riding circuit, and he'd had a good trip, several weddings and funerals, and quite a few sinners had come to repentance. So he asked about me, and they told him I was in the Hole, where of course he couldn't see me. But by then they had themselves another problem in that prison, and they thought maybe he could help them with it.

"This whole prison had got religion or something, and they wasn't satisfied with swearing off chewing, no sir, they wouldn't even *eat* until their assistant chaplain was let out of the Hole. They'd go out there and just keel over by the dozen on the rock pile, from hunger, and every time one did, everybody else would start screaming. The screws didn't care to risk shooting, because you take a bunch of men who simply don't care, numbers count."

Abe said, "Yes, you'll drop a few, but then the others are on you with their bare hands."

"Yes. Anyway they let him fish me out and dry me off, and bring me a cup of water and some cold noodles. He said frankly he never heard of anybody carrying his faith to extremes the way I had, since they quit burning heretics. A heretic is somebody that don't agree with you," Rolf said.

"He said, 'Ledger, I personally think you're more vain than penitent, but you have a start toward being a real Christian. What have you got to lose by going the rest of the way? Do you want these men to die of starvation, or go crazy and be shot by the guards? Don't tell me this is a matter of principle! Tell me this, have you ever been babtized?'

"I said no, unless you could count setting in that Hole. He said that was a form of babtism after all, and why not go for the pure-D form, and own up to my stubborn vanity, and then help get them idiots back to the mess hall. He said, 'What do you want, their deaths and your distinction, or peace of mind?' I said all I wanted was to be let alone and for them fellas to have a square meal.

"He said, 'I can get them the square meal if you can get them to eat it. But being let alone, that's out of my power. We have to rub elbows with our brothers in Christ, as enemies or as real brothers. You can't run from it. All your life you been trying to and look where it landed you! Ledger, the Lord is holding out His hand to you, and you're too cowardly to take it.'

"I said look what I'd been through and hadn't caved in, how could he call me a coward? He said, 'Ledger, a martyr to faith is a hero, but a martyr to his own vanity is a wicked fool.' I tried to hold out, Sheriff, but them noodles was beginning to melt down in me, and I just felt so good I had a moment of weakness, and I said all right.

"He hollered for a trusty to bring a tin cup of water, and he made me kneel down there sopping wet and all wrinkled up from being so long in the water, and he babtized me and made me a Christian. Then he got me some more noodles.

"I told him I didn't feel any different, and I still couldn't swaller everything I read in the Bible, and if the Bible was one hundred percent the word of God, then all I could say was that God had His own problems. He said a little doubt never hurt anybody, just make sure I didn't let it become a vice like I did self-control, you can run anything into the ground.

"So that's how it is, Sheriff. I'll bury your dead atheist, do the best job I can on him, but I don't think it's going to do a bit of good. What goes in a prison is one thing. The Lord has mighty slim pickings there anyway, but I can't see Him taking my word for anything on the outside."

Sheriff Abe Whipple thought this over a long time while they jogged along, and then he said, "Well, I'm afraid I have to differ with you. I reckon your writ runs outside as well as in. Let's see what kind of a sermon you preach."

"I ain't going to preach a sermon. I'll lead in prayer and recite the eulogy, if somebody will give me a few tips to go on, and I don't reckon I'll have any trouble there. In prison, it's hard to eulogize anybody, all you can say generally is he took his weekly bath and never let himself stink, and would share his tobacco or his stub pencil with you. Things like that."

The sheriff said, "You know what I've got in mind, Mr. Ledger. Here's a church that is short a preacher, and here's a preacher that is short a job. No, it won't do you no good to holler at me! Let's see how things work out. If you suit the church board, and we can find some way for you to support yourself, it could solve a lot of problems, one of them being an empty, idle church in an election year. And I might say here and now, young man, I ain't asking you, I'm telling you!"

3

Rolf took a shine to Mooney, Colorado, the minute he seen it. There wasn't no mountains there, but it stood high enough to be seen for some distance off, and was old enough for the trees the old settlers had planted to of growed up pretty good. It wasn't no small town either, claiming 414 people according to the best guesses. It got started as a halfway station during the Indian troubles, or the cavalry troubles as some people said, the cavalry being as much of a nuisance as the Indians at times. It had outgrowed its old wild beginnings, except for one thing.

This was a part of town most people ignored, or if they had to mention it, they only said "across the crick." Mooney laid between two lines of the Burlington, also called the C.B.&Q., or often just the Q, with no rail service in town, but not far from Sterling or Fort Morgan, if you could spare a day for the trip.

If you didn't have a whole day, you made do with what was in Mooney or across the crick. You might as well come right out and say this was the red-light zone, with five or six hotels, and a couple of saloons with a game usually going in them, and if you had the money to afford it, Huey Haffener's Jackrabbit Club, where they offered the most refined and expensive worldly pleasures. They had a store or two, and a livery barn strictly for their own people, and Dr. Sidney Nobile's office, a better doctor in many diseases than the ones in Fort Morgan or Sterling, especially for female complaints.

The people that lived there, and the cowboys and freighters

that spent their money there, called it Lickety Split, but in Mooney they only said "across the crick." It laid kind of low, and about every other spring it got flooded when the spring backed up, and they always had mosquitoes. There used to be a saying that a man never noticed the mosquitoes until he was *leaving* Lickety Split, but this is just a point of human nature and has nothing to do with Rolf Ledger.

It was onto dark by the time they got to town. Abe took Rolf to his house, and had his woman feed him, and give him a room where he could put on his brown wool pants and prepare himself spiritually for his ordeal. Mrs. Whipple was the former Edna McHenry when she married the sheriff, only he wasn't sheriff then, just another cowboy with nothing to mark his future greatness except his nerve. She had a ham boiling with spring greens, and a dried-apple pie, and she was famous for her good, strong coffee with plenty of bite in it, and if Rolf needed any proof that he was in a nice homey town, this was it.

Edna took his gun and hung it in the closet, and then he shaved and put on his brown wool pants, and when she seen his shirt, she decided she had time to whip up a clean white one for him. She cut one out, and basted it to his fit, and got it all done except the buttonholes before it was time for him to go, so she pinned it on him with the buttons sewed on the outside. "There, nobody is going to notice the difference, Reverend," she said.

Abe was hustling around town, organizing the crowd. There was some doubt about using the church, since the diseased had been a devoutly outspoken nonbeliever, and had turned down many a chance to write off a four-hundred-dollar church mortgage that he held. But in an election year, Abe wasn't going to be denied. He got the church.

Mooney had an embalmer, a builder by trade, very good on ornamental doors and bay windows, and he made his own coffins. Liz Saymill, the bereaved sister, told him to shoot the stack and bill the estate. The embalmer, Bernard Petty by name, had a bolt of lavender satin he had been saving for years. Most men called Bernard are going to end up Bernie or Barney or Benny, but this one stood on ceremony for the dignity of the dead, and was always called Bernard.

He done a good job on the colonel, and he had him laying there on lavender satin, outlined by a ruffle he cut with his wife's pinking shears, and he really slathered on the witch hazel and bay rum, so there wasn't hardly any smell of the chemicals in the colonel. He delivered the body in its coffin, stained ebony, to the church without any extra charge, and put on his pearl-gray gloves and stood watch beside it, not moving at all, not so much as to wrinkle his face to scare off a fly now and then, or bending his eyes to see whose kids was peeking in the windows. He just stood there reverently.

Abe got back when Rolf was ready to push back his chair from the table. "You'll have a good crowd, Reverend," he said, "and I can remember that church being filled only twice. Once was a revival that seemed to catch on one real dry summer eight years ago, and once when a Texas cowboy tried to devil an Indian by the name of Excuse Me Bill. He picked on the wrong Indian. I had to put Excuse Me Bill in jail for a day or two, the town being full of cowboys. At the funeral, we had one side of the church full of cowboys and the other side full of Indians. Brother Richardson got gas on his stomach from nervousness, and belched two or three times during the service, but I had my men swore in and scattered through the audience. There wasn't no trouble and they had better than thirty dollars in the collection plate."

"Getting up in front of a bunch of convicts was one thing," Rolf said, "but getting up in front of a lot of strangers kind of spooks me."

"You'll do fine! You look real good in them brown wool pants," Abe said.

"Your wife ironed them for me with a wet rag. I never seen that before," Rolf said.

"The only way to iron wool is with a wet rag over it, didn't you know that?" Abe said.

"No, as I say, I never seen it before," Rolf said.

"That Kansas must be a backward state if they don't even know how to iron wool. Let's go, Reverend," Abe said.

The closer Rolf got to the church, the worse he felt, but he was in for it and he knowed it. And when he seen that crowd, he would ruther have died himself than Colonel Saymill.

Most people could of walked there, but at a funeral it's human nature to want to ride, and spare your frail flesh all you can. The First Methodist was a big brown wooden building on log sills with the bark still on them, and them windows was something to behold. The Q had wrecked a passenger train up north of Mooney once, and turned over some fine new coaches with colored ornamental glass over the windows, and the Methodists got there even before the wrecker.

"Son of a bitch, there's Huey Haffener with some of his Jack-rabbit ladies," the sheriff said. "He's asking a lot of a bunch of Methodists. What do you think?"

"If they was friends of the departed, I don't see how you can bar them," Rolf said.

"Well, but this don't seem to be the time and place to call attention to that friendship. I'll interduce you to Huey. He can tell you all you need to know about Peg, the good and the bad," Abe said.

People was going into church with that grim look people wear to funerals, but the sheriff put his fingers in his mouth and ripped out a whistle, and then he took off his hat and waved it to Huey, and Huey and his three girls come down the sidewalk and met them behind a lilac bush. Abe interduced Huey and Rolf, and then Huey interduced Amy, Babe, and Cherry, which he called the A, B, and C of it.

Huey was a twitchy man, kept rubbing his nose with his fingers and pawing the dirt with his shoes, and tightening and loosening his stomach muscles. His eyes was what you might call snot-colored, with big flabby suitcases under them. He dyed his hair black and parted it in the middle, and some said wore a corset.

"I had great respect for Peg," Huey said. "I can remember a dozen times he handed out money to down-and-out men, not your worthy cases, and he never expected to get any of it back, or any credit in heaven. No, Peg had no interest in a man until genteel society had give up on him."

"Our Lord was kind to the same kind of people, when He walked the earth," Rolf said.

"I doubt for the same reasons," Huey said. "Peg just liked to take a long-shot bet against the world. He paid cash for everything and you never seen him in liquor. I can't think of anything else you could use in a sermon."

"Likewise," said Babe, and Amy nodded, and Cherry said, "Peg cursed freely, but he never talked dirty, and he respected Albert Sidney Johnston as the best general on either side in the war except his own commander, a man by the name of Gibbons that was killed young. I can't think of anything else."

"Thanks for trying," Rolf said, and Huey and the girls went back to the church and went in, and Rolf said, "My, they sure are pretty girls."

"Just as nice as they are pretty," Abe said. "You don't see Amy or Babe or Cherry getting drunk or diseased or tarred and feathered. But somehow they're always glad to move over and get a job with Bea Cunningham."

"Mr. Haffener must be quite a ladies' man," Rolf said.

"Well, he likes to be thought of as such, but I've knowed him for fifteen years, and his girls all treat him more like a sister. Let's talk to somebody else," Abe said.

They circulated around, and Rolf scraped up what he could get for his eulogy, but the pickings was thin except that Peg had wrote a beautiful hand and once had raised the best fighting chickens in Colorado, until his sister made him cut it out, and things like that. And Rolf met Bernard Petty, and Bernard said, "After the services, I would be glad to have you partake of a little brandy in the settings of my funeral parlor, a toast to the departed and a restorative to we who preside."

"I never touch the stuff," Rolf said, "but I appreciate the thought, Mr. Petty."

He met Liz Saymill, a smart little old woman about as big as twenty cents' worth of salt, with highborn manners that went all the way back to her great-grandmother in Maine. She said, "So you're not ordained, well I'm sure a patient and tolerant God meant it to be. My brother was a quarrelsome rascal and a cynic, but he deserved better than to be shot down like a dog. I hope you won't have to compromise your own convictions to say a few words in behalf of one so hell-bent as Pegler."

"If he's hell-bent, I don't know it," Rolf said. "I doubt the Lord has even had time to find your brother's brand in the book let alone run him down the lower chute, ma'am. With all respect, I wouldn't bet a cent either one of us could predict how He's going to rule."

"That's a comfort," Liz said. "I took a quick judgment for granted, and that was wrong, wasn't it? I can shed a few tears now, and start worrying about my own soul, instead of pitying Pegler's in hell."

Rolf said he reckoned he had enough to slide through, and he wanted to get it over with before he lost his nerve, so they went in the side door, and the people still waiting out in front went in the front door. There was a little private room inside the side door, with a desk for the preacher, and a nail where he could hang his raincoat during services, although it wasn't safe overnight, and a locked cabinet for the communion wine. The sheriff took a book off'n the shelf and said, "This is the songbook they use. Pick yourself out what you want and I'll tell Mable, although I personally favor 'Lead, Kindly Light,' 'Up from the Dead,' and 'Till We Meet Again,' and the thing is, I know Mable can struggle them out of the organ. The others are a gamble."

Rolf said any tunes would do, just give him the numbers. So the sheriff wrote down the numbers, and went and told Mrs. Mable McMurdoch that these was the ones the reverend wanted, and she said, "Mighty curious that *he* favors the ones *you* favor, but I ain't going to question anybody's word at a time like this."

Rolf could hear the people stomping and kicking around to find seats, and when they quieted down, he knowed it was time for him to come out. And all of a sudden, it didn't bother him no more. It was like waiting to get on a horse you had bet you could ride that had throwed everybody else: you was nervous until it came your time, and then you just got on and rode him. Or got throwed, as the case may be, but it wasn't nerves that throwed you.

So he went out and found himself on the stage, on the lectern side. That's the left side from the preacher's standpoint in the Methodist faith, whatever it is elsewhere. He had both the Holy Bible and, on a hunch, the Book of Common Prayer. He went up and laid his two books on the lectern, and the only thing he really wished then was that he had a pair of glasses he could put on, and do it up right.

He took the sheriff's note out, and opened the book of hymns that was on the lectern. He looked around him, and he seen the coffin down there with this old white-headed dude in it, and every lamp in the church burning and one of them smoking, and the light twinkling off'n them red, blue, green, and orange glass panels from the Q passenger cars, and he just had the feeling he had catched his fourth jack and this pot was his'n.

He said, "The Lord is in His temple. Let us all rise and supplicate His mercy with a moment of silent prayer. When the organ begins, let us lift our hearts and our voices in 'Lead, Kindly Light,' which you will find on Page 147 of your hymnals. Let us bow our heads."

"Not for a minute, young man. You just hold it a minute, young man!" a woman said.

It was Mrs. Stella Landsdown, a former Babtist who wouldn't unite with any other church, who was dead against sin of all kinds, especially carnal sin, and she knowed more Deuteronomy on this subject than most preachers. She was standing up pretty close to the front, and pointing across the church at a woman who was just setting there with her hat on with a feather in it, in the same pew as Huey Haffener and his three Jackrabbit girls.

Rolf said, "What's the matter, ma'am, what ails you?" and

she said, "I suppose we have to tolerate Mr. Haffener, the Methodists are notoriously lax, but even they don't have to put up with the likes of Beatrice Cunningham. This is a house of worship and either she leaves or I do! I don't have to tell anybody why either, and I bet I take plenty with me, the cream of Christianity in this town too, and will you look at that silk dress. Silk! Out, I want her out of here!"

She was just screaming at the end. Rolf knowed that all he had to do was look to Abe, in the front row, for a hint, or to Miss Liz Saymill for a hint, and play the hand from there. But he made up his mind that if he had to run this funeral he was going to run it his way, and nobody was going to hone his spurs for him.

He said, "Please set down, ma'am. I agree with you, if there's anybody here unfit to face the Lord in His sanctuary, we're going to have an angry God on our hands in about a minute. But the Good Book says, 'Let the women remain quiet in the temple.' So I'll ask the men here to take the necessary steps, and heave out anybody that would offend the Lord, and the only advice I'll give them is what the Savior said on a similar occasion, 'Let him who is without sin cast the first stone!'"

"Amen," somebody said, and somebody else said, "Set down, Stella, you heard him, remain quiet," and somebody else said, "Amen, who is without sin in this town? Nobody, amen!"

Well, Stella knowed she was a one-woman army if she marched out, so she set down, and Mable McMurdoch sneaked into "Lead, Kindly Light," and everybody stood up and whooped that song out from the belly up. Then Rolf led them in a kind of a meandering prayer, searching out the territory you might say, in case Stella Landsdown stood up and heaved another chunk at him, only she didn't. Then they sang, "Up from the Dead He Arose, with a Mighty Triumph O'er His Foes." That's a corker that the average Methodist can't sing, it takes a steam soprano that can go plumb to the top, and you need a couple of men with good deep whisky voices to bleed everything there is out of it. But they done pretty good.

Then Rolf thought he'd gamble a little, and he took his Book of Common Prayer and began reading, "Man, that is born of woman, hath but a short time to live, and is full of misery," and so on. Then he went into his eulogy as he called it, and this is just about what he said, word for word verbatim as the saying is:

"We commit our brother to the judgment of the Lord without judging him ourselves. What we do instead is beseech Him in His mercy to stretch things as fur as He can in favor of this poor fella, because nobody here knows it won't be himself here tomorrow, needing everything that can be said in his favor.

"Colonel Pegler Saymill fought to preserve the Union, and he carried the scars of battle right into that coffin, but he did not carry vengeful hate against his foes, no sir he had nothing but kind words to say about Albert Sidney Johnston, for example.

"He owed no man a dime when he died. He paid in cash as he went along through life, and nobody's loser by his death in that respect.

"He took care of his sister the way a man ought to, and he didn't ask no special credit for it. She was his sister and that was enough for him.

"He claimed he was an atheist, yes he did, but he never tried to talk anybody else out of his faith; if you wanted to believe him, that was up to you, but you really disappointed him if you didn't give him a good lively argument on the subject.

"He drank like a gentleman and was never drunk.

"He seduced no man's innocent daughter or sister, and lusted after no man's wife.

"He consorted with some low-down riffraff, yes he did all right, but so did Jesus when He was here on earth, and Peg Saymill caught criticism for it and I reckon Jesus did too, but enough of that.

"Not many called him friend but nobody called him an enemy either. He lived up to his code, and it was a gentleman's code, and maybe not a Christian code but the next best thing at least.

"So now we consign him to the earth, to become ashes, to become dust, and I who has been in prison tell you this, you can't trust half of the testimony that people are convicted on. There ain't no more Colonel Pegler T. Saymill, we have lost him to God, and this here town is poorer if I'm any judge, and in our poverty and loss, what can we do but pray?"

He cut loose on a prayer that like to ripped the roof off. It added to his confidence to be burying a colonel who had died rich and respected, not some rapist or strangler or horse thief, and he was talking to people that knowed the difference between right and wrong, or at least thought they did. He come down toward the end of the prayer real quiet and friendly and solemn, never whooping or pounding the lectern, and then he give Mable McMurdoch the signal, and she bore down on the pedals and began walloping out "Till We Meet Again, Till We Meet Again, Till We Meet At Jesus's Feet."

He motioned them to stand up, and he hauled off and gave them a benediction, something he hadn't planned on doing at no time, and he got them to filing past the coffin in good order, only he never did catch Abe Whipple's signal to take up a collection. Except for that, it was a mighty well-run funeral, and Colonel Pegler T. Saymill could afford to skip the collection if anybody could.

4

The custom of grave site services hadn't took root in Mooney because the graveyard was so neglected it took the heart out of the strongest believer in the Resurrection, and was uphill besides. Weeds everywhere, and fences down, and prob'ly somebody's milk cow staked out to graze on the graves. Besides it was coming on to rain, with thunder already rolling, and anybody with a lantern wanted to get on home, and not fool around in no graveyard. So Abe deputized four good single men to go with Bernard Petty and get the job done in decent privacy, you might say.

Beatrice Cunningham, who ran Bea's Place over across the crick, waited while everybody else come up to tell Rolf the usual lies, how much they was comforted and so forth. Then she slipped up and interduced herself, and said she prob'ly erred in coming to the obsequies, but it was hard to pass up the funeral of the last true gentleman in town.

Beatrice was about thirty or forty or fifty, with a big pile of yella hair, and nice blue eyes, and she was a well-turned woman as to shape. She used plenty of good French perfume, and you have to remember that Rolf had been two years in the pen away from women, and then had swore off all these things including women.

"I do appreciate the stand you took, Reverend, and I'll never forget it," she said. Rolf just said yuh sure, something like that, and then she said, "I won't embarrass you further, better get in out of the rain, and I'll get across the crick while I still can." He was so strangled on that perfume he hadn't even noticed it was sprinkling good and hard.

Abe was going around with his lantern, telling everybody that Rolf was the former assistant chaplain at the Kansas pen, and not attached to any church, and was a single man, frugal in his tastes. When Rolf went to look for him, to find out where he was going to spend the night, and to get the five dollars from Liz Saymill that Abe had bragged about so free, Abe was just meeting up with this family that had come up in a nice top buggy and had missed the funeral.

"Abe, I just don't understand you going around telling everybody this was a six-hundred-dollar *quarterly* payment," this man was saying. "My business is my business. I regret the tragedy, but it catches me by the short hair; that's a call loan and if the estate calls it, I'm in trouble. And you have to go around telling everybody I have been paying Peg six hundred dollars every *quarter*."

"I didn't get you into debt and I didn't kill Peg, and it'd come out in probate proceedings anyway, Cal," Abe said. "Evidence is evidence, somebody else knowed he had that money; what am I going to do, go around saying it was six bits he died for?"

"I admire your industry," this fella said, "but I wish you had been half as industrious last winter, when I was losing a couple of hundred head of hay-fat cattle."

Abe said, "Now don't start on that; by the way, I want you to meet Reverend Rolf Ledger. Rolf, this is Cal Venaman of the Flying V, and this is his wife Opal, and this is his daughter Sammie, and this is his daughter Winnie."

"Don't call me Sammie," the one girl said.

Now if you had to single out one big family in Mooney, it would be either Cal Venaman of the V, or Alec McMurdoch, president of the State Bank of Mooney and wife of the organist, or husband ruther. Rolf figured the Flying V owner, or the V as they sometimes said, would be a big old raunchy ignorant type, because the cow business wasn't no place for a vanilla salesman in them days. Your average money-making cowman, he had to pull his shirt tail out to tell what day of the week it was, by how dirty it had got since he changed it last Sunday.

But Cal was kind of a gant whippy fella in brown side-whiskers, educated up to the point of college or maybe a little beyond, and usually quite neatly dressed. His wife Opal was a mighty handsome woman, and they made a mighty handsome pair.

The oldest girl, Samantha, had pretty much missed out on the family good looks. Sammie they called her in school, till she put a stop to it when she put her hair up. She was exactly twenty-four years old then, and was as tall as her father, and whippy-built like him, making her too limber of build for a real good-looking woman. She had blue eyes and brown hair almost red, but the thing about Samantha, and this is not an easy thing to say about a woman, was her big mouth. She'd share her opinions with you on short notice, and you didn't have to provoke her to it, all you had to do was be within range.

The younger sister was Winifred, better known as Winnie. Now there was a girl for you. Just seventeen, a head shorter than Samantha, and you talk about built, she was the lonesome cowboy's dream on a cold night, as the fella says. This was the one that Thad Rust was hanging around to his mortal peril. A sweet womanly critter that knowed her place, and none of Samantha's big mouth.

"Ashamed to get here too late for the service, Parson," Cal said, shaking hands, "but we didn't hear of it at all. Are you looking for a charge? You can't say the church is looking for a minister, truthfully. I'm on the board, and it will put off spending a dime for anything as long as possible. But there is a vacancy."

Rolf struck hard and he struck fast, like a diamondback. He said, "No sir, Mr. Venaman, I ain't an ordained preacher, I'm just a cowhand. I was on my way to ask you for a job when I got sidetracked for this."

"An ex-convict, I understand," Cal said.

"Yes sir, pardoned because I wasn't guilty," Rolf said.

"Well," Cal said, "I wouldn't necessarily hold that against you, but I'm afraid I couldn't use you. On the Flying V, I'm the sole source of the gospel. No, I couldn't risk a rival moral leader, to be quite frank."

Abe said, "Well it's sure been nice talking to you folks; don't rush into anything, Cal, we still got to talk over who's going to fill this pulpit someday."

"You're the one rushing things," Cal said. "Why can't we chat a moment with the parson?"

"Because it's going to rain is why," Abe said.

"It'll rain on the just and the unjust as usual, Abe. I only wish you was half as conscientious about what happened to my livestock as you are in finding a preacher for the First Methodist Church," Cal said.

Abe mopped his face with his sleeves, and said, "Cal, if you couldn't track your steers through the Goddamn snow, excuse that, ladies, how do you expect me to do it in spring grass? You don't bother to get out and rustle around in a storm, oh no indeedy, you're too comfortable there by the fire rubbing your sock feet against each other! Well a cow thief can't take things so easy. He's got to ply his trade when he can, and then you can only think to blame the law enforcement officers."

Cal had already stopped listening to him in that highhanded way he had, and as soon as he could, he said, "Parson, are you interested in this church?"

"Not in any way, shape, or form," Rolf said.

Abe said, "Now wait a minute!" But Cal slid in between his words and his ideas, and he said, "My feeling is that your experience in prison would be more useful in the pulpit than in a crew on a working ranch. I've worked a few ex-convicts. They were all unjustly convicted, and they're hard people to get a day's work out of."

Rolf said, "Well, you do lose your touch with a horse or rope, after fondling a sledge hammer a few years. But I reckon I'll make out when I land me a job."

"You might try a neighbor of mine, Jack Butler," Cal said. "It's a one-man outfit, and Jack has no moral boundaries that I've ever discerned."

Abe said, "Cal, do you mean you suspicion Jack of running off your steers?"

"You've got more sense than that. No neighbor ran them off one at a time. They were driven north in a herd. I sent a man to get Jack to help us track them, but he was laying drunk, I won't mention where, and had been for three days. But he needs a man if he can afford one, and an ex-convict may not be too particular about bachelor cooking and the suspense of waiting for Jack to go on one of his periodic toots," Cal said.

"It may be an idee at that, Cal," Abe said. "Reverend Ledger could help him fight his fiend, and Jack's place is close enough so he could get in here Sundays to preach."

"I ain't going to preach and I ain't got any patience with drunks," Rolf said.

It was still making up to rain, showering every now and

then, but Cal and Abe went on talking and paying no attention to him. Cal said it would amuse him to see a man of real experience with sin and suffering in the pulpit, and Abe said that was exactly his own idee, and Cal said preaching wasn't a lazy man's job in *this* town, and Abe said no, it sure wasn't if it was done right.

Samantha spoke up and said, "Reverend Ledger, before I form an opinion, how do you stand on the theory of evolution?"

"Darwin, you mean?" Rolf said.

She snapped, "Do you know any other theory of evolution?"

Rolf said, "No, but for all I know there could be a dozen. The chaplain in prison gave me one of Darwin's books to read, and he explained it to me later. Darwin's a little foggy to push through, but if you don't let go too easy, he can be read."

She said, "Well, are you for or against it?"

Rolf said, "How can you be for or against it? Either it happened or it didn't, it ain't like getting out the vote to close the saloons, we're talking about backwards, not forwards, you might as well vote on a comet."

"You evade the question. Do you or do you not believe in the theory of evolution?" Samantha said.

Rolf kind of walled his eyes like a bronc being pushed into the saddling chute, and he tried to hold it in but she had savaged him just a little too hard. He said it was an insulting question and if she was a man, he'd tell her it was none of her business. Cal said, "Sickem, wolf, go to it, bulldog!" He had come out loser in too many arguments with Samantha himself.

"Do you or do you *not?*" Samantha said.

Rolf said, "I'm a workingman, and I don't believe in it the way I do low prices and high wages. Them things make a difference to me. Since the wheat farmers plowed up the range from Texas to Saskatoon, a workingman has got more to worry about than whether his ancestors was apes or ant-eaters. You go up there in the Black Hills and see men working twelve hours a day in them gold mines for a dollar and a half, and coming out with no fingers, or their eye put out, or deefened by careless blasting for life, where did I leave off? Them is the things that count with me. Whether they come down from apes, and before that lizards, and before that some kind of jelly fish, today they're breaking their rear ends for a dollar and a half. Or you take the railroads; now these automatic couplers is supposed to make railroading safe as clerking dry goods, but how about the cars that's still link-and-pin? Them highbinders ain't going to burn all them old man-killing cars! I seen a man that stepped in between two cars to link up, and his foot slipped, and you should of seen him after that link went through his meat in the middle. I'll tell you what, ma'am, *he* didn't care a whoop about his remote ancestors, all he wished was it had cut his backbone so he could die easy, and I'd feel the same way. So when you ask about evolution, I say how about outlawing link-and-pin today, instead of after them death-trap ancient cars wear out! Now there was a certain kind of a bird Professor Darwin seen on some island, and it was almost the same as the same kind of a brown bird he seen somewhere else, except he claimed that natural selection had changed a few little things. That was interesting, sure it was, laying in a cell in prison with nothing to think about except how I got there, and how I was going to get out, and if Professor Darwin himself was to come up right now and ask me if I was for him or against him, I'd tell him he's just making a nuisance of himself. What I want to do is make a living. The same with transubstantiation, now if you want to believe that way it's all right with me, or if you're for consubstantiation instead, that's all right with me too, just show me where I can get a job to make an honest living. But if you insist that I've got to pick between the two, then I've got to say that I just don't *know*. And if you ask me what was my practice as the assistant chaplain in prison, why, I'll serve out the wafer and the wine to all comers, and I only wish that the transubstantiationists and the consubstantiationists and the evolutionists had to make a few couplings with link-and-pin on a dark track on a wet night, or you look at life on a cow outfit for the hired hand, how many men have you seen going around with a limp from being throwed or walked on by a horse, or with a finger tore off at the roots by a rope, or– Where was I? Oh yes, evolution."

He catched his breath, and Samantha just stared at him like she had swallowed a frog, but that woman had the doubtful gift of a ready tongue. She said, "I don't think that's sound Methodist doctrine or any other kind of doctrine I ever heard of. Not that I care! I believe in evolution, and I'm only glad I don't have to compromise my beliefs, well look at it rain, so nice to of met you, Reverend, we must have another chat sometime."

It was coming down in bucketfuls. The Venamans run to their buggy and got the side curtains up, and Abe and Rolf started for town. Abe said, "I want you to talk to Jack Butler, and he's laying drunk in the Jackrabbit if he hasn't come out of it, and tomorrow the crick may be too high to cross. So come on."

Rolf wasn't anxious to talk to no drunks about a job, and he wasn't about to let this sheriff run his life for him. But you might as well holler down your stove pipe, or up it, as argue with Abe Whipple when he had one of his enthusiasms going.

There was a big cottonwood log forty inches thick across the crick, with the top adzed flat, and an old rope for a handrail that went out with every high water, and stayed out until somebody found some more old rope and strung it up. This was all the bridge there was, and the rigs had to go a quarter of a mile up the crick to the ford. The water was still normal when they crossed.

It being come on to rain, you wouldn't expect a crowd in the Jackrabbit, but the shooting of Colonel Pegler T. Saymill had brought folks to town, and a storm was all the excuse they needed. A couple of the Jackrabbit girls shook their tails at Rolf, but Abe said, "Goddamn it, this man is a minister of the gospel!" One of the girls said she had problems with her soul and was willing to exchange blessings, but Abe told her to get the hell out or he would be forced to jail her a few days.

"How do you know, maybe I could help her with her problems," Rolf said.

"Not the one she's got," Abe said.

"How do you know?" Rolf said.

"I thought you swore off!" Abe said.

"I did, but life goes on, and it ain't life without a few things. Maybe at your age, but not mine," Rolf said.

Abe just about boiled up, but then he seen that Rolf was just making fun of him. Rolf said, "We'll keep the Commandments, Sheriff, but don't make up my mind for me! I'll tell you something else, the chaplain said that for every fallen woman, there's some man that pushed her, and maybe that girl does need help."

"There's some that was pushed," the sheriff said, "and some that fell, and some that just laid down. Some things you can advise me about, Reverend, but not that."

They sent a girl to call Huey, and they both turned down a free drink on the house, even strawberry syrup in water, Rolf because of his vows and the position he was in after preaching a funeral, and Abe because a woman had put knockout drops in his cherry water once in San Francisco, and took his poke away from him. They'll do that in San Francisco every time.

Huey come in, and Abe told him to go get Jack Butler. He grumbled somewhat, but he went down into his cellar and brought Jack up. "A good thing, too," he said, "because the water is rising down there. Welcome back to life and Lickety Split, Jack."

"Oh God oh God oh God oh God," Jack said.

"You may well say that, you sot, you miserable whisky fiend, you hopeless drunkard," Abe said.

"Oh God oh God," Jack said.

"How about a drink to damp your fuse?" Huey said.

"It would kill me," Jack said. "One taste would stop my heart. Oh God oh God oh God."

Jack Butler was about forty-five years old, give or take a few years. When sober he was just a plain decent-looking fella, usually a very serious expression, not very big and not very small, just like any old batch of forty-five that minded his own business. But coming out of a bout with his demon, like to-night, he wanted to puke and couldn't, and had the look in his eye like he'd been scraped out of the saddle when he let his horse run under a low limb.

Abe give him a good talking-to, and the Jackrabbit girls brought him black coffee and peeled raw potatoes, which he always craved coming out of one. He tried to pull his mind together, to keep it from tracking all over. Abe told him he wanted him to hire Rolf for twenty-five dollars a month, and Jack said, "A man can't make a decision like that in my shape, Abe, so let's put it off. I know you're looking out for my in-terests, but—"

Abe said, "Don't you bet on that, Jack. I can lose patience with you mighty fast. You're going to give him Saturday after-noon off, so he can scratch a sermon together for Sunday, and a good horse so he can make it here and back."

"I ain't going to preach no sermon," Rolf said. But Abe didn't pay no attention to him, and he kept on until Jack said sure, he could use a good man if he didn't mind batching, and he'd let him use Fanny to go in to conduct the Methodist services. That was a brown mare, four years old, three white stockings and a narrow blaze on her face, that he just doted on, and rightfully.

"It may be just what I need, Abe," Jack said. "Maybe the reverend can help me with my problem too."

"Nobody can help a drunk but himself," Rolf said.

"You never spoke truer words," Abe said, "but at least you won't lead this pitiful son of a bitch into temptation. Look what this will mean to the county!

"Why, an ex-convict, the former assistant chaplain in a prison, comes riding up to the church every Sunday on the prettiest little gaited mare you ever seen, to preach to his flock. Same time, it comes out that I'm part Sephardic Spanish Jew. You said it yourself—people like to be different. We'll be the standout county in Colorado!"

Rolf said he wasn't going to preach nowhere, and Abe might

as well brag his ancestors was monkeys, and so on. There's something about a saloon that just about makes it impossible to end a conversation without starting a fight, and Little Dick Silver kept wandering in and out, and he could distract them if anybody could, and he did. Dick was an old Army scout, and he wore his white hair in long curls down over his shoulders, and a big white mustache and goatee, and stayed drunk a good part of the time, and couldn't be trusted with a pistol any time. He had went out on the prairie and picked some pink and white Sweet Williams, and he went around handing everybody flowers and saying, "The message I bring is loving kindness for everybody free of charge," and finely Abe had to tell him where he could put his Sweet Williams.

"There's a little thing called ordination, Sheriff," Rolf said. "I ain't ordained and I ain't going to be ordained, and you can't preach unless you are."

Abe said, "That could be a poser except I'm sure it's a legal technicality. I'll talk to Jimmy Drummond about it, and if there's a better lawyer on these technical propositions, I ain't heard of him. The way I look at it, I can't swear in a regular deputy without the county commissioners authorizing it in an ordinance, and they're so mean and stingy that look at what I can afford, Thad Rust, a well-meaning boy, but too prone to fire his weapon, and he couldn't handle a hen-house robbery alone.

"But in an emergency, I swear in a *posse comitatus*, on my own authorization, and I lead them out to make an arrest or a corpse as circumstances provide, and any court in the country will back me to the hilt. I look on this as a similar emergency. Why can't we have a preacher *comitatus*? A divine militia you might say, keeping the spiritual peace in the absence of the regular ordained troops.

"It don't stand to reason you've got to leave a pulpit empty in an emergency, waiting for somebody to blunder along that's been ordained. What if the Lord Himself came back for His Second Coming, and didn't have the papers to prove He was ordained, why He couldn't even take the pulpit to talk to a few Methodists that was already all for Him! Or they say they are. Sometimes I just wonder."

"An empty pulpit and a full saloon, they're the brand and earmark of a backwards town," Jack Butler said. "A preacher *comitatus*, well say, Abe, you sure do come up with some fertile ideas. But it may hold water at that."

5

At least Rolf had himself a job, so as soon as Jack Butler could set on a horse with a reasonable hope of not swooning off'n it, they went out to his place, the J Bar B, and it was a real pleasant surprise to Rolf. Jack had himself a shelf up in the hills, with timber and water in addition to grass. Not a big spread, but you couldn't of told it from the best parts of Wyoming, and you can't say no more for cow country.

Jack didn't have much of a herd, but what he had was good-looking brood cows, and bulls of the whiteface persuasion. But he had the best fences Rolf ever seen, fences across draws that snowed in during the winter and could starve cattle, and fences around hayfields that he cut for winter feed, and fences that kept his cows out of Cal Venaman's grass and Flying V cows out of his'n.

He had a nice three-room log house without a draft in it, and a fireplace for heat and a cookstove to cook on, and nice big mattresses on the beds, not just straw ticks, and plenty of chairs that didn't teeter, and even curtains on the windows.

"They're scrim," Jack said. "I sent off to the mail order for them, and Mrs. Bloodgood at the post office helped me make out the order, and she said scrim was the thing."

"Scrim. Well you learn something every day," Rolf said. "Looks to me like you're putting everything you make back into your property, and in time your natural increase will make you a rich man."

"I hope so," Jack said, "but it ain't planning, Rolf. I spend it for bobwire and things before I can spend it for drink, in case a fit comes on me."

"It would be a blessing if your fight against the drink made you a rich man," Rolf said. "The Lord moves in a mysterious way, His wonders to perform."

"Well," Jack said, "the first thing, we've got to haul some more bobwire from Fort Morgan. I already got more bobwire than I know what to do with, but I ordered this when I felt a fit coming on last winter, and I waited a mite too late, and was already drunk. I knowed there was something I meant to do, so when I remembered what it was, I done it, so I sure am going to be well fixed for bobwire."

They et their supper together real pleasant. Like most cowboys, Jack was a pretty good cook with beans and oatmeal and bacon and the like, and Rolf had worked in the prison kitchen and knowed a few fancy tricks himself. There was not going to be any problem about food.

The next morning, Rolf hooked up a four-horse team before daylight, and took along some cold beans and some bacon sandwiches in biscuits, and a bottle of coffee, and headed for Fort Morgan. He got there and lo and behold, here was a whole carload of bobwire. Now that's just a mountain of bobwire. When Rolf got his load on, just spool after spool of it, he seen he hadn't hardly made a dent in that load.

He got back about dark, and Jack told him to unload behind the stone barn, and when Rolf pulled around behind the stone barn, there was a stack of bobwire almost as high as the stone barn. Rolf asked him how in the world he expected to use all of it, and Jack said, "I don't know what you can do with it except build fence, I honestly don't. But look at all the liquor that would of bought."

"You're going to have your place fenced horse-high, hog-tight, and bull-strong, as the fella says. You could fence yourself away from all the liquor in the world with the bobwire you got here," Rolf said.

Jack said, "Rolf, I could climb a red-hot fence a mile high, barefoot and blindfolded, if you tell me where a bottle is hid when I've got a thirst on me. Don't poke fun at a man's weakness."

Rolf was three weeks hauling that bobwire, and he tore his hands up a little, but he made some muscle too. In the pen he had learned how to be alone without getting fidgety and vile-tempered from lonesomeness, and mostly he sort of lined up arguments in his mind in case him and Samantha Venaman ever butted heads again on a question of theology. He had her hobbled and belled and blindfolded every time, as a man will when it's all in his head, and he could just picture her apologizing for putting her female arguments up against his'n.

Now all this whole three weeks he was hauling bobwire, he didn't so much as mention going to Mooney to preach, and neither did Jack, and neither did Sheriff Abe Whipple come out to make an issue of it. At first Rolf figgered he had wore that old sheriff out, but Jack said you never could trust Abe Whipple, just when he ort to be throwing in his hand, here he comes tilting the pot like he had aces back to back. He was that kind of a man, Jack said, crafty as an old dog-coyote, and could wait with his nose in a rabbit hole as long as it took to get him that rabbit.

After he finished hauling the wire, Rolf plowed up a potato patch, and then started planting some potatoes so they wouldn't have to depend on beans all the time next winter. He was planting away when he seen a nice top buggy coming, pulled by two nice matched bays, at a nice easy canter. Now nobody owned that kind of a rig but Cal Venaman, and when he made out three female figgers in it, it didn't take no brains to speak of to know it was Opal and her two girls, Samantha and Winnie. Their place was only six miles cross-country from Jack's, or eight by wagon road, with only one gate to open.

Samantha was driving. She flourished up to where Rolf was

planting potatoes, and Opal give him a nice smile, and said, "Reverend Ledger, my girls and I have a surprise for you and Jack."

"Please don't call me reverend, ma'am," Rolf said.

"Take note I didn't," Samantha said.

"Now, Samantha!" Opal said. "Sammie beat up a sponge last night, and she got up this morning early, and rolled out the dough and made some real nice light rolls. Then we thought of you two lonely bachelors, and we decided while they're fresh we'd bring you some."

She fetched out a big pan of nice light rolls from under the seat, and whipped off the dish towel over them, and held them out to him, and said, "Just smell that!" Rolf leaned over and smelled them, and he thanked her and said there was nothing on earth, not even roses, that smelled as good as fresh bread.

Winnie said, "We brought you some butter, too, see? From our own press." She showed him the round pound of butter, with the Flying V in the middle and a row of braided design around the edge. Having your own butter press with your own brand is something most cowmen wouldn't bother with, because in the first place not many cowmen milk cows, let alone make butter, and in the second, your own hand-carved hardwood press could cost you as much as three or four dollars in Denver.

"Well say, ladies," Rolf said, "you're going to have us two batches just crying our eyes out from pure gratitude."

Samantha said, "I've made better bread in my time, and I'd be ashamed if I couldn't, but it won't poison you. Just don't make hogs of yourselves. You know how heavy fresh bread lays on your stomach."

"Not this kind, ma'am," Rolf said. "This would be as light as butterflies on your stomach."

So far they was doing fine, passing the peace pipe around in good shape, and burying the hatchet too. Only just then Jack Butler ambled up in his gum boots, from where he had been mucking out the horse barn, and was enough to kill anybody's appetite.

"Fresh light bread!" he said. "Too bad you had to bring them today, right after Rolf made us some yesterday. You talk about light-bread buns, these is mighty good homemade ones, but homemade ain't in it with the way Rolf learned in prison."

Opal's eyes bugged out, and she got red-faced, and she started laughing and whooping, until it was all she could do to say, "You mean Reverend Ledger can bake?"

"The best," Jack said. "He says that when you can bake for the warden's family, the only better job in the pen is assistant to the chaplain."

"Well I declare," Opal said, and she just leaned back and let herself go. But Samantha said, "Mama, don't be entirely an undignified idiot. You'll recall I was against the whole idea, I said it was a waste of time, casting our pearls before swine."

"I don't know as that's fair now," Rolf said.

"Fair or unfair, I'll scatter that bread in the timber for the deer first!" Samantha said.

Well Rolf's mane crested a little, and he said, "Don't pick on the poor helpless deer, ma'am, us swine will take care of these pearls, as you say."

Opal just laughed until she cried. She said, "Well I never seen two workingmen who couldn't work their way through two batches of light bread; just bring the pan back sometime when you're riding our way. And if you want to fill them with Reverend Ledger's light-bread buns, that will be fine with me."

"Mama, you infuriate me," Samantha said.

"Because you have no funny bone," Opal said. "Oh dear, we'll never live this down."

"I'll see to it that you don't," Samantha said.

Jack said, "Remind Cal he was going to put that off mare to his black stud. I do believe she's coming in, and what he wanted was a spring colt."

Samantha let out a bleat, "Pet—Lottie— Git!" She cracked the whip over the team, and out of the yard they went.

Rolf said, "Jack, that was about the most ignorant thing you could of said."

"Why, I used to own Lottie myself," Jack said. "I raised her out of a mare I traded an Indian out of, let's see, Willie Bonfire was his name, her sire was half mustang and half Kentucky hotblood. Cal had this mare he called Pet, a perfect mate for my filly—"

You get Jack on a horse story, and the dam has broke, and you're up on the ridgepole, and you could fire a cannon between his feet and he'd never lose his grip on where he was in the horse story.

"I don't mean about the horse coming in heat," Rolf said. "I mean letting on we already had fresh bread."

"Well we did," Jack said.

"Jack, do you know what a gentleman is?" Rolf said. "I heard this from the chaplain; a gentleman is somebody that never *unintentionally* causes pain."

"How does he know if it's unintentional?" Jack said.

"That's the whole point. Think, Jack, think!" Rolf said.

Jack thought, and said, "It's too deep for me. You can swear off'n intentional things, I can see that, but the other is too much to ask of human flesh; you might as well swear off'n unintentional sneezing, or unintentional farting, or unintentional yawning. I'd like you to show me in the Bible where that is about what a gentleman is. I bet that ain't the whole verse."

That was how Jack Butler was, if you let him he could drive you crazy, and you might as well hang yourself in advance as to be snowed in with him, but Rolf could get away from him now and then, and get his bearings, so he didn't feel he was on a runaway merry-go-round listening to Jack talk.

The trouble was, Jack really didn't need a hand, just somebody to amuse him so he wouldn't fall into drink. But with all that bobwire, there was no excuse for not building fence, so that's what they done. Building fence ain't a bad job, if you don't get too much of it at once, because a short stretch of fence gives you a nice change. First you go out and cut your posts. Then you hitch up your team and haul your posts to where you're going to string your fence, and you lay them out in a line. Then you dig your holes, and you've got to set your posts right away, so some critter don't step in the empty hole and break his leg. Then you get the stretchers out and hang your top bobwire. Then you go along and steeple it down. Then you hang the next wire, and so on, until you've got as many wires as you need, or as you can afford.

But where you're stringing a long fence, first you've got all post-cutting, and then all post-hauling, and then all post-setting, and then nothing but stretching your wire day after day. And Jack Butler lost a lot of his charm after you'd heard his stories a few times. Most of them was horse stories, with a few mules throwed in for variety, and a couple of famous poker hands he had seen, and a reformed train robber he had met, and a woman who picked his pocket in Kansas City. He had a couple of stories about widows he had courted, but he said they wasn't the kind you'd ordinarily tell a preacher, and Rolf didn't give him no encouragement.

Jack came to feel the same way about Rolf and his life in prison, until one evening he said, "Rolf, I don't know about you, but I need a change from yarns about prisoners cutting each other with spoon handles they sharpened on the stone floor, and betting who can find the most worms in the salt pork, and so on. I'm frank with my friends, and I consider you a friend, and I'd appreciate knowing how you feel about it."

Rolf said, "Jack, spoken like a man! I swore off the liquor, but you can drive me so close to drink with your same old stories that I can understand your weakness for it. I think you drive yourself to drink with them stories of yours."

"You see, we're getting on each other's nerves! I say let's go to Mooney," Jack said.

Rolf squinted at him and said, "And get drunk, you mean? Do you feel a thirst coming on?"

"Oh Lord no!" Jack said. "Just for a change, before we come to blows and you force me to kill you."

"I'm sorry to disappoint you on that score," Rolf said, "but you won't kill me. I learned to fight before I went to prison, and I learned more after I was in there, and I'd have you picking up your own guts before you could trip on them."

"That's what you think," Jack said, "but this only proves it's time to go to Mooney and see somebody else than each other for a change."

So they saddled up and rode in, the first time Jack had let Rolf ride this Fanny mare, the most beautiful little mare he had ever rode, and only five years old. By the time they got to Mooney, Rolf was so enchanted with her, he was even considering preaching. The only thing he could fault her with, he wished she had four white feet instead of three. And like he said, that was pure vanity, that was criticizing the Lord's judgment in one of His finest creations. Next to a pure woman, you've got to rank an innocent child as the Lord's best work, but a good horse ain't going to be fur behind in third place, even ahead of a good hunting dog or a lifelong friend.

They put their horses in the livery barn on the respectable side of the crick, and Jack went over to Lickety Split, and Rolf went into a store and bought a nickel's worth of candy corn and a pair of socks, and then just about every other amusement in town was ruled out by his vows. He walked up and down the streets watching the dogfights, and a drunk who was fishing a penny out of a crack in the plank sidewalk, and a rooster that was scaring himself to death on top of an upside-down washtub. Every time he'd haul off to crow, he'd have to flap his wings, and when he whanged the tub with them wings it would boom out and scare him cross-eyed. The minute he got over it he'd try it again, but he never did get to where he could let out a crow. He'd get his neck craned and his beak open, and then BOOM, BOOM, BOOM he'd thump that washtub with his wings, and he'd jump a foot in the air and come down cross-eyed. Finely he had to give up, and he slunk off looking like he'd swore off ever crowing again, and he went into the blacksmith shop, and then under a tree where it was shady, and he stood there shaking his head for a long time.

A young fella figuring on what his life's work is going to be, he ought to consider how he'll spend his time off. A blacksmith or anybody that works with his muscle, he can put his feet up on another chair, and he don't need to read or think or nothing, and if he's got a couple of days off, why fishing is tailor-made, he don't care whether they bite or not. A storekeeper can go to Denver or Cheyenne or San Antonio or Sioux Falls, and let his wife go to concerts, and have wine with his supper, and maybe slip away from her for a couple of hours while she's trying on corsets. Or a liveryman can take a hotel room, as far from horses as he can get, and have the bellboy bring up a bottle, and a couple of sporting newspapers, and some cigars, and he don't need anything else. But what is a preacher going to do when he gets some time off? If he ever does.

So it came to where Rolf thought he had better look Jack up before he yielded to temptation, so he clumb down the crick bank and went over on the foot log, and he seen Jack right away, setting in Bea Cunningham's front parlor, drinking coffee with her where they could watch across the crick in case there was anything to see. She tapped on the window and said, "Come in, Reverend Ledger, I'm sure you won't do your future prospects in Mooney any good, but Abe Whipple and Jimmy Drummond are looking for you. They said they'd be back."

Rolf said he had just come to check up on Jack, and she said Jack would never get a drop on her premises. So he set down and had a cup of coffee with her and Jack, and pretty soon Abe showed up with this lawyer. He said it saved him a long ride out to the J Bar B, and this was as good a place as any to get things straight.

Rolf liked this Jimmy Drummond right off. Jimmy Drummond was a fairly old man, and he spent his time working or reading, and there wasn't much legal business for him in a town the size of Mooney, but his wife was buried there and he reckoned he'd stay to lie beside her in the end. He said:

"Abe's problem is one I've been prepared to deal with for years, and never expected to. I read law in a firm whose senior partner spent his life in research on the subject. He wrote a treatise that will never be published, because it isn't litigated as often as you may think. Religion causes a lot of arguments, but you'd be surprised how few times it gets into court."

"I wouldn't," Rolf said. "Any time you settle a religious argument, you take all the fun out of it."

"True, true," Jimmy said. "I can tell you what I think, based on a unique work in the history of law."

He had this fellow's life's work with him, a stack of paper six inches high, that he had entitled *Principles of Ecclesiastical Law,* and he had been through it from front to back, and had threshed out a few kernels that might be called wisdom or might be just weed seeds, depending on your point of view.

He said, "Of course the surest method is that of consecration by consecrated authority, to wit, a bishop or authority of equal rank. But the Congregationals don't have bishops, and they developed the system of ordaining by laying on of hands by the congregation, or by board members, deacons, elders, or vestrymen. There is also ordination by convention, when a candidate is examined publicly in faith and doctrine, or certified as reliable by a legally constituted examining board, after which the convention votes his ordination."

And so on. Or you could get yourself a Bible and go out and free-lance, and nobody could stop you from calling yourself Reverend, and the state would recognize marriages you performed, because the state wasn't going to get itself into no cat-fights about ordination, no sir, if it satisfied the married parties, it satisfied the state. Or you could go to a college, or for that matter start your own college, and along with your diploma you got ordained, and from that minute you was free to tote the light unto the Gentiles.

But Jimmy said, "I think the best thing for this young man is for the board to examine him in faith and doctrine, and lay on their hands, and declare him ordained, and then send the record of the procedure to the bishop. This isn't a two-bit congregation, and if the Methodists fool around too long, the Congregationalists or the Babtists or the Lutherans or somebody is going to step in here and take over a going concern, and the bishop knows that as well as anybody. Now that's what I would do, if I was you."

"Well thanks," Rolf said, "but you went to a lot of trouble for nothing. Nobody's going to examine me and nobody's going to lay any hands on me, and that's that. I've got a good job punching cows, and that suits me."

"Building fence, you mean," Abe said. "What a way for a good horseman to make a living! Why do you think I let you alone out there all these weeks, why, to come to your senses is why, punching cows my eye, you've forgot how to saddle a horse."

They jawed it over for a while, but Rolf's mind was made up, and finely the sheriff got up and clamped on his hat and went out, and Bea said, "I never saw Abe in such a state. It means a lot to him to get a preacher for that church. He's wiser than you may think. Discord in a church is a serious thing. It can wreck a town."

"I hate to see it happen myself," Jimmy Drummond said. "Of course I haven't got the stake in it that you have, an investment like you have in this place, I mean."

Bea said she wished Rolf would change his mind, and he said he wouldn't, and she seen his mind was made up so she let him alone.

6

Rolf seen that Jack was not in immediate peril of drownding his sorrows, so he started back to the other side of the town, but on the way he picked up a nice soft white-pine stick somebody had dropped, so he set down to whittle and think on the crick bank. He was just going good when here came old Abe Whipple looking for him again.

Abe said, "Listen, Reverend, we've got about as pitiful a case over there with one of the Jackrabbit girls as you ever seen. Her name is Lois. To make a long story short, she hasn't been at the Jackrabbit very long, but already she's one of his most famous girls. There was a fella come all the way from Greeley today to see her, based entirely on what he'd heard. He should of had better sense, naturally, and I won't go into details with you, but some of the things he heard about her is just an absolute impossibility.

"He brought along fifty dollars, a princely sum for even a Jackrabbit girl. Now here's the tragedy, Reverend. The minute they met, it turns out he's her brother, and she's his baby sister that he ain't seen since she was twelve years old back in Cincinnati. Almighty God, you can imagine the shame. It throwed her into a convulsion, just the pure shame of it. Doc Nobile says she'll die of it."

"What happened to the brother?" Rolf said.

"He went out the back door, right across there not more than a hundred yards, you could see it if it wasn't for the brush and Huey's privy, and he took a knife and cut his own throat. He made a bad mess of it, but he got the main job done all right, it killed him deader than hell. The thing is, even if this girl comes out of the convulsion, they've got to tell her about her brother, and she'll prob'ly flop right back into it again."

"Why are you telling me this?" Rolf said.

"Well, Dr. Nobile calls it catatonic hysteria, and he says it's beyond medical aid. He said you might have a chance to fetch her up," Abe said.

"What does she look like?" Rolf said.

"Reverend, she's just stiff as a board, with her eyes walled back to the whites, and her eyelids only half open, and my God you ought to see her mouth! It's like a grin only no grin you ever seen before, more like a wolf that has died hard from strychnine."

Rolf said, "I seen a prisoner go catatonic once, only he didn't stiffen up. He got limp as a rag, and he just tapered off breathing until he quit entirely."

"I reckon it's different with a woman, they must get stiff as a board. Doc Nobile says it's a sickness of the soul, and you're a better physician than he is for it. That's quite an admission for a medical man to make. I'd say it checks the bet to you."

Rolf shook his head slowly and went on whittling. "No, Abe. I know my powers and I ain't ashamed of them. I've got guts enough to bury a man, or forgive his sins, or lead a Sabbath chapel lesson. But there's a thing called a 'call,' and either you feel it or you don't, and I don't. And if I was the Lord, and somebody I hadn't called turned up trying to heal somebody in My name, I'd consider he had took a lot onto himself."

Abe laid his hand on Rolf's shoulder and said, "I see what you mean, but listen, I went to look for you at Beatrice Cunningham's place first, and she said tell you this. She says she *knows* you have the power to heal this girl. She says you can give her back her life, her pride, her hope, and her soul. She says *she* can get along without a soul, but it's plain that Lois can't. She said to tell you that, Reverend. You know as well as I do that you're not going to get any spurious spiritual talk from a madam in a whorehouse, this woman says she *knows*, because she's seen it in your eyes whether you feel it's there or not. Maybe you can argue with her, Reverend, but I'm older than you, and by God I can't."

Rolf leaned down and rested his forehead on his hand, and done his best to think of a decent way to get out of it, not because he was afraid of the job, but because he was satisfied with the way things was and he didn't want to risk any change in his life. But there wasn't no way he could talk himself out of it, he had to go see that girl and do his best.

So he put his pine stick away where he could find it again, and closed up his jackknife, and him and Abe went over to the Jackrabbit. They had laid this girl out on her bed of sin, on her back, and had took off her shoes and hair net. She had a crucifix hanging around her neck by a chain, and Rolf thought sure she was a Catholic, but one of the other girls said no, Lois won that in a crap game with a fellow from Idaho only last night.

This girl was so white she was blue, like she had been washed with bluing in the water, and her mouth was just like

Abe said, more a snarl than a smile, and you couldn't see her breathe. Jack Butler broke out sobbing the minute he seen her. There wasn't no way you could keep that man out of something like that.

"I wish I had brought a Bible along," Rolf said. "This will be like dealing with my eyes shut. Well, the rest of you get out of here and lock the door."

They seen him kneel down before they closed the door, and Huey said, "What good will it do to save this poor little whore? How else can she make a living? She can't sew or cook or raise garden or chickens, and this just about disables her for the trade. Some people sure have tough luck in this life."

"Shut up and bow your Goddamn head," Abe said, so he did, and they all shut up and listened. It was a mighty thin door, which ought to be a good lesson to anybody goes into one of those places thinking he's got any privacy to speak of. They could only hear a word here and a word there, and at first Rolf wasn't praying at all, he was just kneeling down there talking to this girl with his mouth to her ear, in a nice soft voice.

He told her the Lord Himself when He walked the earth had a mighty good friend by the name of Mary Magdalene who was in the same business, and He just gave her one good straight look, and she was new and white and clean like she'd just been born. He said there was another hooker that fixed herself up by just reaching out and touching the hem of His shirttail. He told her she might think she didn't deserve a friend left in the world, but he was going to be her friend, and Jesus would be her friend too, and anybody that mistreated her would have them both to account to.

He said life was a tough old trail to ride for poor folks, and she had spent her whole life getting into this fix, true enough. But he said there was savages all over the world *born* in worse shape than she was, and the Lord held out His arms to them. He said he had seen the Canadian Indians hire their daughters out when they was only nine or ten years old, but they was still children, and of such was the Kingdom of Heaven. He said the Lord would put His arm around them when the time came and never think He wouldn't. He said that in China, they throwed girl babies into the river to drownd them, or else they raised them to be ten or eleven and sold them to be whores in the seaports, and at least her folks hadn't done that to her.

He said that when she got stiff as a board it was trying to punish herself for her sins, and that wasn't none of her business at all, Judgment is mine saith the Lord, and who do you think you are? Throwing around the wrath of God like you was God Himself, when them kids in China had it a lot worse than she ever had! He said he had seen men in prison, so vile and miserable that she was pure as an angel compared to them, a whorehouse wasn't half as bad as prison if only people knowed what went on there, and he could testify that the power of the Lord got through them steel doors anyway, and every now and then brought somebody to his senses in time, and he'd seen it happen. Not to mention any names, he said, he knowed one prisoner that was just about the stubbornest fool he had ever met, and the Lord didn't let *him* down, in fact this fellow was pardoned soon after.

He said the Lord cautioned people about being stiff-necked, and here she was being stiff all over, when all she had to do was let herself go limp and feel the arm of Jesus go around her. He said that it was sure enough true that Jesus hated sin, but He loved sinners, and if He could meet her, all He'd say was, "Lois, go and sin no more!"

Well at this she started to breathe so a man could see it, and he kept on talking to her, and then he seen her eyes unwall, so the dark part showed as well as the whites. Then she began to cry, and then to scream, and he thought he was going to have to slap her to keep her from going stiff on him again.

But he just said, "All right, you're limbered up again, now here's what I want you to do. I want you to get down on your knees and pray for peace of mind and heart and soul."

She said, "Oh bullshit, my own brother, he always took such pride in the family, and in me, he used to bring me paper flowers and kerchiefs and things when he come back from his trips, I say bullshit to you."

He said that was fine with him, if that was the way she felt about him. But he said, "I'll tell you one thing, you've got more guts than your brother had. Your brother is dead."

She said she knew it, she knew it, oh my God he killed himself. Rolf said, "Yes he did, and what you and me can only guess at, he knows now. Maybe there's no heaven, and no hell, nothing but cold meat when we die. If you know that, then go ahead and do it your way, but I sure don't, and if I's you, I'd look at the other side for a change. Just in case it turned out there *was* a heaven, and there *was* forgiveness, and there *was* a merciful God who forgave the sinner. I'd try to picture your no-account brother up there trying to square himself fast—not because he's afraid of burning up in hell forever, *but for your sake!* I don't see how you can take a chance, Lois, because what if he is up there trying to do something for you, and you're down here refusing even to say a prayer."

He wore her out, or something, because she did get down and pray, but she couldn't think of no words. Rolf said he'd do the praying, and all she had to do was let out an "amen" every time something went past her that she agreed with.

Abe reckoned now was the time for them to get out of there, so him and Huey and Jack tiptoed out and went down to the bar, and Huey called for buttermilk for himself and Jack, and whatever the sheriff wanted. Abe said he'd take strawberry water with a little whisky in it, to celebrate the first time in history that Huey Haffener had stood treat for anything. To jump ahead, Lois got well, and she had almost nine hundred dollars saved up, and she took this and went up to Kimball County, Nebraska, and married a fella there, and made him a good wife. A happy ending to a sad story. He was a wheat farmer, but nobody can be all bad.

7

When they catched up with Rolf, he was back at his whittling, with his boot heels hooked in the bark of the rotten old log he was setting on, staring at the mud of the crick bank with his old hat on the back of his head. He gave them a look like he'd just as soon they'd let him alone. But Abe set down beside him, and Huey and Jack set down on the other side, and he seen he was cornered.

"Dr. Nobile is with her," Abe said. "He says she's going to be all right."

"He does, does he," Rolf said.

Huey said, "In fact, I never seen Lois look prettier, and I would of bet anything we was going to have to bury her stiff as a board."

"I never did think that, not after I talked to Bea," Abe said. "She might not know religion, but she knows whores, and I know enough about religion to feel sure of my ground. My grandmother was a Sephardic Spanish Jew, you know, and a lot of them Bible people was Jews."

"I never knowed that," Jack said.

"It's a fact! Ask Rolf," Abe said.

Jack asked him, and Rolf said why sure. He said, "In fact, our Lord Himself was a Jew, didn't you know that?"

"I may of heard it, but if I did, I forgot it," Abe said. "For all anybody knows, I may be descended from Him. I could have in my very own veins that Precious Blood they're always talking about."

Rolf said, "Abe, you're a fool! Our Lord died a single man, executed, you might say, as a felon. They railroaded Him, and they convicted Him on perjured testimony, and they executed Him fast so He couldn't take it up on appeal. Nobody on earth ever had a rawer deal than Him, and believe me, I'm a man who knows what it is to be unjustly convicted."

Abe said, "Well, I could still be related to Him. Over in Blessed Sacrament, they got a statue of Jesus that could pass for a Spaniard. I'll bet we both come down from the same line of people."

"Tell you what, Abe," Huey Haffener said. "Let's go down to the crick there, and you turn that water into wine, at least try your luck at it."

Rolf looked at him and said, "Mr. Haffener, I can't speak for a patient and forbearing God, but I'll tell you that from a personal point of view, you're being as offensive as a wet goat by a hot stove."

"Oh what are you so touchy about?" Huey said.

In former times, Rolf would of busted anybody that talked like that right in the nose, but he said, "Don't try my patience! I've had a hard time of it with that girl, and I saw the Lord heal her, and I'm in no mood for the kind of jokes you put out."

Huey twitched and grinned and batted his snot-colored eyes. He said, "Oh look here, you don't really mean the Lord come into that room and cured Lois, do you?"

Rolf said softly, "You don't believe that?"

Huey said, "Oh hell, of course not, do you think I was born yesterday?"

Rolf stood up off'n the log, and snapped his knife shut, and laid his whittling stick down, and put his hands on his hips. "Then you look me in the eye, Mr. Haffener," he said, "and tell me in plain short easy words what you see in me."

Huey said, "In you? Why a plain old cowboy, a nice enough fella, and you've got sand, nobody could of stood up to that old bitch that wanted Bea run out of the church without plenty of sand. Let's say, Ledger, I'd give even money on you to ride a bronc or skin a dead cow faster than anybody else. But on whomping up a miracle and summoning the Lord into a whorehouse, why you're on the short end of a million to one."

"So that's how you see it," Rolf said.

"Yes, and don't take offense. You asked me fair and square, and I told you fair and square," Huey said.

"I don't take offense. You got me pegged, I'd say. Now, you seen that woman in a rigid convulsion, didn't you?" Rolf said.

"No mistake about that, she was sure stiff," Huey admitted.

"You seen Dr. Nobile throw in his cards?" Rolf said.

"Yes, he's an honest man. If he can't help you, he says so, he don't just give you a sugar pill and send you a bill for a dollar," Huey admitted.

"You seen me go into that room with her, and you yourself helped lock me in there, didn't you?" Rolf said.

"We all seen that. What's your point?" Huey said.

"Well go see her now," Rolf said, "cleansed and well and happy, turned over a new leaf with her sins washed away. I was the only human bean in the room with her, and I couldn't heal a dog of the slobbers of my own power. Now if *I* didn't heal her, tell me this—*who did?*"

Huey just set there twitching and batting his eyes, and Abe said, "He's got you by the balls, Huey. Either Rolf did or God did, now one or the other."

Huey shook his head. "I'm only glad that it happened by daylight," he said. "It sure gives you the creeps, son of a bitch if it don't! The Lord Himself in that room, why I'll never be able to use it again."

Word of that healing spread over Mooney so fast you'd think there was a dozen wagon bridges over the crick and a brick road to each of them. They just deviled that poor cowboy to death. Everybody that had a hair crosswise, they wanted him to heal them. This one-legged man that worked in the livery barn, he wanted his leg back after thirty years.

There was some opposition. Frank Mueller, the butcher that had been the only witness to the escape of whoever killed Peg

Saymill, was a socialist. He wanted to know if Rolf could work a miracle, why didn't he raise the colonel from the dead? That was a good question, and Rolf admitted it.

He could only say that he wasn't a healer or a miracle worker, all he did was pray, and he'd done this plenty of times before, and never had no such crazy unexpected results. But he said he wasn't ashamed of it and he wouldn't back down on what happened, not if they lynched him. But he said he wasn't going to try it again, he felt too let down to work himself up like that, and they could like it or lump it.

There was one person wouldn't take no for an answer, Mrs. Mable McMurdoch, organist in the church, and wife of the banker. She pinned Rolf to a brick wall and leaned against the wall to shut him off on one side, and she shook her finger in his face to herd him back on the other.

She said, "Pastor, I know the power of prayer, and I know the limitations of those who pray, but I've got a little boy, a nephew I'm trying to raise, that I think falls within those finite limitations. You can help him. He got throwed from his pony a year ago September, and hurt his back. Dr. Nobile says it's healed long ago, but poor Emmet is afraid to try to walk, afraid of pain and failure, and I haven't the heart to make him because, God forgive me, I'm afraid too."

"So am I," Rolf said when he could pinch a word in by its thin edge.

"Well just roll up your sleeves and pretend you're not, Pastor," she said, "because I think you can get to this boy's cob, you might say, where nobody else could. No use asking my husband, he don't care much for Emmet anyway and he only puts up with prayer, but this is a case for a man."

"You expect too much of me," Rolf said.

"No I don't," she said. "I only expect you to try, but I have faith in you if not in myself, and I think you'll hearten that boy, and that's what he needs if he's going to take up his bed and walk. If he don't, Pastor, he's going to be a bedfast cripple all his life."

She catched Rolf by the arm, and dragged him home to

where she lived, and here was this kid, Emmet James Day, laying in a hammock under a tree, Day being her maiden name. Emmet was the son of her diseased brother. He was just laying there, looking up through the leaves. He was a puny little thing, and he didn't take no interest in Mrs. McMurdoch, and even less in Rolf.

A lot of people had follered them home to see the miracle, and they was tromping down Mable's flowers and taking turns getting a drink at the pump. Rolf told them to get out and give him elbow room with this spoiled little brat, and Mable made them get out of there. Rolf picked up a wooden box, and stood it on end beside the hammock, and he set down on it and started in.

Nobody seen or heard what happened, and Rolf never talked about it and neither did the kid, and the only sure thing was that the kid was right, it did hurt something awful, and he didn't pick up his bed and walk that day, not by any means. But he did get up on his feet, and he cried and cursed Rolf something awful, and Rolf got him back in his hammock and began showing him tricks with a deck of cards Emmet had. Rolf had always been good at card tricks, and in prison an old-timer had taught him a few that could of made him a rich man if he hadn't of swore off gambling. It wouldn't of been no gamble by then, though, the way he could deal a deck.

Later on that day, Mable heard the kid crying, and she went out in the back yard, and there he was up on his feet, trying to hobble from tree to tree, and saying, "Oh God it hurts, Goddamn but it hurts, my son of a bitching back anyway." Mable cried, first because he was trying to walk, and second because he used that kind of language. But Rolf told her that everybody had his own way of praying, and first you got the kid up on his feet, and then you broke him of swearing. One thing at a time.

The next day he was going tree to tree, and then to the pump, and then to the woodshed, and before summer was over he had learned to spit between his teeth and skin the cat on a tree limb, and was a sore trial to that poor woman, he was so full of hell.

That's jumping ahead, but there was enough early signs for it to be another miracle, so before anybody else could make an offer, the Methodist board got together and voted to tie Rolf up. They would go as high as $2.50 a sermon, and fix the leak in the roof over the pulpit. They had a parsonage they could rent for eight dollars a month, so they was coming out of it dirt cheap. Although somebody said $2.50 for an hour's sermon is more than a single man has a right to expect, if he's holding down a steady job during the week, and can't visit the sick or comfort the dying between weekends.

Rolf must of said "no" a hundred times, as patient as possible, which wasn't very patient by nightfall, and he would of stuck to it except for one thing. This thing was Jack Butler, and Jack said, "Well if you ain't going to preach, what do you need with a fast horse to make a trip in every Sunday? You won't need Fanny then, will you? Pick out any other horse on the place for your working string, and let's put her back in the barn."

That was more than you could ask Rolf to stand, but he had this bullheaded streak in him, he quit saying "no" but he still wouldn't say "yes." So Abe got the board together quietly at Jimmy Drummond's office, and he got Rolf to go up there with him for some reason or other, and they broke the news that he was to be examined on faith and doctrine.

"That's what you think," Rolf said. "This job is over my head, and I know it, and you ain't going to examine me in faith and doctrine or anything else."

One of the board members said, "I don't know what it is you object to, Reverend; you believe in the Apostle's Creed, don't you?"

"More or less," Rolf said.

So they looked at each other, and then one of them said, "I believe we can pass this candidate for the Christian ministry with a thankful and joyous heart, and I so move." The others said they would too, and they skinned him through the examination before Rolf knowed what was happening.

"Now you had better bless him with the laying on of hands," Jimmy Drummond said. "Reverend Ledger, you get down on your knees, and let them form a circle around you."

"That I will never do," Rolf said.

"I see," Jimmy said, "you're a proud old cowboy that can work miracles, a lot of gall anybody has got to expect you to kneel before the Lord."

"Somebody is going to pay for this," Rolf said. He knelt down, and they all put their hands on him, and Jimmy Drummond told somebody to pray that their candidate be acceptable unto God, that being a form he had found successful in *Principles of Ecclesiastical Law*. So old McMurdoch, he said, "Lord, we bring Thee a preacher to preach Thy word, and before Thou findest fault with him, consider our need. We ain't much of a congregation, and the longer this pulpit stands empty, the worse it will be. Look with pity on us, Lord, hung up on this side of the Continental Divide, neither frontier nor farm nor good honest cow country, drifters passing through like the dispossessed Children of Israel, and half of them don't have no idee where they're going. Thy beaver is gone from Thy streams, Thy buffalo has vanished, and Thy Indians with them, and when we look at some of the riffraff that has took their place, we see we have only went from bad to worse, because there's nothing worse than a bad white man, as Thou knowest. Oh Lord, we need preaching and guidance, and a strong hand on a severe bit, or here goes another of Thy churches the way of the beaver and the buffalo. If our candidate for Thy ministry don't look like suchamuch, look at what's left to pick from, and who's doing the picking. Make the best of what we have, oh Lord, and help him as Thee did across the crick, because we need it as bad as that woman, amen."

Somebody helped Rolf stand up, and Abe took off his neckerchief and wiped his eyes. "I may hear worse prayers than that before I die, Mac," he said, "but I'll never hear a better."

"A man does the best he can," McMurdoch said.

Jimmy Drummond drawed up an affidavit for them to sign, saying they had examined Rolf in faith and doctrine, and found him sound in wind and limb. It stated that the examiners knowed of their own knowledge of a healing caused by the candidate's prayers for a contrite sinner he had brought to penitence, and that the congregation was all good Methodists, and that they hadn't heard nothing repugnant in his preaching to the good old Methodist creed, and that his unjust term in prison had taught the candidate how firm a foundation his life rested on, and so forth. They all signed it, and Jimmy swore them in as a notary public.

"This'll go to Denver by the U.S. Mail," Jimmy said, "but the gossip about healing that poor woman will beat it there. The bishop will either take you up on it, or there'll be a stampede of the other denominations in here, with more ordinations than you'll know what to do with."

"I still ain't going to preach steady in that church and I don't consider myself an ordained minister," Rolf said. "I don't mind helping the church out in a pinch, but enough is enough."

"That's up to you," Jimmy said. "You remember, though, that the church property follows the pulpit, and any time there's real estate at stake, ecclesiastical law is no different than the civil law—it'll find a good sound loophole to secure title. You may not feel ordained, but you'll get the patent or whatever they call it in the mail, and you take notice, it'll be dated today."

They thought they had themselves a minister, but they didn't know that old cowboy. He made up his mind right then that he would stay long enough to buy himself some new pants and a shirt, and maybe a suit of underwear, and if he could stand it that long, a new hat. And then he was going to light out some night, and change his name if he had to, because this was just more responsibility than he wanted to take on. Swearing off a few things is all right, most people backslide on them resolutions sooner or later, and Rolf looked on his oaths as a way of sliding back into civilian life a little at a time. But they wasn't fooling *him*, ordination was worse than getting married for tying a man down, and he meant to be long gone and unheard from before that bishop replied.

The truth was, Rolf was rattled bad by what had happened to that girl and that little boy. He never had backed down on a job or a dare, no sir, especially if there was one chance in a million it would work, and he went into both of them deals in that spirit, what did he have to lose but a little time? He had seen prayer fall flat as a pancake many a time, like every summer in Smith County, Kansas, when people a lot more righteous than him never let up petitioning the Lord for rain, and it never did rain, and a few times people prayed not to let somebody die, and they went ahead and died anyway. It just beat the thunder to him, how his prayers had worked on that poor miserable whore and that little boy.

He kept trying to get out of town to think it over, so's he'd have a ready answer for people that pestered him, but they kept coming up wanting to shake hands, or just to touch him, especially women, and what they wanted to do was grab and not just touch. A lot of people brought babies for him to bless.

He told them, "I can't bless nobody. I can only ask the Lord to do that, and you can do that much yourself." But you know how well that went over; no, they just wouldn't let him alone until he had put his hand on that baby's head, and shut his eyes and said a quick little short prayer, and then if he couldn't get out of it, kissed the baby. People are that kind of fools about their kids. Even if they don't take much stock in religion most of the time, they won't take a chance on their kids missing out on something.

There was going to be a full moon, but it was all clouded over, and was darker than a yard down a cow's throat before he busted away from people. He didn't know that town at all, and he walked into a couple of fences and one clothesline, and he started some dogs to baying, and he finally found himself blundering around down on the bank of the crick. He tripped over something and fell down on his knees, and he reckoned that as long as he was there, he might as well try a prayer or two for himself, and see if it done him half as much good as it did that girl and that little boy.

Well, finely he had to get up without no answer whatever, not one indication that the Lord was taking in any filings that day, court was closed as far as Rolf could tell. He was getting hungry anyway, so he pointed toward the lamps and pretty soon got back into town, not any more of a mess than you might think except for the knees of his pants, where he had went down in the mud. And the first people he seen was the Venaman family, in town to buy their month's groceries at the stores. Cal had already heard the news, and he wanted to shake Rolf's hand, and he seemed to be amused anyway at the news.

"You have unique qualifications and a unique opportunity, Parson," he said. "I'd like to have your own story of that girl's miraculous healing sometime."

"I ain't going to talk about it," Rolf said.

"Well, I'll respect your reticence. I hear it even gave Huey Haffener a jolt," Cal said.

"Well, he stopped twitching for a minute, and when he does, he just looks flabby all over," Rolf said.

"You've got Huey sized up. We'll see you day after tomorrow. Like everyone else, we'll make a special effort to get to church," Cal said.

"Day after tomorrow? Me and Jack thought this was Saturday!" Rolf said.

"No, it's only Friday. Don't feel badly about losing track of only a day. Living with Jack Butler, I can see how you'd lose a week easily," Cal said.

Rolf shook hands with Cal again, and then with Opal, and then with Winnie, and when he turned to shake with Samantha, she just deliberately didn't put her hand out to shake. She looked down at the muddy knees of his pants instead.

"I see you didn't lose any time putting on the public badge of your trade, Reverend," she said.

Rolf said, "I was just walking in the dark, ma'am, and I plainly and simply fell, that's all."

"I see!" Samantha said. "I'd clean those pants if I were you, Reverend. You're liable to mislead people into thinking you had been praying."

"They'd be right, ma'am, if they thought that. As long as I was down there, I thought I might as well."

"Oh?" she said. "If it isn't too personal, what does a new minister pray for immediately after the rite of ordination, or whatever it was?"

Rolf said, "Humility, Miss Samantha. I never was any too well stocked with it, and it seems to be in mighty short supply in sections of this congregation, too."

Cal laughed, but nobody else did, although Opal and Winnie swallered a little air, and got a little purple in the face, and couldn't look at each other. Rolf just walked off and left them, wondering what in tarnation had made him say a thing like that, because he never in his life had so much as used that word before, only read it, yet "humility" sprung to his mind as quick as a mouse trap snapping. And he knowed that words could be a vice too, yes they could, and he'd have to watch that in the future.

8

He found Jack pretty soon after that, blessedly sober as a judge, but spiritually buoyed up by what had happened to Lois until he just talked Rolf's leg off on the way home. He had some of the peculiarest idees about religion, like they was going to have a regular parade of women coming out there to the J Bar B to own up to their sins, and he said he didn't want a lot of fallen women giving the J Bar B a bad name, but what was really ailing him was that he had women on the brain. But Rolf let the talk roll off like water on a duck's back, and before the week was out, Jack had to face up to it that life was just stringing fence, nothing more.

They knocked off early Saturday morning, when Jack said he wanted to go into town and buy some bolts and washers and stuff. Rolf said, "Are you sure you don't want to liquor up, now? You don't have to lie to me."

"I never was in better shape to stand off my demon," Jack said. "All I want is some half-inch carriage bolts and washers."

They got an early enough start, but then they found one of Cal Venaman's horses bogged down in the mud, and they had to stop and pull it out, and then go back to the J Bar B and change clothes, so it was suppertime before they got to Mooney. Jack went over to the Jackrabbit where he always stayed, and Rolf was going to blow four bits on a room over the livery barn, only he run into Marcus Sippy and nothing would do but what he'd come there. It was his first experience with how women will flourish their cooking at the preacher, and trot out fruit jars their families didn't know they had, when their own husband was lucky to get bread and bacon-grease gravy for supper. Rolf went with Marcus, who sold harness and saddles, and his wife Blanche taught a Sunday school class and made missionary didies out of flour sacks. Everybody called her Blanche, whether they knowed her well or not, because you try saying "Mrs. Sippy" over and see what comes out.

Their supper was over and the kids was in bed, but Blanche took out the back door on a dead run when she seen Rolf coming with Marcus, and Rolf heard one strangled squawk and then another, and then a lot of flopping in the dried weeds, and he knowed two big fryers had been sacrificed in his honor. Marcus set Rolf down in the parlor, and give him the album to look at, and then he excused himself and went out.

Pretty soon he come back and set down too. Marcus had soldiered in the cavalry, and been in the Black Hills like Rolf, but somehow they couldn't get a conversation going, and Rolf knowed why. Marcus had excused himself to have a little snort, and then that wasn't enough, after he set down again he slipped off his boots, and there was a hole in one sock that let his big toe stick out, and he didn't know whether to put his boots back on or just pretend nothing had happened.

Then one of the kids hollered he had wet the bed, and all they could do was set there and rock and try to talk about the weather. But it had been clear and warm and dry for so long, with summer coming on, that finely they was both saying things like yes that's true, it certainly was a good open spring this year, that's right. Rolf knowed he had to take the bull by the horns or they was never going to stop pulling against each other.

He said, "Mr. Sippy, I hope the fact that I'm temporarily your minister don't make you uncomfortable in your own home. There couldn't be nobody commoner than me."

"What mortifies me," Marcus said, "is that Jacob wet the bed, and he's the one you're going to sleep with. He ain't done that in a long time."

"Don't worry, I don't mind a bit," Rolf said, and it was his first white lie as a preacher, and he reckoned it prob'ly wouldn't be his last.

Pretty soon Blanche said, "Five minutes! I set three places, Papa, because I know you'll want to eat and I do too; my, we'll be both as fat as Watertown geese, but land sakes how often do we get to enjoy a meal without the kids?"

Rolf and Marcus washed up, and then Marcus excused himself again, and had another little nip to steady to his hospitality chores, and he steadied too hard. He got to preening on Blanche's cooking, and how she could raise a chicken to be four or five pounds without getting too tough to fry, and so on.

"It sure is delicious," Rolf said. "I never et better fried chicken in my life, and there's nothing I love more than milk gravy from chicken grease."

"Blanche is part Scotch-Irish and part German," Marcus said. "You can't beat that combination."

He talked so much that he got Blanche nervous, and the way she kept watching him made Rolf nervous, and Marcus knowed it. He was one of these men who like to have a thing out in the open, even if it does embarrass you, so finally he blurted it out.

He said, "Reverend, I take a little nip every night before supper, but to my shame and sorrow, tonight I took a second one because I'm a poor host without something to touch off my kindling. That's a mighty poor excuse for imitating Jack Butler, but it's all I got."

Blanche just glared at him, but Rolf said, "I don't know why you feel you have to confess to me. I'm white-ribbon myself now, all the way, but in my time I have downed my share of the rotgut, and I figger it this way. So long as you carry it like a gentleman, and don't have to charge it at the saloon, and don't bring shame on your family or pass out like Jack Butler, what you do is your own affair."

"Reverend, Methodists is temperance!" Blanche said.

"I know that," Rolf said, "and it's their own affair, but you just show me where it mentions temperance in the Ten Commandments, ma'am."

Marcus said, "There, ain't that what I always said? Temperance means being temperate, and I'm a temperate drinker. Did you ever see me stewed?"

Blanche began to leak tears, and she said, "I have to say that's the truth, Reverend, it's not a problem for Papa, but we get the church papers and they're *so* down on liquor! A body don't know what to think."

"I know what I think," Rolf said. "Drunkenness is a sin, like sloth and lust and usury and lying, and I'll pray over a sot as long as anybody will hold him down, or until he's redeemed. But if we keep out everybody that takes a nip for his nerves, or a cold now and then, we shut the door on some of our best Christians."

She busted out weeping and said, "Have some more chicken, have some more fried potatoes, have some more creamed baby turnips."

Rolf was beginning to see he had to watch himself, because he had a gift of loosening people up he'd never suspicioned before. Until he went to prison, he had more of a tightening gift. He could go into a perfectly calm store or saloon or auction barn, and look the material over, and pick his man, and in two minutes all you'd see was elbows and feet, and all you'd hear was grunts and people yelling not to upset the stove. Them good old days was gone forever, but he meant to do the best he could as long as he was on this job, with no regrets. Just watch himself that he didn't loosen people into loading him down with a lot of nasty personal problems he couldn't help with.

Word had got around considerable, that Rolf was a good sound preacher, and single, and everybody with unmarried daughters anywhere from thirteen to fifty was there, and no Abe Whipple to help herd them. They said Abe had went out to see about some kind of a robbery, and the board wasn't no help, in fact it looked to Rolf that most of them favored somebody's daughter, usually one that needed all the help she could get.

He preached to a mighty good crowd, taking as his text Romans 11:1, I say then, Hath God cast away His people? God forbid. You can make just about anything you want out of that, so it's a mighty safe text for a new preacher, and when Rolf went into the pulpit instead of the lectern for the first time, he needed something good and safe. It just scared the dickens out of him, that pulpit. He said the difference was, when you spoke from the lectern, you was just any old body reading the Bible or something else, anybody could do that, some claimed even women, although that was going pretty far. But when you went into that pulpit, you was delivering a message from God, or at least *for* Him, and it was like the difference between transubstantiation and consubstantiation, it might be only a word, but so was hell only a word in a way. It depended not just on *what* you said, but *where* you said it and *how* you said it and *why*. Even if you talked like a fool, if it was from the pulpit, some fool was going to take it for the Gospel.

But he skinned through all right, claiming that they might feel cast away out there in Colorado, but the opposite was true; if they had that feeling it was because *they* had cast away God. He paid his respects to them that had struggled to hold the church together, although not at any great expense to anybody, and he said if they thought they had problems, they should of read up on them Romans that Paul was writing to. He said they was some of the most miserable people he ever heard of, with a perfect right to think they had been cast away. They had to hide down in the tunnels where they buried their dead, because it was against the law to be a Christian in them days, and they was all on the dodge.

And so on. They took up a collection, with Marcus Sippy and Alf Constable, the ushers, taking it up, with everybody keeping a mighty sharp eye on them. Then they sung another hymn or two, and Rolf asked Alf to lead them in prayer, because he looked like a man who could do it, and he could. They had another song, and then Rolf prayed and give the benediction, and then Mable McMurdoch pinned the people down with some music until he could get outside to shake hands as they marched out.

It was like slipping into any other job; you done the best you could and copied the workmen you admired the most, and that was all anybody could do. He shook hands with everybody, and they all told him how much they was inspired by his sermon, and he thanked them one and all. When Liz Saymill shook hands, she slipped a ten-dollar bill into his hand and whispered, "I hope you never lose your refreshing innocence, Reverend," and so he could really thank her with deep feeling.

He told Alf Constable he'd be proud to have Sunday noon dinner with him, because he didn't see no way out of it, Alf was just busting with pride over being picked to lead in prayer, but Rolf said he had to look up Jack Butler first, to make sure he wasn't yielding to his demon. Nobody could really follow him across the crick to make sure that was all he was going to do, but they made sure they hung around that part of town to see how long it took him.

He was just starting down the bank of the crick when this Irishman come across the footlog. His name was Bill Ahern, and he owned a half-interest in an eight-horse freight outfit that was making a little money, and he had been married to a local girl until she died suddenly. A well woman one day, and three months later dead of a terrible eating tumor in her female organs. Bill claimed to of fought fifty-eight rounds with the champion of Wales, and knocked him out.

Bill got to be a problem when his wife died, getting drunk every time he got lonesome, which was every time he got in from a freight trip, and then going out and looking for somebody worth whipping. Most of them wasn't, but he whipped them anyway. It took five or six men to arrest him, and volunteers had got scarce, so mostly Abe Whipple tried to reason with him. Sometimes he could and sometimes he couldn't and today he was out of town on this robbery.

Bill had quite a brogue, especially drunk, so you could tell by it how much he had drunk. He had on hobnailed teamster boots and was carrying his shirt over his shoulder. He always took his shirt off when he was looking for somebody worth whipping, so he wouldn't have to stop and take it off then, and risk a chance the fella would get away.

Rolf didn't have no idee who Bill Ahern was, only that he was a big drunk with no shirt on, on a Sunday, but he stepped aside and said, "Good morning." Bill stopped and looked at him, and he seen there wasn't no fair fight in anybody Rolf's size, and all it done was annoy him to be spoke to when his mind was on a fight.

He said, "Well, Jesus Christ, what difference does it make what kind of a morning it is? I'm tired of that kind of talk. You can't do nothing about what kind of a day it is."

His brogue was so thick it was hard to understand him, but Rolf did, and he said, "Well, what we can't help, we can either endure or enjoy, I reckon."

"Jesus Christ, are you saying you're going to *make* me enjoy it?" Bill said. "Even if I don't feel like it?"

Rolf said, "No, my friend, and this is twice you've used the name of the Lord in vain to me. I'm a sort of a deputy minister of the gospel, and I resent it, and you don't hurt me, only your own immortal soul and what manliness you have, if you have any. Just a reminder."

"You're a piss-poor specimen," Bill said.

"I know when somebody's twisting my tail to make me beller," Rolf said, "and I ain't going to beller. But I'm purely tired of standing here arguing, and I ask you man to man to let me pass."

Bill swang at him, and Rolf seen it coming and rolled backwards uphill, staying out of the mud, and coming up on his feet again hardly spitting any blood at all. You could hear Bill all over town, and most of the men from the church suddenly passed up propriety in favor of not missing anything, and if you'd passed the hat up there on top of the bank, you'd of had the cream of society to deal with.

Not that anybody made any move when they seen Bill knock the new preacher down. There was enough of them to swarm over him like bees, and weight him down several deep, but a thing like that takes leadership, and leadership don't necessarily pop out when it's most needed. Rolf felt his way back uphill backward when he come to his feet, and he dusted his clothes off a little and said:

"You hit like a man who knows how to fight, then you ought to have sense enough to know you didn't land that one. Well, then you ought to have sense enough to know I can whip you if I have to."

Them people up on the bank just purely panted at that, not a gasp but a whole gale of panting, like they was thinking has this young preacher gone crazy or what? Talking about whipping Bill Ahern.

Bill said, "You can what? Jesus Christ, you couldn't lick the cream crock with the cat."

"That does it," Rolf said.

He come down the path, and Bill smiled and throwed away his shirt, and doubled up his fists, and he had fists the size of the hoof of a Shire horse, and about as hard, and arms like cottonwood limbs. Well he come at Rolf swinging, and then there he was sliding back down towards the crick on his hind end, blood puddling out of his nose and one eye closing up.

He said, "Say that was some trick, let's see you do it again." He stood up and licked his thumb, and people knowed that when Bill licked his thumb, watch out because he was getting ready to enjoy himself.

Rolf said, "My friend, I learned to fight in prison. You're prob'ly fairly tough, but where your kind of fighting leaves off, that's where prison fighting begins."

So Bill jumped him again, and come down on nothing, and then Rolf was all over him, hitting him with his fists whenever he seen his chance, but also with knees and elbows and boot heels, and the top of his head. Every time Bill got up, Rolf knocked him down, until finely he did let Bill get up and catch hold of the bushes to stay up. He asked Bill if he had enough, and Bill said no he was just getting started.

He come in for more, and this time he really got it, and there wasn't no way Rolf could quit, because as long as Bill could move, even his little finger, or one toe, he was ready to fight. Finely he couldn't even move them, and a couple of men had to come down from the top of the bank and help Rolf carry him up.

"He is just a troublemaker," Rolf said. "Anybody that fights on Sunday only wants to make trouble."

"That's right in a way," somebody said, "but Bill used to be harmless except on payday, but since he lost his wife he has been pure poison."

"Well why did he have to take it out on me?" Rolf said.

"He had already took it out on everybody else, Reverend," this fella said.

"That's a mighty poor excuse," Rolf said, "but leave me alone with him. I never lost anybody near and dear to me, but it must be pretty bad," Rolf told him.

"She was sure dear to him," this fella said. "He just doted on that girl."

Bill come to, and him and Rolf was alone except for two or three dozen people that had stepped back to a decent distance. Bill said, "Give me a few minutes, and I'm your man again. You're a good dirty fighter, my kind."

Rolf said, "I found out why you want to fight everybody, because you lost your wife."

Bill said, "Drop that you slobber-mouth pious son of a bitch, you're not fit to mention her name."

Rolf said, "I don't even know her name, I only say my heart goes out to you, and I forgive you wanting to fight me, because that kind of suffering comes only from love, and God has nothing but mercy for a heart full of love, and who am I to argue with Him? But I'll tell you this much, Bill, that wife of yours is now with Him, and my hunch is she feels this foolishness has to come to an end, she prob'ly didn't like your fighting when she was alive, and it don't seem logical she'd be for it now."

"I *wish* you'd shut *up* about her, how *much* can a man *stand?*" Bill said.

Rolf said, "As much as he has to. The Lord giveth and the Lord taketh away, blessed be the name of the Lord. You can't fight this with your fists, or with the hardness of your heart if you've got any. Only grace can help you, and don't ask me what grace is because I can't tell you, only that if you had it you wouldn't go around shaming your wife's memory the way you do. And you look me in the eye and tell me this, Bill—besides being a sin and a public disgrace, what good does it do you?"

"Nothing, but I can't stand it if I don't," Bill said. "She was the best woman! You just get your hands on something good in life, and it slips away from you. The only thing really good in my life was that woman."

Rolf said, "I ain't got no answer to you. I never had your experience, and anyways I'm only a man, and not suchamuch of a one at that. Who you need to grab hold of the other side of this heavy pail handle is God. You've tried everything else,

Bill. If you want, I'll be glad to lead these neighbors of yours in a little prayer. What have you got to lose?"

"Nothing I reckon," Bill said.

So they all bowed their heads, and them that had hats on took them off, and Rolf opened by reminding the Lord that He was responsible for this man's mess by taking his wife, and it was up to Him to ante up now. He said it surely wasn't no offhand whim of the Lord's to take her, but part of a plan, and he wasn't trying to tell Him how to run His business, but he did feel some responsibility for this poor bereaved trouble-making Bill Ahern. He said it wasn't going to be no easy job to touch Bill's heart with grace, but it couldn't be much harder than turning water into wine, like he done at the wedding in Cana. He wound up with an over-all general apology for the worthlessness of people in general and Bill in particular, and then he said, "Let Bill know some way, and You can do it if You put Your mind to it, that Bill's wife is still doing the best she can to take care of him, only he won't let her, this we ask in Christ's name, amen."

Bill was still setting down, and at this he covered his face with his hands and let out a yell. "I can see her face in my mind! I see her, I see her, I had forgot her dear face, but now I see her again!"

"That's grace, Bill," Rolf said.

Bill started blubbering around, and pounding the dirt with his fist, and he said, "I forgot what her face looked like. That was what hurt. You just have no idee how it hurt! She wasn't a pretty woman, you ask anybody though and they'll tell you that Grace was a good woman, really good, and now somehow it's like I partly got her back."

"Was her name Grace?" Rolf said.

"Why sure, what did you think?" Bill said.

Rolf said, "Well all right, just cut out this trying to whip everybody. I don't care how good you are, you're going to run into somebody that can whip you."

"You for instance?" Bill said. "We'll try that again sometime, when I'm sober."

"Not me," Rolf said. "God. Nobody can whip Him."

9

A healing is all right, there's prime material for popularity in it, but for downright public idolatry, nothing equals winning a good fight over a man nobody thought nobody could whip. Even Huey Haffener come out of his prairie-dog hole to shake Rolf's hand, and Rolf said it was like handling a piece of hog liver.

"I only regret I missed the spectacle," Huey said. "I'm a great admirer of the manly art."

"I'm sorry it happened," Rolf said, "and I'm sure Bill wasn't at his best, was at his worst in fact."

"It's when Bill is at his worst that you want to worry, padre. Tell you what I'm going to do, I'm going to make a donation to your church."

Rolf said, "Well that will be appreciated, Huey, the Lord don't take no account of where money comes from, but you might examine your spirit in giving it." Huey took out his purse, and fished around in it quite a while, and made up a dollar out of quarters, dimes, and a nickel, and on second thought added another quarter to it, making $1.25.

Rolf said, "Are you sure you can afford this, Huey? I don't want your impulsiveness to run you short of the necessities of life."

You couldn't get Huey's goat any way about money, but he did scowl and scrounge around and come up with another $1.25 in silver, making $2.50 in all.

Rolf said, "Tell you what I'd ruther do, Huey. You take this back, and I'll go down there and take up a collection among your girls, and you match it."

Huey said, "You're a hell of a bargainer for a man of the cloth," and he handed Rolf a $10 gold piece, and got out before Rolf could twirl his rope for a foot catch. Making $12.50 in all, a record for Huey. Bill Ahern had turned Huey's place upside down more than once, and Huey himself once, and sloshed his head on the floor and into his spittoons, and it should of been worth $100 to Huey. But try getting it out of him.

A man likes to be liked, but Rolf had learned to make do with what human kindness leaked through the bars of a prison, which is just about none, and this overflow of appreciation had him edgy, so the harness was beginning to gald. Also he couldn't find Jack Butler, and he feared the worst.

So it was a relief to get free of people and go home with Alf Constable to dinner, which was roast pork loin with fresh spring greens and canned gooseberry sauce from last year's crop, and cinnamon rolls with raisins in them, and then green-apple cobbler from this year's crop. Alf run a feed and seed store, and also handled some horse medicine, and he raised garlic, and also fed about two hundred hogs a year. This was a nice two-hundred-and-fifty-pound barrow that accidentally got himself kicked in the head the night before, but Alf stuck it less than a minute after it happened, and an old-time butchering man like him, it didn't take him no time at all to boil up water to scald it in. A real good loin of roast fresh pork. One year, Alf shipped more than one hundred and forty pounds of garlic to Denver, where there was a lot of foreigners working around there in the mines who would eat it. His wife, Keziah, wouldn't have it in the house. Keziah was a Travis and originally a Presbyterian, but she made the switch to Methodist without any strain.

After they had finished eating, and Keziah went out to give the scraps to the dogs, Alf said, "Reverend, you look pretty peaked to me. Are people pestering the dickens out of you? It looks like that to me."

Rolf said, Well, he couldn't complain of the kindness they intended, but it was beginning to raise his sweat. So Alf said, "All right, you come with me, I'll show you the best little old hide-out in town. Nobody else knows about it, but you feel free to sneak in here and use it any time these people bear down on you too hard."

He showed Rolf a hammock he had slung between two trees out beside his hogpen, under some Concord grape vines that was just setting on green grapes. He said, "Reverend, do you know what, I killed a man once." Rolf said no, he hadn't heard that, and Alf said, "Well, I did. I didn't go to, it was over a woman, and the shame is, it was after I was married to Keziah. I was fooling around with her, and it's no excuse that she was a loose woman and easy to fool around with, a man makes that decision himself. Well there was another fella fooling around there too, and to make a long story short, him and me came to blows, and I knocked him pizzle-end upwards, and he come at me with a knife. Now I don't know what was in *his* mind, but I know that in *my* mind, all I wanted to do was knock that knife out of his hand and get out of there once and for all. Well what happened, I hit him with a chair and knocked him down, and he fell on his own knife and cut his own throat."

"That's a sad story," Rolf said.

"Yes it is. You can't give life back. Well this woman said for me to light a shuck out of town, this poor misguided dead bastard had often enough threatened to hang himself over her, and it wouldn't be no problem making people believe he'd cut his throat instead. This was down in Waxahachie, Texas. I was down there looking for some likely feeder steers for a fella on commission, and I was on the first train out of there you can really believe, headed back to St. Louis where me and Keziah was living. She don't know about this to this day. I never told it to anybody but you."

"I don't know what to say," Rolf said. "It ain't my place to say you're forgiven, although I'm sure in my heart that you are. Most forgiveness, if you ask me, comes from a heart that's heartily sorry."

"I hope I am," Alf said. "I'll tell you this much, Reverend, when that thing troubles me, or anything else troubles me, I just lay here and look up through them grape leaves to the sky, and prayer seems to mean more here than it does even in the church. I hope you won't take offense at that. It's a kind of a pagan way of looking at things, but that's how it is."

Rolf said he could sure enough understand it, he'd laid in a prison cell too many miserable days and nights not to appreciate being outdoors, and he was the last man in the world to say God wouldn't come close to a hogpen. Alf said, "Well, Reverend, you ain't old and you ain't learned, but you talk straight from the shoulder and you whipped Bill Ahern, and you may have more of a power in you than you suspicion. I'm glad I told you. I do feel better—maybe not entirely forgiven, but like I was getting there."

Alf went back to the house, and Rolf laid down in that hammock and thought, My goodness, what a lot of unhappiness people got themselves into, and then dumped it all on the minister, and all he could do was try to keep his knees from buckling and take it. He said to himself, Well I ain't up to it, that's for sure; imagine me trying to give comfort or guidance to a man like Alf Constable, why he ought to be guiding me, ruther.

He stretched out, and loosened his feet in his boots, and it felt mighty good. He could look up through them grape leaves that twined back and forth between them two trees, and there was a nice fresh breeze blowing, toward the hogpen instead of from it, and it blowed the grape leaves and the hammock too. Every now and then the hammock ropes would creak, and every now and then he'd see a twinkle of blue sky up there through the leaves, or maybe the white of summer clouds, and you can just guess what happened. He got two and a half hours of the best sleep he ever got in his life.

When he woke up, his first thought was that he hadn't been so rested since he went to prison, he could go out there and rope cows from hell to breakfast tomorrow, or do the branding and cutting if he was told, and go until dark. For a minute there he was carefree as a jaybird, a plain old no-account cowboy with not a worry in the world except where his next meal was coming from.

And then it come over him, the job he had took on, and he whipped both of his hands over his eyes, he felt so bad all of a sudden. He had never had the least desire to be a preacher, even temporary, and had agreed to be assistant chaplain only to get out of that clammy cistern. He said out loud, "No sir, I can't do it, it's too much, it's just ridiculous that's what, and I'd only fail so why ruin my own life and everybody else's too?"

He never knowed a preacher that enjoyed life, and their families was usually peaked-looking and timid, dressed in hand-me-downs, and cutting each other's hair. Their wives had to be nice to every woman in town, and when you consider the women the best Christians marry, there's no heavier curse on Adam's daughters. If a woman said to the preacher's wife, "That's a beautiful dress you got on, I don't see how you do it, I know I can't afford anything like it, I surely do admire how you manage," what she really meant was, "I know how much your husband makes, not much and it's still more than he's worth, and either somebody give you that or something funny is going on, and in either case, you ought to keep your place and not try to be fancier than the people that support you."

When a preacher's son got into a fight, he was a renegade bully, and when he didn't, he was a coward. He had to go to prayer meeting as well as church, and set there and look at the other boys, and wonder whose hand-me-down clothes he'd get next, so it was a wonder they didn't all turn out to be train robbers. When a preacher had daughters it was even worse, and if they was pretty, he was better off hit by a cyclone. If they played post office like the other girls at Halloween parties, on October 31, you bet on November 1 it was all over town how wanton they was, and if they didn't play, you wondered who they was kissing on the sly. If they married well, people said they had to, they'd been caught doing it, and if they married badly, people said what did you expect, girls like them.

If a preacher went into the barbershop, you can bet it wasn't for a haircut, it was to ask for a free calendar or to borrow his extra scissors because his wife had broke hers and he couldn't afford new ones. When he went in, everybody stopped talking, and some fella would say, "Well, Reverend, I was in the middle of a story, it's a little raw, but I reckon you like to let out the curb of your bit now and then, so I'll go right ahead." If the preacher walked out, why he was a hypocritical old son of a bitch all over town, and if he stayed, why *that* was all over town too, that the pious old son of a bitch had a dirty mind.

Rolf had had no use for preachers as a boy, and laying there in that hammock, he suddenly remembered why. When he was about ten years old back in Smith County, or maybe eleven, there was an old retired preacher, Reverend Hood, who come around every second Sunday with his wife, for chicken and dumplings with the Ledgers. They drove a gray mare so old she had gone first white and then sort of yellowish, by the name of Birdie, that they had raised from a colt. They had a creaky old top-buggy Reverend Hood kept shined up like a new saloon, it being the only way he had to pass the time. The other preachers in town wouldn't cut him in on calling on the sick, the aged, and the bereaved, because they said the next thing they knowed, he'd be cutting himself in on weddings and funerals too, and there went all semblance of regularity, and without regularity where was Christianity?

Reverend Hood wore an old derby hat, and a celluloid collar, and a ratty old black silk tie, and he was so nearsighted that if Birdie hadn't of knowed the roads, he just never would have got anywhere. His wife was about as ugly as a woman can be, so maybe it was just as well his eyesight was bad. She was always sewing, setting there in her buggy stitching away, with a black lace cap on her head, and her thimble on, and it was that thimble that was Rolf's mess of pottage as the saying is.

When old Birdie slouched into the yard, dragging the Hoods in that old wobble-wheel buggy, Rolf and his older brother Eddie was supposed to lope down and take care of the horse. They also had to help them out of the buggy, the

Reverend first and then Mrs. Hood, and Eddie wouldn't do it because he said they smelled bad. So it was always Rolf had to.

Reverend Hood would pat Rolf on the head and say, "Take care of the mare, lad, she has served me loyally for many a year, give her a measure of oats, that's a good lad," and you could bet if she ever got any oats they was mooched at the same time the Hoods was mooching their chicken and dumplings. Then when Rolf went around to help Mrs. Hood out, she said, "Give me your hand, boy, look lively now!" She come down on him like the smokehouse caving in, and then she had to huff and grunt and belch getting turned around and aimed towards the house. All this time her weight was on Rolf, and she wasn't no small woman, no, not by any means. Then just when she was aimed right, and ready to be fired, before he could duck loose from her, she'd rap him over the head with that thimble.

He thought he could have stood anything else, the long prayers that Reverend Hood spooled off before dinner, and the Hoods getting the best parts of the chicken, and the biggest slabs of pie—they was welcome to that for all of Rolf, but *why* did she have to whack him on the head with that thimble?

One hot Sunday in August, old Birdie come slouching up the lane, and Rolf knowed he should of expected it because his mother had killed a hen, but he had been living in a fool's paradise as a boy will. He had a new horse in fact, and while he hadn't rode him yet, and could barely lead him around, he was laying there in the shade dreaming of when he'd be old enough to be a train robber on that very horse.

It wasn't really a horse, just a little spotted Shetland pony stud that Rolf's father had picked up in a swap. Three years old, not much higher than hip-high to a tall Indian as the saying goes, and so mean and spoiled it took a good man to handle him.

This pony stud, Trinket, was carrying on something fierce from his lot behind the barn. Rolf helped Reverend Hood out of the buggy, and then he helped Mrs. Hood out, and she whacked him over the head with her thimble, and they went creepy-crawling up towards the house the way real, real old folks will. Rolf and his brother Eddie unhooked the mare Birdie, and was going to put her in the barn and give her a bait of oats, as per usual.

But the old mare was cutting up real frisky, whipping her tail and stomping her feet, and finally she let out a blast at the pony, poor old undefiled preacher's mare that she was.

Rolf said, "Eddie, you know what? This Goddamn old mare is horsing, that's what?" Eddie said that couldn't be, she must be twenty years old, too old for that stuff, and Rolf said, "Well just look at her. Eddie, I feel sorry for this old mare! Listen, take her into the barn and peel off the harness, but leave her bridle on. I'll put a bridle on Trinket, and when I holler, you bring her out back of the barn to the tank."

Eddie was the oldest, and if he had ever had a dishonorable thought in his life he suppressed it well, and this just shocked the hell out of him. But even if he was the oldest, Rolf was the boss buck there, and Eddie was prob'ly just as curious as Rolf to see if that religious old mare was capable of it.

The barn was built on a sidehill, with the horse barn on the high side, and the cowbarn on the low side. There was a tank from the windmill set in a fence, to water both cows and horses, and on the low side, so the cows could get to it, Rolf's father had built a platform of dirt, held in by a brick wall about two feet high, with a ramp up both sides of it.

This is where they tried it out, the mare on the low side with her hind end up against the brick wall, and Trinket on the platform. It was the first time Rolf ever tried to handle that pony alone, but Trinket had only one thing on his mind, and he got onto it mighty quick, what they expected of him.

To make a long story short, if horses enjoy it as much as they look, Birdie paid off for twenty dry years in that one day. They let Trinket cover her twice before they went up for their prayers and chicken and dumplings, and while they was eating, they was so ashamed and guilty they couldn't look at each other. Especially Eddie. Only then Mrs. Hood asked them if they had give Birdie a bait of oats, and they said they had forgot, so she told them to get up right now and go do it, and this time she give Eddie a whack on the head with her thimble as he slid past her.

That put the iron in Eddie's soul for a while, and so they let Trinket cover her twice more before they give Birdie her oats, and this time they didn't have a bit of trouble handling Trinket, he was an old hand at it. Then they hid out until it was time to hitch up the mare for the Hoods to go home.

Now nobody is going to expect a mare twenty years old to get with colt when she has never been bred before, especially from a little stud no bigger than a butchering calf. It couldn't happen one time in a thousand, but this must of been the thousandth time, because that's just what happened. Birdie kept getting fatter and fatter, and Reverend Hood kept letting out her bellyband, but nobody suspicioned the truth. Rolf and Eddie kept track, and when July come, they both felt like running away from home and becoming train robbers, but they couldn't bear to miss the fun.

One Wednesday there was a package for the Hoods from a church they used to pastor back in Ohio, some free second-hand clothes and crumbled cookies and so forth, and he had to hitch up Birdie to go get it. He left her standing in front of the post office, and while he was inside, she started to throw her foal. Somebody seen what was happening, and even if he couldn't believe it, he dropped her tugs and let her step ahead so she wouldn't drop the colt on the singletrees. Sometimes a mare takes a long time having a colt, but this was only a Shetland, and she got rid of it like spitting out a cherry pit.

A little spotted stud, the image of Trinket. She had done had it, and half the town of Smith Center was standing around watching it stumble to its feet and suck, when Reverend Hood come out of the post office with his package. Old Birdie looked just as proud as could be, throwing her head around at people like she was saying, "You didn't think the old mare was up to it did you, well now who's the fool, you or me?"

Reverend had two choices. Either his mare had had carnal

knowledge of a he-horse, or he had himself the first virgin birth of a horse in history. Well there was only one spotted stud in Smith County, and all anybody had to do was count back eleven months, and they could pin down the exact day. What made it worse was that his old mare fell from grace on a Sunday.

Eddie cried and said he was sorry, so their father only give him a couple of licks with a strap. But Rolf said he had been whacked once too often on the head with that Goddamn thimble, and he reckoned he had went insane, and he couldn't remember what happened. So he got two good larrupings, once for breeding the preacher's mare to the pony, and once for cursing and making light of it.

Reverend Hood come out of it all right in one way. He sold the colt as a two-year-old for seventy-five dollars, more cash than he had ever had in his hand since he got paid off from the Union Army, after laying in a stinking hospital outside of Washington for two months, after being shot in the knee at Fredericksburg.

He didn't even scold Rolf and Eddie, although he did talk to them. He said he didn't blame the horse and he didn't blame the pony, no, that was animal nature, they couldn't help themselves. But he said human beans could either yield to animal nature or conquer it, and they knowed that as well as he did. He reckoned boys had done worse things than this, only he said he couldn't figger out why they done this one to him. "Why, boys?" he said. "You knew it would humiliate me. If I could understand that—but you don't know yourselves, do you?" And they couldn't bring themselves to tell him about his wife whacking them on the head with her thimble, because she died not long after the colt was born, and before Reverend Hood got around to questioning them.

10

Rolf laid there in the hammock and tried to go back to sleep, but he couldn't get them Hoods off'n his mind. The Hoods raised a little patch of corn, and they had a coffee mill that they used to grind their meal in, and they said there just wasn't no meal like that you ground fresh before baking. But when Reverend Hood died, and they laid him out and seen how skinny he was, and they found only $2.08 in the whole house, and nothing in the cupboard but a little tea, the truth come out.

Them poor old people was hungry, that was why they went around mooching Sunday dinners, they prob'ly lived on cornbread and weak tea most of the week. The old woman whacked kids on the head with her thimble to let out her misery, where others would of took an ax and called attention to it by mass murder. No two ways about it, a retired preacher is a cast-off cull, unless he's managed to put out a little money on mortgages, or married it. And if he did, he's an object of revilement for serving Mammon, so he can't win.

Well not me, Rolf thought. I never felt no call to preach. I got caught in quicksand, and everybody pushed.

He made up his mind to get up there and preach them one more farewell sermon next Sunday, and apologize for taking up their time, and the next day he'd be on his way out of Colorado. He wouldn't even ride Fanny home, it was going to be too hard parting with that horse, but it was worth it to get rid of this load. And the next thing he was thinking was, Anyway how do I even know there is a God? If there was, what did He ever do for Reverend Hood?

Well then he heard a voice say, "What do you mean, cowboy? It's not what I done *for* him that really bothers you, it's what *you* done *to* him."

Rolf never claimed it was an out-loud voice that anybody could of heard. He knowed it was all in his own mind, but the funny thing was, when he looked away from that patch of blue sky he stopped hearing it, and when he looked back, here it was talking at him again. The wind had let up, and the leaves was still, and here was this little patch of blue. And being as he wasn't the kind to drop an argument with anybody, he made the most respectful reply he could, and it went about like this:

ROLF: You mean, Lord, that I'm not even with You yet for what I done to Reverend Hood?

THE LORD: The man was in his seventies. He may not have been the brightest vessel that ever bore My truth, but he fought the good fight and he kept the faith, and you crowned him with ridicule and humiliation.

ROLF: A joke is a joke, Lord. It wasn't all that bad.

THE LORD: Cowboy, when you're in your seventies, and standing in the only patched shoes you own, afraid to bend over because your pants are liable to bust, and you been on bread and tea for six days, wait until then and tell me if a joke is still a joke.

ROLF: Then how do I get square for what I done?

THE LORD: You'll know when you're forgiven, cowboy. You have to forgive yourself, that's about it.

ROLF: Well if You'll excuse me, Lord, it looks to me like I'm just heaping more ridicule and humiliation on Reverend Hood when I pretend to be a preacher myself.

THE LORD: That could be true, cowboy. You flourish around right smart, healing people, getting into fights and then comforting the loser, things like that. But I just wonder what's in your heart all this time.

ROLF: So do I. That's what bothers me, that's what I can't face up to, what business have I got preaching?

THE LORD: Yes, I can see how you'd wonder that.

ROLF: Getting back to Reverend Hood and his mare, I plead guilty to worse than just nasty, it was cruel to an old man and woman, but in all modesty, let me ask You this: Ain't I almost even after helping Lois out of her convulsion?

THE LORD: You may even be ahead of that game, cowboy. But when your heart tells you that you're forgiven for what you done to Reverend Hood, then you can start paying for the blessing that saved you from the gallows, or at least hatred and despair for life in prison. You was well on your way in that direction when My chaplain pulled you out of the Hole, and you know it as well as I do.

ROLF: You mean I've got to slash away at trying to preach here, until I pay off *all* of my debts?

THE LORD: Do what your heart tells you to do, cowboy. Why don't you want to do it?

ROLF: I'll turn my hand over face up, Lord. I can't get Abe Whipple or these other people to understand, but maybe You will. I didn't mind slopping around helping the chaplain in prison, anything you do there is better than nothing, and I did take babtism, and I'll go through with a deal I've made, clear to the line fence. But these people expect more, and Lord, they're *entitled* to more. It just seems I'll be forever, paying back in pennies for debts that I owe in dollars, don't You see what I mean?

THE LORD: You just bet I do, cowboy.

ROLF: Looks like a long job.

THE LORD: Oh no! You can get up out of that hammock and go do as you please, any time. Nothing's got you by the seat of your pants except your conscience.

ROLF: You know me better than that, Lord.

THE LORD: I thought I did, cowboy. I didn't think you'd let these people down.

ROLF: Well, Lord, I'll stay until they can rustle up a genuine preacher, how's that?

THE LORD: Suit yourself, cowboy.

ROLF: No sir, I'll try to suit You. I'll stay here a few more Sundays, and do my sincerest best to give these people what they're looking for, if they know what it is. I sure don't! Look at Alf Constable, already he unloaded a murder on me, how do I know what else I'm going to run into in this congregation of strays? You know what we get out here on the frontier, Lord! But if I've got it to do, I'll do the best I can.

THE LORD: That's all I asked of My own Son, cowboy.

11

That was something to sweat through, even if it was all in his mind, enough to make Rolf shun that hammock like it was full of bedbugs. Well then, when he come out from under them grapevines, after the wind swung around and started blowing from the hogpen, he blundered into the Constables' house and discovered a whole lot of company had come there, trapping him. And listening to them, he found out that the preacher was expected to put out *two* sermons every Sunday, one in the evening.

He didn't feel in shape for it, no he didn't, but he skimmed back and forth through his Bible, and he finely found something he reckoned he could whomp up a sermon on, "A new Commandment I give ye, that ye love one another." It prob'ly wasn't the best, because it's generally considered best for the Easter season, and here it was early summer, and besides, there is prob'ly more dirty cowboy jokes about love than anything else. But they told him he didn't need to worry, the evening crowd generally didn't amount to a hill of beans, mostly old maids or families with daughters they was trying to marry off, so not to worry.

They couldn't of been more wrong. Blessed Sacrament was only a mission, and Father Lavrens that run it had other flocks to herd, and this wasn't his Sunday in Mooney. And all of them sects had got careless about property lines anyway. Father Lavrens's bishop was always having him up for drumhead proceedings on the way his flock rambled after every whooping evangelist in forty miles, and one of the reasons Brother Richardson had finely hauled off and quit First Methodist was that every time Blessed Sacrament had a carnival, or a feast day, or any reason for trotting out the altar boys in their lace gowns, why the Methodist crowd thinned out, and everybody went to Blessed Sacrament to see the show. There was a good deal of ignorant discussion of doctrine, and now and then some intermarriage, and a general loosening of the laws of regularity, and the loss of money that goes with it. A person he's a guest in some other church, he feels called upon to be a little liberal about it, and he ponies up two bits instead of a dime, or four bits instead of two, and it really ain't fair. Suppose you owned a saloon, and your own bartender never touched the stuff on duty, but the minute his day was over, he went across the street and handed out a dime of your money for somebody else's whisky. You'd take offense too.

There was some French Kincaiders who come a long way to Mass, only to find out Father Lavrens wasn't in Mooney, most of them named Beauseigneur, pronounced Bossinner, but one family of Lally, and a few of other names, including one young single unmarried bachelor by the name of Bob Gaston. They all come to the Methodist church, and so did all four Venamans. The collection was $31.75, mighty good, plus a $1,000 check from Harold DuSheane. He was the town halfwit, and not French at all despite his name. He was perfectly harmless except that he'd take a leak just any old where, and was always writing them big checks. There was a few atheists too.

After the services, when the people marched out, them

Frenchmen all wanted to kiss Rolf's hand, and it was just short of a rassling match to keep them from doing it, and then this Bob Gaston wanted Rolf to interduce him to Samantha Venaman. He seemed to feel it was his duty. He spoke perfectly good English, and he said, "I'll go this far, Reverend, if anything comes of it, I won't bear down on her to join my church, I'll come a-helling to yours. Now is that a fair deal or ain't it?"

He couldn't get out of interducing her, and then he had to stand there part of the party while Cal tried to get away, and Samantha deviled him by shining up to this Frenchman, knowing how Cal felt about Frenchmen. Finely Bob asked Cal if he could call on Samantha, and Cal said, "I don't see how the hell I can prevent it if I can't even start for home," and the Frenchman took the hint and left.

Rolf thought he never seen Samantha look so pretty, after all that gushing from that Frenchman, and he was in a moody state of mind anyway. She said she could see that he had put a lot of thought into his sermon, and he said he didn't know whether to thank her for that or not, and she wanted to know why not.

He said, "Well, that's the kind of compliment your lawyer would pay the jury, after they come in with guilty. You've got to say something."

She laughed and said, "You're too sensitive, Reverend. When I vote to hang, no one is in doubt. No really, the highest compliment a preacher can pay his congregation is merely to *think*, and make them think too."

He said, "I hope somebody was thinking, man, because I was bogged down in the quicksands of indecision as the fella says, and I just couldn't find the words, I reckon because I wasn't sure what I was trying to get over."

She said, "Oh that was quite clear, but it's the seeking that counts, truth plays hide-and-seek with all of us, and we count on you for guidance—not answers so much as leadership in our seeking," and so on.

Cal said, "If you're through instructing our pastor, daughter, let's get along."

She fetched up short, and seen how excited she had got, and she must of thought it made her look foolish, but it wasn't in her to apologize, not ever. She'd stand pat on what she had dealt herself, that was her nature and nobody was going to change her.

Cal said, "Have you seen that nitwit sheriff, Parson? I expected him to be at services, but he's never around when you need him."

Rolf was still gaping at Samantha, and it took a minute for that to soak in. He said, "Has Abe done neglected you? That don't sound like Abe to me."

You can see how he was already getting the swing of being a minister, bringing peace and goodwill to his flock, instead of the normal human tendency to act the son of a bitch, just to see the fun.

Cal said, "Oh no, not much, my house is robbed, that's all!"

"Why," Rolf said, "I heard that Abe was out investigating a robbery."

Cal said, "He sure was, mine. I lost forty-eight hundred dollars in less than a year I figger, first my best hay-fat beef, and now sixteen hundred in gold. Abe came out and looked wise, and then went plodding off on his horse to look for tracks. About as much chance of him finding tracks as an elephant. They shot both of my dogs, too! Nobody could have gotten past my dogs. I had two of the best watchdogs in the country, and I regret them more than the money. They died for me, and redressing that is as important as getting back my money. You tell Abe I said that!"

Rolf said, "I thought you worked upwards of thirty or forty men, and now you tell me some of your beef was run off, and now your house is robbed. Where was your crew when your dogs was shot and your house was robbed?"

"Working, where they're supposed to be! I can account for every man I've got, Parson. No man of mine did it. Some two hundred head of prime steers vanished last winter, between snowstorms. Now they come into my very home. This isn't some hungry, out-of-work cowboy's work. It took a gang to do it after a leader planned it, and you can tell this distinguished Sephardic sheriff of ours that I said so," Cal said.

Opal said, "Reverend, Cal holds Abe responsible for everything from drouth to the bots, just because he supported him for sheriff. And he'll hold you responsible now too, because you're Abe's nominee. You may as well be prepared, you're expected to have at least five or six angels looking after Flying V interests."

Cal grinned like he had his temper back, and said, "Five or six, the dickens, I'm entitled to a squadron of them at least."

Rolf lost his head completely. He said, "Well, Mr. Venaman, you already have a couple of them, these two daughters, and I'll get you the rest of your ten thousand when you need them."

Samantha put out her hand without warning to shake hands good-by, and then Opal and Winnie, and then Cal, but you bet he didn't get no inspiration out of Cal's handshake. Cal said good-by, and he told Rolf, "Ten thousand, that's a lot of angels, you just conjure up one old loudmouthed sheriff, and I'll tie him to an anthill until he's paid in suffering for my two dogs."

They headed on home, and Rolf woke up and seen it was time to hunt up Jack Butler, only then this town halfwit, Harold DuSheane, come running to say he'd found Jack drownded in the crick. Jack wasn't drownded, only half so. He was upstream from the footlog a quarter of a mile, where nobody but a drunk would of been blundering around, and nobody but a halfwit could of found him.

They took him to Huey's place, and renched off the mud, and started pouring black coffee into him, and now and then they'd slap his face to bring the blood to his head, and pretty soon it was even money he was going to live.

Abe Whipple didn't get back into town until nigh midnight, just when Rolf was about to start home with Jack Butler. Abe said no, put it off until tomorrow, anyway Jack had soaked up so much he couldn't stand another drink, and he wanted to talk to Rolf. He took Rolf to Bad Lim's place, a Chinese place that put up a good bait of Chinese food for two bits, something Rolf had never et before.

"Once you give up wondering what that meat is in it, there ain't none better than the Chinese grub," Abe said. "I like it so well, I wonder if maybe I haven't got some oriental blood in me somewhere."

"It's possible," Rolf said. "The way I feel tonight, I wouldn't bet a plugged lead nickel on the chastity of my own grandmother."

Abe said, "I'm with you there, and I think I love my son of a bitching fellow man as much as the next man, or maybe more, and I include that sterling citizen and leading cattleman, Calvin Venaman. I'm glad I missed him. Cal's all right in his way. He'll set up all night with a man of his that gets sick, and pay for his doctors, and every man that dies on his place, he gets a place in the Flying V private graveyard. But when it comes to abusing an animal, there's no moderation in him. He'll favor the animal every time. I keep telling that fool kid deputy of mine, Thad Rust, he'd be better off to have himself gelded in the long run. He's just at the age, and so is Winnie, and one of these days they won't be able to help themselves, they'll just rip their clothes off and go to it. A rooster is a rooster and a hen is a hen, and nature will have its way."

"The Lord gives us power over our natures," Rolf said.

"A dime's worth of power and a dollar's worth of nature. You can't blame these kids. It's the wrong way to go at it, but with spring weather and the hot weather coming so close together, the strain don't let up until somebody's knocked up. Green as a gourd, that's the word for Thad, and you've got to look at the practical side too. If them kids do get married, Cal ain't going to be satisfied to have no son-in-law in a deputy's job, oh hell no, he'll run Thad against me for my job, and them Rusts breed like flies. They're related to the Cooks and the Vandermeers and the Spurlings and Januarys and Warnocks, and what you've got to watch out for in politics is what they call a natural coalition. This one is so natural it would curl your hair," Abe said.

Rolf asked him what he found out about Cal's house robbery, and Abe got sick at his stomach, and shook his head a long time, and said, "Not a thing, not a damn thing. I'm in trouble, Rolf, plenty of trouble! This ain't no little old two-bit home-town robber gang. We're close to Nebraska and close to Wyoming, and it looks to me like somebody from one of them two states is coming down here and helping himself to our wealth. State lines are a damn nuisance, Rolf. We didn't used to pay no attention to them, you lined out chasing your desperado, and you run him till you caught him, and you hung him on the spot, and that was that. I never knowed of no foreign sheriff from the other state interfering, and I never interfered when they trailed their horse thieves down here, and believe you me we had law and order. Now it's all law and no order."

Rolf said he wished he had Thad's job instead of the one he had, and any time Abe had a vacancy, he wanted to be considered for it. Abe said no sir, where Rolf was now was where he was needed; anybody could be a deputy sheriff with a little training, but preaching took special talents that you didn't pick off'n every bush.

"Well I ain't going to stay with it, and you might as well get used to it, Abe," Rolf said. "I'll be on my way soon, I reckon. Soon as they can rustle up another preacher, be he good, bad, or indifferent."

"What in thunderation has got into you?" Abe wanted to know. "I swear, you ain't the same boy I last seen!"

Rolf said no, he sure wasn't, and Abe asked him what had happened, and Rolf said he didn't care to talk about it, and Abe said he could understand that and he didn't want to pry, but it worried him when a man got that dreened-out look in his eyes that Rolf had. So Rolf said it was partly Samantha Venaman, he was afraid he was getting to be a goner for her, and he knowed what chance an ex-convict preacher had with her, but that wasn't really what had changed his mind. Abe kept after him, kept sidling and circling and backing around, and he had a lot of practice in snaking your soul out backward, he'd get the kernel out without cracking the nut, and that's what he done to Rolf. Pretty soon, Rolf was telling him about laying there in the hammock at Alf's place, and carrying on the most logical and lifelike conversation with God you ever heard of, and he didn't expect Abe to believe him, but he'd had a revelation that proved he wasn't fit to preach and would go on doing it at peril of his immortal soul.

Abe said, "Well, maybe it was a daydream and maybe it wasn't, I'll bet you won't find it in no dream books, but if you're asking me do I think you've went insane, why no I don't. I reckon it was like when Moses went up there on Sinai, he purely had to be by hisself a while to cipher things out, them people of his'n was enough to drive a steady man frantic, and Moses never did seem to me very steady. A drifter, not satisfied no place. He may of been a prophet, but any man that can ramble for forty years, he's got to be unsteady, Rolf, he's *got* to be! I don't mean an unsteady man can't be a prophet, no sir, but I ain't going to take an unsteady man's literal word necessarily, either. I reckon he went up there on the mountain, and hid out from them people before they drove him plumb out of his mind, and set down on a rock, and said to himself, 'Moses, look here, you ain't getting nowhere with these folks, and there has to be a reason, and until you know what's wrong, how are you going to figure out what to do?' Like you done there in the hammock. Well it come to him what was wrong, them people didn't have no *rules;* they believed in the One and Only God true enough, that's all right, I don't quarrel with that, but a God without rules might as well not be God at all. So he come up with these rules, and he laid them out simple and stiff, there it is, take it or leave it, foller the rules or get out of the tribe. He had to stretch it a little when he come down from Sinai, and give yourself credit, Rolf, *you* didn't, you told her just the way she happened to you, no blast of thunder and fire, and no carved stones either. It's the difference in times, see. We're ignorant enough here on the frontier, but we ain't a caution to them people. Why they even had a rule to cut the end of your pecker off, I reckon because it got dirty on them, and it's mighty skeerce getting a bath in the desert. Well that's all right as a last resort, but a man can spit on it and keep it clean, why trim it off?

You can't blame Moses for telling a stretcher to people like that. They was just a bunch of blanket Indians on the warpath, looking for somebody they could whip, and take his land away from him, and rustle his cattle. And I'll tell you something else, Rolf, except that some of us can read and write, and we don't mutilate ourselves except in fights, *we ain't a Goddamn bit better today!*"

"You're sure in a cheerful state of mind, Abe," Rolf said. "A man comes to you already feeling low, and you send him away fit to cut his own throat."

"Well it's the truth!" Abe said. "I'll tell you what I think, the time is coming when people are going to look back on us and say, 'My God, and they called themselves civilized!' and they'll be right! Look at us, shooting each other, and cutting each other with knives, and hanging each other, why if you see a man going around unarmed, you know he's either a preacher or drunk or lost it in a game somewhere, and you call that civilized. Look at the way we treat our women! Edna has got it pretty good now, compared to some women I know, but I knowed the time she was no better than a pack animal, same as most women on the frontier, before I woke up and said to myself, let the Goddamn county support us! What has a woman in this country got to look forward to? The whores is the lucky ones, at least they price their own ass, that's something, but the average rancher's wife is just livestock. Have her babies alone on a dirty old straw tick, and try to make milk in her breasts for them from nothing but beans and hog meat and corn meal, no beef for her, oh no, the Goddamn beef has all got to be shipped and sold! And a Kincaider's wife is even worse off, you might as well hitch her to the plow with your ox and be done with it. Their kids grow up mean and wild, all wanting to be train robbers, all packing guns from the time they're thirteen, and not worth the powder to blow them to hell. When there's no hope for the young people except raising hell and shooting and peddling their ass, your country's on the road to ruin. The time is coming, and you mark my words, Rolf, that people are going to look back and say one and all that this was the worst part of the history of mankind, and the cowboy was the lowest, meanest thing that ever walked on two legs, and yet you want to go back to riding for a living!"

"You sure can cheer a man up," Rolf said.

Abe said, "Don't take it so personal. It's just that I hate to see a young fella ruin his life twice."

"I can't be a hypocrite."

"You could if you tried. It only takes a little. Look at Moses. The thing that's important ain't whether the Lord dynamited them stone tablets out for him personally, it's the rules that count. Rolf, this here country is about as lean and raw and worthless as the Holy Land was then. It's got a little more water, but not much, and a little more grass, but not much, and about the same kind of people. But the Lord valued that property enough to send His angels down there again and again, to line them ungrateful fools up, and to help them against the Hittites and the Assyrians and all them other worthless tribes. Now if He thought that much of a few acres of stony old desert, how can you just ride out of here and completely abandon and desert a country that needs you as bad as this country does?"

"I never seen no angels of the Lord around here," Rolf said. "I don't think this is angel range, Abe."

Abe just glared at him. "If there's one thing I can't stand, it's a smart-aleck, but go ahead, be a cowboy, and may the Lord have mercy on your ignorant soul!"

"Amen," Rolf said.

12

Rolf and Jack got a late start back to the ranch the next day, because Jack had the bull-shakes and the whisky trots, and couldn't trust himself on a horse. Rolf was pretty impatient with him, and he rode Fanny as hard as he thought Jack could foller, and he had him in pretty good shape by the time they got home. Jack had bought two gunnysacks full of groceries and stuff, and when they got home he dumped them in a corner, and said he believed he'd turn in and get some sleep.

"Oh no you don't," Rolf said. "You and me are going to build some fence, and sweat some of the whisky out of you."

Jack said, "The hell with that, I'm sick as a dog, and if there's one man in Colorado caught up on his fences, I'm that man, and whoever said work is the healer never felt like I do." But Rolf made him go out and help as long as he could, which was only until about noon. Jack seen by the shadows that it was midday, and he said he hadn't et nothing for thirty-six hours, so Rolf let him quit, and they both went in. Rolf took care of the team, and when he come into the house, Jack had unpacked the groceries, and was standing there staring at them.

"What do you call this?" he said.

Rolf said, "Why, I'd call that a quart of Tom Sanderson's Old Bluetick sourmash whisky thirteen years in the wood. Jack, you have run from that stuff long enough. That bottle is going to stand there on the table and reproach you. Any time you feel like taking a drink, tell me about it man to man, and I'll help you stave it off. If that don't work, we'll try something else."

"That sure is hospitality to your worst enemy," Jack said, "but we'll do it your way. No danger now, I can tell you! The very idee gives me nowsea."

For three days that black bottle set on that table, with the picture of that bluetick hound on it. Jack got up in the morning talking about it, and he talked about it while they worked, and while they et dinner, and all afternoon, and at supper too, and it was the last thing he mentioned at night.

The evening of the third day, Jack took a bucket and went down to the horse tank and had a bath, and stropped up his razor and shaved himself, and put on some new Levis he got out of the drawer of his dresser, and a new white shirt too. Rolf said, "What in the world do you aim to do with all of them clothes? Why you've got enough clothes there for a store!"

"I like to be well dressed when I go out," Jack said, "and I'm always losing clothes, or getting them tore up or filthy dirty when I'm drunk."

"Where do you think you're going now?" Rolf said.

"You expect too much of me. I can't set there and look at that bottle and grit my teeth. I've got to get out of here, that's all," Jack said.

"Where to?" Rolf asked him.

"Nowhere. Anywhere. A long hard punishing ride to get my mind off'n the drink," Jack said.

"You didn't need to clean up for that. You're heading back to Mooney," Rolf said.

Jack swore he wasn't, he just felt unclean with a fit coming on, but Rolf said to set down, they was going to start talking this thing out.

"I won't set down and I won't talk," Jack said. "I'm so nervous I could scream, so don't push at me!"

"Then get down on your knees and we'll ask the Lord's help," Rolf said.

"I don't want His help, He'll only say torture myself for greater glory, and glory is something I can do plumb without," Jack said.

"All right, you won't set, and you won't talk, and you won't pray, all right, go ahead and drink. Here, I'll pull the cork for you, so's you can smell it," Rolf said, and he did.

"Don't try to shame me, Rolf. I'm past shame," Jack yelled.

Rolf unbuttoned his shirt and peeled it off, and he advised Jack to do the same. Jack asked why, and Rolf said, "Because you and me and your demon is going down into a tangle over your immortal soul, winner take all this time."

"What do you aim to do?" Jack wanted to know.

"See you get your fill of whisky for once," Rolf said.

"You are like hell! You're fired. Get off'n my place!" Jack hollered.

Rolf come at him, and he had an advantage not having any shirt for Jack to get hold of. Jack wasn't a big man, but he was hard-built and quick on his feet, and he put up a pretty fair scrap. But Rolf got him down on his back, dead to the world from a clip on the jaw, and was setting there on top of him when he come to. Rolf had the bottle in his hand, and as soon as he seen that Jack was awake, he tipped it into his mouth.

"Drink or drownd, you miserable sinner!" he said, and kept it there until Jack begin to lose it out of the corner of the mouth, and waste that good whisky. Rolf let him get his breath again, and then it was "Drink or drownd, you miserable sinner!" again. That system is calculated to take a lot of the pleasure out of getting drunk, and Jack finely passed out without ever getting more than relief, no enjoyment at all.

Rolf put the bottle on the table, where Jack could find it when he come to, if he did, and then a rider from Elias Petty's little Lion Track ranch galloped up, and he said that Mrs. Petty's aged mother, Mrs. Urma Perkins, was dying and wanted to be comforted going over the hump. Miz Urma, as they called her, was in her eighties, and had come to Colorado in a covered wagon pulled by a span of good brindle Ohio oxen, and had been burnt out by Indians twice and scalped once, so she had this little bare pucker on top of her head where there wasn't no hair. She was originally a deep-dip Babtist, but had went to the Methodist until she got too feeble, and was entitled to all the privileges of a communicant member.

Rolf loaded his books into his saddlebags, and they went out on a gallop, and Rolf got to the Lion Track in time to give the old lady a boost when she needed it, and she died full of grace. It was coming on to rain then, so they hitched up a team and wrapped the remains in quilts and put them on the bed of a wagon, because she wanted to be buried in town. Well then when they got to town, Bernard Petty, the embalmer, a cousin of Elias, said there wasn't no use embalming the old lady, it was too hard to find her veins, and anyway people as old as her was so dried-up they didn't rot, they couldn't for lack of juices. All they done was sort of tan like a cowhide; however, it was hot weather, and a good idee to conduct the burial with all decent haste.

So Rolf conducted the funeral, and used the Book of Common Prayer again, and enough of Miz Urma's kin showed up on short notice to make a nice walking cortege, and the rain held off. About midnight, the Lion Track bunch started home, because they had left some wash on the line, and Rolf thought he might as well go back to the lonely bachelor quarters he shared with Jack.

When he got there, he found Jack gone, and his new clothes in a pile in the middle of the floor, all over puke, and the bottle missing, and so was Jack's saddle. Rolf went to bed, not as worried as he might of been, because as the saying is, the Lord takes care of children and drunks. He slept late, until almost six o'clock, and then a bunch of Flying V boys rode in and wanted to borrow all of Jack's wagons.

Jack only had two, and he wasn't around anywhere to say aye, yes or no, but Rolf told them go ahead, help themselves. The Flying V boys had brought along extra harnessed teams to pull the wagons with. Rolf thought it was kind of curious that Cal Venaman would need extra wagons, so he asked why.

One of these riders said, "Why the Q mixed train went on the ground, a real interesting wreck, and Cal usually gets the job of teaming and hauling whenever they have a wreck or a washout on the line."

Rolf said, "Then if he's going to be paid in cash, he can pay cash rental for them wagons, and you tell him I said that."

This rider, he said it was unneighborly to take that attitude, but he'd tell Cal; however, they'd always borried Jack's wagons before and never had this question come up, and Rolf said, "That's a rich man for you. To them that have shall be given, well I reckon not in this case, somebody's got to take care of that poor sot's interests."

They went off with them two wagons, and Jack finely come in an hour or two later, looking like the wrath of God, and unable to tell where he'd been or what he'd done, only that by now it was clear that a long hard punishing ride wasn't the answer to his problem. He set there holding his head and saying, "Oh God oh God oh God oh God," and then he'd jump up and throw hisself at the door and try to puke, and couldn't, and then he got to seeing lizards all over everything. Not snakes but lizards. He'd scream, "There they are, coming down from the ceiling on that rope, swat the shiny green sonsabitches somebody, oh my God cut that rope, they're all over me, I got shiny green lizards down my shirt collar," and so on.

It was an original change from snakes, but a drunk is a drunk and that's about all you can say for them, so when Jack finely went to sleep on the kitchen floor, Rolf totted it up in his mind and concluded he'd lost this bout with the devil for good. He packed up all of his few belongings, and left a little note for Jack saying he was quitting and that he had loaned his wagons to Cal Venaman, and got on his horse and rode out of there.

He went up north to the Q to see this wreck first, and it was an interesting one all right. The engine was still standing, but it was astraddle of one rail and could of tipped over pretty easy, and the combination passenger and baggage and mail car was on its side, and so was two box cars. This was a swampy stretch of track built up on a fill, and they had to put in a rip-track detour around it, to get trains through, and to let the wrecker come in and set the wrecked train up again.

Cal had seven teams hauling dirt in wagons, and five teams on grading slips, and was setting on his horse making sure they put out a day's work and didn't abuse his horses. He nodded to Rolf and said, "So I'm expected to pay Jack rent on his wagons, am I? I've never had this demand made on me before, Parson."

Rolf said, "It's up to Jack. I was responsible at the time, and I thought it was the fair thing to do. If Jack don't want pay, it's nothing to me."

"So I'm a rich man, am I?" Cal said. "You know of course that I have to pay Liz Saymill six hundred dollars every quarter, if you don't you're the only man in Mooney County that don't, old bigmouth Abe Whipple saw to that. I'll tell you how that verse really ought to go, Parson, to them that has shall be given trouble and taxes, until all they have is taken away from them, and then some."

"As I said, fix it up with Jack," Rolf said.

"Mighty decent of you, Parson, I appreciate your attitude," Cal said, and rode off a little ways where Rolf couldn't talk to him no more.

It really put a chill on Rolf to be treated like that by the father of Samantha Venaman, and yet he didn't see how he could of done any different about the wagons. Four bits a day for a wagon, or a dollar for both, wasn't going to break Cal, it wasn't bean soup to the six hundred dollars he had to pay Liz Saymill every three months, and yet it would mean a lot to a poor man like Jack Butler, because a thirst like Jack's was as expensive to support as a family. It was the same old thing Rolf had seen all his life, people in Cal's position expected too much of people in Jack's position, and Rolf's position. They took it as their right, and a cowboy with nothing in his pocket could say yes sir you bet sir or get out of the way, and it was the same with the preacher. Cal would let the church board fool around for a while, even let them hire a preacher without consulting him, but he'd pull them up short when he took the notion, because in his mind he run that church the same as he run the Flying V.

No, no question about it, he had let Rolf know where he stood, partly because Rolf was Abe Whipple's friend and he blamed Abe for his troubles, and partly because Rolf had the gall to ask him to pay for Jack's wagons, when the sot ought to be grateful for a chance to loan them. So Rolf headed toward Mooney, pushing his old worthless horse right along, and saying to himself, Well this does it, I give it a try, it could of been some good experience for me but I done everything wrong, like I always do.

He couldn't feel the presence of the Lord at all that morning, and he couldn't of prayed if somebody had put a gun at his head, and in a way it was a relief because now the strain was over. He could go get a job riding somewhere, and slide back into cursing and drinking and fighting a little at a time, and never get as obnoxious as he used to be, and stay out of prison this time. But at least have some fun out of life.

But a man can plan all he wants, and there's still times that circumstances does the deciding for him, and this was one. He was still three miles out of Mooney when here come a spring wagon at a good hard gallop towards him from town, and he pulled up and said to himself, Say now, I've seen that team before!

And he had, because it was the good Flying V buggy team pulling the spring wagon, and it was Winnie Venaman and Thad Rust in it eloping. Winnie broke out crying, she was so glad to see him, and Thad almost cried too. He had run them good buggy horses of Cal's until they was lathered and winded and wouldn't answer the whip no more, and he had a crick in his neck from looking back expecting to see Cal coming after them with both guns blazing.

"You've got to marry us, Reverend," he said. "You're our last hope. Oh my God, if that old fire-breathing daddy of hers catches us before it's legal, why I'm as good as a dead man."

"I don't see how I can do it," Rolf said. "I don't owe Cal

Venaman anything, but I can't do something like this behind his back, either."

"You'll never do it any other way," Thad said.

"Please, please, *please*, Reverend," Winnie said, and cried harder. "Do I have to shame myself and spell it out for you? I missed my time this month, and Thad will marry me, that's a lot more than most men would do, but Papa will just kill him if he finds out."

Rolf said he wasn't no expert, but it seemed to him he'd heard that a woman could miss her time for other reasons than the one she mentioned, however that did put a different light on things. Them kids had done just about everything else wrong too. They had went to the courthouse before Earl Sheffield, the county clerk, got his hind end out of bed, and Minnie Newhouse was the only person there. Minnie was deputy clerk, deputy treasurer, deputy registrar of deeds, and deputy everything else. She was getting on in years, and was kind of deef, and maybe a mite foolish. She forgot to ask about parents' consent, and anyway she knowed that Winnie was above the age of consent, so she wrote them out a license to marry.

There was a justice of the peace, Ed DuSheane, father of the town halfwit and some other kids, but he had went to Colorado Springs about an old family lawsuit there, and the county judge, Andy Obers, was a personal and political friend of Cal Venaman's, and the Catholic priest, Father Lavrens, wouldn't of married a couple of Protestants even if he'd been in town.

The truth was, Rolf was their last hope unless Winnie had missed her time for some other reason, and the odds was against that, and to tell the truth, Rolf wasn't in no particular mood by then to consider Cal Venaman's pride anyways. Not after the way Cal had treated him over that proposition of paying rent for Jack's wagons.

So they turned the spring wagon around, and they went into Mooney together with Rolf plodding his old horse alongside, and they went to Liz Saymill because Rolf thought she would be more independent of what Cal might think and do about it. She was all right, it just pleased her like nothing on earth to be asked to hold the wedding, and she went out and rustled up another old maid for a witness, and Rolf got the Bible and the Book of Common Prayer out, and married them there in the parlor where Colonel Pegler T. Saymill had been murdered. He filled out the certificate and signed it as the officiating clergyman, and then he asked what the kids planned to do while Cal was getting used to the idea.

"Don't ask that question, because if you don't know the answer, you won't be held accountable," the bridegroom said.

Rolf said all right, he wouldn't ask it, but he heard about it later. The kids knowed about a nice cabin out in the willer brush along the creek, down in the homestead country closer to the Platte. There was an old Kincaider, Luke Sweeney, who lived there first, before he bought up some other homesteads and built a bigger house, and he ran a few steers and done a little farming, and made a little white whisky that he sold privately. He was a sort of anarchist anyway, and didn't care what Cal Venaman or any other person in authority thought, and wouldn't even vote.

They rented the cabin for a week, and had Luke bring them some groceries. Luke had a boy of eleven, Grover, who was learning to play the cordeen, and the family made him take it out in the willers to practice it, so they couldn't hear him. But if they couldn't, the happy young couple could. This kid Grover had learned to play several songs, and he had one song he was learning to sing while he played it, and this was what he was working on at the time. They heard it so often they got to know it too, and it went like this:

I went to the river
And I couldn't get across,
So I paid five dollars
For an old gray hoss.
The hoss wouldn't go,
So I traded for a hoe.

The hoe wouldn't dig,
So I traded for a pig.
The pig wouldn't squeal,
So I traded for a wheel.
The wheel wouldn't run,
So I traded for a gun.
The gun wouldn't shoot,
So I traded for a boot.
The boot wouldn't wear,
So I traded for a bear.
The bear wouldn't holler,
So I traded for a dollar.
The dollar wouldn't pass,
So I flung it in the grass.

Grover got up early to practice, and in the evening after he had did his milking and unharnessed the teams and got the cobs in for the stove the next day, he went out into the willers and practiced again, and if a dog started a bobcat or a coon and got to baying at night and woke him up, he'd grab that cordeen and head for the willers to practice, or any reason. Luke said if that kid was as dedicated to a harrow or scythe as he was the cordeen, he'd be a big property owner someday. But a happy young couple on a honeymoon, they don't object to being woke up early in the morning, or in the middle of the night, or any old time for that matter; they just kept the shades pulled down and let him holler and play the cordeen all he liked. For years after that, every time Thad and Winnie heard that song, they'd clasp hands and just sigh all over the place. It got to be their song, you might say.

13

Cal didn't miss Winnie until late that afternoon. Winnie told her mother she was going berry-picking, and she took a pail out, and she hitched up the buggy team to the spring wagon because she knowed Cal would have a fit if she drove the good buggy out there in the rocks to the berry patch, and where she made her mistake was in leaving her berry pail in the barn. Cal didn't have no way of knowing she was a sort of a have-to case, but he figgered from the first she had run off with Thad, and all he wanted was to get her back and kill Thad.

Tired as he was from the train wreck, Cal rode into town with a dozen of his boys, looking for her. He looked for Abe Whipple first, but Abe had rode up to the train wreck to investigate it, although as Cal said what business it was of his how many trains the Q wrecked, he didn't know, and then he run into Earl Sheffield, the county clerk, on the street. Earl said he hadn't issued no marriage license to Winnie and Thad or to nobody else, business was bad in that line, and so far this year death certificates was thirteen to ten over marriage licenses, divorces far behind with only one so far, and births leading everything with eighteen.

Cal said he didn't trust any son of a bitch who had had his head in the public trough as long as Earl, so he went down to the courthouse to see for himself, and there was the record of the license Minnie had issued, and the certificate of marriage that Rolf had filed. The question now was whether to hunt up the minister and kill him, or go after the runaways. He couldn't find nobody that had seen which way the kids went when they left town, at least anybody that would talk. So it was the preacher's turn.

Cal started out to the J Bar B, not knowing that Rolf had quit there, with his cowboys behind him. About five minutes after he left, Abe come into town from investigating the train wreck, to say it was a busted rail that had throwed the train off. There was plenty of people to tell him that Cal Venaman had been in town looking for Reverend Ledger, to kill him for marrying Thad and Winnie, only they hadn't found him yet.

Abe was tired too, but he started out to the J Bar B to keep the peace, only he happened to think of looking in the church first just for luck, and there was Rolf's old bony horse tied behind it, and when he went in, there was Rolf setting in a pew staring at nothing. Abe went in and set down beside him and said, "Well, saying farewell to it all, I reckon," and Rolf said that was about the size of it, his one folly had been to tackle preaching in the first place, but he kind of liked this dark old building at that.

Abe said, "Well it'll miss you too, Rolf. I'm one of them people that believe that people leave their mark on a building, and this gloomy old place will be a little different because it was your church for a while, and my only regret is that some otherwise good memories has to be discolored by quitting under fire."

"What do you mean under fire?" Rolf said, and Abe told him about Cal Venaman going around looking for him to kill him. Rolf said that was just talk; one of the curses of the frontier was that people were always going to kill somebody, only usually they never did, and even when they did, he never heard of a preacher being killed. Cal would think twice.

"I ain't worried about Cal," Abe said. "I'll put an ax handle on his pulley and run his belt off, but it don't sound good for the church, no it don't; you'd never catch Father Lavrens leaving Blessed Sacrament under threat of death, now there's a man who'd just as soon be a martyr as not, poor old frail narrow-minded man."

Rolf said a Methodist made just as good a martyr as a Catholic any day if it came to that, not that he took any great stock in martyrdom as a blessing, it seemed to him more sensible to skin through somehow and go on serving the Lord alive. Abe said then there was Samantha, now *there* was martyrdom for you, she'd really catch it from Cal now.

Rolf said well, he wasn't in no particular hurry and he didn't like to run out on the church, and he might stay a couple of weeks just to prove his point, so Abe said let's go find him a place to stay.

There was two women that took in visiting missionaries, one a widow, Mrs. Rachel Wyatt, and one an old maid, Thea Pickering, who had been the other old maid that stood up with Thad and Winnie at their wedding. Rachel had the biggest house and was the best cook, but she had this daughter Lettie, about thirty-five and still single, and hell-bent on helping some man of God to discipline his congregation. Lettie wasn't ugly, or deformed, or anything like that, she was just too eager. You let a clerical male man get within a mile, and she started rolling her eyes and getting red-faced, and heaving her bosom, and she really had one to heave. There was some old talk that a visiting middle-aged missionary from the Ivory Coast had found her in his bed in the middle of the night when she was only fifteen, and before he knowed what to do about it he had already done it, and this was why her father had hung himself to a pear tree in the back yard.

The worst problem at Thea Pickering's place was her cats, seven or eight of them, and all over the house. But they was safer for a single unmarried bachelor clergyman than Lettie Wyatt, so Abe took him there. A little later, when Thea and Rolf was having supper, Abe brought Opal and Samantha Venaman there, so Rolf could assure them that Winnie was not living in sin somewhere.

"It's as legal as I could make it, ma'am," Rolf said. "They had the license, and they claimed there was no impediments, and I performed it before two witnesses, the way it said on the back of the certificate."

"I'm so glad!" Opal said.

"Well I'm glad you feel like that," Rolf said. "I hear your husband is having a fit, though."

"Yes, and he has had so many reverses lately. Money you know, and he has been stolen blind. He's a proud man, and these are hard blows," Opal said.

"He's a stiff-necked man," Rolf said. "Come now and let us reason together, that's still a good motto."

Opal laughed and said that was one way of looking at it, and too bad the people that run off their cattle and killed their dogs and robbed their house didn't feel the same way. She said that Samantha had a personal problem she wanted to talk over with him if he had the time, and she'd just wait in the buggy out in front until Samantha came out if Rolf had the time for her. So he said sure, if she thought her husband wouldn't object, and want to kill him twice.

Opal went out, and Rolf and Samantha set there a minute, and finely he said, "Was it about your sister, Miss Samantha? Because I don't know what I could tell you that I haven't already told you." He wasn't going to be the one to break the news that she had missed her time, and was going to come up with an eight-months grandchild to plague Cal still more.

Samantha said, "Oh no, I'm glad for her sake. I was in school with Thad, you know, and I'm not critical of him. It has been my observation that men have to go through a period of aimless, witless, worthless male lunacy. Thad may come out of it. I suppose Winifred's pregnant."

Well Rolf just turned red as a beet at that word. It would knock him over coming from anybody in mixed company, and Samantha just out with it like it was any old word, and the word didn't bother her and neither did her sister being in that condition.

She said, "No, I want to ask your frank opinion on the Catholic faith. Of converting."

That hit him harder than pregnant. He said, "Lord God of hosts, are you thinking of that?" and she said yes she was, and he said why it was worse than what Winnie had done, she might as well of got married.

She said, "Only no one asked me to do that, and the Catholic Church does ask all of us to unite with it."

He said, "It sure does, Miss Samantha, but it's a hard old row to hoe, and you've got your daddy's headstrong nature. In fact, you're as much like him as your sister is like your mother, come to think of it."

She said, "Thank you for your frankness although I'm not sure how you meant it. Certain things about the Catholic religion bewilder me, certain things repel me, and certain things attract me strongly. I might even think of becoming a nun."

"Lord God of hosts!" was all Rolf could say. "I must say, Miss Sammie, that when you say you've got a problem to talk over with the preacher, you come up with a dandy."

She said, "Well what do you think? And please don't call me Sammie, I hate that name."

He just couldn't stand the idea of this girl going for being a nun, and wearing that burlap underwear they're supposed to wear, and shaving their heads, and having to get up and pray on a stone floor so often, and like that. And yet he didn't feel like the kind of a fatherly old preacher that ought to be handling a proposition like this anyway. But she had asked him the question, and he just told himself that by George, he was going to give her the straightest answer he could.

"What I think," he said, "is that you hate too many things beside your nickname. Hate is a bad word for a Christian to point around recklessly, loaded or unloaded. Instead of arranging your life around what you hate, you ought to start thinking about the things you love for a change."

She said, "Oh indeed," and he said, "Well that's how I feel," and she said, "I see that I have wasted your time, I apologize, good night."

She jumped up and retch for her shawl, which had dropped to the floor while she was being so enthusiastic about being a nun, and he leaned over for it at the same time, and they knocked heads hard enough to put them both on the floor if either one of them had of been soft-headed. They stood up, each of them holding onto the shawl, a sort of brownish-gray one with a fringe she had knitted herself, and Rolf realized he hadn't seen her from this close before. In fact he hadn't seen *any* woman from this close since going to prison.

He said, "Miss Sammie, I reckon I barely know you, and shouldn't make judgment, but it seems to me there is nothing on earth you couldn't do if you set your heart to it. You've got the mind, and you've got the courage, and you ought to be the happiest person on earth, seems to me. All you have to do is just let yourself be yourself."

"What good does it do," she said, "when other people won't be their own selves?"

She was kind of squeaky-voiced and saucer-eyed, and he knowed it wasn't no spiritual problem that had drove her to this. No sir, this was just the way her sister had looked this morning. He said, "Say, is it this Bob Gaston that has caused this onset of interest in the Catholic faith? Because he told me he was willing to turn Methodist, the dirty double-crosser!"

She just looked at him awhile, and he could hear the old clock ticking away, and Aunt Thea's, as they called her, cats prowling around the back door wanting to be let in. And then she said, "No, it isn't Bob, although he has come to call on me, and that's a novelty if nothing else. Reverend Ledger, I'll presume to advise *you,* if I may. The next time a young woman comes to you with a problem, don't compliment her on her mind and her courage."

"I don't know anything better than them," Rolf said.

"Neither do I," said Samantha, "or I'd use it. Good night, Reverend Ledger."

Abe Whipple knowed Cal and his rowdies would be back in town soon, and they was. He heard them pound in at a gallop, and he began to meander over there to see what they had in mind, or thought they had in mind. But just then, here came

Opal and Samantha in the buggy, on their way back from their visit to the preacher.

Them women heard the Flying V riders too, there couldn't of been anybody in a mile that didn't hear that bunch clatter up, and nobody had to tell them what the next move was. They'd go after Rolf sure. Well just then they seen the sheriff, so Samantha hauled in on the lines and hollered "Whoa," and Opal sang out Abe's name, and he come over to the buggy in the dark.

Opal's teeth were just about chattering, she was that scared. She said, "That's Cal and the boys just got back, that bunch of riders, I reckon."

"I reckon," Abe said.

"He's looking for Reverend Ledger," Opal wept.

"I reckon," Abe grunted.

"Oh, Abe, he's out of his mind!" she said.

"Well I ain't out of mine," Abe said. "I declare, what's in that white kittle between your feet, Opal?"

"That?" she said. "Oh we had some chickens on frying for supper, and then when Cal took off with the men, without even coming to the house, we didn't want to stay to eat. We just put it in the kettle and brought it along."

"Well say! I wonder if you could spare an old man a wing, or something," Abe said. "I been so busy today I ain't hardly had time to eat. Don't you worry about Cal. He ain't going to breach the peace in *my* town."

They told him to help himself, and he took a couple of drumsticks and a couple of wings and his favorites, the gizzards. He went over to his house and got a couple of .30-30 lever-action rifles, and a 12-gauge shotgun, and a 16, and ammunition for all of them. So when Cal picked up the news that Rolf was boarding with Aunt Thea Pickering, and came riding with his crew to take him out and horsewhip him, here was Abe standing in the middle of the road with two .45's on him and a .30-30 under his arm, eating away at fried chicken from his shirt pocket.

"Now listen, I won't stand in the way of anybody who feels

there's a principle at stake," Abe said, "but if any of you twenty-five-dollar-a-month Ulysses Simpson Grants think you're going to abuse a man who never done you no harm, you're going to find out you're only George Armstrong Custers after all, with a Crazy Horse behind every horse turd. Cal, you ignorant son of a bitch, why can't you fight your own fights and not try to get a bunch of well-meaning cowpokes shot or jailed?"

This is what cold raw nerve can do. They woke up that they was only getting twenty-five dollars a month for risking their blood needlessly, and it wasn't their blood that was going to be mingled with that of Thad Rust and his tribe, and there just wasn't no way they could break even. That war party just faded away on the spur of the moment.

"I'll remember this to my dying day, Abe," Cal said. "I'm not a forgiving man, not where my family is concerned."

"Don't tell me your troubles, I'm not your rabbi," Abe said.

"What do you mean, rabbi?" Cal said.

"A rabbi is a minister to the Jews, and I'm part Spanish Jew, but I'm only a sheriff, not a rabbi. I can keep peace in the town, and don't you ever dream otherwise, but nobody can bring peace to that miserable worthless cinder you call a heart," Abe said.

It just made him sick, because he knowed he was through as sheriff with this term. He could look fur enough ahead to know that Winnie and her father was going to make up, it always happens that way, and then instead of killing Thad, Cal was going to try to figure out some way his ignorant worthless son-in-law could make a decent living for his wife and baby. And there was only one thing Thad knowed, sheriffing, and his tribe had the votes, and it was one of them natural coalitions instinct told Abe to fear. Abe could always make a little money cleaning out livery barns and so on, and sleep any old where, and he was bound to make out for himself. But it was a rough deal to put on Edna in their sunset years, and no consolation that he had brought it on her through devotion to duty. Women don't take duty and things like that as seriously as men do.

14

It seemed to him it hadn't no more than started to get daylight, and he'd barely been to sleep, when here they was, pounding on his door again. But Abe Whipple could wake up fast if he had to, action was his maiden name you might say, and all he said was "Oh lordy, lordy," and then while he was still buttoning his pants, he was loping over to Aunt Thea's place and pounding on *her* door, and Rolf was just waking up and thinking *he* had barely got to sleep. Here's what had happened:

It was a busted rail that wrecked the Q, near a siding called View Point, although there wasn't nothing to view there. A few miles away they had a section house, and an Irish foreman by the name of James Hegan, and some shanties for his help. Hegan's brother worked for him, by the name of Bill, and they was both married to Indian girls, and was related to most of the rest of the gang.

So James Hegan sent Bill out to stand watch on the train that night, and one brakie, an Irishman by the name of Pat Dunne, stayed too. Long before daylight, James took the pump car and a push car and all thirteen of his Indian hands out to start getting ready for the wrecker.

Not a care in the world. There wasn't no reason to leave a guard there, nobody was going to steal a wrecked train was there, and the only reason was to give his brother Bill a night away from his wife, who was in one of her mean streaks. The only reason Pat Dunne stayed, he was lame in the back from having got throwed off'n a car in the wreck, and it would be easier than riding back into town on a hand car, and then coming out again.

No sir, not a care in the world! Yet when they got there, Bill Hegan and Pat Dunne was both dead. Bill had been shot twice in the back, so prob'ly whoever it was sneaked up on him, but Pat Dunne had tried to run away, lame back and all, and had been finely cornered and shot in the top of the head with a .45, prob'ly, like he'd been on his knees begging for mercy.

"Rolf, these ain't no gang of chicken stealers going around and lifting a fry off'n somebody's roost, no they ain't; I got some murdering sons of bitches here, and I've got to raise a posse and go after them," Abe said.

Rolf said wait, he'd go with him, but Abe said, "No, Father Lavrens ought to be down around Dalton somewhere, that's a place southeast of here used to be a stage station but it's dying now, but he's got a few stray Catholics there, and he stops in and combs and brushes their faith now and then. Both of these dead men was Irish, so they'll be his to bury, unless the railroad decides it's less trouble to haul them to Denver. I don't want that old Norwegian priest on my tail. I'll take the blame, it happened in my jurisdiction, but I wish you could find a way to urge him to ask the Lord to temper the wind to the shorn lamb, because I'm clipped close to the hide this time," Abe said.

He rode off with his *posse comitatus,* the usual bunch of loafers, and Rolf saddled up and took off down the Dalton trail. In a little while he seen the priest coming towards him on a big old horse almost as old as he was, and Father Lavrens was seventy-seven then, a big old red-faced Norwegian. He never had much use for the other Protestant preachers that came and went around Mooney, but he took a liking to Rolf right away. Partly it was because Rolf was half Swede, although at other times Father Lavrens said a Swede was only a Norwegian with his brains knocked out.

Father Lavrens's horse wouldn't stir out of a walk, and he didn't want it to. He said, "Abe's up against it, I'm afraid, and it's too bad because we're sure to get worse. The scum always floats to the top if you roil the waters enough."

Rolf said, "He'll be relieved to know you feel this way. You've been a powerful worry to him."

"Because of this Sephardic Jewish nonsense? Or it may not be nonsense, we're all God's family, only some of us behave better than others, as in any family," the priest said.

"That goes for even Methodists?" Rolf said.

"Even Methodists. You're willful and blind and stubborn, you're undutiful children of a loving Father, and you flee from the affectionate discipline of the one true Church, but I've been commanded to love you and I try to be an obedient son. Which I don't think is true of yourself, since you served a prison term," the priest answered him.

"I don't know as that's a fair statement. I was unjustly convicted and I got pardoned out," Rolf said.

They sloshed that argument around some, and then Rolf found himself telling the priest about that business in the hammock, although he hadn't intended to, because ordinarily it was the kind of thing any man would keep to himself, especially somebody like Rolf.

"I haven't a doubt that it was God you heard," Father Lavrens said. "Keep listening for it, and I'm just as sure that someday you'll hear from Him again, and He'll tell you to go the rest of the way, and unite with the one true church."

"I doubt that," Rolf said, "and I couldn't cut it if He did. I hope you won't take it the wrong way, but somehow I can't swallow the pope."

"Why not?" Father Lavrens said.

Rolf tried to explain, how Jesus went around with the worst hard-up riffraff in town, and had to mooch His grub and a place to stay, and He told them to give all they had to the poor and follow Him, and so on. And here the pope was on a golden throne, wearing golden robes, and you had to kneel down and lick his hand, and Pontius Pilate and Herod both never had it as rich.

"Never forget, young man, that the pope is a man," Father

Lavrens said, "as every pope before him has been a man, and as priests always have been, still are, and always will be men. Don't ask that we perform the miracles necessary to revive the simple creed of Jesus Christ. The miracle is that in a world of thrones and kings and empires, of wars and rebellions, of wholesale murder and the desolation of nations, the Holy Church has survived at all. When power was used to exterminate us, we asked God for power to help us survive, and He gave it to us. We erected our own throne, and made the heir of St. Peter as glorious as the richest and most ignorant king. We showed the Holy Father reverence, clothing him in golden robes and kissing his hand, to demonstrate to jealous kings that we were ready to die for our pope, our church, and our God, though every jealous king in the world threw his armies against us. Yet all this time, beneath the robes of the pope was the student of the simple fisherman he succeeded, do you see that?"

"In a way," Rolf said.

Father Lavrens smiled. "But in a way no, is that it? The time is coming when it will be no longer necessary to impress kings and emperors—when mankind will have progressed to the point where we can again live in peace and trust and brotherhood, and a simple fisherman can again lead us. I don't expect to live to see those times, but they can't be far off, say the turn of the century, yes sir about 1900 the last throne should have toppled, don't you think?"

"I couldn't say," Rolf said.

Father Lavrens said, "I look forward to that, young man. Imperfect republics take their places, but they're still republics because man is better than he used to be, thanks to the mercy of God, and he will be better still. Change comes faster and faster! Prophecy can now be carried over the electric telegraph wire, think of that! So can sin, you will say, but sin has always been a fast traveler, and still the truth outruns it because it has what a cowboy calls 'bottom.' You know how, when his horse founders in a race, the cowboy says he 'bottoms out,' well, the truth of God never bottoms out! No, I won't see God's golden age, but you will, when the pope will step down off his throne at last, and the love and peace and brotherhood of the golden age will have arrived, and there will be no rich and no poor, no strong and no weak, only the children of God. And when that happens, young man, remember that it was an ignorant old cow-country priest who told you so, in his seventy-eighth year."

He could really talk when he got wound up, but he was talking to a man who had did time in the pen, and it seemed to Rolf that he knowed more about miserable human nature than Father Lavrens did, and the golden age was a good deal further off than he thought. Another thousand years was more like it, as these two murders at the Q would kind of demonstrate.

Father Lavrens was played out when he got to Mooney. He said any ride of more than a couple of miles was getting too much for him, he felt fine except for a little prostate trouble, but he didn't have the strength he had fifty years ago. Rolf helped him into his shack behind Blessed Sacrament, which wasn't more than a shack itself, and brought him a pail of fresh water, and picked some cucumbers for him from the vine by his back door, and took care of his horse. Cucumbers was all he needed, having priested a hitch in the desert, where they're raised for both food and drink.

"Find out where the bodies are going, if you can," Father Lavrens said. "If they're to be buried here, I'll have to get my strength back."

"I'll do the best I can," Rolf said. "I'd bury them for you if I could, but I reckon I couldn't, and they didn't live long enough for me to hear their dying confession and grant absolution, so it's past the point where a mere Protestant can do any good."

The priest said, "What do you mean, hear their confessions and grant absolution? You're uttering a grave impiety young man, this verges on sacrilege." Rolf told him what he had got from the chaplain, and they argued about it awhile, and the priest said that at best it would be a pretty makeshift sort of unction, and the Protestant that dared to tackle it had better be in a high state of grace himself. He said he'd look into it when he could get to his books again, and he hadn't had time to read much in the last twenty or twenty-five years, and maybe he had slipped up on something, but he said, "I would hate to rely on you to grant peace to my own sinful soul, for example. I want something other than a cowboy hearing my last confession!"

Rolf said he didn't blame him, most cowboys was pretty ignorant, and then Father Lavrens complained that his feet burned, so Rolf got a gourd of water and washed them for him. He asked him if he didn't have no clean socks, and Father Lavrens said he didn't think so, when summer came he usually turned his feet out to grass in sandals, but he hadn't got any sandals yet. So Rolf washed out his socks for him too, and hung them up in the sun to dry, and a mighty wore-out pair they was, too.

So then Rolf got his nerve up, and asked Father Lavrens if he could get his advice on something that didn't have nothing to do with religion or the church, just an idee of his own, a hunch that bothered him. A priest gets used to giving out the advice he's hired to give, so there's nothing in it for him any more except getting impatient with the same old cussedness he hears all the time. But you ask him for some man-to-man advice, nothing professional, and you've got yourself an interested priest, and Father Lavrens was.

Rolf told him about this secret hunch that was bothering him, and he said, "I'm taking a lot for granted. I'm putting my own judgment up against the whole county, including Abe Whipple."

Father Lavrens said, "Let me ask you this—how strongly do you believe in what you call your hunch? Do you have an overwhelming conviction in your heart as well as your mind, that it is this way and no other?"

"I sure don't," Rolf said. "If I felt that way, why would I need advice?"

"If you had given me any other answer," the priest said, "I

would have told you, 'Shoo, boy, forget it, don't bother me!' But I'm afraid to say it's your prison-wise knowledge of mortal man, which I envy you not at all, that bares the truth to you."

"But suppose I take a chance, and I'm still wrong?" Rolf wanted to know.

"Why then you'll be sincerely wrong, and I trust sincerely penitent for it. Now let me sleep. You can be a pest, you know, burdened with a conscience almost as heavy as your ignorance. Shoo, boy, shoo!" Father Lavrens said.

Rolf got on his bony old horse and headed back into Mooney, and this was the very minute that the old Zimmerman house fell in, the oldest house in town, and always a lot of talk about saving it as a historical relic, it being the town's first post office, and some people had been murdered there, and the first twins in Colorado born there, one on the way to the bed and one in the bed. But people kept talking about preserving it, and the house kept getting older, and the last Zimmerman was living in Denver and wanted two hundred dollars for it, and nobody could make up his mind to put in some of his own money to start the pot going.

It was an old log house with a fireplace, and it had had a roof of hand-split cedar shakes, but most of the shakes was gone, and the old pole rafters leaned every which way, and the town milk cows scratching against the corners had weakened the joints. There was five boys in her when she went down, the pole rafters going first, knocking each other over like dominoes, and then the long west wall, and then the short south wall with the fireplace. The fireplace stood though, in silent tribute to whoever built it. A lot of people wondered what them boys was doing in there, the general opinion being some kind of nastiness, and they was prob'ly right. But most of the grown men in Mooney could remember being in there as kids, and she didn't cave in on them. So there wasn't as much talk about the hand of God as you might expect, because none of the boys was killed, or even hurt, and when people talk about the hand of God, what they usually mean is some kind of death and disaster.

15

Abe was back so soon it was clear he had rode hard both ways. His posse was worth the price of the ride, and no more, and his deputy had disappeared into a honeymoon fog, and Abe was so stumped he had kind of a horrified expression. He said they had took the remains of Bill Hegan and Pat Dunne on to Denver, so Father Lavrens could forget about that.

But the extra train had come in with the wrecker, and it had thirty-three Irishmen on it and eighteen Italians, a total of fifty-one tough young bucks, each fresh from his own Old Country, and still smelling of the immigration louse powder. They had been roughed up somewhat on the long trip, and was as spooky as brush calves when they was finely dumped out on the free arid soil of Colorado. And then the first thing they heard about was the murder of two fellow Catholics, because any time you find an Irishman or an Italian who is not a Catholic, it's like a double-yolk egg for scarce.

Their families had prob'ly warned them against this country, saying they'd either have to join the Protestants or be gelded, and then the Q expected them to horse that train up without a meal, until the cook in the kitchen car sobered up enough to fry some eggs or beans or something. There could of been real trouble if Abe hadn't of showed up then, but he went out there without his guns on, and offered to take them foreigners on two at a time if they'd wait their turns, and fight the fair American way, anything went except knives.

You tell an immigrant Irishman or Italian to fall in like a soldier, and call him a son of a bitch, and offer to whip him two at a time, and one of two things is going to happen, either you've got to make good or he's going to love you. These boys was hungry for a familiar word, and they throwed down their pick handles and told Abe their troubles, and he could understand enough of the Irish brogue to get it straight. He turned the cook out of bed, and put him on the end of his rope, and led him at a nice steady trot in his underwear for a mile or two, and he decided he was in shape to wallop a pot or two after all.

"Just when I think we've got peace on earth," Abe said, "this is when they discover somebody has robbed the Goddamn train, prob'ly the same miscreants that killed them two men, because who else had the chance? Rolf, you can't have no idee what they got away with! There was three bales of Chinese silk worth six hundred dollars each, and ten cases of good whisky, and a crate of twenty-four rifles with twelve thousand rounds of ammunition, and five cases of dynamite, and a gross of primers, and two cases of paregoric in pint bottles, and a gross of butcher knives. The rifles and ammunition and dynamite, they're bad enough, but with good whisky selling for eighty cents a quart, it's that paregoric that upsets me. You take an Indian, and sell him whisky made of water and caramel syrup and paregoric, and you've got an Indian who's going to wake up and go on the warpath, and you arm him with some of them old cheap butcher knives, somebody's going to have to kill the poor son of a bitch before he hurts somebody. Rolf, this is the most fiendish thing I ever seen! That stuff went out of there on a wagon, we know that, it had to, but it rained like hell up there just before daylight, and there ain't no more tracks than on a brick road."

"Yes, what I wanted to—" Rolf tried to say.

Abe hit a tree with his fist, and skinned his fist a little, and the tree too, and busted in, "And that train was deliberately and fiendishly wrecked. Some bold son of a bitch dug out from under three or four ties about four feet from a rail joint, and then he chiseled the angle-bar bolts of the joint off, and that took some time. He couldn't expect that rail was going to break and part of it turn over, but it did, so he had himself not just a simple derailment, but a first-class wreck. Now here's something else that puzzles me; this has to be the work of a gang, no one man or even two is going to pull a job like *this'n*, but the signs show that when them big heavy bales of silk was loaded, they was pinched along a little at a time by pinch bars. Now that's a lot of trouble to go to, and what are they going to do with it now they got it? You can't just load nearly a thousand pounds of Chinese silk up in your saddlebags, and go around peddling it to various women. Rolf, this thing is creepy! It's like a crow picking up pieces of glass and tin to hide in his nest, there's no sense in it, but no harm either except to waste his time, and what's time to a crow? But these ain't crows, and I put it to anybody, if he's got a plan to dispose of three bales of Chinese silk, then this is the same miscreant son of a bitch that run off with Cal Venaman's steers last winter. *That* wasn't no home-town pilferage either!"

Rolf caught him temporarily breathless, and he said, "Rest your mind and your mouth a minute, Abe, and tell me one thing if you can. What kind of a winter did Jack Butler have last winter?"

"The usual kind, drunk. I don't know why you plague me with the problems of a common sot at a time like this, but I know that during them January blizzards, there was twice the ignorant son of a bitch would of froze to death if some of the Flying V boys hadn't come along and pried him out of a snowbank. Why do you bother me with a common drunk at a time like this?"

"Because," Rolf said, "I don't think he's a common drunk, is why."

Abe didn't say nothing, but he knowed Rolf wasn't a word waster, not out of the pulpit anyway, but he come to a point like a bird dog. Rolf said, "Abe, I took a quart of whisky out to the ranch with us last time, to break Jack of his habit or drownd him. When I seen a fit coming on him, I took him down and poured it down him like drenching a sick horse. How much do you think it would take to get that man drunk?"

"Why," said Abe, "if you only had a quart, you'd only have a starter."

"A half pint done it," Rolf said.

"*What?*" Abe said.

Rolf said, "From the first, he was just too pitiful a sot to me, Abe, every cent he had ought to of gone into his thirst, but he's got a nice tight cabin with even scrim curtains, and fences like he was raising race horses, and bobwire enough to put a fence around the county, and a dresser full of nice new clothes he never wore. You never seen a good whisky sot that et very much, but Jack is a pure hog for his grub, you couldn't bake enough light bread to fill him, and he wants butter on it too, and bacon boiled in his beans, and anything you bring home to eat, he'll eat it. Now look here—he was passed out drunk when Colonel Pegler T. Saymill was murdered, and was beyond suspicion. He was passed out drunk when Cal Venaman's house was robbed and his dogs killed, and was beyond suspicion. And I can testify personally that he was passed out drunk when that train was wrecked and them men killed, or at least he had that excuse, because I personally poured half a pint down him. Then he went out for a long hard punishing ride to sober up, and I'll tell you this, he looked punished all right when he got back. *But he left most of that whisky in the bottle, Abe.* What I think, this man can't drink at all!"

Abe shook his head. "Only listen here, Rolf; I trailed them critters of Cal's as fur as Keith County, Nebraska, last winter. I talked to two men that said they heard they was sold for eight dollars each to somebody that paid cash, and then drove them north by east, and there wasn't a couple of hundred like Cal thinks, there was three hundred and two of his steers. Cal would hang himself if he knowed that, and you can't blame him, but you can't blame Jack Butler either.

"Because we're talking about $2,416 worth of cash steers, and $1,600 in gold from the house robbery, and $600 from Peg Saymill, and Jack Butler is a man that bets one-cent chips in two-cent raises, what the hell is he going to do with three bales of Chinese silk, and all that other stuff? Jack Butler is just *nobody,* he couldn't talk nobody into being his gang, why any robber worth his salt would laugh himself sick at the idee of being part of Jack Butler's gang!"

Rolf said, "Abe, in prison we had a little old nobody fella too, nobody took him serious either, so he'd go around and make a mysterious sign on things, a circle with a line drawed through it was all. It didn't mean a thing, but we felt sorry for the poor booger, and we didn't want him to feel neglected and slip a knife into somebody, so we took it serious. Like we'd all shiver when he was around, and say my goodness what does this mysterious sign mean, scratched on the wall in the can, and in the dust on the surgery table in the hospital, what are we coming to? It made this poor ignorant convict as happy as if he had good sense.

"This is the kind of robber Jack was, a plain old scrabbling two-bit cowman, but in his mind he's simply next to God. Killing don't mean a thing to him; behind that face he's laughing himself sick at us because he knows who done these killings and we don't, and he'll do some more if he ain't catched. The prisons is full of men that think they're too good for the rest of us. They don't need a woman, they don't need money, they don't need a dog or a cat, or even a prison rat that can be trained to come back for some crumbs. All they need is just to know that, in secret, they're smarter and better than everybody else in the county.

"There's just one thing wrong with the whole idee, Abe. Brains! Jack Butler couldn't plan how to empty a bootful of you know what, he'd cut a hole in the toe first; he could drive a four-horse team to a wagon, if somebody supplied the horses and wagon, or he could do the killing, or use a pinch bar to load three bales of Chinese silk. But he ain't got the brains to lay out the plans for this, he's hardly got any brains at all, he can't even make a convincing drunk!"

Abe kept nodding and sighing, and nodding and sighing, and then he said, "What gravels me, Rolf, is Jack ain't the only ranny that thinks he's smarter than us, there's another one just like him only worse, and the hell of it is, he *is!* Well, man may toil from sun to sun, but a sheriff's work is never done, as the poet says. I'd like to contribute one more thought before we have the closing ceremonials, I'll enjoy arresting this twitchy little son of a bitch more than I do most arrests."

"Don't go off half-cocked on my surmises, Abe," Rolf said. "I been wrong in my time, you know."

"You ain't wrong about this. This has stared me in the face for months, only I never spent two years in the pen to learn the sad truth about my fellow man, that the son of a bitch is even more unreliable than he looks," Abe said.

He went out of there calm as a cucumber, and Rolf could only hope he didn't walk into an ambush in that cold but angry frame of mind. Forty minutes later he was back, empty-handed. He set down and took off his hat and shook his head like he was getting rid of a buzzing in his ears, and maybe he was. He said:

"Rolf, ever notice that big bay gelding in the back box stall at the livery barn in Lickety Split? Well you missed a horse, son! Well that horse belonged to Huey Haffener, and Tattooed Emily, his Number One girl, told me he rode out on that horse last evening and ain't been seen since. He dug up the floor of the cellar, so he prob'ly took his valuables with him, and he even borried money off'n some of the girls before he left. A total of $144 he beat them poor hard-working girls out of, can you beat that?

"Rolf, I'm whipped, and I deserve it. I might just as well hand this star to some six-year-old girl for all the good I am. But I'll have to say this in behalf of myself, if Thad Rust turns out to be worth two whoops in hell on this job, it'll be because of what I learned him, not any native talent, because native talent is one thing he hasn't got, unless it's one he's keeping employed right now. He's your next sheriff sure as hell!"

Rolf said, "Don't give up yet, Abe. Lend me a good horse, and you just keep the eggs warm on the nest until you hear from me again."

"You can have any horse of mine any time, you know that," Abe said, "but you little piss-ant you, what are you up to? You're a minister of the gospel, like it or not! You've put your hand to the plow, and you can't turn back just because an old wooden-head sheriff overstayed his time on the job."

Rolf said, "I ain't taking no chances of no kind, Abe. I'm just doing what I knowed had to be done a long time ago, and would of been done if I hadn't got sidetracked on this preaching foolishness."

This was when he come to see me. I'd been looking for it for a right smart, and when I heard the dogs, I got up and went out, and there he was on one of Abe Whipple's horses.

First thing I noticed was how middle-aged and steady he looked, not like the wild old nothing kind of a kid he used to be. He seen I didn't have no gun on, and I seen he didn't have one, so he pulled in his horse and just waited, but I figgered it was his move to speak.

So he said, "Hello there, Holbrook."

I said, "Howdy, Rolf, but I don't go under the name of Holbrook Cohelan no more. I'm Peter S. Heath, Pete Heath, around here."

He said, "I know that. Mr. Heath, you owe me one."

I said how did he figger that. He said, "Well, partly the Red, White, and Blue deal but mostly the Missouri Pacific, and if that wasn't the most ignorant kind of a robbery, it'll do till one comes along."

I had these two dogs, a mostly mastiff bitch by the name of Spot, and one of her pups that I called Foolish, and as long as you was on horseback with them you was all right, but get down on the ground and see what happened. I had to tie them in the dugout where I stored my spuds, and then Rolf got down and we went into my place. I had this little old shanty down near the Platte, in the homestead country, called Pete Heath's Place, where you could buy groceries and tobacco and so forth, and ammunition, and I run a little game there. I never set in myself, only took a penny out of every dollar in the pot, and there wasn't a crooked dealer anywhere that dared set in there. I knowed them all.

Rolf didn't offer to shake hands, but he set down and said, "You're looking mighty fit for a man carrying so much metal in him."

I said, "Well, I have a lot of pain, and a regret or two, but mostly I'm satisfied with life. So you are a minister of the gospel now."

He said, "Not for long. I've got to ask you for something, Pete Heath, and I'm going to overlook the Missouri Pacific proposition entirely, and just say three words to you, Red, White, and Blue."

This went back to when him and me went up into the Black Hills. We worked first in a gold mine, but you take a cowboy that has always earned his dollar a day on a horse, mucking in a mine is a low-down way to earn an extra four bits, so we quit in disgust. There was this Red, White, and Blue saloon there, run by a fella by the name of John Hamilton Shaefer, that had been a captain in the cavalry, but had to resign when he was caught raping a squaw. If she had been an officer's squaw he could of been in bad trouble, but he was only a sergeant, Sergeant Backsy, so there was only an inquiry by the colonel, and John Hamilton Shaefer got the choice of resigning or taking a court martial for conduct unbecoming.

When he said he'd resign, Sergeant Backsy got up and said what the hell kind of justice was this, he'd kiss your foot if this was justice, so they busted him back to private and give him ten days in the stockade. John Hamilton Shaefer started this gambling hell called the Red, White, and Blue, the rawest games you ever seen. So when Rolf and me went broke, we decided to relieve Mr. Shaefer of some of his ill-gotten gains, so we went in the morning about 4 A.M., and put our guns on him, and took what gold there was in the strongbox, about $110. Only when we took out the back way, Mr. Shaefer ups with a damn little old .25 caliber derringer and shot me in the intestines, and I dropped the gold, and only had time to pick up four ten-dollar pieces, less than Rolf and me had lost in his dirty crooked games.

With that little slug in my intestines, I could of died if Rolf hadn't took care of me, so I owed him one for that all right. He wanted to know where Huey Haffener and Jack Butler would be headed with their loot. I didn't know about the train being robbed, only about the wreck, so it was shocking news to me.

I said, "So they're finely out in the open. It was a pure marvel how long they got away with it. I'll tell you what I can, Rolf. There's a freighter in Cheyenne, Louie Isbel, that runs a freight line. He got in over his head for some fancy imported horses, and it was him that brought a couple of men down to help Jack move them Flying V cattle they stole, and he said they just froze their hind ends off for less than fifty dollars apiece. Now you tell me there's three bales of Chinese silk and quite a bit of other heavy stuff, now that spells Louie Isbel to me, because he can move it and warehouse it until Huey finds somebody to buy it. There's a little old grassy canyon where Louie Isbel will hole up, and rest his horses, and wait for the fuss to die down, and he hasn't got any more guts than Huey or Jack. All Abe has to do is go in shooting, and he's got them."

He said this was what he wanted to know, and how could he find this canyon. I tried to tell him how, but he didn't know the country up there, and he said he'd have to have a map to give Abe. I said no sir, I was through with crime, but now and then somebody came through that wasn't, and I didn't want none of my handwriting on anything to put me in a bad position.

He said he'd make the map if I'd tell him how, and we rustled around and couldn't find a single piece of paper anywhere, and neither of us had the habit of carrying paper on us. I had this piece of slate I had quarried from the creek bed, with a three-corner chip of it for a slate pencil, and he drawed the map according to my directions.

He got up on the sheriff's horse, and I handed him up the

piece of slate, about a foot and a half square, and he said, "I told you I'd call it square between us, and I will, Holbrook, or rather Pete. But I come into this country to kill you for letting me go to prison on that Missouri Pacific deal, and it still rankles. It ain't easy to give up two years of your life that way."

I said, "I bet it ain't, but sometimes one man draws the Queen of Spades, and sometimes the other'n. I just wonder how you can have the guts to remind me of the Red, White, and Blue, after you played me false on the Missouri Pacific proposition."

He said, "Me played you false? How do you figger I played you false?"

I said, "There's no profit in digging up the dead, but by God I wouldn't of went into that with no such fool as Bobby Dale if you hadn't gone into it! Here I am a fugitive with a price on my head, and you're in prison it's true, but if you didn't light on your feet I'd like to know who did, assistant to the chaplain! I heard you was down on me because of the Missouri Pacific job, and I wasn't surprised because you always did have a short temper, but by God I got deadfalled into that one, and I wasn't going to shoot it out with you! No sir, I would of plugged you from behind with a rifle the minute you showed up here!"

He said why didn't I, and I said I'd heard he was preaching in the church in Mooney, and it was just like that unpredictable son of a bitch, and let's see how long it lasts. I said, "Rolf, you was the best sidekick I ever had, but don't throw up that Missouri Pacific proposition to me, because you're set for life with one of the easiest jobs in the world, and I'm scratching a living the meanest kind of way. I ain't one to complain that life ain't fair, or you'd sure hear me complaining now!"

He said, "Mr. Heath, I swear to you I never knowed Bobby Dale in my life, and I never knowed anything about that Missouri Pacific robbery until I was arrested for it, and I don't have no idee how you possibly figgered I could be in on something as foolish as that."

I seen it all then, this Bobby Dale had lied to me to get me to go in with him; there couldn't be no other explanation because Bobby Dale would lie to his own mother, and I never knowed Rolf Ledger to lie to anybody. We shook hands, and I felt mighty good about that, and I reckon he did too, because he said, "The hardest thing in the world is to believe that a friend has let you down, and that's what I've had to believe all these years."

I said me too, and we shook hands again, and I said maybe someday I'd get up early enough to come in and listen to him preach. He said it would prob'ly do me good to listen to anybody, but he was giving it up.

I said if he was giving it up, I reckoned I never would get started on it, and he said religion would do me good and bring me peace of mind. I said, "I already got peace of mind, it's a hardscrabble way for an old cowboy to live, but I brung it on myself and I know it. Religion is a cash proposition, and I can't afford it. Prob'ly Jesus meant well, but if there's been a clergyman since then that wasn't out for the dollar, history has overlooked him. It's like a bunch of these new mail-order stores, all fighting over the same business. The pope has got one store, and the archbishop of Canterbury has got one, and there's a couple of other pretty big ones, and a regular epidemic of little crossroads bargain places dealing mostly in secondhand goods. Whenever they scrape the trade dry between them, they load up a nice stock of piety and go over to Africa and pester the cannibals, and all *they* want is to be let alone the same as me. I'd love to hear you preach once, though, Rolf Ledger, just to see the spectacle. I bet you ten dollars you couldn't get up there in the pulpit and look me in the eye."

He said, "You'd lose that bet, Mr. Heath," and he turned his horse around, and I let Spot and Foolish out, and hoped nobody would ever find out it was me that told on Louie Isbel. Not that I owed him anything, but it's a matter of principle.

16

Rolf had his doubts about that map, but Abe just said, "Oh yes, I know the area well, and it seems I've seen this piece of slate before too."

"It's pretty common around here," Rolf said.

"Yes," said Abe, "but this is an uncommon good piece. I hope you didn't go to a lot of trouble getting it."

Rolf knowed what he meant, and he said, "I didn't. A nice profit for both parties."

Abe said, "I watched that Peter S. Heath for quite a while, let me tell you, until in my judgment I decided he was keeping his tugs tight and his crupper buckled, so I let him be. Some sheriffs might of rode him clear out of the county, but I didn't, and here's the bread I cast on the water coming back to me. So we'll just rub it out, and there you are, a nice clean slate again."

He spit on the slate and rubbed the map out, and put some more .45 shells in his belts, and throwed his saddle on another horse. Rolf said he was going with him, and Abe said, "No you ain't. I'm only grateful I haven't got Thad Rust to handicap me, a man of the cloth would be more than I could stand. Thad never was much help, and he'll be a month getting over his backache and catching up on his sleep; no thank you, Reverend, I've got problems enough without you along."

He picked Bill Ahern and Alf Constable and Johnny Wyatt, a nephew of Rachel and cousin to poor old eager Lettie, all good steady men, good shots, and used to his highhanded way of doing things. Not every man could ride to Abe's orders.

It was almost dark when they left town, and they went a roundabout way in case anybody was keeping watch for Huey, which wasn't likely. Abe told his men, "Huey won't be no trouble. Staying alive is always his main concern. But this fool of a Jack Butler prob'ly imagines he's some kind of a damn tornado of a badman, and he'll draw his weapon. Let's don't stain our souls with killing that deluded riffraff. Let's save him to hang."

"What I want to know," Bill Ahern said, "is where we're going."

"You'll find out," Abe said. "Discipline, that's what puts steel into an attack! Learn to do as you're told without a lot of questions, and you'll be steady on the firing line. Just notice where my suspenders cross, and keep that between your horse's ears, and you'll get to the right place at the right time."

"Your rump is a lot easier to follow, nobody could miss that," Johnny Wyatt said.

They got up on the Flying V range, and Abe told them to lay down and catch a little sleep, he'd watch the horses, and so they did. He booted them out a while later, and kept them amused by quarreling with them until almost daylight, when they come to where these fugitives was holed up.

They had to admire the place all right, plenty of feed for the teams, and a nice spring of sweet water, and in grass so deep the tracks wouldn't last long for anybody to foller. As near as anybody could remember, the spring was a good half mile up from where they had to stop, around a bend.

"Now let's see, here's how we'll do this," Abe said. "You all wait here. I'll dismount and go around them afoot, and see what we're up against."

Bill Ahern said, "You old fat aged fool, it'll be noon before you get anywhere afoot. I'll go see myself what we're up against."

Abe said well all right, but use his head for a change. Abe and Alf and Johnny stood down and held their horses and

Bill's, and Bill sauntered off through the grass until he had to get down on his hands and knees, and that was the last they seen of him for a while, and all they could do was stand there and slap mosquitoes and make sure the horses didn't make any noise.

Bill got up on the rise, and he could see the camp of the desperadoes, and them four big beautiful draft horses just catched his breath, they was so beautiful. Four matched Clydesdales, two browns and two chestnuts that would average nineteen hundred pounds each in working flesh. The wagon was turned around already, so they wouldn't have to fool around turning it when they got ready to move out. There was only one other horse Bill could see, Huey Haffener's big bay.

Huey was setting on his knees beside the wagon, with his derby hat on and a cigar in his mouth, and it looked to Bill like he was counting his money. There wasn't no sign of Jack Butler or this Cheyenne freighter Louie Isbel, but Bill figgered they'd be around somewhere, because Huey couldn't even harness one of them Clydesdales, let alone drive a four-horse hitch of them.

Bill got down on his hands and knees and started around them. There wasn't no trees nowhere, but about a hundred yards from the camp there was this spring, with a lot of brush around it, the nearest thing to cover in miles. Bill got there, and had a nice drink of fresh water, and made himself a cigarette, because he didn't figger Huey would notice if he was to fly a kite.

In a few minutes, Jack Butler crawled out from under the wagon, rubbing his eyes and yawning. Bill throwed his cigarette into the mud and squatted there listening. He could hear every word they said.

Huey said, "Morning, Jack, did you sleep well?"

Jack said, "No thanks to you if I did."

"Cheer up, Jack! We got the world by the tail with a downhill pull," Huey said.

"Maybe you have, but I left a ten-thousand-dollar property

back there and I never can go back, the prettiest little property in the world," Jack said.

"You stupid son of a bitch, you owed so much on that property, you couldn't of sold out for six hundred net," Huey said.

"I had more than that in bobwire," Jack said.

"The more fool you! Man that can't handle money, he don't deserve it. But that's behind us. I was just computing; you've got eight hundred and forty dollars coming right now, more money than you ever had in your life," Huey come back.

"I had more than that from Cal Venaman's house. I took all the chances, and like a fool I just handed that money over to you," Jack kind of whimpered.

"Fair is fair. I was the one told you the money was there, wasn't I?" said Huey.

"You never do anything except *tell.* Somebody else has to take the chances. Where the hell is Louie?" Jack said.

"You know where he is, Cheyenne, to find us a place to hide this stuff. You can't just go driving into Cheyenne and start looking for a place in broad daylight. Don't try to think, Jack. That's where you get into trouble every time, when you try to think. Get us some breakfast and feed these horses of Louie's, and let me do the thinking," Huey said.

"Why did he have to ride my horse? That Fanny mare is the only thing I got left from the days when I was a cattleman on my own J Bar B property," Jack complained.

"He had to ride something, and I don't allow strangers on my horse, you know that, Jack," Huey said.

Jack said he had to have a drink of water, so he come down to the spring and got down on his hands and knees and leaned over, kind of complaining to himself about how he was doing all the work and what was he getting out of it, sore hands was all. Bill got up and leaned down and hit him in the back of the neck, and then fished him out of the spring before he could drownd, and then hit him again to make sure he stayed asleep.

Nothing looks sillier than a city fella trying to get by on the prairie. It don't matter how shrewd he is, setting in his own saloon in his checked pants and deerskin vest, surrounded by beautiful fallen women and drinking them rotgut French wines, he's just an orphan calf if you get him out in the prairie. Bill dragged Jack a ways by the ankle, and then he started to come to, and Bill had to wallop him again, and then he got up and throwed him across his shoulder, and Huey never did even suspicion how close he was.

"Well well, so here is one of our miscreants," Abe said, when Bill carried Jack up over his shoulder. "I judge he didn't give you no trouble. What are the other two doing?"

Bill said that Huey was counting his money, and Louie Isbel was gone to Cheyenne on Jack's Fanny mare, and they might as well forget him for a couple of days. "You ought to see them beautiful Clydesdale horses, Abe," Bill said. "Somebody's going to get them horses. I want you to help me figger out a way to bid them in."

"You don't want Clydesdales in this country," Abe said. "A Clydesdale will eat as much as an army remount, that horse has got to be grain fed, that's not a horse for the frontier, you don't want Clydesdales."

Bill said he reckoned he knowed what he wanted, and Abe said Bill might as well drink his money up as pour it down a Clydesdale's throat in oats and rolled barley, and so on. They tied Jack's hands behind him good and tight, and left him lay there sound asleep. They didn't tie his feet, because he wasn't going no place anyway, and it might be fun if he tried to.

They went down and gathered Huey in without much trouble, although he was expecting Jack Butler and lost his head when he looked up instead and seen the sheriff and a posse, and he yanked out a pocket gun and tried to shoot. Abe slapped him across the mouth for that, and made him drop the gun, and that took all the fight out of him. He had put his money away in a tin box that he had kept buried in the floor of his cellar in the Jackrabbit, and they took the key away from him and opened it up and counted out $15,980 in gold pieces.

"That money is mine, nobody lays a hand on that money, it's mine, leave my money alone," Huey kept saying, until they had to slap him again. They tied his hands behind him too, and Bill hitched up them four Clydesdales, calling them darling and sweetheart and so on while he done it. He asked Huey what their names was, and Huey said the leaders was Betty and Candy, and the wheelers was Dolly and Bonny, but Bill went on calling them darling and sweetheart. They walked out of there with that big heavy overloaded wagon like they was dragging a piece of grocery-store string behind them, with Huey tied on behind on a ten-foot leash, so he had to trot to keep up.

Abe and Johnny and Alf rode ahead, and the first thing they noticed was that Jack Butler wasn't nowhere in sight, and Abe said he wondered where the fool had went to, and just then a rifle bullet plunked into Johnny Wyatt in the side. He fell off'n his horse, and the others jumped off'n theirs, and just in time too, because here come another rifle bullet that didn't miss Abe by more than an inch or two.

Abe hollered back for Bill not to come no closer, some son of a bitch was shooting at them. He asked Johnny how he was, and Johnny said, "Why I'm shot, how the hell do you think I am? You led me out here on a wild-goose chase and got me shot."

Abe had him pull his shirttail out so he could look at the hole, and he said, "It's not the worst I ever seen, Johnny, but I can well believe it stings, so you take it easy and the rest of us will handle things from here on out."

"Small comfort to me," Johnny said.

They had let the horses run, and that's what they done, they run. Abe said, "Bet you a nickel this Louie Isbel didn't go to Cheyenne after all, because nobody but a fool teamster would let a man get down in deep grass where he had to hunt him out. Let's kind of fan out, everybody stay low to the ground, and let him come after us. This could take quite a while now, boys, so don't get impatient, remember how the Indians did it; that's the game, boys, we play it like Indians."

They spread out and stayed hid in the grass, and pretty soon they seen this fella on Jack Butler's mare Fanny, setting up there with a rifle in his hand and the butt on his hip. He knowed he was safe, because he had got a good look at them, and he knowed none of them had rifles.

There wasn't no sign of Jack Butler, but they knowed Jack wouldn't be far away. They knowed this fella had come back and found Jack and turned him loose, and knowed how things stood, the camp captured by now, and the four Clydesdales and the wagon in the hands of the law.

This fella hollered, "Sheriff, hey, Sheriff!" Abe just set there in the grass and sucked on a piece of grass, and didn't pay no more attention than if somebody else had been sheriff.

This fella hollered again, "Sheriff, I'll make you a deal. I want my teams and my wagon and a free start, and you don't come bothering around and ask where I went to. You can have Huey and Jack and there's right at sixteen thousand dollars in gold that goes with them, now how can you beat that offer?"

Abe looked over at where Johnny Wyatt was laying, and said, "He calls that an offer, why I've got the teams and the wagon *and* the sixteen thousand dollars in gold!"

Johnny said, "Yes and you got me shot."

This fella hollered a few more times, and Alf Constable crawled over and asked Abe if he wasn't even going to answer him, and Abe said no, let him holler his head off, play it like Indians.

This fella wanted to know why they should kill themselves for the C.B.&Q. railroad, they had everything else and the railroad was the one that would have to pay for the stuff on the wagon. All he wanted, he said, was to get out of the state of Colorado with the teams and the wagon, he'd take his chances from there, fur as he was concerned, nobody would ever know there was sixteen thousand dollars in gold in that wagon and *he* didn't care what ever became of it. He said they'd never get another chance to divide up that much gold, but Abe just kept shaking his head and saying, "Why he calls that an offer, why he must think I'm green as a gourd!"

Johnny said, "Somebody else does too, oh my stars will you look at that fool!"

Abe looked, and here was Rolf Ledger standing up in the grass behind that fella on Jack Butler's mare. He didn't have a gun on, not so much as the sign of one, but he had rode that mare enough to know her as well as Jack did, or maybe better, and he knowed she was touchy about being brushed between her hind legs. He got up to her hind end before the fella seen him and turned around to point the rifle at him.

He brought his hand up between Fanny's hind legs, and she went up in the air like he knowed she would, because some horses are that way, you just can't break them of it and it's as much as your life is worth to brush them between the hind legs.

The bullet went into the ground somewhere, and Louie Isbel had to let go of the rifle to hang onto the saddle horn, and by then Rolf had hold of the bridle, and had Fanny turned so fast it didn't do him no good to have hold of the saddle horn.

Out he went, and then Rolf jumped on him and took a pistol away from him that he carried in his pants pocket, and when the fella still wanted to fight, Rolf was forced to hit him. He only hit him once, and he proved that in all the years he hadn't forgot how, because that one was all it took to lay him low.

"Well, Reverend, you shortened things up for us, you sure did, I'll have to give you credit for that," Abe said. "But you took a long chance too."

"Not much of a one," Rolf said. "He's no cowboy, he's just a teamster; why he couldn't ride the family milk cow, and he was getting real nervous when you wouldn't answer."

"The wicked flee when none pursuith, but the righteous are bold as a lion," the sheriff said. "He had reason to be nervous, yes he did."

They had to rustle around then and find Jack, and then run him down and rope him like a calf, and then tie his hands and turn him loose again. They started back to town with Huey tied on behind, trotting along and complaining that his feet hurt. They didn't pay no attention at all to Jack Butler, and pretty soon he come lolloping after them, scared to death he was going to be left out on the prairie with his hands tied. They tied Louie Isbel up and let him ride on top of the load, along with Johnny Wyatt, because Isbel had a boil on his neck and one on his thigh, and Johnny had this wound in his side.

Now some people might think it was an easy capture that don't know anything about it, but it was easy only because there was some mighty good men on the trail, with a good man in command. Abe made a mistake about leaving Jack Butler's feet untied, and not leaving anybody to guard his rear, yes he did, but all in all he planned it pretty good and come out of it all right, and how you come out is what counts. After that, everybody called this place where the capture occurred, "Outlaw Canyon," although it was so shallow it was more of a draw than a canyon, and when you call the likes of Huey Haffener and Jack Butler and Louie Isbel outlaws, people like the James boys and the Daltons and Youngers are prob'ly turning over in their graves.

17

Abe gave Rolf the dickens all the way back into Mooney, about taking his chances the way he done, and violating his oath as a minister. But Rolf's mind was made up, and he never was one to tell you when he'd made it up, he just done it and you figgered it out by yourself.

But the truth was, he felt as useless as a freemartin, which is a heifer calf that grows up with all of the rigging of a she-critter, only she never takes no interest in the bull, and when you finely give up and butcher her for beef, you find she's got a little old undersize pair that never did come down. A free-martin is neither all he, nor all she, nor anything but a dead loss.

They got into town before dark, and such a to-do you never seen before, with people going down to the jail and demanding to see the prisoners, even respectable women that as a rule would of died before you'd ever catch them around a jail. Rolf got his few traps together, and was all set to ride quietly out of town and be on his way, only he thought it was only fair to tell Abe first. He went to Abe's house, but Edna said he was down to the courthouse.

When Rolf got to the courthouse, the sheriff's office door was closed, and Alf Constable was keeping guard over it, and he said nobody could see Abe for a while. Some of these women was waiting to see the three prisoners, and one of them was Mrs. Stella Landsdown, who had made such a fuss about Beatrice Cunningham going to Colonel Pegler T. Saymill's funeral. She started in on Rolf about the Zimmerman house falling down, and she wanted to know what them boys was doing in there when she fell, and she said it was a pity the Methodists was so flabby in their stand against carnality, you could bet if there was a Babtist church in town, them nasty little devils wouldn't of been there. She asked Rolf how about things like that going on in his own congregation, and he had his mind on other things, so he only asked her back what did she expect of him?

"Why," she said, "raise up a child in the way of his going, and when he is old, he will not depart from it. If the minister of their own church ain't going to train them boys, who is?"

Rolf wasn't hardly paying any attention to her at all, and he just said, "That ain't something a boy has to be trained in, ma'am, it comes natural." That shut her up all right, and give the boys at the livery barn something to talk about for years to come, and in the barbershop too. If Stella hadn't been a red-neck who had already helped run two Babtist preachers out of town, because she didn't like their idee of the Babtist creed, it could of got Rolf into some trouble.

He waited awhile, and then he seen it was coming on dark, so he just told Alf to tell Abe he had said good-by, and he slipped out and got on his horse and rode on out of town. What was keeping Abe all this time, Bea Cunningham had come to see him, and it was her idee that the girls wanted to take up a collection to buy Jack Butler's mare, Fanny, for Rolf, on account of the way he'd healed Lois. They had raised two hundred and fifty dollars, but Abe didn't want to have anything to do with the proposition, and he didn't like to discuss it with her even.

But Bea kept after him, and finely he said, "Bea, Goddamn it, you're just making it unpleasant for both of us. After this, you don't think this town is going to put up with that mess across the crick, do you? I'm going to have to close you down, and run all of you out of there."

Bea said, "Oh shoot, Abe, we're all packed and ready to go. Why the minute we heard that Huey was mixed up in those robberies, we knew our time had come."

He said, "Well I purely hate to do it, Bea. A good red-light district is important to a town, and you run a nice clean orderly place. Huey's wasn't no great shakes, but it was different, it got talked about, so Mooney became a well-known town. Although them shows he put on every Saturday night didn't amount to much after you seen them a few times, and besides a girl that would put on a show like that will also pick your pocket."

Bea said, "Huey ruined it, but times aren't the same, we wouldn't have lasted anyway, Abe. I'm not losing any sleep over it."

"What are you going to do?" he asked her.

"Why, money's no problem to me," Bea said. "I think I'll go to Custer County, Nebraska, where I've got some land, and try wheat farming."

Abe said it seemed to him like that was just going from bad to worse, but Bea was a farm girl born and bred, and just charmed with the idea of owning her own land, and having a good string of work horses, and a buggy team of her own, and her own butter and eggs, and to wake up at night and listen to her own windmill squeak.

Abe said all right then, he'd try to make a deal with Jack for the horse, and to wait there. He went back to the cells, and there was three women viewing the prisoners, and Huey Haffener was setting there on the edge of his bunk, making dirty remarks to them, so dirty they couldn't understand them. Abe told him to shut his dirty mouth or he'd shut it for him, and then he offered Jack two hundred dollars for the horse.

"That Fanny mare is worth a lot more than two hundred dollars," Jack said.

"Try and get it," Abe said. "If Cal Venaman chooses to file on her, he'll get her along with everything else you've got."

"And everything else everybody else has got, all the way across Colorado," Huey said. "Mark my words, Abe, he's going to make money out of being robbed. He'll bill me for a thousand dollars apiece for them two dogs, mark my words."

Abe said, "Where you're going, it won't make no difference to you," and Jack said on second thought, he'd take the two hundred dollars. So Abe went back and got a bill of sale out of his desk, and filled it out, and had Jack sign it, and then he told Bea he had saved her fifty dollars. He said the horse was worth every cent of two hundred and fifty dollars, but you didn't make your first offer her true worth, that's contrary to every rule and custom in dealing for a horse. Bea said to give the rest of the money to Rolf, or to the church, however he liked, and then her and Abe shook hands, and he told her again how sorry he was to have to close her up, and she went out of the courthouse.

But only about two steps. She come running back in, white as a sheet, so scared she could hardly talk. A lynch mob was coming toward the courthouse, and Cal Venaman and some of his boys was trying to hold them back, and wasn't having no luck at all to speak of. "They'll kill you along with them,

Abe," she said. "This is the worst bunch of hard-cases this side of the Barbary Coast."

She was right about that, too, because it was the extra-gang crew from the railroad, all eighteen of the Italians, and thirty-two of the thirty-three Irishmen, the other Irishman having been killed unloading a rail that afternoon, when it dropped on him. He never knowed what hit him.

Cal had this foreman, an old Arkansas boy who stuttered, that had formerly rode the Chisholm Trail, but his stuttering kept him from telling the usual lies about it. For some reason, his stuttering had got him the nickname of Shoo Shoo, but it hadn't done nothing to his nerve, no sir; that old bony bent-back Shoo Shoo didn't have hardly a tooth left in his head, nor a hair on top of it, but he was out there with Cal doing his best to hold back the avalanche as the saying is. Them crazy Italians and Irishmen had took Cal's own teams and wagons away from him, and had whipped them horses at a deal run all the way to Mooney, and this alone was enough to bring Cal to a boil. You never run a team with a loaded wagon for him.

Shoo Shoo had his weapon out, and Cal was trying to make him put it away, saying, "No guns, Shoo Shoo, for God's sake, they'll tear you limb from limb." Meanwhile he was backing down the street, yelling at the Irishmen, because the Italians couldn't understand him, "You'll go to prison for this! I'm your friend, you know this, stay out of trouble, boys, those men will hang anyway! Whisky for everybody that will follow me!"

If he had hollered that in time, it might of helped, but it was too late for that, and anyway somebody shied a clod at Shoo Shoo and hit him in the mouth, and he started to bleed. You let somebody start to bleed at a time like that, you might as well issue a proclamation that all laws is repealed, because the sight of blood is all they need.

They swarmed over Shoo Shoo and Cal, and that was all that stood between them and the courthouse until they got there. Then there was Sheriff Abe Whipple and a few good men like Alf Constable and Frank Mueller, the socialist that ran the meat market, as well as Bernard Petty, the embalmer, and Dr. Sidney Nobile and County Judge Andy Obers. Even Thad Rust showed up just in time to throw himself into the breeches, as the saying is, looking a little peaked but not as bad as Abe expected.

They could stand off the mob from the front door as long as they had to, and Abe knowed it, because the mob had to climb seven steps to get to him, but sooner or later they was going to discover that there was a side door that led straight into Abe's office. Not many people knowed about it, because Abe usually ran that county from his house, and said that anybody that wanted to see him could come there, but the door was there and there wasn't no way to keep them from finding it out.

Rolf Ledger had got a little piece out of town on his horse, but not fur enough he couldn't hear the yelling and shouting and screaming and so on, and he had been in prison long enough to know how a voice sounds like when a man has gone crazy, because every now and then, somebody went crazy in the pen. He had a pretty good idee what was happening, without anybody having to tell him. He jumped off'n his horse, because if he was in a hurry, he didn't want to be bothered with *that* horse, and started back.

He didn't know what he aimed to do, and in fact was pretty hopeless about the whole thing, but he had heard a little lynch talk around town, mostly from people like the loafers at the livery barn and Mrs. Stella Landsdown, and he knowed it wasn't no way to dispose of these cases. He didn't have no gun, not even a pocket knife, not even a shingle nail to defend himself with, all he had was this one idee in his mind, that this was the wrong way to go at it. And when Rolf got the idee in his mind, anybody that knowed him could testify that you wasn't going to get it out with dynamite.

He reached the side door, just as the mob give up in front and come running around, looking for some other place to bust in. Rolf never seen such wild men in his life, even in prison, and he seen some wild ones there. He got to the door first, and he braced himself into it good and strong, and they made the mistake of coming at him too fast. So all they done, on the first charge, was just pile a few up on top of each other in front of him.

They hadn't hardly hurt Rolf at all, just enough to close one of his eyes, and start him to bleeding at the nose, and make him lose his temper for the first time since he took the oath not to lose it again.

"Stand back you sons of bitches, stand back you riffraff, it's my night to howl so stand back!" he yelled at them.

They seen him bleeding, and it upset them more than they already was, so they untangled themselves from the door, except for a couple that had to be carried out of the way. Then they started at him again, and howl! say you should of heard them.

But just then Father Lavrens slid in beside Rolf and lifted his hand. He was in his gown or robe or whatever you call it that Catholic priests wear, and there wasn't no way them fellas could make a mistake, he was one of their own kind of clergyman and not a black Protestant ready to put the knife to their manhood.

Only they had already started throwing things, and something catched Father Lavrens in the chest, and something else catched him in the stomach, and down he went. *That* fetched them up short, you just bet it did, they had dropped their own priest, and not meaning to was no excuse. A couple of them was going to help him up again, but Rolf seen the old man was hurt pretty bad, and he yelled at them to STAND BACK, and this time they done it.

He squatted down beside the priest and got his handkerchief out and dabbed away some of the blood that was coming from his mouth, although Father Lavrens hadn't been hit in the mouth, and he said, "Take it easy, old-timer, just lay here and we'll get a doctor for you right away."

Father Lavrens said, "Oh no, it's too late for that, I've burst my heart I'm afraid, receive my last confession."

"I've been thinking it over," Rolf said, "and I doubt I've got the jurisdiction after all."

"Receive my sins and forgive me them!" the priest said, and so Rolf took his hand, and Father Lavrens started to go through the rigamarole, and he got as far as "heartily sorry" before he played clear out. But he was still breathing, at least a little, so Rolf hurried up and made the sign of the cross over him like the chaplain had taught him, and said, "I forgive you your sins, in the name of the Father, the Son, and the Holy Ghost, amen."

Everybody else practically was down on their knees by then, the whole bunch of railroaders that wanted to lynch Huey and Jack and that Cheyenne freighter, Louie Isbel, even Stella Landsdown, who got carried away every now and then by religion, and the town halfwit Harold DuSheane, and quite a few more. The railroad boys got their beads out and started to say their Rosaries, and them beads clicked so fast it sounded like payday on an army post, a dozen crap games going.

Old Rolf he folded Father Lavrens's hands over his chest, he seen he was dead all right, he didn't need no doctor to tell him that, and then he looked up at the sky. He just set there listening a minute, nobody else breathed a word you just bet, and nobody else heard anything, but finely old Rolf he just nodded and said, "Well, all right, if I have to stay, I guess I have to."

18

I went there myself to see him bury Father Lavrens, about the only way you'd get me into a church unless they carry me in against my will after I'm dead. Rolf was all for holding the services somewhere else. He said it would be sacrilege for him to officiate in a Roman Catholic church, and sacrilege to drag a poor dead priest that couldn't help himself into First Methodist, but Abe Whipple took charge and in it he had the support of Jimmy Drummond, who looked it up in *Principles*.

"You can't celebrate the Mass, all you can do is recite a eulogy; you can't even face the altar legally, but have got to stay down on the floor with your back to it, no better than the rest of us," Jimmy Drummond said. "But you can recite the eulogy, and I say we better get at it, because in this heat, he ain't going to keep forever."

So they held it in Blessed Sacrament, about as shacky an old place as it could be and still be called a church, old yella-painted wood, and a dirt floor, and no windows to speak of because all but two of them had been boarded up after the glass got broke. I went because me and Father Lavrens used to have many a good argument about just about anything you could name, anything but religion, he wouldn't argue that with me. He used to stop there at my place and water his horse, and I'd make him his favorite restorative, whisky and water, with a little brown sugar and cinnamon, and some raisins on the side to eat. That's the only way you would of catched me in a church, to bury the old man.

They couldn't of held the crowd in the Methodist, and it barely got a toe hold in Blessed Sacrament, but Abe was bound Father Lavrens was to be buried from his own church, so they did. Rolf didn't really throw much of a celebration at all. He read them the twenty-eighth chapter of Matthew, verses one through six, and then he said, "I can tell you something along this same line, either this man here is risen or we're all of us fooling ourselves, and I for one ain't fooled, no not a bit."

Then he said a little prayer, mostly asking forgiveness for them dirty no-good lynch experts that had killed their own priest, trying to get at Huey and Jack and that Cheyenne teamster, Louie Isbel. Then he said there would be a couple of moments of silence while we each prayed according to training or conscience or habit, after which people could file past and view the remains.

I tried to catch Rolf's eye, but he knowed I was there, and you wasn't about to trap him that easy, and he never so much as looked at me. When he put it to us to pray, each his own way, I was stumped, but I jogged the man next to me to share his book with me, and he done it, and we knelt down together. Only he was one of them Italians, and I couldn't begin to read it, not a word of it, so I just made a mumbling sound, and he thought I was saying the Hail Mary in my own language, and to tell the truth, it didn't sound much worse than it did in his'n.

In the back of the room I seen Cal Venaman and his wife and daughters, including his new son-in-law, Thad Rust, Thad looking a little patched up here and there. He had got beat up pretty good there at the door of the courthouse, before the mob give up and went around to the other side, mostly on his face. Some men wear wounds well and some don't, and Thad didn't. He looked like he'd been in a fight, was all.

When Rolf skinned out so he could shake hands with people, everybody got up and went past the coffin to view the remains, and quite a few of them wept, and Stella Landsdown fainted. I was one of them close to her, so I had to help tote her outside. We set her down on her feet, and she revived and told Rolf she thought his choice of a text was excellent, the Resurrection was one of her favorite funeral texts, and he said a man didn't have much choice at a funeral, it was Resurrection or nothing.

I managed to get in line to shake his hand, and I said, "I really appreciated the send-off you gave the old man, Reverend, he deserved it if anybody did." He said, "Well, Mr. Heath, I only hope it does you some good too." I said at least it hadn't done me no harm, and I stood back a little ways because I wanted to talk to him again, because if he was leaving Mooney and Colorado forever, I might want to tie in with him.

Then I seen the Venamans go up to him and shake hands with him, and Cal said it was too bad if Rolf held to his threat to leave the town and the church, he had enormous possibilities here and would be missed. Rolf said, "I thought it over, Mr. Venaman, and if the people want me, I reckon I'll stay."

"Well say, that's good news!" Cal said. "You must come out to dinner one of these days, and let's get better acquainted; how about tomorrow, or even today?"

Rolf said he reckoned he was too busy tomorrow and today, and he turned to shake somebody else's hand, and the Venamans got nudged plumb away. I seen Samantha looking back, dying to say something to him, but she didn't have no more idee about what to say or how to say it than a hog does about Sunday. Rolf wasn't going to leave Mooney, that was a cinch, so I thought, All right, old buddy, let's have some fun.

I edged a mite closer to him, until I was only a couple of feet behind him, and I said "HIPE!" real loud. Rolf dropped his Bible and spun around and slapped at his leg like he was wearing a gun. Now how this come about was this way; when a man is making a fast draw under peril of death, he'll let out a grunt with the violent motion. It may be his last one, but you don't worry about peculiar noises at such a time, you just do it. There was this fella by the name of Cockeye Britton, from Beaumont, Texas, that come up to Kansas when Rolf and me was kids about fifteen or sixteen, quite famous for the fast draw. His eyes crossed so you never could tell if he was looking at you or over in the corner, and prob'ly that was a help in beating people to the draw, because if they thought he was looking over in the corner, it would be their last thought. So instead of being called Charles B. Britton, his real name, he was called Cockeye. He was as fast as they came, and when he drawed his gun he said "Hipe" instead of just grunting, and it got to be quite the thing among us young bucks of fifteen or sixteen. If you wanted to notify somebody that this was it, all you had to do was say "Hipe," and it shortened the ceremonies considerable. Cockeye Britton was killed in Valentine, Nebraska, by an old cowpuncher by the name of Harry Casper, in the town wagon lot, over a bucket of axle grease. Harry Casper never claimed to be no gunman, but it was his turn with the axle grease, and he wasn't letting nobody push in ahead of him, and he killed Cockeye before he could get his "Hipe" out. But them old customs is hard to break, and this one lingered to keep alive the memory of one of the fastest men with a gun that ever lived, until he met somebody faster.

Rolf looked like he was going to strangle, and would be disappointed if he didn't, because he couldn't say what he was feeling at Blessed Sacrament in front of all of them people. What he wanted to do was kill me. But I just give him a big old smile, and I put my hand out and made him shake it, and I said, "Well so long, Reverend, drop in out at my place sometime and have another go at me, but I won't hold you up now because I see your girl is waiting for you."

I had them both mad at me now, because the last thing in the world Samantha Venaman wanted was for people to notice her waiting for Rolf, but she was, and too late to run for cover. I give old Rolf a little shove, and he stumbled over there and catched her by the arm, and she just looked at him and stumbled along with him, and Abe Whipple limped up to me and whispered, "I couldn't of done it any better myself, but what did you mean by saying 'hipe' to him?" Abe looked in bad shape, his face just pounded to a pulp, one eye closed and the other'n half closed, and both lips cut.

I told him it was just a joke between me and Rolf, it didn't mean nothing, and he said, "Fine, I'm glad to hear that, because that word stirred some memories in me going away back, and I thought to myself, maybe I ought to go out and have a talk with this Mr. Heath. But if it was just a joke between you and Rolf, let's forget it."

I said let's do, and I got out of town while the getting was good. Early in August, the Methodist bishop himself come to Mooney, to consecrate Rolf in the ministry as he called it, and read the marriage service over Rolf and Samantha, and you never seen a prouder girl in your life, she'd finely made it. Or a prettier. Then I had to stay for the sermon, which Rolf himself preached, on the text, "Behold I stand at the door and knock." He was a sort of lukewarm preacher it seemed to me, didn't stir around hardly at all in the pulpit, but just stood there and sort of argued with you, no shouting or weeping or threatening, here was the truth as he seen it and you could take it or leave it. Well that's a simple text, "Behold I stand at the door and knock," but he made a pretty filling sermon with it, one that sticks to your ribs, because every time anybody knocks at my door now, I'm a son of a bitch if I don't jump a foot.

BOOK II

THE BLOWHOLERS

For
ERMA McCUTCHEON CARSON
Who Knows Better . . .

CHAPTER 1

It was fixing to blizzard, a Ground Hog Day storm out'n the Rockies, with sixteen inches of January snow still on the ground, and the sleet rattling off the cabin like birdshot, and the wind whooping in the eaves. It was a good time to get a winter shave, about five of an evening, but dark as midnight. I was in my kitchen with a lantern and a lamp, stropping my razor while my whiskers soaked, with the tops of my underwear hanging down around my belt. I'll never forget.

I thought I heard Ownie Cope complaining to me, so I said, "What? What you bellyaching about now?"

Ownie was a worthless kind of a kid who was holed up with me until I could think of a way to get rid of him. He didn't answer, and when I looked into the common room, he was still laying asleep on a bench, nine points drunk.

I heard it again then, and knowed it was this new dog of mine, that an Indian left with me for security, when he stole a bridle. If you're going to do business with tame Indians, you've got to do it their way, and this was my dog until the Indian wore out the bridle and brought it back. Its mother was half wolf, and its Indian name sounded like V.G., so I called it V.G.

My other dogs, Spot and Foolish, began to bark. I pulled up my underwear and put on my coat and earflap cap, and went out with my lantern. Spot and Foolish was in the root cellar, and V.G. was on a chain where he could get into the barn, only he never did, and liked to sleep outside in the worst weather.

Spot was the mother of Foolish, and a good watchdog. They had heard the noise too, and had come up the steps and was looking out through a crack in the door of the root cellar. Her and me looked at each other like we both wanted to know what was wrong, so they had just been barking because V.G. had barked.

I went over to V.G. and saw him leaning against his chain, trying to smell downwind, and not even a wolf can do that. Most people needed a club in their hand whenever they got close to V.G., but I never had no trouble with him.

"What's the matter there, dog?" I asked him.

He made that kind of a whiny, howly noise that went for a bark with him, and I knowed something was down there. I hollered, "Is somebody out there? Who's there? What do you want?"

Not a sound answered, and I wished I'd had sense enough to put on my gun, and when I get that feeling, usually it's right. A man can't always pick and choose who his visitors are going to be, especially somebody like me.

I had this place near the homestead country in northeast Colorado, Pete Heath's Place, where I ran a poker game, and sold groceries, and a little whisky, and could fix you a meal if you was content with stew or good plain fried cooking. A few pilgrims stopped there, that didn't dare show up nowhere else. They knowed me and I knowed them from old times, and there was a rule that nobody ever made trouble for me, because then they wouldn't have no place where people in a hurry could fill their bellies and rest their horses.

I had been on the wrong side of the law in my time, I admit that freely, and Pete Heath is not my family name, but after I got a few wounds in me I had swore off the outlaw game, and everybody knowed it. I was prob'ly the safest man in Colorado without a gun, as a general rule.

But the only general rule about people I believe in is that you never can tell. I started to blow out the lantern, but I changed my mind, because if somebody is about to ambush you, this is just daring him to take his shot while he can. I headed back toward the house with it, and here came Ownie Cope, blundering around in the dark.

"Why didn't you leave a light on?" he said. "Who was you hollering at out there?"

The lamp in the kitchen had blowed out when I went outside, and Ownie had banged himself on the side of the head on a shelf, and he wasn't either drunk or sober to begin with, but just mean. "I don't know if it's anybody," I said, "but I'll get my gun and find out."

"I'll go with you," he said.

"You'll go back inside is what you'll do," I said.

"You don't give me no orders," he said.

"This time I do," I said. "I don't want to hunt down some fool sot that fell down and half froze to death."

"Did you call me a fool sot?" he said.

"Yes I did," I said.

Ownie was maybe twenty-two, a big tall lean skinny big-boned kid that had been around a lot. Born of a woman that rode the Mississippi steamboats, he said, and she died when he was about ten. He lived with her relations in St. Louis, but they kept dinging him about his mother being a loose woman, and they fed him sparingly and whipped him generously. So he went over the fence when he was thirteen, and it seemed to me he had never stopped running.

Ownie was a cowboy by trade, a real nothing job, and he fancied himself a hellion with cards and a gun. He was a good poker player until he started to win, and then you could see through him like he had a glass head. He played a good hand when he was losing, but you ain't going to make no money playing good losing poker.

Ownie was always practicing the fast draw, and he loved to talk about the gunfighters that had left their name and fame wherever people take it serious. He had never killed nobody, but he was a cinch to do it someday if I was any judge, which I was. Or get killed himself.

Ownie had the big hands a gunman needs, and you couldn't fault him for nerve, but a good gunfighter ain't fighting the bottle if I'm any judge, and I was. Ownie had long yella hair and blue eyes, and a kind of a pitiful look like a lost dog, until you got him mad. When Ownie Cope got mad, he had the meanest blue eyes you ever seen.

He got mad now, and said nobody was going to call him a fool sot, and took hold of my arm. I give him a good shake and got rid of him, and went back to the house and got my holster down off'n its nail. Ownie blundered along after me.

"You son of a bitch, what do you mean, calling me a name like that, Pete?" he said. "I thought we was friends."

I pulled the gun out and stuck it in his belly, and thumbed the hammer back slow, so he could hear both the safety click and the full-cock click. "Only my true friends can make free with that name, boy," I said, "and nobody's a true friend who makes things worse when they're already bad enough. Cover the lamp when I go out."

I lit the lamp and went out and left him grumbling. Oh but it was dark! I couldn't hear a sound except V.G. whining, but I had this strange odd feeling I wasn't alone. Spot and Foolish had went back down where it was warm, where there was a weighted door to let them in and out without freezing my potatoes and onions and turnips. But V.G. was still leaning on a tight chain, and when he seen me coming, he whined and wagged his tail.

I unsnapped his chain from the steeple in the barn wall and said, "Let's go then, V.G." He took off down the wind, pulling like a colt, me blundering along behind on the other end of the chain.

It had started to snow, hard and fast, and my lantern just wasn't no use at all. I had a kind of a winding, twisting road from the Mooney wagon road to my place, because when I chopped the brush out for it, I was looking for easy brush to chop, ruther than a straight road. Right down that winding road through them light trashy trees we went.

V.G. stopped suddenly, and here was a man on his face in the middle of my road. "Damn it, somebody has got himself shot on my doorstep practically," I said to myself, "and I'll have that sheriff over me like a swarm of bees, what a Ground Hog Day this has been."

You'd expect a quarter-strain wolf dog just to tear a man's throat open that was laying helpless like that, but V.G. didn't. I put the lantern down where it wouldn't tip over, and holstered my gun, and got down on my knees as fast as I could, considering my old wounds.

I turned him over and seen he was no more than a boy, with his whole front one big slab of frozen blood. I never seen nobody lose that much blood and live, but he was still warm to touch, and he had got this far. It was up to me. I couldn't get a sound out of him, and he didn't so much as twitch, but when a person is still warm, you've got to figure he still has a chance.

I've got no business packing a load, the shape I'm in, but there's times when you've got no choice. I eased this boy up without straining myself, and hefted him over my shoulders. I picked up my lantern and started back toward the cabin, feeling my way through the snow.

Somehow I lost V.G.'s chain, and he streaked off into the storm, and I didn't know whether to curse him or me. I just kept hobbling along, one grunt at a time, with them old bullet holes pulling at me. If I'd of cut that road straight, I'd of been all right. But I only got around one hairpin turn, when I knowed I wasn't going to make it all the way, not with this kid on my shoulder.

Just then here come Ownie hanging on the end of the chain, with V.G. on the other end, dragging him along. Ownie could always get along with a horse or a dog, and once he even tamed a chipmunk to come to him, and once a blue jay, and he never had showed no fear of V.G. But I didn't expect nobody to catch that dog once he got loose.

"How did you catch him?" I said.

"Catch him? Hell, he like to tore the door down, trying to catch *me*," Ownie said. "What have you got here? Let me have him, before you tear your fool guts out. Why, he ain't no bigger than a pound of hen feathers!"

He took the kid over his arms like a baby. Ownie could sober up fast when he had to, and he surely had sobered up when V.G. started fighting that door. Now you tell me why a dog would do a thing like that, for human beans that kept him on a chain, and hardly had a kind word for him! But that's what that dog had done, he went back there and got Ownie to help me.

I packed the lantern, and Ownie packed the kid, and we got to the cabin. When I opened the door, V.G. shot in ahead of me, the first time he had ever been in a human house that I knowed of, and went straight to the bedroom. Now you tell me how he knowed where it was!

The lamp blowed out again, but I still had the lantern. While Ownie was putting the boy down on the bed, I got a big two-burner coal-oil lamp from the common room, and brought it to the bedroom, and lit both wicks.

"Why he's just a kid!" Ownie said. "What a hell of an age to get all cut up or shot, whichever it was."

"Let's peel him down and dress his wounds," I said. "You got to figure he's got a chance, if he's still warm."

All the kid had on was a canvas jacket, and an old cowhide vest, and farmer overhalls half wore out, and no shirt or underwear. He had on cowboy boots without socks, but he sure didn't look like no cowboy, and the dirtiest feet you ever seen. He had long black tangly hair, like an Indian, and a few black whiskers, but if he had ever shaved in his life, it was just showing off.

But there wasn't a wound on him anywhere! Nothing but two big juicy welts across his back, where somebody had whipped him, and a few bruises here and there.

"He's stove up bad inside, to bleed so from his mouth," Ownie said. "He's as good as dead. God damn anybody that would beat a kid like that!"

I told Ownie to set with him while I got him something warm to eat. I'd made a nice big stew earlier in the week, beef and cottontail rabbit and venison, and two teal and a canvasback, with potatoes and onions and turnips and carrots and okra and some Mexican chilis I'd been able to raise in my rocky old garden. I kept it froze in a big kettle in the lean-to off the kitchen.

I chopped off a chunk with the hatchet, and put it in a pot on the kitchen stove, and throwed some pine knots into the fire. I got it thawed out fast, but then I couldn't get more than a little dribble of the gravy down this kid.

"His guts is ruined," Ownie said. "The poor little pitiful son of a bitch, to die so young!"

"Let's try the sovereign remedy," I said, handing him the key to the chest. "The store whisky."

"The creek shine is better," Ownie said. "You know, Pete, this is the first time you ever let me have the key to the whisky chest."

"And the last time, and make it store whisky," I said. "Them nesters out on the creek make shine out of anything, even boiled corncobs. Just pour a little in the cup and lock the chest."

"Don't take any myself, you mean," he said. "You sure are a friendly sociable bastard sometimes."

He brought me the cup and my key, and I poured a little of the tanglefoot into the kid's mouth, and like to strangled him. I had Ownie put a little water in it, and some sugar, and tried it again.

The thing about whisky, it'll bring the spit when food won't, and an unconscious man will swallow it when he won't swallow anything else, because of the flow of spit. The kid kind of wiggled and moaned, and I started slopping it to him, a sip of whisky and water, and then a spoon of the stew.

I got almost a cup of the stew down him before he just kind of slid off asleep. "If his guts is ruined," I said, "he'll die anyway, and if they ain't, and he's just asleep, maybe he'll live."

"He's got some red in his face now," Ownie said. "He looks better to me. If he don't make it, he'll at least die drunk, that's some consolation."

"He's a dirty little varmint," I said. "I sure hope he don't bug up my bed."

"Lice or bedbugs would starve on what's left of his blood," Ownie said. "I sure would like to know who done that to him. I'd take a blacksnake whip to him, and when I had cut him up a little, I'd put a .45 in his mouth and pull the trigger with a clean conscience."

I told him he made my hind end tired with that kind of bloodthirsty talk. We put a blanket over the kid, and left the bedroom door open so the fireplace in the common room could warm it up in there, and went back to the kitchen. I finished shaving. Every now and then, Ownie would take a candle and tiptoe in and look at this dirty little naked kid on my bed.

"He ain't so pale, and he seems to be just nice and sound asleep," he said each time. Then finely he set down and said, "Pete, that kid is going to make it! I'll make you a little bet, four bits against two, he lives."

I was getting pretty tired of him. I said, "What do you care? What's it to you, Ownie, if he lives or dies?"

"What's it to me?" he said. "That's a hell of a thing to say!"

"Why is it?" I said. "When did you ever think of anybody but yourself before in your whole life? Now here you are, slobbering like a missionary with pity. Do you mean old worthless Ownie Cope has turned over a new leaf?"

He had to think that over. "Maybe I been waiting for somebody in a worse fix than me, and finely I've found him," he said.

"I don't know what you've got to complain about," I said. "Ownie, life is what you make it."

"The hell it is," he said. "Tell that to that kid in there, if he lives long enough to listen. A fine chance he's got to make a life, at his age!"

"How about at your age?" I said.

He asked what I meant by that, and I told him he was old enough to know better and young enough to change his ways, and still was one of the most worthless people I knowed. I told him the mother that bore him might as well of dropped him on a rock, and saved the world the trouble. He said the mother that bore him was only a steamboat whore, and I said I was tired of listening to him complain about her, and he said if I wasn't already so stove up, he'd pound them words back into me. I said to go ahead and try.

Thus we passed the night, not what you'd call sociable, but at least interesting.

CHAPTER 2

Late in the night, the kid began clawing at his hair and screaming about snakes, and we couldn't quiet him down and we couldn't wake him up. We just had to hold onto him until suddenly he quit fighting and dozed off again. We went back into the kitchen.

"He don't act like somebody all busted up inside," I said.

"It's that store whisky, Pete," Ownie said. "He's got the delirious trembles, that's all."

But he agreed with me, the kid wasn't as bad hurt as he looked. A while later, we heard him moan, and when we went in with a lantern, he was wide awake. I had the stew in a pot on the back of the stove, so I left Ownie with him while I fetched it. He let me spoon a little of it to him, and then he grabbed the spoon and wolfed it down himself.

"That's all they is?" he said, when it was gone.

"There's plenty more, but you better take it easy," I told him. "A little at a time, that's the ticket."

He didn't thank me, just laid down and looked around liked a trapped coyote, trying to figure out where he was, and who Ownie and me was, and how he'd got there. Then his eyelids sagged, and off he went to sleep, just like that.

Hour or so later, we heard him rustling around. We went in with the lantern and caught him stumbling around in the dark, trying to be quiet. He grabbed a quilt to cover himself and said, "Whar's my clothes? Who stoled my clothes? I got to go find my sisters!"

"What's left is in the woodshed," I said. "I'll find you some clothes when you're able to go out."

"Able hell!" he said. "God dang you, git me my clothes, I want my clothes, whar's my clothes?"

He didn't talk pure hillbilly, but it was mostly that, and he didn't have no more manners than a hog. That old narrow dark face of his was just mean as a cornered skunk, and his eyes glittered through that hair of his like they'd catch it afire.

"You can't go nowhere in this storm," I said. "Get some more rest, and then eat some more if your guts is up to it. You was just covered with blood, and there ain't a mark on you except some whip marks, so likely you throwed up the blood."

"That's my pappy's blood, and from my nose," he said, and began to cry a little. "God dang you, git me my clothes so I can go look for my sisters!"

"Pete, he can eat," Ownie said. "Let's feed the little varmint some more, and see if we can tame him."

"You do it," I said. "I'll get him some clothes."

Ownie hacked off another lump of stew and het it up, and I got some clothes out of the chest. Somebody comes along now and then wanting clothes, usually so they won't answer somebody's description, and they know they can make a swap at Pete Heath's Place. I found a shirt and pants, and some drawers and an undershirt, and a blanket coat. When I come back through the kitchen with them, Ownie was filling up the stew bowl again.

"Movers!" he said. "Why didn't we let him freeze?"

"I reckoned he was a mover when I heard that hillbilly talk," I said. "Did you find out who whipped him?"

"I was too busy watching him eat. You could feed a teaming crew cheaper, I swear to goodness," Ownie said.

We took the clothes and the stew to the bedroom. The kid ate while I laid out the clothes. "Jesus, drawers! I never had drawers before," he said.

I didn't say nothing. He just set there huddled up in a blanket and pumped the stew into himself.

"I had a bad dream, didn't I last night?" he said.

"You sure did," I said.

"Once when I was little in Tennessee, I walked under a tree limb, and there was a big old copperhead wropped around it, and he dangled against my head," he said. "Every time I get sick, I dream I got that snake wropped around my neck and can't get him off."

"So you come from Tennessee," I said.

He narrowed his eyes and just shivered. "You'ns get out of here, so I can get dressed," he said.

Nobody is as particular about being seen naked as somebody so poor he can't afford under-drawers. Me and Ownie went back to the kitchen and closed the door.

"Movers, by God!" Ownie said. "Stomp on them before they can multiply, I always say. Movers!"

Movers is the most hopeless people on earth. They say they're going to the gold fields, or Oregon, or the Sacramento Valley, or the Qu' Appelle Basin, someplace where a poor man has got a chance. But they ain't going nowhere, they're going *from*, not to. They couldn't settle down and amount to anything where they was, and they ain't going to settle down and amount to anything anywhere else, either.

They're mostly hillbillies, the men poison mean, always packing pistols and knives, and a rifle in easy reach, and the women usually just dirty sluts. The old ones is ugly and toothless and always chewing snuff, and the young ones is usually trying to get you off into the brush, only if you get caught at it, you're as good as dead or gelded. Sometimes you can hand the man a five-dollar gold piece, and he'll forget it unless it's his own wife. If it's his sister or daughter, he'll whine he ought to have more, in case she gets your child, and she was a pure girl until you tolled her off into the brush. Who prob'ly tolled her off the first time was her uncle or cousin, because movers is like pigs out of the same litter, they don't care who they breed to.

They have some old sore-backed horses to pull a covered wagon with, and a couple they can't drive, because they're something wrong with them and all they're good for is to trade. You trade a mover out of a decent horse, you can be sure he stole him.

They'll trade harness too, or pigs or dogs or pots and pans, and while your back is turned they'll steal you blind. If you run them off your place, they'll come back at night and burn you out, or kill your own pigs or sheep and throw them down your own well.

They live their whole lives in them wagons, going from New-Brasky to the gold fields or Oregon or someplace, and they hate everybody that's settled down, and you offer one a few days' work, he's insulted. They live on game, rabbits and squirrels and ground hogs and the like, or somebody's chickens or shotes, and all it takes besides that is a little corn meal and salt.

The kid come slinking out of the bedroom in his new clothes. "Howdy," he said. "I'd like to borry a horse now, please, to go find my sisters."

A mover that will say "please" is the albino in the litter for sure. I thought maybe this kid could be tamed after all. I said, "Look at how it's storming, kid. You wouldn't get a hundred feet in this weather."

"You try to holt me!" he said.

"I won't hold you," I said, "but leave your clothes behind, because they won't be no good if I have to break them off'n your corpse when this storm lets up."

He made a jump and grabbed a meat cleaver off the wall, and come at me screaming, "Give me my own clothes then, God durn your soul, or I'll cut your heart out!"

I retch behind me for the broom, but Ownie said, "Pete, leave this cub catamount to me. He reminds me too much of my own self at the same age, only he's dirtier."

I went into the common room and waited there. I heard Ownie and the kid talking in the kitchen, and then the kid went into the bedroom and slammed the door, and then Ownie went in after him. They was in there at least half an hour, and then the door opened and Ownie come out and closed it behind him. He set down in a chair in the kitchen and began cursing, just God-damning everything, starting with the day the world was created and working up to the present time, going at it slow so he wouldn't miss anything.

I went into the kitchen. "Where is he?" I said.

"Asleep," Ownie said. "Pete, there's a kid who had even less chance in life than me."

"I hope he makes more of what little he's got," I said. "Did you find out anything about him?"

"I found out everything," Ownie said, "and it would just make you crazy mad at the world, when things like this can happen to people."

The kid's father was named John Houten Swiverton, only the kid called him his pap, not father, and said Pap was dead now. The kid's name was Houten Saul Swiverton, and he went by the name of Hoot. He was fifteen, and his sister Alice was fourteen, and his sister Liddie was seventeen. Their mother was dead a long time ago.

They come from Lapland, down in the Ozarks, where Arkansas laps over into Missouri, and before that Tennessee, and before that Kentucky, only the kid couldn't remember that. The mother had died in McDonald County, Missouri, and Pap was on his way to file on land in Wyoming, where a poor man had a chance.

"And by the Eternal, Pete, this one I believe!" Ownie said. "This wasn't no ordinary mover trash."

In Nebraska last summer, one of their horses give out and died, and Pap had to work in the hayfields to earn another one. Then Pap gave out too. Hoot and the girls between them made a haying hand enough to buy a horse, and two weaned heifer calves, and they lit out for Wyoming again. The old pap swore to get them kids out of the wagons if it was the last act of his life.

"He almost made it, too," Ownie said, "and it sure wasn't his fault he didn't. God damn such a world as this one! Where is your law when things like this can go on?"

They had come through here week before last, missing the towns and the main roads, keeping to their own selves all they could. The horses was getting tired and they knowed a storm couldn't help but hit soon, and if they was going to be snowed in for the winter, they wanted to pick the place.

A couple of days ago, they found a nice flat canyon full of bluestem that hadn't all been snowed under, to the north and west of my place some eight or ten miles. I thought I knowed the canyon they meant. Anyway they made a camp there, and butchered one of the calves. They hated to kill a calf that would make them a milker in Wyoming, but they had no choice, they hadn't seen a deer or antelope in weeks, and the old pap didn't have no ammunition left for his guns even if they had.

They staked the team out, and hung up tarps so Hoot and Pap could sleep under the wagon, while Alice and Liddie slept in it. They killed the calf and cooked the liver the first night, and cut the rest of it up to smoke over their fire.

Yesterday morning they was just going to go out and get more firewood, when they looked up and seen four riders on a ridge about half a mile away. They didn't do nothing, just set there watching, and the old pap began to get worried. He told Hoot he wished they'd been harnessed up, but there wasn't no use trying to move out now. That would just dare them four to come down and devil them.

He had the girls get in the wagon and stay there, and he made sure he had his knife handy. The girls got in the wagon, but it was too late for that. Them four riders come jogging their horses down slow, like they didn't know what they wanted. But the old pap did.

"Hoot," he said, "you take my slatto, and I'll take the meat knife, and you promise me this: If they kill me, you kill your sisters before you let anybody have them."

A slatto was what the hillbillies called a long thin stabbing knife, a stiletto. Hoot said, "Oh God, Pap, you cain't mean that, I got to kill Alice and Liddie!"

"You'll be sorry if you don't," Pap said.

They was four of the raunchiest, dirtiest, worst-looking roughnecks he'd ever seen, Hoot said, only to save his soul he couldn't tell now what a single one of them looked like. What happened was just so horrible his mind had went blank, and he only remembered what his old pap had said because Pap was right, he was sorry he hadn't got a chance to kill his sisters.

He remembered seeing one of them chasing Liddie on his horse, and he remembered Alice fighting with two of them inside the wagon, and his pap going at them with a knife. He didn't remember the shooting, but he did remember his pap laying there on his back in the snow, his chest and belly just shot to pieces. That's how he got all that blood on himself, when he throwed himself down on his pap and blubbered, "Oh no, Pap, you can't be dead yet, Pap, oh my God, Pap, git up and help me help the girls."

He remembered one of them four men on his horse laughing, and he went at him with the slatto, but the man hit him over the back with his quirt and just kept hitting him until he could catch him over the eye with the heel of his boot. Out he went.

When he come to, they was trying to burn the wagon, only it wouldn't burn. They throwed the calf meat down so the coyotes could get it, and just rode out of there. And Hoot couldn't describe a single one of them! It had just went out of his mind, how they looked.

He didn't have no idee where his sisters was, and when he hollered for them, nobody answered. He started to foller the tracks of the four horses. He follered them all day, but when night came, he was in amongst some trashy softwood trees. He knowed he couldn't foller nothing through the dark amongst them trees.

He pulled some dry grass out from under the snow, and got out his flint and steel and made a little fire. He aimed to night there, and start again in the morning; only then it started to blizzard, and he knowed that by morning, the tracks would all be gone.

He broke off a couple of limbs and made himself torches, and he follered the tracks through the dark to a little winding road. He come to a place where them four had stood their horses quite a while, before they rode off in another direction, almost due west, at a gallop.

Hoot knowed he was at least a day behind them, and afoot in a storm. He just wanted to set down and cry, only that wouldn't do no good. About then, he thought he seen a light through the trees and brush. He started towards it, and that was the last thing he knowed before he woke up in my bed.

"Them four was from the blowhole," Ownie said.

"Like as not," I said.

"And I tell you something else, they was heading here for your place, Pete," he said.

"Ownie," I said, "I been in trouble in my time, and I get some curious people in here, yes I do. But I run a legal way-side inn, and the sheriff trusts me, and he's got a perfect right to. Nobody from the blowhole feels free to stop in here, and so let's not have any of that kind of loose talk starting around."

Ownie was headachy from the drinking, and nervous as a spring bear. He drummed on the table with his fingers a minute like he hadn't heard me. He said, "I didn't mean they figured they could hole up here," he said. "You'd of got the same thing old pap got. They meant to hole up here, and you know what scared them off? Me!"

"I just bet," I said. "A man with your virtuous reputation, why it would just scare them to death!"

He kept drumming with his fingers. "Have all the fun you like," he said, "but by God, Pete, one of them murdering bastards knows about me. He seen my horse in the stable is why they changed their minds about raiding this place. Four of that kind, why they're only about six men short of making it an even fight against me, and they damn well knowed it!"

He set there cursing, calling them every filthy name he could think of, and he had a mind that run to that kind of words. But he wasn't fooling me. I knowed that what made him so all-fired bitter was that, in his heart, he knowed he wasn't a whole lot better than they was.

He hadn't fell that low, not yet anyway. But give him time, he was headed for the blowhole sure.

Northwest by west of my place about fifteen miles was this big hillside that you could spot as far as you could see it. There was this big bald ten-acre sand hole on the side where nothing would grow, not even cactus. There was a little brush around it, but nothing in it, and this was what you call a blowhole.

In wet weather, sometimes silky sleeper-grass or milkweed thistles would start there, but they died the minute it dried out. Then the blowhole changed like the ocean, sometimes making nice even ripples, other times big rough waves. It all depended on the wind.

The color changed too. Wet, it was a kind of a dirty brown, but when it dried out, it was a light tan or sometimes kind of an orange, depending on the light. There wasn't no feed to speak of for several miles, and no water, and no reason for anybody to pass there.

That's how this riffraff got to hanging out there. There's a kind of person that seeks his own level, and he sure ain't going to find it in a prosperous cow country, or even amongst the nesters. That means work, and there's this kind of man that won't work, that only wants to drink and raise hell and rob somebody, and once you get west of the Missouri River, the country is full of them.

Men like them drift into the Badlands, or up the Gila, or into the Superstitions—any place too worthless for decent law-abiding working people. The blowholers wasn't what you'd call a gang, not by any means. They came and they went, and most of the time there wasn't nobody there. Then some cowboy tracking a lost calf would see a fire up there, and he knowed where his calf had went, and he also knowed better than to go asking questions up there.

Instead he went to the sheriff of Mooney County, Sheriff Abe Whipple. Abe rode up there when he got these complaints and kicked their camps to pieces, and burned their shanties, but generally they seen him coming and he never got so much as a look at the blowholers themselves.

That was the lonesomest place! When you get run out of a place like that, you're about as low-down as a man can get. It was no wonder Ownie Cope felt so mean. He wasn't no more than a step and a half away from the blowhole himself, and I reckon he finely faced up to it.

CHAPTER 3

The storm let up at daylight. Me and Ownie dug my wagon out of the snow and harnessed four horses, and fed them a good bait of oats. Ownie saddled up his horse. We would of left Hoot behind, because he wasn't in good shape at all yet, but we'd of had to tie him. And he had the right to go, you couldn't deny that.

There was a little blue sky when we left, and patches of fast-moving sunlight, but it was only a hole in the storm. Ownie rode ahead, breaking trail. I had all I could do with four horses on an empty wagon behind him, in places. Hoot set there on the seat beside me, trying to recognize things, but it was all strange to him.

A couple of eagles was out, cruising for something to drop on, but nothing was alive and moving closer than the homestead country, and you can bet the Kincaiders was out with guns to protect lambs or pigs or even dogs caught out in this one. By the way them eagles was tossed around, I knowed the wind was still blowing hard up there. I was in a pure frenzy to get where we was going and back, before it set in to blizzard again.

We stopped every now and then to rest the horses and eat some cold biscuits and pork sausage I'd fried up. Hoot would just nibble was all. Then we'd go on again.

We come to this stand of light cottonwoods, and Hoot set up straight and looked around. "I allow I come through these trees," he said finely.

I said, "I reckon you did, Hoot, but we got a ways to go yet, if I know where we're going. And I bet I do."

We wasn't heading for nowhere near the blowhole. We had to go around them trees on account of the wagon, and the minute we was in the clear, Hoot set up straight again and started to feel for his knife that he'd lost.

"Whoa now, boy!" I said. "That's just a tame old tramp Indian, Charley Polk. He wouldn't harm nobody."

Charley was up in his sixties and had never done a day's work in his life, and he drank too much and stole a little, but me and him always got along. Charley was over there in the foothills where the timber got heavier, waving to me. I waved back to him and told Ownie to rest the team and let me have his horse.

"A God-durned lazy Indian, well I like that!" Ownie said. "We got to stop what we're doing to see what he wants."

But he let me have his horse. I rode over to where Charley was waiting.

"What are you doing out with a four-horse team in this kind of weather, looking for a woman?" Charley said.

"Yes, a couple of them, Charley," I said.

"Only got one," Charley said. "I found her running around yesterday. This one go crazy, Pete. Crazy!"

"I'll take her off'n your hands," I said, "and then let's see if we can find the other one."

He got up behind me, and we rode to his place in the trees, half cave and half wickiup, with a nice stone fireplace, and room for him to curl up in, and not much else. He had put this girl in there last night, and he slept out in the storm. An Indian has got a lot of respect for somebody that's out of their mind, and she sure was.

She was just setting there in the dugout and staring, wilder than any squaw you ever seen, with the same black eyes and black hair that Hoot had, only her hair was down to her waist, and tangled up with twigs and grass and dirt. She was barefoot, and she had on an old brown dress and an old tore shawl.

"Which one are you?" I said to her.

She didn't answer, and Charley Polk said, "I don't think she talk, Pete. Crazy!"

I said let's try again. I got down on my knees so I could see into the dugout better, and asked her which she was, Liddie or Alice. She didn't pay me no attention, none at all, and I knowed if I went in there after her, I was going to have a wildcat on my hands, poor thing.

"I don't know what to do, Charlie," I said. "There's supposed to be two of them. We got their brother, Hoot, with us. Hoot made it as far as my place. Some of them blowholers savaged them considerable yesterday."

"Oh, them sons of bitches," Charley said.

"Hoot," the girl said. "Hoot. Hoot."

I thought I might be getting through to her, so I went on talking to Charley. I said, "Hoot is fine. He's a good boy, that Hoot. He wants to find his sisters real bad. Hoot is nice and warm and safe, and he wants Alice and Liddie to be nice and warm too. Hoot is a good brother, Hoot is."

It was like breaking through the ice. She come out of the shanty like a cork out of the jug. "I'm Liddie," she said. "You say you've got Hoot? Is Hoot all right?"

"Yes," I said, "and he's a mighty good boy."

"Not a boy," she said, and began to cry and blubber and wring her hands. "Not a boy. He fit like a man and he cursed like a man, and he'll never be a boy again, never!"

She didn't know where she was or how she'd got there, but when I told her, she tried to shake Charley Polk's hand, and when he was ashamed to do it, she grabbed it in both of hers and kissed it. Then I got up on Ownie's horse, and Charley hoisted her up behind me, and we headed back to the wagon.

She told me what she knowed, which wasn't much. She'd got away because the minute them blowholers rode up, she had sense enough to run and keep on running. One of them rode after her and tried to rope her, but he was drunk and missed her three times.

The fourth time, he got a loop over her, but she was ready for it. She catched it and jerked it off and swang the loop at the pony's face. It stood up on its hind legs and throwed this man right on his back.

What this wildcat aimed to do was steal his horse and ride off, and if that ain't pure undefiled gall, I never heard of gall. She would of made it except the horse got away. She picked up a rock instead, and hit this fella over the side of the head, and then she outrun him.

Run was all she could do, and once he caught his horse, he was going to rope her again, and this time he wasn't going to let her pull him out of no saddle. He caught his horse and finely did spot her, but she got across a little canyon with an icy crick at the bottom, and he couldn't make his horse cross.

He took a couple of shots at her with his .45, but she got away. At least she thought she did.

An hour or so later, here they come again. They must of talked it over and decided they couldn't take a chance on her getting away to live and tell on them. She got into the trees then, and dodged and hid and backtracked, and five or six times at least, she was laying there in the snow behind some brush while they set and talked it over less than a dozen feet away.

They finely give up on her, and she started walking again, until she went out of her mind. She couldn't remember Charley Polk finding her, or anything. All she knowed was that there was a fire and a soft place to sleep, and she could rest and warm her feet at last.

Her and Hoot hardly spoke to each other when we got to the wagon. Movers is a curious people. They don't like to have you looking on when it's family business, so I just let her have my seat on the wagon, and I walked ahead of the team to help break trail for them.

In another mile, their camp come in sight, just where I knowed it would be.

The most curious thing was the other girl, right out there in plain sight! She had a fire going, and the crane rebuilt, and a pot hanging from it, and water boiling so hard you could see the steam from a mile away. She seen us coming and run towards us, laughing and waving.

"Y'all's just in time, Hoot," she said. "I'm fixing a bait, just venison and dumplings is all, but I got salt too. Dumplings without salt ain't fitten."

Hoot jumped out of the wagon and grabbed her by the arm. "Where'd you get venison and stuff to make dumplings? Where'd you get salt?" he said to her.

Liddie jumped down in the snow, bare feet and all. "Let her be, Hoot, let her be!" she said.

"But God durn it, what's she talking about?" Hoot hollered. He was about to cry.

Ownie rode over to the fire, and then over to me. He said, "Pete, my God, there ain't nothing in that pot but plain water. She's crazier than the first one!"

"Maybe it's better this way," I said. "She was the one got caught here, poor little tyke."

We had an awful time trying to get her into the wagon. Them blowholers had wrecked the covered wagon, but Alice couldn't see that. No sir, as soon as they got another team, they'd go on to Wyoming and file under the Kincaid Act, and get out of the wagon the way Pap promised.

She showed us where them blowholers had shot the two horses, and she showed us her pap's body. "Sh-h-h!" she said. "Pap's sleeping late today, poor old man. Pap works so hard for us!"

Hoot just cried like a baby. Liddie wanted to cry too, but there was a girl that could save her tears when she had to. Her job was to get Alice into our wagon, and one way or another, she done it. We loaded the old pap's body in, and covered it with what was left of the wagon sheet, and I got them four tired horses turned around again, and we started back to my place.

Ownie rode back and kicked that pot of boiling water over the fire. He had to do something violent or blow up himself.

Alice set on the wagon seat with me, while Hoot and Liddie rode in the wagon box with Pap's body. I tried to talk to her about these four blowholers.

"What did they look like, honey?" I said.

She laughed and said oh, she couldn't remember what they looked like. "Only they was mean, real mean," she said, and laughed some more.

"Did you hear any of them use anybody's names?" I said.

"Oh, I didn't pay no 'tention to names," she said, and laughed. "But I scratched them. I scratched them good! They cursed something pitiful. Oh how they could curse!"

She laughed. I wasn't getting nowhere, and it was making Liddie and Hoot cry. When I left her alone, Alice just set there beside me, snuggling up to keep warm, and talking about how nice it was going to be when they got to Wyoming and could put in a garden and set some hens.

"And never have to live in no wagon no more!" she said.

"Pap said it ain't fitten to bring up girls in a wagon, and Pap keeps his promises, he does."

She wasn't like the other two so much. Liddie was kind of a tall girl, and dark like Hoot, but Alice was one of them little chubby girls, and her hair was brown instead of black, and it curled up at the ends and around her ears. It would just break your heart, she was so pretty and happy and carefree. Her mind had went completely.

I pushed them four horses worse than I like to punish a horse, but I got there before the storm got too bad. I let Ownie and Hoot take care of the team, while I went in with the girls to kick up the fire. I'd left Spot and Foolish in the root cellar, and V.G. chained to the stable, and V.G. wouldn't stand for strangers feeding him.

After I got the fire going, and Liddie to peeling potatoes, I said I had to go out and take care of my dogs. "Oh, let me go too!" Alice said. "I love dogs. We always had a dog back in Missouri."

"No, you stay and help your sister," I said.

"Oh no, let me feed the dogs," she said.

She started to run for the door. I catched her by the bare arm and held her, and when I felt the fever in her, I knowed she was a real sick girl. She was as hot as fire, and she fought me like a tiger.

Ownie come in and seen me rassling her. He let out one yell, "Alice! Stop that now! God dang you, behave yourself and stay in the God-dang house, and get into that bedroom before I have to whale the hell out of you."

Alice stopped fighting and went into the bedroom, not really scared it seemed to me, just out of habit, more. I got some meat for the dogs and went out with it, and Ownie follered me outside.

"That's how white trash talk to their kids," he said.

I said, "Ownie, it worked. That's the main thing. Don't start telling me how bad a time you had as a kid. This is one night I won't stand for it."

"I just wanted you to know why I hollered and swore at her, is all," he said. "Pete, I wouldn't talk to that girl for any other reason that way. I knowed it would work. What kind of a bastard do you think I am?"

"Just the ordinary kind," I said. "Nothing special. Your kind come in herds."

"Oh, listen to the deacon!" he said. "Let me feed the wolf, you pious son of a bitch."

I give him the meat, and dad-blamed if he didn't go over there and get down on his knees beside V.G., and feed him a piece at a time out of his hand. I couldn't even do that with V.G. myself. He'd take your hand off.

I didn't need no lantern to get around my own place. I had a nice snug barn here that would hold ten horses, and Hoot was still in there fooling around with a pitchfork, dunging out from under the horses and throwing them fresh bedding. He had a lantern hanging from a peg to see by.

I started to go in and see what was left that I could do to help finish up. Only just then, Hoot leaned his fork up against the barn wall, and put his face down against one of my horses, and wrapped his arms around his head, and began to bawl like a baby. Just crying his heart out.

So his sister was wrong by that much, he wasn't all a man yet, not by no means. But the kind of life I've led, I've heard a few people cry their hearts out, and you get to be kind of expert in them things. And I judged that this cry was about Hoot's last.

CHAPTER 4

It stormed for two more days, not a lot more snow, but it blowed and drifted until them eight miles to Mooney looked like eight hundred.

I never seen nobody eat like them three kids. Liddie could help in the kitchen, but she wasn't used to an iron stove, and pots and pans and dishes. As fur as she could remember, they'd cooked in an iron kettle over a fireplace, and et out of tin plates, and then just rubbed them down with ashes instead of washing them.

She caught on fast and got to be real good help, except that every time she salted anything, it made her remember her pap. It appeared that old Swiverton had been a caution in his day. He made shine, and drank so much of it that he never really made money at it, and he fit with everybody, especially his wife's kin.

But after she died on him, he changed overnight. He stopped drinking and fighting with people, and vowed he'd get them kids out of the wagons before he died. It was hard for Liddie to think of him laying out there in the wagon, where he'd keep. Hard on Hoot too, but it never bothered Alice none. Nothing bothered her.

None of them kids could describe the men that had done this job. Liddie had got away too soon to see the other three up close, and all she could tell me about the one that had roped her was that he was drunk.

Neither one of them noticed horse brands, nor the kind of guns they wore, things like that. Alice, who seen the most of all four of them, couldn't remember a thing, and she seemed too happy to bother about it.

The day we knowed the storm was going to break, Ownie started for Mooney to bring back the sheriff and the preacher. Them kids had their hearts set on having their pap buried with all the trimmings, not like movers was usually buried, just spaded under beside the road somewhere. Ownie rode his own horse, leading one of mine with a harness bridle on a long rope, so he could drive one ahead of him to buck out trail.

I didn't look for him back for a couple of days, but the next afternoon, after it had cleared up, here they come. Sheriff Abe

Whipple had went to Omaha to meet some of his wife's kinfolk that had come up from the Gulf Coast, and called it a vacation. Anybody that would go to Omaha in the middle of the winter for a pleasure trip, or any other time, is mighty hard up for fun. But that's where he was.

Abe's deputy, Thad Rust, come out in his stead. The county would only pay for cheap help, but I never reckoned Thad to be as no-account as most people. He was green as a gourd, and timid about making up his mind, because Abe never spared his feelings none when he made a mistake of judgment. Thad always hoped every case would turn into a nice simple shoot-out. He reckoned he could get by that way, and it's hard to criticize a peace officer that has the guts to think that way.

Me and this preacher, Reverend Rolf Ledger, was just about raised together back in Smith County, Kansas, although I was some years older. Him and me got into some scrapes together, and I catched a bullet in one of them, and we fell out over it. Then Rolf went to the pen for a holdup he didn't commit, and got to be the assistant chaplain, and was well on the glory trail when he got pardoned.

He was the First Methodist pastor in Mooney, and a good enough one from all I heard, but I wasn't one of the lost lambs he'd rescued. I reckon I'll convert on my deathbed, like most people, when it's too late for me to miss any fun. But so far, me and religion has got along pretty well without each other; it don't miss me and I don't miss it, and I say any deal that works that well is a good deal.

Rolf and Thad was married to sisters, the Venaman girls, and both girls was expecting to drop babies, Thad's in the early summer and Rolf's in the late. You never seen two seriouser young men in your life than the ones Ownie brung out with him. And the way I sized it up, I might be getting rid of my problem, but them movers' kids sure wasn't solving theirs.

"What should I do, Rolf?" Thad said, after he had looked the situation over, and seen it was just as bad as Ownie had said it was.

"I know what I'd do," Rolf said. "I'd borry Pete's wagon and team, and haul the body and these kids back to Mooney, and then find places where the kids can stay. That's what I'd do if it was me."

"I was thinking along them lines myself, but Abe is sure to say I should of shipped them to Denver or somewhere. I never had no case like this before," Thad said.

They went back the same day. It was pitiful to see them leave. Alice didn't realize it was her pap rolled up in one of my tarps in the wagon. She set there laughing and talking to herself, and at the last minute she had to jump out and go throw her arms around V.G. and say a special good-by to him.

They say dogs can tell when a person is insane, and their hair stands on end, but they won't bite. That's the way it was with V.G., except his hair didn't stand on end.

Finely they was gone, Ownie leading the way, just about tongue-tied because he couldn't curse in front of the minister, and there's no harder handicap to put on a man who has to break trail through the snow. Liddie kept waving to me until the wagon was out of sight, but Hoot just set there staring at his pap, and Alice kept chuckling and weaving her fingers together and talking like she had some kind of a secret.

I was glad to put this whole proposition out of my mind. All I want is to be left alone, and it's a good rule for somebody in my position to live by, and here I had almost got mixed up in one of the rottenest murders ever committed. It was damned if I did, damned if I didn't. I didn't want the law down on me and I sure didn't want them blowholers down on me any more than they already was.

They got back to Mooney late that night, in bright moonlight, but a big crowd of people had stayed up to wait for them. Rolf got four or five men to go to the graveyard and hack out a grave below the frostline, which was nearly forty inches down, so they could have a morning burial. That took until daylight.

They had the funeral at nine-thirty in the morning. There wasn't time to heat up the church for it, and no need anyway. They just carried him up the hill to the graveyard on foot, Thad Rust leading the way, and Rolf following the body with the three Swiverton kids.

Liddie and Hoot never shed a tear. Alice went skipping and hopping along over the ice and through the snow, clapping her hands together and talking to herself, saying, "Oh my oh my oh my, suchy purty town, look at all the purty houses, ain't never *seed* suchy purty town, oh my oh my oh my." She was such a little beauty and looked so happy that she had a lot of them people crying, even old men.

They didn't take time to make Pap a coffin, and Hoot said the old man would of felt kind of tight in a box anyway. They just laid him down in my own quilt, without asking what I thought about it or anybody else, and Rolf read the service over him as short as he could, because Hoot and Liddie was about to play out.

He took all three kids home with him for his wife to watch, while him and Thad went to see Andy Obers, the county judge, to ask what to do about the kids.

"Nothing you can do about the oldest girl," Andy said. "She's above the age of consent and has been emancipated by her father's death. She has all the rights and privileges of an adult except voting and making contracts. If she wants to join somebody in having a guardian *ad litem* appointed for her, a court can deem her a legal infant. But if she won't join in the petition, the only way you can overcome the presumption of emancipation is by showing she's a public charge, or a menace to morals."

"She won't take kindly to having a guardeen," Thad said. "Who would be the guardeen, anyway?"

"Why, you," Andy said, "as a county officer. You have the responsibility *de facto* for all three."

"Let's go on to some other idee then," Thad said.

Andy said the next best thing was have the two young ones made wards of the court, and he'd appoint Thad to find places where they could work out their keep. Thad wanted to get shet of the whole affair before Abe got back. It was his idee that they could ship the kids to some orphanage in Denver or somewhere.

"The only way to do that," Andy said, "is to get them to consent to it, and appoint you guardian *ad litem* for all three, and then you petition me for commitment."

"Judge, by God I expected better of you than this!" Thad said. "You know what Winnie will say, in her condition, if I'm guardeen of a girl seventeen years old, built like that girl."

"The law puts up fences around widows and orphans. There's a reason for everything," Andy said.

"I never seen a fence without a gate, nor a law without a loophole by God," Thad said. "What I want you to do is find me that loophole."

"You hire yourself a lawyer," Andy said. "I ain't scouting out no loopholes for you."

"Oh sure, and you know what Winnie will say if I go spending money on lawyers," Thad said.

Winnie was his wife, and used to a lot more than Thad could provide her on a deputy's pay. They said that her father, Cal Venaman, had four cents of the first nickel he ever earned, and had wore the other one cent out counting it, and while this may be a severe judgment, it wasn't no libel.

Thad had to go to Jimmy Drummond, who said he got two dollars each for drawing up two petitions. One was to have Thad named guardian *ad litem* to all three kids, and the other was a motion to commit them to an orphanage in Denver. Andy looked the petitions over and ordered that the infants in question be brought before him.

Rolf went down to the parsonage and got Hoot and Liddie and Alice, and took them to the courthouse. Andy asked them how they felt about going to an orphanage in Denver. Alice just smiled at him and said she thought it would be nice, everybody was so nice to her.

"I ain't going to no orphanage," Liddie said, "and neither is my brother. Our pap is buried in the ground here. There ain't no wheels between us and that ground, and here me and Hoot aim to stay."

"Miss Swiverton, can you read and write?" Andy said.

"You mean me?" Liddie said. "I kin read and write a little. But I ain't going to sign nothing, and I ain't going to no orphanage."

Andy chuckled and said she had spirit all right, and was within her rights. He would deny the commitment and hold the petition for appointment of a guardian *ad litem* in his desk until Thad come up with a fresh idee.

Thad and Jimmy Drummond went out into the hall to talk it over, while Andy kept the kids in his warm courtroom. "Thad, they hold the trump aces," Jimmy said. "Andy is perfectly right in not overruling the minors' natural and rightful desire to remain near the family grave."

"A hell of a narrow gate you found for me," Thad said. "I reckon you figure you took me for four dollars."

Jimmy Drummond was as good a lawyer as there was west of the Mississippi, and he had his pride, and he was getting on in years, and he didn't enjoy going out in the cold just to have some young badge-heavy deputy scold him. He said, "You asked me to draw you up two petitions, and I done it, I drafted them. Now if you ask my advice on a better way to do it, it'll cost you five dollars but will get you out of a pack of trouble. That's my last offer, take it or leave it, and let Andy *order* you to do whatever he's a mind to."

"Jesus, that's nine dollars already," Thad said. "But what else can I do? Go ahead."

Jimmy drawed up two more petitions. One declared Liddie emancipated, and the other one made her guardian *ad litem* for the other two. Thad just about cried when he seen how simple it was, and was still going to cost him nine dollars.

Andy declared court open, and he swore Liddie in as a witness. She testified her parents was both dead, and that she was the oldest surviving member of the family, and that she was willing and able to act as guardeen to her brother and sister. Andy ruled that way, and held Thad responsible for finding them places to stay. Then he said it would cost Thad a filing fee of one dollar for each petition, a total of four dollars, including the two he had turned down.

"Great God, why don't you put my feet in a vise and be done with it?" Thad said. "I only got $2.35 on me, and I'm supposed to bring home some beans and things out of that."

"I reckon you've suffered enough, Acting Sheriff Rust," Andy said. "I'll give you some free advice that would cost you at least five dollars if you retained private counsel. You can put in a claim to the county for this whole bill, and they'll have to pay it. The statute makes the county responsible, and if Abe Whipple gives you any trouble about it, you tell him to see me."

Thad felt better then, and him and Rolf rustled around to find places for them kids, and got them all located by dark. He thought Liddie would be the one to give him the most trouble. There was plenty of places would take her, all right, for the wrong reasons.

Most respectable homes don't want a mover's kid around, specially a grown woman in every way except knowing how to eat politely, and do housework, and keep herself clean, and so on. After growing up in a wagon, Liddie wasn't much better than a savage in her manners.

There was this rich old maid, Liz Saymill, whose brother had been a loan shark, and got murdered for six hundred dollars, and left her every cent. She needed help and could afford it, but she couldn't keep a girl because her girl had to milk the cow and take care of her buggy horse, because she wasn't going to pay no hired girl eight dollars a month and her keep, and then hire somebody to care for her livestock besides.

"I have no choice, have I?" she said. "She'll have to bathe and put on clean clothes before she comes into my house, however—mark you well that!"

"She ain't got no other clothes, ma'am. She's just barely covered up as it is," Thad said.

"Take her to the store and tell Buck to fit her out and send me the bill, and if he tries to palm off the purple junk he bought to cheat the Indians with, only they was too smart to buy it, I'll have his life," Liz said.

Buck had to guess Liddie's measurements, because he sure wasn't going to go feeling around her with no tape measure, not with all the attention Liddie was getting, but he sent her to Liz with a whole paper sack of new clothes. Liz didn't even shake hands with her.

"What's in the bag, child?" she said. "Let's see how he has outfitted you. Come, come, open it up!"

Liddie opened it up and let it all fall on Liz's carpet, and then she fell down on her knees too. She wouldn't even touch the things, just point to them.

"Shoes, real shoes, not moccasins," she said. "What's this, some kind of underclothes? I never had nothing but flour-sack pants underneath before. Oh look, ma'am, what's these things?"

"They're bandeaus, or as some people say, brassieres," Liz said.

"Stockings too," Liddie said. "Oh, ma'am, I cain't, it ain't fitten, I never had nothing like this, it'd be a sin for somebody out'n a wagon to dress so, trash like me—"

Thump, that was as far as she got, and Liz leaned over and rapped her on the head with her knuckles. "You look here now," she said, "what's your name?"

"Liddie Swiverton," Liddie said.

"It is *not* Liddie, it's Lydia, and Swiverton is an honest English name, and you are *not* trash, no one in this house is *ever* trash; now go take a bath and put on your new things and let me look you over," Liz said.

Liddie dragged the washtub into the kitchen, and had her bath, and managed to struggle into the clothes somehow, and even combed her hair out with her fingers. She come into the room where the old lady was sewing away in her rocking chair.

"Ma'am, how do I look?" she said.

"Why, child, you're beautiful!" Liz said. "Why, Lydia, your beauty is something to live up to, indeed it is, we must make a lady of you to go with all that gracious good looks. For manners and speech are a part of beauty too, Lydia. You must speak properly and act like a lady."

Liddie dropped to her knees beside the old lady's chair, and folded her hands together, and said, "Oh, ma'am, will you learn me manners, and how to talk? Will you?"

"I shall *teach* you, and you will *learn*, lesson number one," Liz said. "That fool of a Buck, I shall have his life yet, what did he think you were to wear while you're washing these things? Why didn't the man send along a change of clothing for you?"

"I kin sew, ma'am, the teeniest stitches if I got a small enough needle. I kin broider too. My mammy learned me—" Liddie said.

"Your mother *taught* you, and you *learned* it," Liz said. "Very well, you shall sew too, but first we'll have Buck send over another outfit. Now your name is Lydia, not Liddie, and I'm Miss Liz to you, are we clear on that?"

"Yes, Miss Liz," Liddie said.

Old Liz leaned over and put her old wrinkled cheek against the girl's clean black hair, and cried a couple of tears, and said Liddie was as bright and sincere as she was lovely, and God moved in a mysterious way His wonders to perform.

That took care of Liddie. Rolf and Samantha Ledger took in Hoot, so he could help them fix up the old parsonage before it caved in. Samantha told Hoot he'd have snow on his bed, but he said he was used to that. The parsonage wasn't much, sure enough, but they'd never had a preacher before with a wife that had been a Venaman, and there looked to be a lot of changes around there before the year was out.

Alice went to Bridey Millsap. Bridey's husband, Elias Millsap, had homesteaded early in the Kincaid game, about five miles from Mooney. He farmed it until he proved up, and then went to brokering horses, and done real good at it, and left 160 acres and quite a bit of money in the bank when he left Bridey a widow. Her real name was Bridget, but everybody called her Bridey, even the men she hired to keep the brokerage business going.

Bridey was a big fat easygoing woman, hard in a horse trade all right, but soft about kids. She hadn't never had no kids of her own, and here she seen a chance to get a pretty fourteen-year-old girl to raise, and it seemed like a blessing from heaven. She wasn't worried because Alice's mind had quit on her. It'd come back, she said.

"She's the sweetest thing, so eager to please, so cheerful to have around!" she told Rolf, when he went out a couple of days later to see how the girl was getting along. "She's already better. As soon as she feels *safe* again, her mind will come back."

The day after Rolf went out to see Alice, Abe Whipple got back to town. He went over the whole case with Thad, and then with Rolf, and then with Andy Ober. He said he reckoned they'd made the best of a bad job, although the county commissioners was going to raise hell at the expense of burial and court costs, but just let them.

"And, Thad, I promise you one thing sure," Abe said. "Sooner or later, I'm going to catch up with the men that done this. I'm going to exercise restraint and not shoot them like I would mad dogs. I'm going to save them for Andy to sentence to death, yes sir I am, and I'm going up to watch them swing, now that's a promise."

Not fifteen minutes after he said that, one of Bridey Millsap's hired hands rode in and asked Abe to come out to the place, and bring Dr. Tattnal with him because Alice was sickly.

Abe and the doctor went right out. They couldn't get Alice to say nothing, in fact she was already so feverish she thought she was floating, and they had to hold her down on the bed.

"She's been losing blood and didn't even know it, poor child," Bridey said. "She left a trail behind her wherever she went, and she wouldn't let me examine her, and pshaw, all the livestock I've handled, inside and out! I'm afraid she's a very sick little girl."

Them movers is strange, they live like pigs in some ways, and they'll go behind a little old bush that wouldn't hide a setting hen's nest when they have to squat down. But they're powerful narrow-minded about nakedness, like Hoot was, and there wasn't nobody going to take that girl's clothes off and look at her body, no sir!

Doc Tattnal had to chloroform her to examine her, and he took one look and said, "God receive her kindly, them wasn't men, them was ravening beasts, filthy ghouls, accursed and bewitched fiends out of hell, and they have killed this child." He was right. She was just all tore to pieces, and diseased besides, and was dead in four days, poor little tyke.

CHAPTER 5

Abe Whipple suffered about as much as anybody, because it was his county, and he run it his way, and it was his fault this had happened. There couldn't nobody talk him out of it, he was to blame. Somebody told him the Lord put the blowhole there to blemish the earth, the state, and the county, and maybe it was all a part of His plan.

"Then it was part of His plan for me to be sheriff, and I let Him down," Abe said. "What can you do with a blowhole? You can't knock it down, or burn it up, or wash it out, or move it away. But you can make it so hot that even a prairie dog won't hang out there, and that's where I failed. Well I never will again. There'll be nothing but dead blowholers camped there from now on, and they'll be under the sand not on it."

Alice was buried out of the church on a Sunday morning, with the best winter weather Colorado could put out. You couldn't get me into a church with a warrant most of the time, but when Rolf Ledger asked me to be a pallbearer for this little dead girl, I just couldn't squeeze out. The others was Bill Weedon and Bill Seek and Otis Paxton, all single men, and not one of them a churchgoer.

It was just Rolf's way of showing us what our lives could lead to, besides showing this little dead girl all the reverence the town could spoon out. I keep calling her a little girl, although she was fourteen when it happened, and many a woman is wife and mother at that age. But if you could of seen her in her coffin, you'd understand. She didn't weigh no more than one cent's worth of soap, and she laid there smiling like she was having a happy dream, with a white ribbon in her hair that Bridey Millsap bought. She looked like she might wake up any minute, and want a mug of fresh warm milk right out of the cow, and some fresh homemade bread.

You could just cry to see her, and the two Bills did, and both of them stone sober. Bill Seek cried all the time when he was drunk, but nobody ever seen Bill Weedon shed a tear before or after. Rolf made a short sermon of it, Suffer the little children to come unto Me, and forbid them not, for of such is the Kingdom of Heaven.

He said, "In her innocence, this child was slain by four ravening wolves, and her clean heart never knowed their vileness. Well, she knows it now, because where she sets now, nothing is hidden from her forgiving eyes, and all ends, as well as all beginnings, are knowed to her."

He said, "The merciful God warns us not to take vengeance. He told us to love our enemies, and I'm trying, oh Lord, I'm trying to obey Thee, and turn my other cheek, and repay evil with good. Lord Thou *knowest* how hard I'm trying, or I'd be out with a six-gun instead of up here preaching Thy stern word."

He said, "The sin of vengeance is a snake, and a lively one at that, and if you chop it in two, like as not them two pieces will become two snakes, and you've got two serpents to fight instead of one. Neighbors, let's look this serpent in the eye right now, and instead of fogging out to lynch somebody, let's try to figger out how the Lord handles these things. Because vengeance is His'n, not ours, and His way is the right way."

He said, "We can go this far, neighbors, in laying our wrath on the heads of this child's tormentors. Let's keep in mind that this girl is up there with the Source of all wisdom and knowledge. Nothing is hid from her forever more, and the earth is only a grain of sand to her."

He said, "Wherever them four murderers is on this grain of sand, I want them to know her eyes are on them, no they can't hide from *her*, not if they dig a hole clean to the center of the earth. Killing's too good for them, and we know it, so let us unite in a wish for a punishment far worse—that this girl's all-seeing eyes follow them until they cry out in torment for death, and can't die until they have suffered as they made her suffer, only worse."

Rolf had heard a sermon like that when he was assistant chaplain in the Kansas pen, and some dirty rat of a prisoner had killed another prisoner, and nobody knowed who done it, and they was about to have a riot. It calmed them convicts down real quick, the idee of a dead man's eyes follering his murderer no matter where he hid. A couple of nights later, the murderer went out of his head and gave himself away, and began yelling that he done it and was so guilty and ashamed, and a few of the others murdered him mercifully, and the riot never did get going.

The important thing about that sermon, though, as I seen it, was that Rolf was the first to understand just how ignorant and innocent them three movers' kids was. When he said Alice never knowed what happened to her, that was the plain truth, and neither did Hoot and Liddie understand. How people can grow up so ignorant is hard to understand, but they live a queer life in them wagons.

You expected Liddie to show up looking pretty good for the funeral, with Miss Liz to take care of her, but the marvel was how Hoot looked, as tame as he could be. Rolf and Sammie had a little trouble with him. Sammie knowed only two ways of doing things, her way and the wrong way, and she set out to shine this boy up overnight. Hoot said he never seen so much soaping and toweling in his life, and if she thought he was that dirty, why did she let him in the house?

Rolf told him it wasn't nothing personal, it was just the way folks lived in town. Hoot said he had lived in a town once, not as big as Mooney, but it had a store and a card room, and he never had to wash up there.

"Hoot, you've got to put up with it," Rolf said. "Once you get used to being good and clean, you won't be comfortable when you're dirty."

"Then what's the use of it?" Hoot said. "You're dirty a lot more than you're clean, and you'll just make yourself that much more uncomfortable."

It seemed to Rolf that this kid was trying to find out who was boss, so he said, "Do as you please, Hoot, but don't be surprised if it gets you knocked on your butt."

"By who?" Hoot said. "I never seed the day a preacher could knock me on my butt."

Rolf knocked him on his butt, and they got to be good friends again, and Hoot didn't cause no more trouble until Sammie told him he had to get his hair cut for his sister's funeral. Hoot had been past the barber shop, and had seen the men in there getting shaved and their hair cut, and the idee just scared him to death. The only haircuts he ever had before was when it got long enough to hang in his eyes, his pap hacked it off with a knife.

"The barber will teach you how to comb and part it," Sammie said, "and Rolf will buy you a comb of your own, and from now on, you comb it every time before you come to the table to eat."

"The hell I will," Hoot said, "and you cain't make me."

"The hell I can't," Sammie said. "Either you get it cut or I'll singe you like a chicken."

She opened up the stove and picked up a piece of wood by the end that wasn't burning, but Hoot just laughed at her, until she rammed the burning end into them long lank black tangles of his. Down he went on his knees. You know how burning hair stinks, well that little old leaky house was letting smoke out until you'd of thought the livery barn was on fire.

"Oh, Goddlemighty, save me, Reverend, save me!" Hoot hollered. "This woman of yourn is burning me up."

Rolf was outside mending something on the house, because that parsonage was so limber it leaned in every wind, and the day never passed that something fresh didn't break down. He loped in panting, and seen Hoot down on his knees screaming, and Sammie stabbing at him with that burning stick of firewood.

"Lord God of hosts, are you a savage, woman?" he yelled at her.

"No," Sammie said, "but he is, and he's going to take fifteen cents and get his hair cut or I'll singe it off."

She stood back with her stick, and let Rolf make up his own mind, and he knowed there was times you could argue with her and times you couldn't. He said, "Hoot, you come out loser this time. I'll go with you and get my own hair cut at the same time, although I just had it cut last month, and I can ill spare another fifteen cents."

Hoot's spirit was broken. He slunk down with Rolf and got his hair cut, and learned to part it on the left, and come home with lilac water all over it. Sammie had put supper on the table, and was so sick she was ready to puke from the smell of cooking, because being a contrary woman by nature, she had her morning sickness in the afternoon.

"My goodness, where's Hoot, and who is this handsome gentleman you brought home to supper?" she said to Rolf.

Hoot grinned and looked sillier than ever, which proves Sammie was a good winner, and that's a lot more important than being a good loser usually. You take a woman who can take that much trouble for an ungrateful brat out of a mover's wagon when she's about to turn inside out from the afternoon morning sickness, you've got a thoroughbred.

Hoot looked more man than boy at the funeral, even when he cried a little, but most of it went over his head. The same with Liddie. Maybe they thought them four miscreants wrung their sister's neck.

Rolf throwed us a signal, and me and Otis and the two Bills stood up to start toting the coffin down the aisle. Liz Saymill come up to Rolf just as he come down from the pulpit and said she wanted to talk to him, and later wouldn't do.

"Your sermon pointed up a worse tragedy, the ignorance of these children, Reverend," she said. "I fear I can't accept the responsibility for Lydia any longer. She'll be eighteen soon, and she has no more knowledge of life than a child of three."

Rolf wanted to get on with his chores, but with Liz, a problem was something to be solved, and right now, not when you got around to it. He said, "Well then, Miss Liz, find some other home for her, that's my suggestion."

"Another home for her?" Liz said. "No one else will take her, or I wouldn't have her in the first place."

"Then turn her out in the street," Rolf said. "Either that, or teach her what she needs to know. What other choice do you have, Miss Liz?"

"I? Why good God, I'm a maiden lady!" Liz said, and she just glittered her eyes at him.

"If you know enough to know she's ignorant," Rolf said, "you know what she's ignorant of. I have to get up here every Sunday and warn people of the agonies of Hell, too, and I never been there. Just because you have got no personal experience with a thing don't mean—"

"Drop it," Liz said. "I'll make out. One thing about us Methodists, we never yet let ignorance come between us and our Christian duty."

Me and Otis and the two Bills toted the coffin up the aisle and out the door, with Rolf coming along behind. Just outside the front door was Ownie Cope, leaning against the wall with his boots crossed, and his jackknife in his hand, opening and closing it.

"Maybe you can set on your hind end and let the girl's eyes punish them bastards," he said to Rolf, "but I ain't, and I just thought I'd tell you."

"You're drunk, Ownie, but not drunk enough to create a scene at this girl's farewell I hope," Rolf said.

"I won't make no scene," Ownie said, "but you and me is going to have a little talk later on."

He stood there with his old dirty hat in his hand while we packed the coffin down to where Abe Whipple had formed up the Honor Society of the Native Sons and Daughters of Mooney County in an honor guard. They was all in their purple sashes, with Abe carrying the flag with the initials and Founded 1862 sewed on in white letters, although Abe was born in Canada or Michigan, he wasn't sure which side of the line.

"Tin-*chun!*" Abe said, and thumped his pole on the frozen ground, and them old Native Sons creaked their old bones and shuffled their feet, and we slid the coffin on the running gears of the wagon, and then lined up two on each side, me and Bill Weedon on one side, and Bill Seek and Otis on the other side.

Every time there's a funeral, everybody says they've got to fix the road to the graveyard, but nobody ever does, and we had to walk beside and hold the coffin on the wagon. Sammie Ledger leaned on Hoot's arm like he was a grown man, and Liddie walked along with her arm around Liz Saymill to comfort her instead of being comforted, and you never seen two handsomer people.

There was a lot of milling around while people went to their buggies and wagons, and Abe said, "Fall in," and the Native

Sons formed up in double file, and off we went. Rolf had this beautiful mare that he rode on his pastoral chores, and he led her behind the rear guard, and we kind of staggered up the hill, with a couple of dogs fighting beside the road the way they do at every funeral.

Ownie Cope slouched along clear at the tail end, carrying his old dirty hat, and opening and closing his knife. If he sorrowed any, he didn't show it. He looked his usual mean self, was all.

At the graveyard we put the coffin on a pair of old castaway ropes, in case they got stuck under the coffin and had to be buried with it, and lowered that little girl into the cold frozen ground. How light she was, and how cold that old dirt did seem! Yet it was kind of like going home to her, because at least she was out of the wagon, and her pap was right next to her.

Sammie Ledger raised two geraniums in two pots, one dark red and one kind of orange, and she'd brung along two flowers. She give one to Liddie and one to Hoot, and they stepped up and dropped them in on their sister's coffin, and me and Bill Seek picked up the shovels and began throwing in the clods. I ain't got no business doing that kind of work, with a bullet in my abdomen somewhere; so in a minute, Rolf told Bill Weedon and Otis to spell us off.

We got her buried at last, and that whole town had come out to honor a little mover's child, even a few people that had no business out in cold weather. That's the kind of neighborly people they was, outside of the normal ornery streak you expect in everybody. I won't say they'd come through every time somebody got in trouble, but they would as often as not, and they had this time.

I walked back with Rolf, leading his horse. Going down the hill, Ownie Cope ranged up on the other side of Rolf, no drunker than usual, but no soberer either.

"Reverend," he said, "I ain't an expert on sermons, but one thing you said up there really puzzled me."

Rolf said, "If you spent half as much time in church as you do in saloons, I reckon you'd understand."

Ownie thought this over. "I reckon not," he said. "It don't take much to get me drunk. I can support my thirst a lot cheaper than I could my remorse, if I was a dues-paying Christian. I reckon you don't feel like explaining religion to me now, though."

"I will if I can," Rolf said, "but if you're only trying to hooraw me, Ownie, this is the wrong time and place."

Ownie stopped, and Rolf stopped to face him, and Ownie said, "You said if you wasn't trying to turn the other cheek, you'd be out with a six-gun. What I want to know is, *where the hell would you be with it?* Nobody else knows who to shoot. What do you know that we don't know?"

"What are you hinting at?" Rolf said.

"I ain't hinting, I'm asking," Ownie said. "You done your hitch in prison—did you meet somebody there that you later met here, that could of done this Goddamn murder?"

Rolf kind of looked off at nothing and said, "Ownie, looking back on my time in prison, I met so many that could of done it that I wouldn't know where to start naming them."

Ownie's hand shot out and took Rolf by the arm. "That ain't no answer! Who did you know in prison that you have seen *here?* Say somebody gets out, and hears that his old pard is now a preacher in Mooney, Colorado. Say he rides here to borry four bits from him, and maybe he can and maybe he can't.

"But one thing sure, his old pard, the Reverend Rolf Ledger, sees him and remembers him! Maybe this ex-convict goes on out to the blowhole and camps there. Maybe he's got three trail-pards out there, maybe the reason they hang around is the Reverend Rolf Ledger could help them if the son of a bitch only would. Maybe the preacher-man turned them down once too often, and they're riding back to the blowhole, and they see this mover's wagon with two girls in it—"

Ownie choked up like a schoolboy and started to cry, and had to start cursing under his breath to shut it off. Rolf said, "Ownie, I promise you one thing. If I ever have the least suspicion of where to lay hands on the men that done this,

Christian forbearance will not stand in the way of my going straight to Abe Whipple."

"Then you do know somebody," Ownie said.

Rolf shook his head. "I don't know anything," he said.

"I dare you to come right out and say like a man that you don't even *suspicion* nobody," Ownie said. And when Rolf didn't answer him, Ownie said, "Oh *shit*, you're no better than they are." He closed his knife and stumbled down the hill like a blind horse, and when old Rolf and me went on, Rolf wouldn't even look me in the eye.

CHAPTER 6

Rolf took his job mighty serious. The Catholic church was only a mission, and the bishop hadn't got around to sending out another buck nun after their last one died, and the other Protestant sects didn't flourish, and Rolf you might say had a monopoly. He was getting twenty-four dollars a month when he could collect it, plus feed for his horse, plus that shacky old parsonage, plus a fresh cow to milk, and new potatoes and garden truck in season.

A man can make out on that, but his wife was used to a lot more, and he wouldn't let her take nothing from her father, Cal Venaman. It was probably a good thing them movers' kids come along when they did, because he was running out of work. He had that town policed up pretty good, and a man like Rolf has got to have something to fight, and he was in a mood to go out missionary to the Apaches, or some other way of proving his zeal.

Rolf set about learning Hoot the things a grown man needs to know, like where babies come from, and what causes it, and all the other trouble it can cause. Liddie used to come visit Hoot every few days, and once her and Sammie got to talking about the same subject, and Sammie told Rolf that the girl was remarkably well prepared to face life in them subjects.

So maybe it wasn't just theory to Liz after all, but the past is the past, and it's her business anyway. The important thing is, she learned that girl what she had to know; yet neither Liddie nor Hoot ever seemed to realize what had been did to their sister.

Hoot was good with tools. He helped Rolf fix up the parsonage, and clean the dead dogs and old whisky bottles out of the well, and put up a new well sweep, and dig a new privy hole and move the privy. When spring come on, they never did let the weeds get a start, and he was prob'ly the first Methodist preacher in that town that could see out of his front window all the way to the street. Them weeds had discouraged other preachers pretty bad.

In May they had a family dinner one Sunday for all of Sammie's family at the parsonage. Sammie's parents, Cal and Opal Venaman was there, and Winnie and Thad Rust, her sister and brother-in-law, the deputy sheriff. After they et, while the women done the dishes, the men went out and set on some nice clean boxes that Rolf had put in the shade to set on.

Cal Venaman was a tall skinny well-dressed man. Even in his own cow camp he stayed well-dressed-looking, and Hoot was really smit at setting at the same table with the likes of him. He never had a word to say.

They just made themselves comfortable on them boxes, when Cal said, "Mr. Swiverton, may I compliment you on your appearance? You have a remarkable dignity, young man, indeed you do."

"Ha?" Hoot said.

"You're a credit to your family," Cal said, "and if my clerical son-in-law has no moral reservations about it, I should like to offer you a cigar."

"Have your fun, Cal," Rolf said.

"Well do you or don't you?" Cal said.

"If he's going to take up the weed," Rolf said, "why start him on something that can cost a nickel a day? He ain't a rich man, to go around smoking them cigars."

Cal handed Hoot a cigar and said, "Mr. Swiverton, that's an excellent five-center, and I trust it may inspire you to earn the good things of life. That's what good things are for—inspiration, not envy."

"Thank ye, sir," Hoot said.

He lit up and smiled all over. Them movers smoke early. Their mothers give them a puff of the corncob pipe for the nursing colic or the toothache, or just to shut up their crying, and by the time they're ten most kids have their own pipes. The reason Liddie and Hoot didn't, there wasn't no tobacco raised in Colorado, and anything they couldn't raise, they done without.

"Like it?" Cal said.

"Sweeter than a yam," Hoot said.

"Good!" Cal said. "You have no trade, have you? How would you like to work for me, and learn the cattle business?"

Hoot almost strangled on his cigar. "Sir, I'd love that better than anything else on earth!"

Cal looked at Rolf and said, "Have you any objections? How does the idea strike you?"

"He'll have to make a living someday," Rolf said. "So long as he goes on with his reading and writing and ciphering, I'm for it."

"Opal will teach him," Cal said. "Very well, let's consider it settled."

"Hold on there!" Rolf said. "How much did you figger to pay him?"

Cal paid his cowhands twenty-five dollars a month, extra in the haying season. He said, "Hoot's skill with tools is not in demand at the Flying V. I thought of this more as a learning apprenticeship, Rolf."

"I bet," Rolf said.

He looked at Thad and kind of grinned, and Thad squirmed on his box like he'd like to second the motion if he dared to. Cal got kind of red-faced.

"I don't need a carpenter or a mason," he said. "The lad wants to learn the cattle business, damn it!"

Rolf said, "There's always something needs fixing, and a man is earning something even if he's only shagging gates at the branding pen. How about half pay?"

That's what they agreed on. Samantha raised some hell when she heard about it, when Cal said he'd sleep in the bunkhouse and grub with the crew. Sammie said he'd learn more in the bunkhouse than he would at any branding fire, and all of it he could do without.

Rolf knowed this was a fact, but you can't keep a growing boy from learning them things anyhow, and there wasn't no bedbugs in the Flying V bunkhouse, and for all his nasty talk, Cal wasn't a hard man to work for. They made the store open up and sell them an extra change of clothes for Hoot, and he went out with Cal and Opal that same day.

It turned out just fine. Hoot was a humble, quiet kid, anxious to please, not afraid to work, and strong for his age. He had the soul of a cowboy, as the saying goes, being early to rise, first to the privy, and first to the table.

Hoot hadn't never handled horses except the old bonebags

movers have, that you drive with rope lines, and keep a prod pole in your hand. The Flying V was famous for its horses, and kept three good studs, and raised one hundred to one hundred and fifty horses to sell every year. Cal put him to helping a man he had there breaking colts.

"Hoot is an animal himself, I think," he told Rolf later. "He doesn't have a thing to learn about a horse somehow. He can get his bare hands on a range colt faster than anyone I have ever known, and once he touches it, it's his horse."

He paid Hoot a hand's full wages from the start, and pretty soon Hoot had his own saddle string, and Cal got on his tail the same as he did his regular hands, and by summer's heat, the mover's kid was a cowboy. Now you could listen to old cowboys set around all day, telling what a low-down miserable hopeless thankless job it is, only they never seen it until too late.

But nobody could of made Hoot Swiverton believe that. The only thing that stuck in his craw, he had to go to the house every evening for some lessons, and the crew teased him about that until he whipped a couple of them, and he fretted considerable until he seen it was part of the price of his job. Ruther than give up being a cowboy on the Flying V, he would of learned hemstitching.

Nothing like that for Liddie, though.

For Liddie it was just work and study, study and work, work and study. Liz Saymill said life was hard for the poor, and harder for the rich than the poor suspicioned, and you had to bluff your way to the grave by knowing how to do many things well. She learned Liddie to cook and bake and sew and make jelly, and set hens and raise garden and milk the cow, and even paint the window sashes and put back some bricks that had fell out of the chimbley.

You'd of thought Liz didn't have no feeling for the girl at all. Do this, do that. Straighten up! Don't go about humped over like a pot-lickin' dog. Pick up your feet, don't drawl your words. Look a person in the eye and smile, like you had some pride in yourself!

"I'll make a lady of you or kill you, Lydia," she said, "and as God is my witness, I wonder which!"

"Don't aim me too high, ma'am," Liddie said. "The upper the leap, the downer the tumble."

"Don't you believe that!" Liz said. "You can do anything, be anything, have anything, that you aspire to in Christian humility. You can even have it without the humility, but not in my house!"

You wouldn't of thought a girl could enjoy suchy life, but Liddie did. After the shiftless life of a wagon, she just loved having firm rules to lean on, and strong walls around her life, and somebody that thought she was important enough to nag.

Women are strong for rules in little things, at least most of the time, although when it comes to running off with the wrong man, the sensiblest of them can jump the fence, buggy and all. This was what worried Miss Liz the most, that Liddie was old enough to get into trouble, and in spite of everything she'd learned her, stayed just as innocent and helpless as the day she was born.

Some women are that way, just too trusting and good, and it's all right if they happen to trust the right man at the right time. But how often does that happen? And like Liz said, why is it the tenderest and fairest flower in the garden that always gets strangled by a big overbearing weed?

Spring stumbled along into summer, and the heat come on, and it rained on the Fourth of July and not again until the twenty-ninth of August, and the cattlemen's range and the nesters' crops just went to hell. Liddie spent an hour a day lugging buckets of water to the garden and flowers, while Liz set under the grape arbor and fanned herself and wondered if it was worth the trouble, if the Lord had lost countenance with Colorado or what.

Liddie had got into the habit of taking some flowers up to the graveyard every Saturday, and putting them on the graves of Pap and Alice, and keeping the weeds pulled so the grass could root in if it ever rained again. And it was on the twenty-eighth of August, the day before it finely rained, that Liz come running to Rolf for advice and consolation. She was more wrought up than Rolf had ever saw her, and Liz was a woman who got wrought up easy and often. . . .

It dawned on Liz that Liddie had got mighty pious about them graves all of a sudden, and in the worst hottest weather of all, was toting flowers up there just about every day. It was the way she done it, too. Seemed like it had to be about the same time every afternoon, and when it got along towards that time the girl got restless and moody and pink-faced, and could hardly wait, and then she took longer and longer to do it, and come back moodier than ever.

Liz couldn't believe Liddie was two-faced enough to be meeting no man on the sly, but she couldn't take no chance. One afternoon she just *happened* to go visiting a neighbor on the way to the graveyard, at the time Liddie was supposed to come home.

Her and this neighbor set out on the front porch with a pitcher of water from the well all afternoon, but she didn't see no sign of Liddie, yet when she got home, Liddie was already peeling the potatoes for supper, in a kind of a daze Liz thought. Liz wanted to come right out and ask her where she'd been, or whack her across the bottom with a broom, only she couldn't bring herself to do either one.

But the next day, she remembered there was another way to the graveyard, clear around town instead of through it. There was this one stretch about forty rods long, an old rundown road with a row of trees along one side, and a plum thicket on the other, and the thrashers and meadow larks nested in the plums, and the young cottontails hid in the shade there, and the grasshoppers was always sawing away like a German band.

In the hot dry summer the dust laid thick there, and this was a hot dry one, and the kids loved to splash barefoot in the dust, and whoop and holler at how hot it was, and make tracks like an elephant. Only in the afternoon it was too hot for kids even, and the birds kept to the shade, and the goldenrod and sunflowers drooped in the dust.

"I hid myself there, in all frankness," Liz said. "I stooped to spying, Reverend. I became an eavesdropper and a sneak!"

She give up her afternoon nap to do it, and stood there in the shade of them spindly old trees, what there was of it, and pretty soon, here came Liddie. Liz felt her heart just go *crack* when she seen it was Ownie Cope with her, the lowest of the low.

They wasn't doing anything, not even holding hands, not talking, just ambling along with their heads down, Ownie carrying his old dirty hat, and Liddie carrying a couple of dandelions. In her worst nightmares, Liz hadn't suspicioned it could be Ownie Cope.

"I was going to rage out like a policeman and march her back into town for all the world to behold for the slattern strumpet from the wagons that she was," Liz said, "and if Ownie Cope opened his big mouth, I was going to tell him some things no man would dare tell him without putting the muzzle of a gun between his eyes first."

"Why didn't you?" Rolf said.

The old lady wrung her hands. "Because it looked too holy, that's why," she said.

"Holy," Rolf said. "Ownie Cope. I see. Holy."

"There are moments when one knows that God is both very good and very close," Liz said. "One knows that He made the trees, the sun, the birds that sing, the warm kindly earth under us, the bees to hum and the flowers to bloom and the hot wind to whisper. Such a moment, Reverend, found me hiding like a sneak."

"Go on," Rolf said.

"It came to me in my foolish human vanity, that if God made these things, he made them not just for me, but for Lydia and Ownie Cope too. Yes, for even Ownie Cope! And I could only hide as Adam and Eve tried to hide, and hope to God my sin would not find me out to them."

"Well did it?" Rolf said.

"No. Blessedly they went on, and I was a long time with my head bowed, let me tell you! I still feel I trespassed on something holy, and you'll never persuade me otherwise. What I want from you, Reverend, is this—how did Ownie Cope get into anything holy?"

"I sure don't know, Miss Liz," Rolf said, "but I wouldn't put nothing past the Lord. Your own heart is a better guide than I am, ma'am."

"I knew that," Liz said, "but it's a comfort to hear you admit it. I'll do the best I can by that girl and trust in His wisdom to protect her, for I can't."

Rolf went looking for Ownie, and found him across the crick, where the old red-light district used to be, until Abe Whipple was forced to abolish it by decree. Ownie was setting on an old pole fence, with his heels hooked over a pole, and his hat down over his eyes, carving a little wooden dog out of a piece of wood.

"Howdy," Rolf said, and clumb up beside him, and hooked his heels over too.

Ownie shoved his hat back and said, "Howdy. I don't reckon this is an accidental meeting, Reverend."

"Not in no way," Rolf said. "Liz Saymill is some upset about you meeting Liddie at the graveyard."

"She is, is she," Ownie said.

"Yes, and she's got every right. I wish every man well, Ownie, but you got to admit you're no bargain for any woman," Rolf said.

"You never said correcter words, Reverend," Ownie said. He eased himself off'n the fence and closed his knife up and put it away, and said, "Listen, would you believe me if I said I never spoke a word to that girl that the whole town couldn't hear?"

"Sure, I'd believe that," Rolf said. "If you tell me that, I believe it, sure."

Ownie nodded soberly. "I don't want to make her no trouble. I won't see her no more, Reverend. I wasn't getting nowhere with her nohow," he said.

"I should hope not," Rolf said.

Ownie didn't even seem to hear him. He said, "Reverend, does the name Cappy Sanno mean anything to you?"

Rolf felt he had a kind of a buzzing in his ears, Ownie had

changed the subject on him so fast. He said, "No it don't but it sounds a lot like Capistrano, so maybe you heard wrong."

"Capistrano," Ownie said. "What's that?"

"It's a place in California," Rolf said. "Why?"

"Nothing," Ownie said. "Well, I won't make no more trouble for Liddie. I didn't have no idee I was! Why I wouldn't harm that girl for anything, why what do you think I am anyway?"

"I wonder myself sometimes," Rolf said. "What are you, tell me."

"The son of a steamboat whore," Ownie said, and he went slouching away, and didn't look back, and Rolf felt so sorry for him he didn't know what to do. He knowed that Ownie was in love with Liddie, but he wasn't going to bother her no more because he felt too low-down for her, even if she had come out of a mover's wagon. People can get into some of the worst messes that way.

Rolf dropped in on Liz Saymill that evening, and told her not to worry. He said that Ownie was smitten with Liddie, but an unexpected contrary streak of decency had cropped up in him, and he'd stay away from her instead of getting a job and quitting drinking.

"Even when people do the right things," he said, "often as not they do them for the wrong reasons, and it don't make my work no easier, let me tell you."

Liz cried a little. "It seems such a shame that anything so holy can't survive in our climate," she said. "And it was holy, it was!"

Liddie come in then, just as pretty as she could be with that olive skin of hers kind of flushed, and her black eyes snapping. Rolf talked around with her a few minutes, trying to think of a way to lead up to it.

Some things just can't be led up to. He finely had to come right out and say, "Liddie, I wonder if the name Capistrano means anything to you?"

Liddie turned white, and her eyes popped wide open, and she put her hands to her cheeks. "That's it!" she screamed. "That's it, that's what one of the men was called that killed

Pap and Alice. Capistrano, that's the name they called him!"

Rolf helped Liz quiet the girl down, but when he went to look for Ownie Cope, to remind him that Vengeance is mine saith the Lord, he couldn't find him nowhere. The reason he couldn't, Ownie was at my place for almost a week, staying drunk as he could, and in between times as poison mean as he could be. And he could be as poison mean as anybody I ever knowed.

CHAPTER 7

It was *so* hot you had trouble getting to sleep before two or three in the morning, and more trouble getting up. I got up one morning, and Ownie was setting there at the kitchen table, with a pencil and a paper, sober as a judge.

"I'll be off your hands today, Pete," he said. "Wonder where a man could find a job?"

"A lot of good men are wondering that," I said.

"I reckon so," Ownie said. "Pete, what do you think I could get for my horse?"

"Last spring I'd of said a hundred and fifty dollars, today I don't know, maybe as much as a hundred," I said.

"That's about what I figgered," he said.

"How are you going to find a job if you sell your horse?" I asked him.

"I ain't sure what I'll do," he said, and that was all I could get out of him.

He didn't have the shakes like a lot of men do when they sober up, and he wasn't in what I'd call a real mean mood, and he didn't seem nervous at all. He thanked me for letting him lay around there drunk as a hog, which he never done before, and left real early in the morning.

That was the day Charley Parker's Roofed Lazy 8 outfit turned over five hundred cows Charley had sold to Cal Venaman. Abe Whipple had a fit when he found out Cal was going to take possession in Mooney. Ownie got to town in time for Abe to do all his complaining to him.

"That's a cowman for you, what does he care how much trouble he causes; well, by God, the first wild range cow that gets loose in this town is a dead cow," he said.

"I don't blame you, Abe," Ownie said. "Them days is gone forever."

Them cattlemen used to just turn a herd loose and laugh their heads off to see it tear through a town, running over yards and tangling up in clotheslines, with women climbing trees and wagons getting turned over and now and then a kid killed. Abe had stopped that in Mooney by shooting cows down and then daring them to do anything about it.

A cattleman didn't care if you shot up his help. He could

always hire another cowboy, but a dead beef cost him money. Many a sheriff would of been run out of the country for standing up to the cattlemen the way Abe had, but he had his own system. When the cattlemen was against him, he made sure he had the townfolks and the nesters on his side, and when he had to bear down on the town people or the nesters, he first made friends with the cowmen.

Abe and Thad showed up all garnished up with guns, each with a .30-30 carbine in his saddle boot. Thad looked like he was waiting to mount the gallus to be hung, if Abe took a notion to order him to shoot one of his father-in-law's cows.

Cal had eight men, including Hoot Swiverton, when he come into town. He laughed his head off when he seen Abe and Thad armed like a Mexican revolution.

"Why shoot, this is just a handful of tame cows," he said. "Four men could eat them alive."

"I hope you're right, Cal," Abe said. "For your sake, I do devoutly hope it."

"Have you ever known me to be wrong?" Cal said.

He tied his horse and walked into the store where he was to meet Charley Parker, and Abe choked a little, and then he said, "Have I ever knowed him to be wrong, and, by God, he meant it just the way it sounded, can you beat that for gall?"

"He ain't no worse than Charley Parker," Thad said. "That ain't family loyalty, either, because I don't feel none. That Roofed Lazy 8 outfit is a corker."

Charley loved to put on a show too. He always had men stumbling around over each other out there, and when he come into town, it was like his own private army. The range war days was long since gone in Mooney County, but them old customs die hard, and Charley was old enough to eat with his knife and live in the past.

Ownie Cope had worked for Charley two-three times, and could of run his outfit for him if he was a mind to, because Ownie made a good hand. But he was a restless one, and sometimes short-tempered, and as liable as not to blow up and tell Charley to go to hell over nothing.

Charley left the herd a couple of miles out of town to the

east, with four men to hold them, and rode into town with five men to meet Cal. They loved an audience, and it wouldn't of been no pleasure at all just to close the deal out there at the holding ground. No, the common people had to see the leather bag of gold change hands, and the papers signed, and the cigars swapped, or it wasn't sacred.

Charley was a big old fat man, foul-mouthed and ignorant, and Cal didn't care for him at all most of the time. But he was necessary for this ceremony, so Cal waited in the store until Charley flourished up and tied his horse and went inside.

They closed their deal on the end of the counter in the store, and swapped their cigars, and Charley throwed Cal's leather bag of gold to one of his men to tote, like this was small change to him. Abe come in the door then, and wanted to know how much longer this opera was going to go on, with five hundred wild cows just a sprint away.

Cal picked out four of his men, and said, "You go ahead and start the herd home. We'll catch up with you in a few minutes. Well thank you, Charley, and so long."

"Thank you, Cal, and so long to you," Charley said. "Let's go home, boys."

Hoot was disappointed at not getting picked to help drive the herd. He wanted the people in Mooney to see he was all cowboy and a yard wide, but at least he'd been a witness to the old trail's-end rites, and it was something he could tell his grandchildren.

Charley come out of the store with his men, and one of them was this fellow by the name of Scotty Dundy, who had come from Scotland years ago, and had this beautiful tenor voice. He was a big brawny man that loved to swagger, so he come out of the store singing, letting his R's roll like taters on a cellar door:

Flow gently, sweet Afton
Amang thy green braes,
Flow gently, I'll sing thee
A song in thy praise.

My Mary's asleep by
Thy murmuring stream.
Flow gently, disturb not
Her slumbering dream.

Scotty was vain about his voice, and he could just make you wet your pants when he cut loose sometimes. He took off his hat and swung it almost to the ground in a big stylish bow, when he reached the bottom step and the end of the song at the same time.

Up there behind him, Hoot Swiverton was just coming out of the door, and he looked like he had seen a ghost, or at least heard one.

Hoot let out a long whimpering kind of a squeal, not words just a regular old squeal, and ran down the steps. The nearest horse was Abe Whipple's, with a .30-30 sticking out of the boot. Abe was maybe a dozen feet away, and the only man there quick-minded enough to see what Hoot meant to do.

"No you don't!" Abe yelled, and jumped for the kid. But Hoot yanked the .30-30 out, and took off the safety, and snuggled the gun up against his shoulder, and come around to draw a bead on Scotty Dundy. Nobody ever had to learn a mover's kid how to handle a rifle, and Scotty wasn't but a few steps away.

Abe hit him just as he fired. The slug caught Scotty in the meat of his right leg, about halfway between the hip and the knee. Hoot was whimpering and crying and cursing and trying to hang onto the gun for another shot, and Abe was trying to take it away from him, when the second shot went off.

This one took Abe's hat off and creased him a little, and down he went, and then Ownie hit Hoot from behind and twisted the .30-30 out of his hand. Thad Rust got hold of Hoot and pulled him back and asked him what in tarnation got into him.

"He killed my sister and he killed my pap!" Hoot screamed. "Listen to how funny he talks! I remember, I remember! Well I got even with one of the sons of bitches."

Somebody run for Doc Tattnal, while Ownie and Thad was throwing this kid down and setting on him. It was like holding a full-grown puma. Abe Whipple stumbled up, bleeding down the side of his face, and Scotty Dundy was over there groaning that he was murdered, assassinated, shot from behind by a cowardly Flying V ambusher.

"Cal, take your men and get out of town, everybody but Hoot," Abe said. "You go one way, and Charley, you take your men and go the other, everybody but Scotty, he can stay here until Doc sees to him."

"I wouldn't stay in your filthy town," Scotty said. "Somebody bring me my horse and help me on him."

Abe got them out of town without no more trouble. Even Cal Venaman was too surprised to try to overrule him. Doc Tattnal come up and made Abe set down on the steps while he took eight or ten stitches in his scalp.

Abe set there and let Doc sew him up. He said to Hoot, "Son, you wild little son of a bitch, there's no decenter man in Colorado than Scotty Dundy, what made you think he killed your sister and daddy?"

"The way he talks," Hoot said. "One of them talked the same way."

"Does he look like anybody you remember?" Abe said.

"Well no, I don't remember seeing him," Hoot said.

"Well now look what you done, you shot an innocent man and you'll have to stand trial, and when it comes to that, you shot me too," Abe said. "I ought to kick your ass clear out of Colorado, that's what I ought to do."

Hoot was still white as a ghost, and weak in the knees, and a lot more scared kid than cowboy then. "I kin still hear that man in my mind, Shurf," he said, "and that's just exactly how he sounded."

"That ain't enough to kill a man for," Abe said, "and now you know it. You go on down to the jail with Thad, and wait for me there, until this damned old clumsy fool of a doctor stops fumbling around and trying to saw my head off. All of you get out of here. Everybody out, out!"

Everybody left but Ownie and the doctor, and finely the

doctor left too, and Abe set there a minute until he got his strength back.

"Ownie," he said, "what do you think?"

"I seen them dead people," Ownie said. "Scotty couldn't of did that in a million years."

"Way I figure it," Abe said.

"Scotty might come at you just for the fun of it, or if you said something nasty about the Queen, or any good reasonable cause for a fight," Ownie said. "But he wasn't one of them murdering blowholers."

"Way I figure it," Abe said. "We'll find out that Scotty didn't have nothing to do with it."

"Likely," Ownie said, "but this still puts it up to you to bet or check, don't it?"

Abe felt around of the bandage Doc had left on his head, and cursed a little, and said, "Bet or check how?"

"Why," Ownie said, "Hoot's mind unfroze enough to give you a clue to one more man. That makes three of the four you've got a line on."

"What line?" Abe said.

"One of them talks with a Scotch brogue," Ownie said, "and one of them has been in the Kansas pen, and one goes by the nickname of Capistrano."

"How do you figure all this?" Abe said.

Ownie said, "Abe, Rolf Ledger has seen somebody he suspicions, he wouldn't admit it but he did, and where would he know that kind of a murderer except in the pen? Liddie remembered something like Cappy Sanno, and Rolf says it's more'n likely Capistrano. That was what they called one of them, either Cappy Sanno or Capistrano, and you know damn well which it was."

"I've been having a bale of wool pulled over my eyes," Abe said, "and I don't like it a damn bit! This is what happens when you do something for somebody. I put Rolf in office, I give him power and responsibility and a chance to marry money, and when he's got information on a felony in my own jurisdiction, do you think he came to me with it? I'll kiss a pig he didn't. Come on, you and me is going to see Rolf right now!"

"I'll wait for you down to the courthouse," Ownie said. "I want to see how Hoot is getting along."

Hoot was just scared stiff, was how he was getting along. He was laying on one of them bunks on his back, with his arm over his eyes, and one boot toe swinging back and forth a little. He wouldn't look up to talk to Ownie, just laid there and twitched that one foot.

Abe came back a while later, with his head about to split with the headache from being grazed with a .30 bullet. "He said yes, he did see a man he remembered from the pen," he said, "but he hadn't ever knowed his name because the man got out just about the time Rolf went in, but his nose had been busted once and healed with a dent in it, and he claimed to be a gunfighter."

"What more do you want?" Ownie said. "What are you waiting for anyway?"

"What more do I want?" Abe said. "Did it ever occur to you that maybe we've got clues to just *one* man, that's a gunfighter with a broken nose and served time in the pen, and talks with a Scotch brogue, and goes by the nickname of Capistrano? How do you know it's three men, and not just one?"

Ownie leaned over the desk and said, "Abe, by God you've got a fifteen-year-old kid in your dirty dark dank filthy jail, eating his heart out in there, and you set on your big fat rump and bring up technicalities. You'd ruther hang Hoot for it than get off your can and work."

"Ownie, what do you want me to do?" Abe said. "I know something about this business. That wasn't no gang of organized criminals. They're just no-account human skunks that happened to den up together out there at the blowhole, and they ain't ever going to be seen together again, not *ever*, because they'll be scareder of each other than of anything else. Men like that don't stick together! Now what the hell do you expect me to do?"

"You could offer a reward," Ownie said. "How much is my horse worth? At least a hundred and fifty dollars. I'll put that up."

"You mean that?" Abe said.

"You try me and see by God!" Ownie said.

Abe said, "Well, Ownie, you surprise me, you back your bluffs all right. Keep your horse. Let's go get the printer going on some dodgeroos."

They got out 1,000 of them that same day:

$500 REWARD
for EACH of the following described
members of a gang of DANGEROUS RUFFIANS:
Suspect No. 1–Speaks with a Scotch brogue.
Suspect No. 2–Nicknamed Capistrano.
Suspect No. 3–Gunfighter with bent nose,
formerly a convict in Kansas State Prison.
Suspect No. 4–No description.

THESE MEN MURDERED AN OLD MAN AND A YOUNG GIRL. THEY WILL BE ARMED AND MAY FIGHT LIKE CORNERED RATS. REWARD PAID ONLY FOR DELIVERY, ALIVE, TO THE UNDERSIGNED.

EXERCISE ALL CARE IN APPROACHING THEM!

A. H. Whipple, Sheriff
Mooney County, Colorado

"Who's going to pay the five hundred dollars?" Ownie asked.

"Nobody," Abe said. "This ain't the way to get them sons of bitches, Ownie. Oh, if I was only thirty years younger!"

"Well I am," Ownie said.

"You're what?" Abe said.

"Thirty years younger," Ownie said.

CHAPTER 8

There was a contractor building some county road, and he come into town that afternoon looking for men that could handle four-mule teams, and Ownie was the first man he hired. Ownie holed up in one of them old shacks across the crick, and done his own cooking, and never showed his face in a saloon.

He come around the next evening to see Hoot in the jail. "I'm worse than them people that killed Alice and Pap, you know that?" Hoot said. "I'll be glad when I'm dead and can forget shooting that man."

"You only say that because you never been dead," Ownie said. "Nobody knows anything about death, except that this is the wagon when it backs up to the door, all of us get in sooner or later. Shut up that kind of talk."

"Reverend Ledger says if I'm truly repentant, I'll be forgiven and can forget," Hoot said, "but I reckon he means after I'm dead, because I sure can't forget now."

"He don't know no more about it than you and me," Ownie said. "I'm going to get Jimmy Drummond to take your case as soon as he gets back from Denver, and I'll talk to Scotty Dundy the next time he's in town, and ask him how he'd like to be in jail for an innocent mistake. Scotty ain't a bad person at all, Hoot."

Hoot began to dribble tears, and said, "That's what I hear, and that's what makes it so awful, I shot a good man."

Jimmy got back, and Andy Obers called the case on some kind of preliminary hearing. The county attorney was Miles James, who claimed to be a cousin of Jesse and Frank James during the campaign, although after he got elected, he admitted this was only a family boast. Miles usually meant well, and in his favor it has to be said he wasn't much of a lawyer, and couldn't get people unjustly convicted, and not many justly convicted. But he had ambitions to run for higher office, and no prosecutor ever got very far without a few hangings on his record.

You couldn't hang a fifteen-year-old kid that had only wounded his victim, but Miles shoved in his whole stack, and charged attempted murder, and Judge Obers couldn't dismiss it. He said about a week later they could go to trial.

"No, please the court, I want sixty days," Jimmy Drummond said. "I'll have some motions to file then. I mean to raise the question of defendant's age, whether a legal infant who can't contract marriage or even buy a horse in his own name, is competent to formulate the intent to commit murder. I may even raise the doctrine of attractive nuisance, and hold the county culpable for leaving a loaded .30-30 in reach of a legal infant."

"Why I never heard such law in my life," Miles said.

"That's because you never heard much law of any kind," Jimmy said.

Judge Obers said, "You don't bluff me none, Jimmy, I've read some law myself, and if that big hulking hillbilly kid is an infant, I'm the illegitimate granddaughter of Empress Josephine. You can have your sixty days, prisoner remanded to custody of the sheriff, without bond."

Abe took Hoot down the steps to the side door of the jail, saying, "I can't remember when a prisoner has caused me more trouble than you; now let's see, sixty days, that's the last of November, well you be here about two days ahead, say the twenty-eighth. Don't come for supper, though, because you won't get any."

"Come from where?" Hoot said.

"Why out to Cal Venaman's place," Abe said. "That's where you work, ain't it? Yonder's the door and yonder's the trail, now let me miss you a while."

Hoot just about cried. He said, "I can't go there, after all the trouble I made for Cal, what if there's more trouble, and I'm to blame?"

"A range war, you mean," Abe said. "Tell Cal if I hear any such talk, to remember one thing, no matter who *starts* trouble in this county, I'm the one that *ends* it. There's always a Flying V horse in the livery barn, so go on with you boy, and don't bother me."

Hoot went and got a Flying V horse and rode out to the Flying V, and Cal greeted him like a long-lost son, and the boys in the bunkhouse made the cook bake up a sour apple pie for him. There's always a couple of expert lawyers in a bunkhouse, and they had it all figgered out. Scotty Dundy was still a British subject, and hadn't swore loyalty to the American law, and wasn't entitled to its protection, any more than a Swede or a Dutchman.

They made Hoot feel better, but the next day, Thad Rust come out there to tell about the trouble Abe got into, and Hoot was ready to go back to jail again. Judge Andy Obers sent for Abe, and asked him in open court if it was true he no longer had the prisoner in his custody.

"Why of course it ain't true, Your Honor," Abe said. "Who's going around telling crap like that?"

"Where is he?" Andy said.

"Out to the Flying V, I reckon. If you need him here for more of Miles James's foolishness, I wish you'd give a man notice," Abe said. "I've got a few other duties, you know, besides running errands for this court."

Andy almost choked. "Sheriff," he said, "this court's order was quite clear—no bail!"

"I didn't take bail," Abe said. "Ask your own Goddamn court clerk if any Goddamn bail is recorded."

"But you released the prisoner, you turned him loose in defiance of the court's orders," Andy said.

Abe said, "I done no such thing. You put him in my custody, and that's where he is, and when he's due back in this court, he'll be here. In custody don't mean I have to chain him to me, and sleep with him; a man can go to the can in privacy without dragging his prisoner along with him, can't he? Reason in all things, I've heard you say it yourself, Judge, the law is ninety-nine parts pure reason; you see, I'm quoting your own historic words right back at you. If you want this prisoner handcuffed to me twenty-four hours a day until he's due back in court, say so and I'll resign, let somebody else run this county, just let them try, that's all! I have never lost a prisoner yet, except a couple of misdemeanants that died drunk in jail, a felony prisoner never. Custody is a sacred word to me, it may be just reason to you but this Goddamn job is next to my heart, and you insult me by saying I can't be trusted with a fifteen-year-old kid unless I handcuff him and put an Oregon boot on him I suppose. Any time I lose a felony prisoner there'll be snow up to your butt in July, Your Honor. I want a ruling on *how long* the chain has to be, and do I have to *sleep* with him, and how about when I take a *bath*, lay it out for me, Your Honor."

"I don't want a speech," Andy said when he could slide a word in edgewise. "I want that prisoner."

Abe said to Thad, "All right, go out to Cal's place and tell that kid to fog it in here, this judge is snagged on one of Miles's technicalities."

"Never mind," Andy said. "I'll consider him to be in your custody, if you think you can send for him just like that, and he'll come."

"Why wouldn't he?" Abe said. "I'm the sheriff, ain't I? God help anybody that don't come when I say to."

About a week later, Ownie Cope went to Abe's house one evening and said to him, "Abe, how would you like to buy my horse?"

"That big brown gelding you ride with a three-quarter rig Rockland Myers roping saddle?" Abe said.

"How many horses and saddles do you think I own?" Ownie said. "That's the horse, and the saddle goes with him."

"Well, Ownie," the sheriff said, "you'll have trouble giving that horse away, but I'll go as high as forty dollars for him and the saddle because I feel sorry for a man so down and out he has to part with his horse and saddle."

"Last chance," Ownie said. "I'm selling today. Come nightfall, somebody else will own my horse and my three-quarter Rockland Myers roping saddle."

"I'll go as high as a hundred dollars out of pity," Abe said.

"Make it two hundred dollars and they're yours," Ownie said.

"You really mean business, don't you?" Abe said. "What will you do without a horse and saddle?"

"I thought I'd go to Denver," Ownie said. "I'm sick of the cowboy's life. What does it get you but broken bones and an early old age? As a kid, I worked in a locksmith shop in Kansas City. Maybe I'll go back to that and learn to be a locksmith."

"That's a good trade to have," Abe said, "but one thing sticks in my craw, that you might be going out on the vengeance trail after them murdering bastards that murdered old Swiverton and Alice."

"What made you think that?" Ownie said.

"It was a flash of inspiration, you might call it," Abe said. "Are you selling your pistol too?"

"No, I mean to keep my gun," Ownie said.

"I reckoned so," Abe said. "I'll go as high as one hundred and fifty for your horse, not a cent higher."

"Make it one hundred and sixty," Ownie said.

"All right, one hundred and sixty dollars," Abe said, "and if I've made a miscalculation somewhere, and you're going out afoot after them murderers, just keep one thing in mind, my boy. This is a public crime, not a private feud, and you've got no badge or commission or warrant. So if ever you get any wild notions, just stop long enough to ask yourself the old eternal question, whose ass now."

He didn't see Ownie again, although he heard he had went to work for a few days putting up clover hay for some nesters, a way of making money Ownie wouldn't of spit on in his recless, rollicking prime. And then he seen old Danny Dexter wearing Ownie's old dirty hat and boots, and old Danny told him Ownie give them to him because he was wearing a cap and moccasins from now on.

Abe went to see Mrs. Deeda Meredith, who was married to Bountiful Meredith, who owned the harness shop and made saddles to order, and would tan your deerskins or bearskins for you. Deeda was an Arapahoe orphan that had been raised Methodist by some Methodist people, but she still kept in touch with the Arapahoes.

Deeda said yes, she had made Ownie some cowhide moccasins and a deerskin cap, like she made for the Araps, to make an extra dollar now and then. She said Ownie told her he was going to have to practice a lot, walking without a heel, and that was all he said.

"Deeda," Abe said, "this don't make sense."

"It sure don't," Deeda said, "and this is just when you want to watch out for Ownie Cope. An ordinary man in love is bad enough. Like Bountiful says, you get it in the head and then you ain't satisfied until you get it in the hind end, that's the madness called love. With somebody like Ownie Cope, who can predict?"

"You mean Ownie is in love?" Abe said.

Deeda said, "Abe, few women on this earth ever get loved the way Ownie loves that pretty little Liddie Swiverton. I may be an Indian, but a human heart beats beneath my dirty coppery pelt, and it just plain saddens me to see all that good pure love going to waste. You know what an Indian would do if he was in love like that?"

"Nobody knows what an Indian would do," Abe said.

"Well there you are, you say you ain't prejudiced but catch you with your guard down, and it comes out. An Indian would starve himself weak, and whet up his knives, and build a smoke fire to his gods, and then see how many he could take with him before they gunned him down," Deeda said.

"If Ownie Cope tries anything like that," Abe said, "I ain't going to gun him down, I'll just wear a pair of tugs out across his hind end. The time for that kind of raucous foolishness is long past in Mooney County."

The only other thing Abe heard, he heard that Ownie beat up on a nester who asked him why he didn't either get his hair and whiskers cut, or learn how to braid. Then it seemed to Abe that Ownie just vanished off'n the earth.

Not to me though. I come home one afternoon and seen that my quarter-strain wolf dog, V.G., was gone. His chain was still there, and Spot and Foolish was both all right, and they was always real nervous when there had been anybody around my place while I was away from it. There was only one person could get close enough to V.G. to unsnap him.

I went into the house, and here was Ownie's gun in its holster laying on my table, a real good .45 with walnut butt-plates Ownie had whittled himself, and a nice easy steady touch to the trigger, and as well kept as a lady's hands as the saying is.

Nobody but Ownie Cope could of just walked into my house that way, without Spot and Foolish tearing them to pieces.

I looked around to find what was missing, and it was just what I suspicioned, a fine double-edged hunting knife in a scabbard for wearing under your shirt. It was the best-balanced knife I'd ever owned, and Ownie used to fool with it when he was working at his drinking at my place, and could throw it clear across the common room and hit the ace of spades four times out of five. That's twenty feet.

Well it was my gun until Ownie come back, or until the Indian I had got V.G. from come to claim him, and the knife was just a dead loss. But you get philosophical as the fella says. It's part of the cost of doing business in the kind of business I was in, in the kind of country I was doing it in, and the kind of customers I had. Which Ownie was by no means the worst.

CHAPTER 9

Long before there was a tame cow in Colorado, or a tame white man, or for that matter any place west of the Missouri, there was these old-time mountain men. Trappers and hunters and gold-seekers usually, or sometimes scouts for the Army or emigrant parties, but that was just an excuse to make drinking money before they went back to their lonely ways. They was such mean, silent, solitary people that they made your average mover look downright sociable.

Their time was long gone, it went with the first settlers that dragged along a plow and a yoke of bulls to pull it, and the repeating rifle was their death sentence. Them old mountain men was sheer death with a smooth-bore musket, that always had a pet name, like Betsy or Mother Magruder or Jesus Calls. The repeating rifle evened the odds against the ace marksman, so he could no longer stand off a quarter of a mile and pick off the settlers one by one as they put their accursed plows into his wild free lonely grass, ruining things forever for him.

This is beside the point except that there was still a few of them left, or at least that's what they thought they was. They wouldn't work, and they wouldn't partner up with each other, no they just went their lonely ways, pretending the world hadn't changed, stealing what they needed when they couldn't get it some easier way, and living you might say in the past.

This was what Ownie Cope deliberately set out to be, one of them misfit mountain men with his hand against the civilized world. He had V.G. on a string when he left my place, because any mountain man that goes through a town with a wolf dog along, he better be leading him on a string or they both stand a chance of getting shot.

He had his moccasins broke in, and his long hair bunched up and tied with a string under the cowhide cap, and my good two-edged throwing and hunting knife tucked up against his bosom under his shirt. His whiskers was about an inch and a half long, and had started out yella but had turned sort of brindle brown. He didn't really look wild yet, but give his hair and whiskers a few more weeks.

He knowed exactly what he was going to do, and how he was going to do it, if it took him the rest of his life. From my place, he hoofed it towards the blowhole, taking his time, learning the dog to walk one step behind him, and set down whenever Ownie stopped. He didn't have no impatience in him, not a grain of it, nothing but the good feeling a man has when finely he starts a job he has put off too long.

He was headed for Denver, because that was where everybody holed up for the winter when they was broke and hungry or on the dodge. Others might figger the trail of them murderers would lead to the Texas river bottoms, or to the Barbary Coast, or the Superstitions, or someplace like that. But Ownie had it figgered that these was two-bit skunks that'd be scared to death amongst the badmen of the Pecos for instance, or any place it took any guts.

He hoofed it clear to the blowhole, and looked that ugly old place over, because it was his starting place, and that's the way his mind worked, you started at your starting place. It had been a dry autumn, and that dirty old sand was about as ugly as it could be, and the wind was chasing some clouds across the sky, and flapping the tail of his dirty old jacket.

Ownie walked out into that sand a piece. He stood there listening to the fine sand blowing against his pants legs, like he was listening for voices. There wasn't nothing else to blow there but sand, not a leaf or a limb or a piece of trash, and the wind didn't make no sound at all. Just that hissing sand on his pants legs.

Then he seen Charley Polk, the Indian that saved Liddie's life, standing over there in the cactus beside the blowhole, watching him. Ownie walked over to him, and they nodded friends. Charley was standing in the ashes of an old brush camp that Abe Whipple had burned out some time ago, leaving nothing of value even to an Indian.

"Hi, where you going? Where's your horse?" Charley said.

"I sold my horse," Ownie said. "I'm through with the cow business. I'm going to Denver and get a job."

Charley wasn't no fool. He looked them moccasins over, and that long hair and whiskers, and that wolf dog, and said, "Bullshit. You're going to kill them men that kill the old man and little girl."

"Don't you ever say anything like that to nobody," Ownie said. "I don't mess around in your business, don't you mess around in mine."

"Sure, sure," Charley said. "I show you where one of them is, all right?"

"One of them killers?" Ownie said.

"Sure, you come with me," Charley said.

They walked half the day, and then first they come to a horse that had been dead quite a while. The coyotes and buzzards had worked it over pretty good, so Ownie couldn't make out a brand on it, but it had once been a sorrel horse. Its right foreleg was busted all to pieces, coffin and cannon and splint.

Ownie nodded yes, and Charley nodded back, and they both figgered it the same way. Somebody had rode this poor old tired half-dead bonebag as hard as he could be rode in that blizzard, until it put its foot down wrong on some ice under deep snow, and the whole leg caved in.

Charley led him over a little hump in the ground about fifty feet, to where there was the bones of a man. The coyotes and buzzards had been here too, but it was clear the man had been shot in the head, from up high and behind, just blowing his head to pieces.

"I see this man two-three times," Charley said. "He's always got this thing around his neck."

He made motions like a man playing the guitar, but he hadn't ever seen the man close enough to tell what he looked like. You can pick out a sorrel horse and a guitar from a fur piece off.

They looked around for the guitar, but it wasn't nowhere to be seen naturally. They stood there beside them bones for a while, thinking about it, and then Ownie said, "He was afoot in the blizzard, and none of them other three was about to ride double with him."

"Sure, sure," Charley said.

"I can just see it now!" Ownie said. "The more the sonsabitches sobered up, the more they knowed what a terrible mess they was in, lynching was too good for them, and here one of them's horses busts its leg."

"Sure, sure," Charley said.

"They didn't just ride off and leave him. He must of made them some trouble," Ownie said. "So one of them leaned out of the saddle and blowed his head off, and then somebody said, 'Bring along that guitar, it's worth a dollar or two somewheres.' I wonder which way they went!"

"A kid up there on the tracks got a guitar," Charley said.

Ownie thanked him for his help, and they nodded friends to each other again, and then Ownie began walking toward the C.B.&Q. tracks northwest where Charley had pointed, and Charley went back on his own private business whatever it was.

It wasn't long before dark fell. Ownie made a little camp beside a crick, and V.G. started a deer in the brush and high grass, and brought it down close enough to Ownie for him to get to it.

He built his fire bigger, and built a greenwood rack over it, and sliced up a lot of that meat and started to smoke it. It was getting mighty chilly at night by then, but he didn't feel the cold, and he didn't get sleepy or lonesome, and there wasn't no mosquitoes to devil him.

Except when he had to get up to feed the fire, he set there with his knees hunched up with his arms around them, thinking about various things, mostly that he was on the right track. The proof of it was, he had already found one of them. He felt bad that this one had died before he could look him in the eye and make him scream, but there was still three left.

Pretty soon, Liddie Swiverton come to him in the dark, the last thing in the world he expected, because all day when he tried to imagine what she looked like, he just couldn't see nothing.

Now she was just as plain as if she stood there. She wasn't looking at him, but just kind of over his shoulder, and she was smiling, but she didn't like it that he had hung around her just for to find out if she could remember anything that would be useful on the vengeance trail. But he thought maybe she was glad he had reformed, and was off the tanglefoot and the fighting and so forth.

"I have to be honest with you, Liddie," he said. "I only reformed to save money. I don't want to have to stop and work someplace if the trail gets hot."

She didn't answer him back, but by and by another idee come to him, that she would be happy if he would only stop blaming everything on his mother. How did he know the troubles she had? Why should he take the word of people he despised, the way he despised them that took him in after she died. That he had run off from because he hated them so bad?

Liddie Swiverton was the living proof of what Liz Saymill said, that no matter how fur down you started, you could go as high as you aimed if you walked a straight path and kept at it. Ownie always thought of himself about as low as a person could be, the son of a steamboat whore, but the movers was lower still, and a thousand miles below them was the blowholers.

"All right," he said to her, "I won't blame my mother no more. Say, it's mighty peaceful here, Liddie, with just you and me and V.G., ain't it?"

Before Father Lavrens got killed, he used to dearly love to set down with a sipping drink to work on, and tell about them old saints, and what he called their extasy, although it was more like a fit than anything else. They'd take a fit and go off into the desert, or hole up in a cave, and one of them even shinnied up a flagpole and set there the rest of his life, all so they could see God.

They was an all-fired curious people, them saints, and it's a good thing extasy has vanished from the race, because a thing like that could get you arrested these days. But it must of been something like the fit Ownie had, setting there shivering by his fire, and talking to a girl that wasn't there, and making promises and so on. There ain't a whole lot of difference between holy and crazy a good part of the time.

V.G. woke him up at crack of daylight, and he put his smoked meat in his various pockets, and rolled up his blanket, and hiked on. About noon he reached the Q tracks, and in another hour he come to the section house, and there was a whole bunch of kids teasing their pet billy goat under some old runty trees, and one of them had a guitar.

He was trying to play it and couldn't. Ownie was good at anything with his hands, and somewhere on his travels he had learned to chord the guitar, and change keys, and run back and forth and up and down all over the strings, although he couldn't read music. Ownie stopped to ask where he got the guitar, only before the kid could answer, a woman come to the door of the section house with a .410 shotgun.

"Help yourself to a drink at the pump if you like," she said, "and then be off down the track, stranger."

"I'd take a drink kindly, ma'am," Ownie said, "but the reason I stopped, my guitar was stole from me last week, but I see this ain't the one."

"It sure ain't," she said. "My husband bought this'n for the kids way last winter."

"I sure do miss my guitar!" Ownie said. "I wonder if I could try it out a little."

"You might want to buy it," the woman said. "Tommy ain't never going to learn, and it's in good shape."

Ownie took the guitar, and tuned it up, and tried to get limbered up on a few chords. "Oh my you surely can play that thing!" the woman said. "I wonder if you'd play my favorite, 'Neeterwaneeter.'"

"I don't reckon I know that one, ma'am," he said. "Let me see what I can think of."

He fooled around some more, and suddenly she said, "Why say, I thought you told me you didn't know 'Neeterwaneeter'!"

"Oh, that one," Ownie said, and he lined out a few more chords and started to sing. He didn't have no voice like Scotty Dundy, nothing like that, but it was a nice true voice, and maybe better than Scotty on a low grumbly song like this one:

Soft o'er the fountain
Ling'ring falls a southron moon,
While high o'er the mountain
Breaks the dawn too soon.

In thy dark eyes splendor,
Where the loving longing well,
Tearful looks but tender
Brim a fond farewell.
'Nita, Juanita, ask thyself if we must part!
'Nita, Juanita, never leave my heart.

The woman just cried. She said wait till the crew got in and see her husband about buying the guitar. Ownie took their bucksaw and ax and cut up some old ties for firewood for them, and dug the last of their potatoes, and when the crew got in that night, he gave them one dollar for the guitar. The section boss was sure down on cowboys, and even worse on mountain men, and he couldn't remember anything about what the three men looked like.

"Just saddle bums," he said. "Put them on the ground on their feet, and there wasn't a day's work in the three of them. They kept laughing and joking, though, about how this fella Capistrano wasn't going to need his guitar no more."

So it was Capistrano that was dead back there by the blowhole, and had to be scratched off the list. Ownie thanked the man, and said no, he wasn't used to eating at the table and wouldn't have supper with them, and he hiked off down the track with the guitar slung over his shoulder along with his blanket, and V.G. mooching along one step behind. And I reckon when that section boss seen him go off towards the sunset like that, he thought to himself, Good riddance of riffraff.

CHAPTER 10

Winnie Rust had an eight-and-a-half-pound baby girl and they named it Catherine, the closest they could come to Cal for its grandfather, Cal Venaman, who had all the money in the family, and most of what was in the county. "Wouldn't you know that trifling son-in-law of mine would beget a girl!" Cal said. "He can't do anything right."

"You only throwed fillies yourself, Cal," Abe said.

"You've got a point there," Cal admitted, "but let's see what my other son-in-law yields. I don't see how a preacher can be much good at stud, but there are preachers' sons, so perhaps I'm too critical."

"You are, but it's nice to hear you admit it," Abe said.

A while later, Sammie birthed an eight-pound boy, just about all by herself. Rolf was out on his pastoral chores, helping some old sorehead ingrate woman pray some of the meanness out of her before she died, when the pains come on Sammie. She had bread in the oven and a clutch of duck eggs hatching so they could have winter duckling, and she just about waited too long to send for help.

"A fine big handsome boy!" Cal said when he seen his grandson that evening. "What are you going to name him?"

"Martin Luther Ledger," Rolf said.

"For God's sake why?" Cal said.

"That's it, for God's sake," Rolf said. "Martin Luther was a hero of his times, and in this day and age we can use heroism. Maybe some of it will come out on him."

"They'll call him Marty," Cal warned.

"Not in my house, they won't," Rolf said.

"What's the matter with Calvin?" Cal said. "He's the nearest I'll ever come to a son and heir, and I can understand not calling him Rolf, that's an atrocity to put on a helpless baby, but why not stick to a family name?"

The real reason Rolf didn't want to have him named Calvin was because it would be too hard on Thad Rust, and he figgered Thad needed Cal's goodwill worse than he did. They jawed around about it some, Cal holding out for Calvin Martin or Calvin Luther, until Samantha said it was going to be named James Cooper after her grandfather, Opal's father.

James Cooper had come to Wyoming two jumps ahead of an Indiana warrant for shooting a cook in a restaurant that used a woman's name loosely in public. He was too late to get a job with the cattlemen in the range wars, so he organized the nesters into an army, and whipped the hell out of the cattlemen, and then he run for sheriff and had his army keep the cattlemen's crews from voting.

James Cooper was one of the heroes of Wyoming, but not of Indiana, where he had left a wife and three children. He got married again in Wyoming, first to an army colonel's wife, after him and the colonel shot it out, and the colonel took a bad chest wound and retired from the Army. James Cooper then married Opal's mother, who owned the Virginia Dare saloon in Cheyenne, and settled him down.

James Cooper was fifty-four when he married her, and about ready to settle down anyway. His nickname was Stony, something it was pretty hard to explain to women, because it was really short for Old Stone-Ache, since that man had the most ravenous appetite for women in his youth you ever seen. He got gored to death by a bull in his seventy-fourth year, and they half-staffed the flags all over Wyoming.

Cal almost had apoplexy to have his first grandson named after James Cooper, also knowed as Stony Cooper, but he got over it. "He'll have to go to Europe for a wife, to play it safe," Cal said, "because God alone knows how much of Stony's blood and seed are scattered over the nation. A most prodigious breeder, and this boy could grow up to marry his own aunt without knowing it."

Yes, life was going on in Mooney with or without Ownie Cope, as the saying goes. Hoot Swiverton come up for trial, and Cal and his whole crew took the day off to escort the prisoner to the courthouse, and Charley Parker and his whole crew escorted the chief witness, Scotty Dundy. Abe made them all shuck their guns in his office, in a barrel he kept there for that purpose, and warned them that no matter who started a fight in this county, he was always the one that finished it.

Jimmy Drummond moved to waive a jury, and Miles James objected, because he wanted to lead a cavalry charge past a jury, and fire off his oratorical cannons, and sob into his handkerchief when he pictured Scotty Dundy laying there foully shot down from behind.

"It was from the side, not from behind," Andy said. "This is a simple case and I don't see no reason for taking honest people away from their work and making the county pay jury fees for nothing. So go on with your case, Mr. James, if you please."

Miles made his opening statement, that he was going to prove malice and intent, and then he put Scotty Dundy on the stand. This was Scotty's chance to preen. He said it was the third time he'd been shot but the first time with a rifle, and it was the worst wound he'd ever had because some of the goods of his pants leg went into his meat with the bullet, and stayed there when the bullet went on through.

"It festered up on me," he said, "and I lost three weeks flat on my back in bed, and then was no more than half a man for three weeks after that. So I'm out nearly thirty dollars in pay, besides look how I suffered."

"Do you bear any ill will against the prisoner?" Miles asked him.

Scotty said heavens no, he only pitied the boy and hoped he'd mend his ways before he ended up on the junk heap of life, and he almost got to crying, and he said his own brother had got shipped to Australia for breaking the Queen's peace, and this was what could come of a misspent youth.

Cal Venaman stood up and asked if Scotty meant to say that Charley Parker hadn't paid him while he was laid up, and Charley stood up and said that wasn't the point at all, the point was here was this decent upright cowboy, a visitor in the United States, entitled to all the courtesies of decent human intercourse, and here some of the best blood of Scotland had been spilled.

"Well I'll tell you something, Charley," Cal said. "You must have run those cows I bought from you all the way from your place, the shape they were in. I estimate that they lost ten pounds each between the time I agreed to buy them at your place, and their delivery.

"That's five thousand pounds of beef, two tons and a half. It may not be the best blood of Scotland but it's money out of my pocket. Nevertheless here's what I'll do, I'll pay Scotty fifty dollars out of my own pocket for his lost wages and his pain and suffering, because I know he'll play hell ever getting a dime out of you, a man that would sell another man cattle and then run them to death."

Scotty hit the table with his fist and said, "By God you're a gentleman, Mr. Venaman, nothing like Charley said you were, I'll take it."

"There's one thing I want from you," Cal said.

"I'm at your service, sir," Scotty said.

"I want you to come to the church to sing at the babtism of my grandchildren," Cal said.

Scotty hit the table again and said, "Done, by God! I know all the old Covenanter psalms, and the Church of England liturgy, may God have mercy on me for that, and a bit of Bach that had words set to it—aye, and parts of that one I can whistle like a flute, sir, fit to split your ears. Ye can't beat well-whistled Bach for an infant babtism, sir."

"We have got lost in a box canyon with the brush afire, I'm afraid," Judge Andy Obers said. "Back to the business at hand. I find the prisoner guilty of simple assault and I sentence him to one year in prison. I suspend that sentence and release him to the custody of Cal Venaman for a probation period of five years."

Rolf Ledger said he had scruples about infant babtism, he didn't think it meant a thing except as evidence of the parents' commitment, which shouldn't of been in doubt anyway. He didn't know about whistling in church either, but Cal was in a mood to carry obstacles like a good catch dog chasing a runaway hog, and he had his way.

It turned out to be a real good babtism, with the church packed, and neither baby cried, at least not very much, and Charley Parker gave the little girl a sterling silver napkin ring and the little boy a sterling silver belt buckle. Cal winced a little when Rolf sang out the little boy's name, James Cooper Ledger, and after that he never would call the kid anything but Little Stony.

After the service was over, and before Rolf could break away to get to Cal's buggy to go out to the ranch for dinner, Liddie Swiverton come up to him and asked if she could talk to him a minute. She was still kind of timid, although not rat-scared the way she used to be, and Rolf knowed it took a lot of nerve for her to do it.

"Sure you can, Liddie," he said. "I hope nothing is troubling you, but you know we'll do anything we can."

"Everything's just fine," Liddie said. "I—I only wondered if you had had a letter from Ownie, or anything."

"Why no, I ain't," Rolf said. "Have you?"

"No, Reverend," Liddie said.

He seen how she was suffering, poor girl. He took her by the arm and said, "Liddie, Ownie ain't going to be much of a man to write, I'm afraid. I wouldn't go around asking too many people if they heard from him."

"I won't," she said, about to cry.

He thought to himself, Poor girl, poor innocent, she's the kind that can give her heart but once. He said, "If it will be any comfort to you, I feel this and I feel it pretty strong, Liddie. Whatever Ownie is doing, or wherever he is, he's true to what he believes. No one could ever call Ownie Cope a hypocrite."

That just made her eyes shine. The only trouble was what Ownie was doing, Rolf thought afterward. You can be sincere as hell about the wrong things.

CHAPTER 11

It was getting cold by the time Ownie got to Denver, and his moccasins was broke in, and his hair and whiskers had made their crop. Like in every railroad division point, there was a place where men passing through could jungle up, and there was more than usual of them in Denver, because there wasn't a job in five hundred miles once winter had set in.

Ownie come padding in on his moccasins, with his blanket and guitar slung over his back, and V.G. stealing along at his heels, and he looked just like a mountain man who couldn't own up that his day was long over. There was several camps in this brush near the Q yards. He could of joined any of them, but he went off and built his own fire, and ate some of his smoked meat, and then got his guitar out and played and sang a couple of lonesome old songs.

Men from other camps come over to listen. Ownie didn't pay them no mind, and they knowed better than to try to socialize with a mountain man. When he left off singing, they went back to their own camps, and talked about what a wild mean ornery bunch them mountain men was.

Ownie set there until Liddie come to him through the dark, when his fit of extasy got strong enough. He called her honey but he didn't mean nothing by it, it was the same as he'd call a little child that. He said, "Honey, I'm a-getting there. Your pap and your sister can rest in peace before I'm through."

He rolled up in his blanket and slept, safe as in a church with V.G. beside him. In the morning, he put his blanket and guitar on his back and walked into Denver. The police knowed about these mountain men and left him alone. He was looking for where men hung out to find jobs, because that was how he expected to get onto these other three blowholers.

He went past a store with a sign, S. H. Bosch, Locksmith, and on a hunch went in. S. H. Bosch was Blind Bosch, the best blind locksmith in the business. He said he was always looking for a good hand, but being blind, it had to be somebody he could trust, and did Ownie have any references.

"No, and there's no reason you should trust me," Ownie said. "Nobody else ever did to speak of."

"Is that your dog with you?" Blind Bosch said.

Ownie said it was, and Blind asked him what kind of dog it was, and Ownie said quarter-strain wolf, and Bosch said well if his dog trusted him, he guessed he could. Ownie went to work there, and while it was a long time since he had been in a lockshop, he hadn't forgot much of it and he was always good with his hands.

He went back to the jungle every night to cook himself a little supper, and play his guitar, and go into his fit of extasy with Liddie. One night, when he put the guitar away and started to roll up in his blanket, one of them men that had been listening to him said, "Pardner, you sure can play that guitar."

Ownie acted like he didn't hear him, but he looked this man over pretty good. He was God knew how old, anywhere from thirty to sixty, you couldn't tell because he had drank enough tanglefoot to raise the Platte a foot. He looked like he had the consumption, and his old snag teeth couldn't chew nothing tougher than chicken, but you bet he thought he was some kind of a cowboy. He had the boots and the hat all right.

But there was no rope calluses on his hands, and no stirrup chafes on his boots, and this is how you can tell if a man has been working cows lately. Ownie wondered if he was getting a hunch about this fella, but he just laid down in his blanket and let V.G. snuggle up to him.

The man wouldn't go away. "I wonder if I could ask you where you got that guitar," he said.

"You can ask," Ownie said.

"I will then, where'd you get it?" the man said.

"Do you say it ain't mine?" Ownie said, and set up. "Who are you to be saying it ain't my guitar?"

He chunked a piece of wood on the fire to brighten it up, and he give this old bum a mountain-man stare, and this old bum said, "Bristol's the name, Hart Bristol, why good God, nothing is farther from my mind. It just looked like one that used to belong to a friend of mine."

"Well it ain't," Ownie said. "I bought it from a Q section boss less than a month ago."

This Hart Bristol give a kind of a lurch and a sigh, and he

got up and excused himself and went over and set down at the next fire. Ownie whispered to himself, "So your name is Hart Bristol, well that's a good start, I wonder which one you are? Not the gunfighter sure as hell. Mr. Bristol, your days is numbered, you son of a bitch."

He had the guitar wrapped up in a length of dry goods, and just for meanness he unwrapped it again and set down to play and sing. He knowed it had hit Bristol hard when he said he had bought it from the Q section boss, well let him set there and listen to it a while longer.

The next night Bristol was back; it was just like he was haunted by that guitar, he just *had* to come stumbling over every time he heard Ownie hit it a lick. This went on for quite a few nights.

Then another old mountain man showed up, and come like a bee to Ownie's fire, a real old-timer gone loony like all of them old ones is. Ownie let him sleep there. His name was Pat Edgerton, and he knowed about a gray stallion that had been stole by the Indians in the Uintahs, and had got away from them and went wild. The Mormons would pay five thousand dollars to get that horse back.

The next morning he started talking about that gray stallion again, so Ownie run him away, and Pat Edgerton went over to another camp and began talking about it, and Ownie packed up his camp and left. He told Blind Bosch he would be gone awhile, and might not be back at all, and Blind said, "I expected it, and it's too bad because you have the touch. I'll prove it to you. Here, see if you can pick this lock."

He handed Ownie a lock, and Ownie fiddled around with it awhile, with some wires and the blade of his knife and an awl and some stiff paper, and in a minute he popped it open. Blind said, "There you are, that's one of the best locks on the market, nobody has ever picked it in less than ten minutes before."

"Why did you do that?" Ownie said.

"To give you something to think about, mountain man," Blind said. "You could be a good house robber or a good locksmith, either one. Think about that."

"I may be back," Ownie said.

He bought a chunk of beef and took it back out to his camp. He took out my two-edged hunting knife and stropped it on his moccasin like a mountain man, and then sliced this beef up and began smoking it. Soon as he set down to unwrap his guitar, Hart Bristol come over and made himself to home beside the fire.

"I bet you're heading for the Uintahs," he said.

Ownie plumb ignored him. In a minute, Bristol said, "That crazy old bastard wanted a pardner to help catch that gray horse, but I wouldn't fool around with an old fool like him. I'd go pardners with you though."

"There ain't no gray horse," Ownie said.

"Yes there is, I've heard about him before," Bristol said.

"It's just a lot of talk," Ownie said, and it was, because he'd heard about the Gray Ghost as far back as Little Rock, when he was only thirteen years old. Maybe there was such a horse once, but he'd of been thirty years old by now, and anyway if the Mormons couldn't catch him, nobody could.

"If it's just a lot of talk," Bristol said, "where are you fixing to go?"

It took Ownie until almost noon the next day to smoke his meat, and when he packed it up and throwed his guitar and blanket on his back, here come Hart Bristol again.

"Take me with you," he said. "I want to go pardners with you."

"If I wanted a pardner it wouldn't be you," Ownie said. "What good would you be to anybody?"

"I used to break horses for outfits in Nebraska and Dakota," Bristol said. "I been in a streak of bad luck, but it's time it changed, and if it turns good for me, it'll turn good for you too. Your luck always hits bottom sometime and starts back up, don't it?"

Ownie never did admit he was going after the gray horse. It seemed to him that his pitiful hangdog admirer, Hart Bristol, was just purely bewitched by that guitar. That guitar started me on my downfall, Bristol was saying to himself, and now it's my charm to change my luck back.

Ownie didn't know how he knowed this, but he did, so sure in his soul it was another fit of extasy in him. A hunch is one thing, anybody can have a hunch, but a fit of extasy is different. It's like drawing aces back to back, and waiting for the third one, and it drops on the fifth card, and you just *know* the other man is setting there with a king buried to match the pair showing.

"I'm going," Ownie said. "I can't help if you go along, you old fool."

He just walked Bristol's hind end off. In a week or ten days, Bristol was toughened to it a little better, and being shut off from the whisky, he healthed up whether he wanted to or not. But by then they was high up in the Rockies, right where Ownie wanted them to be. Ownie led Bristol all over, back and forth and up and down.

It wasn't distance he wanted, it was for Bristol to blab something. Bristol wasn't no walking man, but he was sure a talking man. Something was eating at his mind, and he couldn't fetch it out and he couldn't leave it lay there. He was too tired to talk until Ownie fed him, but the minute Ownie got the guitar out, Bristol started talking. He didn't talk about anything in particular. He just rambled, everything from how his family had to eat acorns when the Yanks burned them out when he was a kid, to an old sow that had sixty-six pigs for them in four years, two litters a year.

Not once did Liddie come to see Ownie in a fit of extasy. Bristol just talked her away.

They was up about eight thousand feet the afternoon the fog come in on them. One minute, it was bright and clear around them and the clouds was sliding along overhead, the next, they couldn't see each other ten feet away. The wind was just like ice, not very strong, but it drilled in.

"Have to camp," Ownie said, because a mountain man never said no more than he had to.

"Let's try to get back down below it," Bristol kind of whimpered. "I ain't skeered of lightning or anything else, but I'm superstitious about fog. We could make us a torch out of something."

Ownie just grunted. Bristol felt around until he found some brush, and he got his knife out and cut a torch, and he borried Ownie's flint and steel and somehow got it to burning. But all it done was blind both of them.

"A-a-a-ah hell, no good, no good!" Bristol said. His teeth began to chatter. "Let's make a fire. Fog just drives me crazy! How about a fire?"

Ownie just grunted. Bristol felt around until he found a little old bush growing. He couldn't get Ownie to help him cut it, and he couldn't put the torch down to cut it himself, and he just had to set fire to it where it growed. It didn't burn very good or last very long, and then it was dark again, and all he could do was try to find Ownie in the dark, and set there shivering beside him like a kid that's scared of the dark.

Ownie retch over and unwrapped his guitar, and Bristol said, "God, man, don't play tonight, not in this fog, man, come on!"

Ownie just grunted. Bristol felt around for some more brush and couldn't find any. He couldn't see anything, but he knowed Ownie was still holding the guitar.

"I ask you man to man, don't play it," Bristol said.

Ownie just grunted and fixed his fingers the way he wanted them on the frets, and he drawed his right thumbnail across the strings real slow, *tim, tam, tom, tum, toom!* Bristol let out a bleat and catched hold of his arm.

"I asked you man to man not to!" he said.

Ownie hooked a fingernail under one string and give it a good tug and let go, and quivered his left finger on the fret, and it went *toom-m-m, woom-woom-woom-m-m, wah-wah-toom-m-m-m-m* until it died out. And he thought, Here is where we come out of the chute a-bucking.

"Did you ever commit a terrible crime?" Bristol said. "I tell you nobody knows how it can haunt you, and you get into it drunker than a skunk, a thing you wouldn't do in a thousand years sober. The man that owned that guitar, he was the son of a bitch that got me into it."

Ownie just grunted. Bristol said, "Listen, I'll tell you about it, and you tell me who's to blame. *He* wasn't drunk, you bet your boots on that, he was stone sober, the son of a bitch. He leaned that guitar up against a rock and said, 'Let's go down and jolly them girls around a little, and warm our shanks.' And by God picked it up again afterward without even wiping that old man's blood off'n his hands."

It just poured out. The man with the guitar was Capistrano Erland, born in San Juan Capistrano, and a sailor by trade until he got tired of it. Bristol and Capistrano met on a haying crew near Grand Island, Nebraska, the B Bar B. When they got laid off come fall, they decided to go to Denver because it was a good town to be out of work in.

They got as far as Mooney before winter set in, and there they bought a pint to warm up on, and the next thing they knowed they was broke, and Sheriff Abe Whipple was giving all of them two and a half minutes to get out of town. He didn't know any of the others but Capistrano Erland, but the others turned out to be Jimmy Rackstraw and Doc Harper. They had got friendly somehow on his and Capistrano's whisky.

They all ended up out at the blowhole. Ownie almost let out a yell when he heard them other two names. He knowed Jimmy Rackstraw himself, from when they both worked for a while on the Roofed Lazy 8. He could barely remember him, but he knowed the name.

Doc Harper's name was well advertised among them that kept up with the legends of the speed-gun artists. Doc had the name of being one of the best. Ownie hadn't heard about him being in the pen, but that's where he went, for killing a man in Wichita.

These four holed up out there at the blowhole, four prime specimens of the blowholer, drifters blowed together by an ill wind as the saying goes. Doc had an idee for making some money, and they had to have money or starve. It was a long cold ride to Denver on an empty gut.

"Doc said he knowed a preacher in Mooney that had been a convict himself," Bristol said. "He said he hit this preacher up for a stake, and was turned down just because he'd been liquoring up a little, and the son of a bitch just dripped fat like a goose, he was so rich. He said the four of us could pull it off easy, and hold him until his father-in-law come up with ten thousand dollars."

Nobody would of took any such fool plan serious except a bunch of saddle bums, especially if they knowed how hard it was to pry a dime out of Cal Venaman. The plan was to ride to my place and shoot me through the window, because Doc said I was a no-good son of a bitch anyway.

Capistrano would ride into Mooney, him being the cleanest one, and tell Rolf that Doc Harper was dying out at my place, and wanted to make his peace with God. That would fetch Rolf out if anything would.

It was only too bad they didn't keep their minds on their business, because killing me has been tried, and nobody gets past my dogs. I been an outlaw myself, and I know who to trust, and so do my dogs. I would of learned them a lesson about who to fool around with, and them Swiverton murders wouldn't of happened.

But on their way to my place, they seen this mover's camp and decided to jolly the girls around. Bristol remembered every little thing that happened.

Capistrano drawed a blank at first, because the girl he chased pulled him off'n his horse and got away, and he had to come back and take leavings. Bristol and Harper and Rackstraw all had a shot at the old pap, and it was Rackstraw that quirted Hoot.

All four of them helped kill Alice. Bristol said he couldn't forget, it was so awful. "I can't describe it," he said, "and you couldn't believe it unless you seen her."

Ownie said, "I did see her, you son of a bitch, what do you think I've got you up here all to myself for?"

It was a mistake to blurt it out like that with the guitar still on his lap, but he couldn't help it. Bristol had some hair-trigger nerves himself, and they told him right now that he had picked the wrong man to ease his conscience with, and what to do about it.

Bristol kicked out and catched Ownie in the mouth with the

heel of his boot, and Ownie rolled back and pulled my good two-edged knife out, and he heard the *whk-k-kng* of Bristol getting his own knife out, and he thought what a hell of an avenger he was to get caught like this.

If he was as good as dead, he might as well take his chances, so he come up hitting and slashing, and once their knives clashed and he seen sparks. It was just spooky, them two knife-fighting up there in the fog in the night, but he seen that he had the best knife anyway. Bristol cut his coat a little for him before Ownie made a lucky grab and catched his knife arm by the wrist.

He started to bend it back, and now he could laugh right in Bristol's face because he had the strength over Bristol. He said, "You son of a bitch, I ain't going to kill you yet, I'll see you live a long, long time, hurting every minute of it. But start thinking about it now why don't you, because I know tricks an Indian wouldn't of used."

Bristol give a big jumping jerk and began to scream, but it wasn't a fit, it was old V.G. that come up at him without a sound, purely like a wolf. Ownie couldn't see a thing but shadows as Bristol jerked loose from him, and at more than four feet, not even shadows.

Bristol catched hold of Ownie's leg, and Ownie felt himself sliding. He kicked the leg as hard as he could as fast as he could, and he shook Bristol off, and he managed to stop sliding.

But Bristol didn't. He just kept sliding and sliding and screaming and screaming, and then there was one last bloodcurdler that thinned out fast as he stopped sliding and fell free, and then it was cut off short when he hit somewhere a long way down. A real long way.

Ownie thought he had lost them both into a Rocky Mountain gorge, Bristol and his dog as well, but then V.G. come scrambling up the slope on his belly, clawing like he was digging out a badger, and he got up to where it was safe. Ownie laid there quite a while, and then he began squirming up one little squirm at a time, prob'ly half an hour to climb the length of his body.

But she leveled out under him at last, and V.G. was licking his face, and he could get up on his knees and crawl after the dog to where he had left his blanket and guitar. He just rolled up in the blanket and laid there and shivered, with the dog right next to him.

Well that is two that got away from me, he thought to himself, but I ain't going to complain about my luck, not after making it back up here.

It was noon the next day before the fog cleared. Him and Bristol had been stopped in about the worst place they could of picked. Down below there was nothing but an ocean of fog with the sun shining on it, and the trail wasn't more than five or six feet wide, and then this sharp short slope, and then nothing.

He took it slow going down. He had to camp on the trail another night when the fog closed in, but the next morning it cleared up nice and bright and cold and windy. He let V.G. pick the way, mostly by smelling the tracks they'd made coming up. Finely they reached the bottom.

Ownie's coat was just slashed to pieces, and V.G. had a cut on his ribs.

But Ownie could look back and see the eagles and hawks and buzzards starting to spiral down, now that the fog had cleared out. Hart Bristol had fell about five hundred feet, and then had hit a rock outcrop, and then bounced another two hundred feet before landing in a tree.

There he hung, head down, waiting for the birds to pick him. "A quicker death than you deserve," Ownie said to him. "That's two of you got away from me. Well better luck next time."

CHAPTER 12

Heading back to Denver, Ownie didn't feel so good and he didn't know why, but he didn't seem to have no strength, and he couldn't sleep well at night nor wake up easy in the morning. He passed by a place where a man was running cattle in a nice little mountain valley, and the winter had held off, and he was getting in some lucky late hay.

He thought he'd ask for a job, and he done it, and the rancher didn't exactly kill the fatted calf for a worthless no-account mountain man. But after Ownie worked there a couple of days, and the man seen he could and would do the job, he let Ownie take charge of the gang. His name was Jerry Clyde, and his brand was the JC, so of course naturally his place was known far and wide as the Jesus Christ.

Ownie stayed with him almost to Christmas. It was like his mind had went to sleep on him and the rest of him hadn't. He couldn't make up his mind to anything. He felt sheepish and guilty, like he was dodging his duty, and yet it was just the purest kind of pleasure to get out here and make this winter hay, and work his tail off.

Jerry knowed Ownie had something on his mind, and he give him every chance to talk about it, but he wasn't the kind of a man to pry. He let Ownie live in the bunkhouse, but he found a few chances to put him at jobs where he'd have to eat with the family. He had four little kids, three boys and a girl, and he let them hang around whenever Ownie was doing anything safe for kids, like shoeing horses or banking up around the house against winter.

Then finely one night, Liddie come back to Ownie. He hadn't seen her since before Hart Bristol come to his death up there in the mountains. He was out in the barn all night, waiting for a little pony of the kids to throw her colt. It come to him all of a sudden, what if it was him and Liddie had a place like this away to hell and gone by themselves, and kids of their own to raise, and so on.

And there she was. He had never seen her clearer, not even when they was together there in Mooney before he hit the vengeance trail. She was wearing a white waist she made for herself with Miss Liz's help, with a high ruffly collar, and a row of little pearl buttons down the front, and that black Indian hair was pulled back so her ears showed, and held by a little ribbon behind.

He'd only seen her that way once, on her way to church with Liz, when he was blundering around half drunk and had to slide behind a tree quick to keep her from seeing him. She looked so happy going to church, and Miss Liz looked so proud of her.

"Well hello there, Liddie," he said to her there in the barn, and in his vision you might say, she kind of smiled, and he thought for about a second that she was going to look straight at him and say something.

"I just figgered something out, Liddie," he said. "You want to know what it is? I always reckoned what made you so happy in Mooney was that people respected you. They didn't ever respect me, no not a bit, but they did you, and I was so proud of you because of that! You never knowed that, Liddie, but I was. I seen you in the jaws of hell, and I seen you come back, and I seen you just bud out like a rose bush when people respected you.

"But you know what, Liddie, that ain't the main thing, the main thing is you respect *yourself;* you got out of the wagon and you held up your head, and you vowed to live up to what your pap wanted for you. It's more important to respect yourself than to have people respect you, ain't it?

"Something else, Liddie, I disrespected myself all my life because of my mother, and now my eyes is open I'm so ashamed I could go sleep with the hogs, but it ain't going to be like that no more.

"I mean to respect *my*self too, and I hope others come to respect me like they do you, but if they don't I ain't going to blame my mother or my luck or anything, I'm going to take aim on self-respect and let the world go hang if it has to. This is what old Rolf means when he says look into your heart, well I reckon he ain't such a fool as he sounds at times, well I see you're going to fade away on me and my mare is straining to drop her baby, but I sure do appreciate your coming around.

"So long, Liddie, for tonight."

She did fade away all right, and he tussled with the little mare until he seen it was too much for him, and about one-thirty in the morning he went up to the house and stirred Jerry out, and later Jerry went up and got his wife, and the three of them finely got this nice big living he-colt out alive, and made it stand and suck. There just about ain't no nicer feeling than to win that kind of a battle, and see that colt stilting around, he thinks that box stall is his whole world and my ain't it big! But just wait until he can get outside, you think.

They had their breakfast about four-thirty of the morning, and Jerry got to telling him about this other place he had bought about thirty-five miles to the west five years ago, planning for his sister's husband to run it for him. The brother-in-law worked for a feed and seed company in Denver, and wasn't a bit happy, but when he checked out to work for Jerry, he come up eight hundred dollars short in his accounts.

"I made it up for him," Jerry said, "but you can't have a man like that running your place and handling your own money. I been running it myself in a half-ass way, but in mountain country, you either run your property with an iron hand or it goes back to the brush."

"That's true, it does all right," Ownie said. "It goes wilderness, and the bears get your calves, and snow breaks down your fences, and the wild studs steal your saddle horses. Ain't everybody can ranch in mountains."

"You could. It's too bad you ain't a family man, Ownie," Jerry said, "because there's a furnished four-room house there, and a good buggy and team goes with it, and I'd start you with fifty hens and a dozen ducks and a drake. I'd go as high as fifty dollars a month and ten per cent of the increase for the right man."

"I ain't the right man, Jerry," Ownie said. "In fact it's time for me to move on, but I thank you anyhow."

He dickered with Jerry over what was owed him, and rode out of there on a small but real good five-year-old gelding by the name of Bud, with a good saddle, and a nice big heavy sheepskin coat that Jerry had got too fat for.

He was in good shape for money and things, but the main

thing was, he could get on with his job of finding Jimmy Rackstraw and Doc Harper, and killing them. He seen finely what had just about paralyzed him for a while.

He looked into his heart and seen that he'd been just plain scared to death by nearly going over the edge up there with Hart Bristol. Ownie knowed he wasn't a coward, or never had been before anyways. But it took all the nerve in him to face what made him scared of dying now.

Liddie.

Yes, when he started out to ask himself why life was suddenly that dad-blamed important, the answer was Liddie. Once you've drug your badger out of the hole, you can rassle with him, and Ownie knowed he wasn't the man for her, nothing was surer in life than that. Escape the wagons, and then marry the likes of *him*?

Oh no, he thought to himself as he rode on to Denver, my head is clear now, I've got my nerve back, I won't be dreaming no more impossible dreams, so on with the job cowboy. . . .

It had to be Jimmy Rackstraw that talked with a Scotch brogue. It sounded just like him to Ownie. Jimmy was one of them sneaks with a big mouth that's always in trouble, but you never catch him in a fight, he'll ride you as long as you let him, but just call him up short and see what he says.

"Me? Why what're you mad at *me* for? What did *I* ever do to you? Call you names, why *I* wouldn't call *you* no names, can't you take a little *fun*? You ain't got no better friend than me, stop faunching and let's shake hands, no I ain't going to fight you over no such foolishness."

Jimmy had knowed better than to let his big mouth run on about Ownie, in fact Ownie barely remembered him, and wasn't sure he'd know him if he seen him again.

But Jimmy could of picked up the Scotch brogue from Scotty Dundy, and it was the kind of a thing he'd use to make fun of Scotty with, and Scotty too good natured to know he was being insulted. According to Hart Bristol, it was old weak-kneed Jimmy that hung back, and didn't want to rough the girls up at first, only when Alice got to crying and screaming, he—but it was something Ownie didn't want to think about.

But in some ways, Jimmy Rackstraw was the worst of the four.

Just outside of Denver, Ownie met an old cowboy who was so bitter he started hollering before they was fifty yards apart. "You got a gun on under that coat?" he said. "If you have, just kiss yourself good-by."

"Why should I do that?" Ownie said.

"Them Goddamn Denver police, that's why," the old man said. "They got a new rule now, you can't wear a gun, not even a holster, what kind of a law is that? They'll take it away from you and kick you out of town, well they don't have to kick me out, I hope I never see Denver again, with their Goddamn narrow-minded police."

"I don't pack a gun," Ownie said. "Well so long, old-timer, see you at roundup time as the saying goes."

"Not in Denver you won't," the old man said.

Rolf Ledger was always in favor of a law against packing a gun, but Ownie never heard of nobody else doing it, and it kind of surprised him that a law-abiding town like Denver would stoop so low. Not that it meant anything to him, so long as he got his chance to catch Jimmy Rackstraw and torture him to death with my fine two-edged knife.

He got in late in the afternoon, and decided he'd go and see Blind Bosch first, and find out if it was any use coming back to work there. There was a saloon on the corner down the block from Blind Bosch's place, and it had a good hitch rack, so he thought he'd tie his horse Bud up there, and walk to Blind's place.

There was this policeman, Virg Kling, that walked the beat there, and Ownie had got to know him. Virg didn't recognize Ownie when he seen him. He said, "Hold up there, cowboy, before you tie your horse."

"Sure, Virg, what's the trouble?" Ownie said.

Virg said, "Well I'll be damned, the mountain man himself, what are you doing on a horse?"

"I learned to ride," Ownie said. "A man put me up on a little pony and held my hand until I got done crying, try it yourself sometime. What's this foolishness about not wearing a gun, anyway?"

"Open your coat up and let's make sure," Virg said. "If you was my own brother, I'd have to search you. Well all right, you ain't armed, go in peace as the Good Book says. We had four cowboy fights since Saturday night, or wars is a better word. I never seen such quarrelsome people, just for the fun of it. Come winter they're all broke, and then they find whisky somewhere, they can't eat but they can always raise a drink, and then they have to prove what dangerous men they are. The people of Denver are sick and tired of it."

"I can see their point of view," Ownie said, "but I don't drink and I ain't armed, Virg."

Virg went into the saloon on the corner, Danny Burgoon's place, and Ownie tied his horse and started to walk down to see Blind Bosch. He almost got there, when this fella come out of a place with a sign Gents Furnished Rooms, and started for the corner.

Jimmy Rackstraw!

Jimmy wasn't in range clothes except he still wore boots. He had a long brown overcoat, and a wool cap with earflaps, and he was smoking a big cigar. He looked like a town man for sure, but there wasn't no possibility of a mistake, this was Jimmy Rackstraw.

It took Ownie some time to get his wits back, he didn't know how long, but quite a while because when he woke up, Jimmy was just running up the steps of Danny Burgoon's saloon. And Ownie was suddenly shaking all over, the way Jimmy must of shook when them other three said let's go rough up them girls a little, like his nerve had just left him completely.

What kind of an avenger am I anyway, he said to himself. He unbuttoned one button of his coat, and one of his shirt, and made sure he could get at the knife. He went after Jimmy right there in the heart of Denver, but he might as well of been Blind Bosch himself, because at the bottom of Danny

Burgoon's place he bumped into a strange policeman and didn't see him at all.

"Hold it there, my boy, who do you think you're bumping into?" the policeman said.

"Excuse me," Ownie said, "but I'm in a hurry."

"So am I," the policeman said. "Coat button not buttoned and the right hand inside, now that's interesting, let's have a look at your gun, my boy, like a good boy."

"I ain't got no gun," Ownie said.

He thought he was going to faint, but he didn't. The policeman retch in and took the knife, and said, "A knife is it? By God, you're a cool one, but we'll warm the ass of you in jail a few days, how's that my boy?"

I can't do it, Ownie said to himself. At the last moment I'm yellow-bellied, a hell of an avenger, but at least he ain't going to get away, I swear to God that. . . . He said, "Listen, there's a man in the saloon there that's wanted for murder. Ask Virgil Kling. He's in there now. Get Virg out here, he'll believe me, Virg knows me, I tell you that son of a bitch is a wanted murderer in there!"

And all he could feel was thankfulness that it had been took out of his hands this way. The policeman trusted him, although not very far, because he held Ownie and sent a boy into the saloon to bring Virg out.

"What do you mean, a murderer, mountain man?" Virg said. "I know everybody in there, they're regulars, not a murderer among them. What kind of a sandy are you trying to run, mountain man?"

"I can point him out to you," Ownie said.

"You do exactly that," Virg said.

"He'll be armed, too."

"He better not be. You show us."

Ownie stepped up and took a quick peek by opening the door and letting it close. "Him," he said. "The one at the end, with the ear flaps and the cigar."

"Oh hell, that's only Dutch Johnny," Virg said. "They call him that because he can talk like a Dutchman until you'd swear he was one. He don't amount to a hill of beans, he works in the express company stables, but me and Francis Kennedy here knows him well, don't we, Francis?"

The other policeman said, "Not well enough to go his bond, Virgil my boy. Let's hear more of this from the mountain man."

Ownie said, "I swear to God, let me smoke him out, I promise I can do it! He helped kill an old man and a young girl, the filthiest kind of murder, it makes me sick just to think of it. Sheriff Whipple, Mooney County, got out some dodgeroos on it. I'll tell you what you go and do, ask him if he's a Scotchman, get him to talking Scotch!"

"Now wait a minute, Virgil my boy!" Kennedy said. "I've seen the paper he speaks of, a man with a Scotch brogue, and there's a bit of a reward on him I think. Can it hurt to find out?"

"You stay here, mountain man," Virg said.

They talked it over between them, and they made Ownie wait. Virg went back into the saloon and went over to the door of the can and waited there, so he was behind Jimmy Rackstraw. In a minute, Francis Kennedy went in and took off his overcoat, and unbuttoned the flap of his holster on the sly. He walked up to Jimmy.

"A cold day, Johnny boy," he said. "As me kinsmen in Scotland say, a r-r-raw, drear-r-r-ry day wi'out a wee drappie to war-r-rum the bones."

Old silly Jimmy grinned a big silly grin, and his big mouth took charge and led him right down the chute for fools. He said, "Ah, be ye a Scot, man? Aye, 'tis a cold one, vur-r-ra cold, God pity the puir-r-r," and that was all the farther he got.

"Son of a bitch, the mountain man is right," Francis Kennedy said. "Keep your hands in sight, I arrest you on suspicion of murder—*oh no you don't!*"

Jimmy went for his gun, the worst thing he could of done unless he wanted to die. Prob'ly he'd seen them dodgeroos of Abe Whipple's, and knowed his Scotch accent was his trademark of murder, and realized he had shot off his big mouth once too often.

The two policemen was facing each other, with Jimmy

Rackstraw between them, so they had a problem about shooting. Virg Kling dropped down on one knee and fired upward, and he catched Jimmy where the neck meets the left shoulder, and tore out about a pound of his meat. Francis Kennedy shot him close to the crotch, not right in it but close enough to make him a soprano if he lived.

Jimmy never got off a shot. Francis Kennedy took his gun away from him, while Virg went to get an ambulance. The ambulance got there, but then one of the horses slipped on the ice and went down, and they was twenty minutes getting him up. A doctor from down the street plugged up Jimmy's bullet holes, while Ownie stood there and talked to Jimmy about the murder.

Jimmy denied everything. He said he didn't know Hart Bristol or Capistrano Erland or Doc Harper, hadn't never heard of them, hadn't been in Mooney for three years, and hadn't never been in any trouble with the law.

"You're a lying son of a bitch," Ownie said. "You fired one shot into the old man, and you abused that poor girl worse than anybody, and you're the one that plugged Capistrano when he run out of luck and crippled his horse."

"I swear I didn't, Ownie," Jimmy said. "Why are you doing this to me, Ownie? What did I ever do to you, Ownie? You and me was always friends."

"All right, go to the gallus with that lie on your soul on top of everything else," Ownie said.

Jimmy looked at the doctor that was patching him up and said, "Is it bad? Oh how I hurt! Will I live? It ain't fatal, is it? Oh God I hope it ain't fatal."

"You're through at stud," the doctor said, "but you won't die."

All the way to the hospital in the ambulance, Jimmy kept swearing he wasn't no murderer, and so forth, but then they chloroformed him to sew him up, and when he come out of the chloroform he was blabbing away for all he was worth about the murders. There was two nurses helping, and the things he told, one of them nurses had to go out and throw up, and it's pretty hard to make an old-time nurse in a police hospital throw up.

That night Jimmy ripped his bandages off and deliberately bled himself to death. "The double-crossing son of a bitch, he beat us out of five hundred dollars," Virg Kling said. "Look, the bulletin says delivered alive to undersigned, how do you like that?"

"I'm sorry about that," Ownie said, "but I'm glad he died the way he did. Him and them other two, Hart Bristol and Capistrano Erland, have got a lot to talk over now, wherever they are. And I bet I know where."

"What are you going to do now, mountain man?" Virg said.

"Don't call me that. I just fixed up this way to find these bastards, and it worked," Ownie said. "But now I'm going to get my hair cut and a shave, and go home."

"What about the other one, the gunfighter?" Virg said.

Ownie throwed up his hands. "I don't know," he said. "I ain't the man to avenge nobody, that's for positive. I can plan as mean as anybody alive, but at the last minute, somehow I lose heart. Just one other thing, boys. If you come across Doc Harper, don't give him the chance that you give Rackstraw!"

"We didn't give Rackstraw any chance," Francis Kennedy said.

"It was still too much," Ownie said.

CHAPTER 13

There was this show come to town in April, the Ambrose Repertory Company, or ARC Players as they liked to be knowed as, and they wanted to use the Methodist church, and would pay two dollars a night for it. The board said they'd be guided by their pastor, and Rolf talked it over with Madison Monroe Ambrose, and Ambrose said it would only be selected passages from Shakespeare, and they always left out the gamy parts when they played in a church.

Rolf said he wasn't up on Shakespeare, but there was parts of the Old Testament that would curl your hair, Lot's daughters for instance, and Ambrose said, "Right you are, Parson, we see eye to eye, nothing that will offend the Methodist conscience will be presented, not even the death of Desdemona, and there goes one of our best ones right out the window."

Madison Monroe Ambrose was sixty-eight years old then, and it took a quart a day just to keep steam up in his boilers, but he hardly ever showed he'd took a drink. He was a mighty spry man, quick-minded and a good talker, and he'd been all over the world. He said he had never played before the Queen, but he had entertained her soldiers in Egypt, India, and the Bahamian Islands, and he'd met the Empress Eugénie when times was better for both him and the Empress, and he'd met three Spanish-American presidents, one of which still survived. Me and him got to be pretty good friends. He paid cash for his drink and never made a scene, and that's a good enough recommendation for anybody.

Paying cash for his whisky might of been one reason the ARC Players went broke in Mooney, and had to stay there until they earned their fare out of town; anyway they was still there when Ownie Cope finely come back. He come to my place first, about daybreak.

"I'll take my gun back now, Pete," was the first thing he said to me.

He handed over my knife, and I looked it over and seen it was in good shape, and I said, "I reckon there's no use asking for my dog back, he'll be your dog now."

Ownie said, "I'd miss him and he'd miss me. I wish I could work out a deal on him that I could afford."

"Go ahead and keep him," I said. "Nothing makes you less profit than trying to keep a dog that don't want to stay. I reckon you'll want to turn in now, if you've rode all night."

"No, I camped at the blowhole," Ownie said. "That place has sure become disinhabited. It don't look like nobody has camped there for a long time."

"Abe or Thad rides out there every time they're in the neighborhood, and they've had to wet down a couple of fires and kick a couple of rumps," I said, "but the blowhole has got a bad reputation, and is knowed far and wide as a good place to miss."

"There was shells in this gun when I left it with you," Ownie said. I give him some shells, and he loaded up the gun and buckled on the holster, and said, "It's sure a lonesome old place to camp. You could just about believe in ghosts there, Pete. You can just about hear ghostly footsteps."

He got off on a long story he'd heard, about a man down in Honduras who owned the worst old sandy blowhole anywhere, that he'd heard about in Denver. They had a scourge of dogs that went wild down there, and they was killing off livestock and even people, and the government put a bounty on them and got just thousands of them killed off.

He said this man that owned the Honduras blowhole, he offered the government his land to bury them dogs in free of charge, and they took him up on it, and he just worked his hind end off for a year, burying them thousands of dogs. Then he just set back a few years, and then planted himself a bananner grove, and that blowhole had become so fertile he became a big rich important bananner king.

He said he didn't see no other solution for the blowhole we had, it had to be made fertile some way, and get a crop started there, and wipe the blight off'n the face of Creation. I said, "We're a mite short on dogs for that, and you'd play hell raising bananners here anyway, but keep thinking, Ownie, you'll come up with something."

"Same old joker," Ownie said. "Sweet clover would fertile up that Goddamn hellhole, if you could get it started. If you sowed it every year, sooner or later you'd get a wet year, and it'd take holt."

I said he was getting warm, it was better than the bananner idee, and I'd back anything that had a ghost of a chance to wipe out the blowhole. He grinned more like his old self, and said he reckoned he'd go on into town.

He was a lot thinner, and was shaved clean, and had a haircut, and some decent clothes, and although I didn't know it then, more than a hundred and fifty dollars in greenbacks in his kick. He rode a good little horse with a good saddle, and his old familiar worthless charm was almost entirely gone. He didn't offer to tell me nothing about where he'd been or what he'd been doing, and you sure don't ask in my position.

I told him if he was going into Mooney, there was a man I wanted him to be sure to look up, Madison Monroe Ambrose, who was staying on credit at the Antlers Hotel. He said he would, but it was more of a sociable answer than anything else, because he didn't ask the man's name again and looked like he was just giving me a polite answer.

He didn't get into town until noon, he dortled along so slow. He went straight to Sheriff Abe Whipple's house, and asked Edna, his wife, if Abe was to home. She said he sure was, and as companionable as a bear with a sore tail, and to go on out back and take his chances.

Abe had run out in his sock feet a couple of nights back, to pitch some rocks at some cats that was loving it up in their lilac bushes, and stepped on a piece of glass and bled like a pig. Doc Tattnal had to take four stitches to fix him up, and he told him not to set that foot on the ground for two weeks.

Abe was in an old willer chair, and Thad Rust was spading up his garden for him, and grumbling about it, and threatening to quit the county service for good. Abe didn't act like he was surprised to see Ownie, and the truth is, it took a good deal to surprise that old man. Ownie asked if he could talk to him, and Abe told Thad to get his hind end to the post office and see if there was any mail, and then go see if two drunks in the jail had sobered up enough to know their own names.

"Look at that foot!" Abe said, when Thad had went. "Felled

in my prime by a piece of glass, me that smoked out the Patterson brothers and Eben Twiss with a pretend gun! Did I ever tell you that story, Ownie?"

"Where you used a straight piece of brush for a sawed-off 10-gauge? Yes I heard it," Ownie said.

"You act like you don't believe it," Abe said.

"I believe it all right," Ownie said. "I'll believe anything after what I been through. If you've got the time, Abe, I'd like to tell you a story of my own."

"What else have I got except time, with my foot in this shape?" Abe said.

Ownie started telling him everything that had happened since they last met, how he willfully disregarded Abe's own warning to take the vengeance trail. How he met Charley Polk and they found the remains of Capistrano Erland and his horse. Abe said yes, Charley finely got around to confiding in him about that pile of human bones, although this was the first he'd had a name for them.

He told how he made out to be a mountain man, and Abe said that wasn't no play-acting, Ownie was as near to a worthless mountain man as anybody he knowed, all he had to do was not shave or cut his hair or take a bath, and he'd fool anybody. Ownie said that was just what he'd done.

He told Abe about getting a job with Blind Bosch, and keeping that a secret from them others that was jungled up out there, because no mountain man would take a job and it would of ruined his disguise. He told Abe about how the guitar drove Hart Bristol crazier than he was to begin with, and about how it was 50-50 who was going to knife who up there in the fog, until V.G. moved to adjourn by slashing into Bristol and tipping him over the edge.

He told Abe it got to be a proposition where he wasn't really looking for the other two, just killing time there on Jerry Clyde's place, and would just as soon of put off a showdown a year or two longer. Only just about the first person he run into in Denver was Jimmy Rackstraw, and you couldn't even really say the policemen killed Jimmy, he had a good chance to come out of it except for his knockers being shot off, when he ripped them bandages off.

"That just took all the heart out of me, Abe, can you understand that?" Ownie said. "You hear all the time about these people taking the vengeance trail: there was this Walcott kid in Wyoming for instance, sixteen years old when his daddy was bushwhacked by rustlers, remember?"

"Yes, I heard that story," Abe said.

"That kid stalked them rustlers for eight years before he got the last one, but he got them finely."

"Four notches on his gun finely," Abe said, "and then he come home to find his mother happily married to another man, and he killed that man too, and went outlaw, and a couple of years later was shot down in a bank holdup by the Royal Mounties."

"That's the case," Ownie said.

Abe sighed and cursed his foot some more, and said, "That's about how them stories usually end up. You hear the noble part, somebody with a brain like a rooster vows to go to the end of the earth to uphold his honor. But you don't generally hear about him flopping around in some drunken flophouse later, although that's the way it ends, because he didn't have the brains of a rooster to begin with."

Abe said, "I told you, Ownie, this was a public crime not a private feud, but you wouldn't listen, no you had to jackass yourself up in a disguise, like them knights of old, that made so much damn unnecessary trouble for everybody. It serves you right."

"I admit it," Ownie said. "I've heard of some curious vengeances in my time, but I'll be beat if this ain't the most ridiculous one on record. Jackass is right."

Abe cursed his foot some more, and said, "How about Doc Harper? Seems to me an up-and-coming gunfighter like you used to be, Doc Harper would be hard to pass up."

Ownie leaned over with his elbows on his knees and his cheeks on his fists, and stared down at the ground. "I'll see if I can line it out for you, Abe," he said, "and you tell me if you see any sense to it."

"I'll do that, never fear," Abe said.

Ownie said, "Some people can commit any kind of a crime and get away with it; they're like a doctor cutting into you, they don't think of the pain or the blood, getting the job done is all that counts, do you follow me?"

"Professionals you mean," Abe said.

"I reckon that's it," Ownie said. "Yes, that's the word I was looking for, professional; if you don't make your living at it, don't try to operate on people and don't commit no horrible felonies, because by God the odds is against you, and your own conscience is your worst enemy. Now I know you're going to say that a conscience is the last thing in the world you'd expect in people like Capistrano Erland and Hart Bristol and Jimmy Rackstraw."

"I wouldn't say anything of the kind, they're human beans same as anybody else, sons of Adam as well as sons of bitches," Abe said. "I understand what you mean, Ownie, God damn this foot of mine anyway."

"Well then," Ownie said, "you don't have to chase them people down and gun them to death, or carve them up like a mountain man, the way I was going to. You don't even have to run them down and point your finger at them and say, 'Guilty, you son of a bitch!' because in their own minds, every stranger they see is doing that; the next face they see is going to be a man that knows the truth about them and will turn them in, do you foller me?"

"Clean to the line fence," Abe said. "All you done was speed things up a little, it appears to me. Not for Capistrano, his case was closed before you assumed your damn ignorant jurisdiction, but at least Bristol and Rackstraw. What you made happen to them, it would of happened anyway sooner or later, their own guilty consciences would scream louder and louder in their own guilty ears, and they couldn't get drunk enough to drownd it out. Sooner or later it'd deadfall them."

"Right! You got the idee exactly," Ownie said. "Well then, why should I do any favors for Doc Harper? Let him live and suffer that much longer. Anyway the kind of luck I have as an avenger, some little six-year-old girl would stick her foot out just as we drawed, and he'd trip and fall with his head on a sharp rock anyway."

"Sometimes I almost have hope for you, Ownie," Abe said. "What are you going to do now?"

"I don't know yet," Ownie said. "I'm a pretty good locksmith, no don't say it, I know there's no locksmith in Mooney, but it ain't for me. I had to touch this town again somehow, kind of come a full circle; well, I've touched it and nothing is holding me. I got me some locksmith tools. Maybe I'll try Cheyenne or one of them big cities."

"Want me to tell you why?" Abe said. "Liddie."

Ownie nodded. "That's right, Liddie," he said.

"Your mother you mean?" Abe said.

Ownie said, "No, God rest her soul, I've quit fighting that devil too, I'm to blame for any thing I do, not her. I reckon my mother was no worse than some of Liddie's ancestors, or yours either for that matter. People is people, Abe, that's about how I size it up."

"I could tell you some things about my own family, say there's some corkers," Abe said. "I still don't know why you won't even go see her, though."

"Neither do I," Ownie said, "except that I know in my heart it would be a bad thing, and I ain't going to do it. For one thing, when old Liz Saymill dies, who is she going to leave all that money to?"

"Liddie prob'ly," Abe said.

"There you are," Ownie said.

Abe sighed and cursed his foot again, and said, "What are you going to do this evening? Reason I ask, Ownie, there's this big show in town, the Ambrose troupe as it's said professionally, and Edna went with some of her hen friends last night and said it's pretty good. I'd like to go if somebody would help me hobble around. I'm entitled on my badge to get us in free, so don't worry about squandering one of your precious two-bit pieces."

Ownie's idee was that a show was the last place in the world he felt like being, all he wanted to do was set under a bee tree and challenge his luck, but Abe had been pretty decent to him for a policeman, and he was a hard man to say no to at any time.

Ownie et dinner with Abe and Edna, and then him and Abe went down to the Methodist church, Abe hobbling along, leaning his weight on Ownie and cursing every step, and saying he never seen anybody clumsier than Ownie in his life, he might as well be leaning on a buffalo bull. Ownie said he was ready to turn back right now if Abe wasn't fully satisfied with the service he was getting, but they finely got there.

The lamps had already been blowed out, and Madison Monroe Ambrose was up there with one of them dazzling coal-oil reflecting spotlights on him, explaining how this funeral oration he was going to give next come about. It was just a funeral oration to the authorities, he said, but who was the authorities? Why the murderers of Caesar themselves, that was who. They had murdered Emperor Caesar and took over the government and God help anybody that took Caesar's side.

Well, he said, this fellow Marc Antony had been Caesar's friend, but he had been their friend too, Cassius and Casca and all of them, and they couldn't very well turn him down if he wanted to say a few kind words over the carcass of the diseased. "Now listen, friends," Madison Monroe Ambrose said, "and see if you don't think this is one of the most daring, as well as one of the cleverest, defiances of authority in history."

Well he really had them there, because this was a country settled by people who wouldn't of been here if they hadn't defied authority somewhere, and he dropped his voice down to a nice ringing growl, and looked down at where the coffin of Caesar would be, and then out over them people in the Methodist church like they was Romans, and began to say, "Friends, Romans, countrymen, lend me your ears, I come to *bury* Caesar, not to praise him, the evil that men do lives after them, the good is oft interred with their bones. So let it be with Caesar!"

Well this hit Ownie right where he lived, he liked nothing so much as a good successful honest double-crosser, and he was on Caesar's side to begin with, and when Ambrose said,

"So let it be with Caesar," he thought to himself why the hell with that, let's tear the town to pieces instead.

That Ambrose really had them gentled to the snaffle, there wasn't a sound in that whole churchful of people until he come to letting loose the dogs of war, and they seen it wasn't all going to blow over like they feared, and Rome was going to get a good tearing up after all. Well they just rose up and hollered, "Go to it!" and "Amen, amen," and "Give them hell there, boy," and it seemed to Ownie that this man Marc Antony must of been one of the prime sports in all of history.

Well then Ambrose had to rest while they moved the scenery around for the next act, and they went around and lit the lamps on both sides of the church, and Ownie let out this big sigh and sort of come sliding out of Rome a little at a time, you might say, and back to Mooney. He looked around him to see if there was anybody he knowed, and he got the surprise of his life suddenly, he really did.

It seemed to him that he was back on the vengeance trail somewhere, having a fit of extasy, and Liddie had come back to him. She had her black hair kind of loose on her head, but tied with a little ribbon behind, and she had on this white waist she'd made, with the high ruffly collar he liked so much on her.

Only this time she talked to him, for the first time in all his fits of extasy. She said, "Oh, Ownie, you came back, didn't you?"

Abe leaned over and said, "Why howdy there, Liddie, howdy, Liz, imagine running into you here. I reckon you remember Ownie Cope."

Liz started to sob all over the place, but she got out yes, she did seem to remember him, what a coincidence to meet, and so on. Ownie seen he'd been deadfalled worse than Cassius and Casca, God have mercy on their souls, but he didn't hardly see what he could do about it.

He said, "Yes, I come back, I don't know why except it was like I was being pulled by the bridle. I made a total complete mess of everything, but I'm back."

Liddie touched his cheek with the ends of her fingers, *she* didn't care how many people was watching, not that girl, and she said, "That's all that counts, you're back. You see prayer does help, I prayed every night you'd come to no harm, oh if you'd died, Ownie, if I'd had another grave to mourn—!"

"You knowed what I was doing?" he said.

Liz Saymill said, "You idiot, the dogs in the street knew and gossiped about it, you're as transparent as any other vain headstrong willful *thing* of a man, what do you care the evil you wreak, if your vanity is soothed? But so help me Father, Son, and Holy Ghost, you'll live up to your brief moment of holiness now, you renegade you!"

Ownie catched both sides of his head in his hands and said, "Goddlemighty, Miss Liz, you mean you'd stand for it yourself, me and her?"

"Out, out, out," she said.

Ownie got out, and Liddie got out, and the two of them went stumbling back through that church with the whole town watching, and then when he got her outside he couldn't make himself say it, he just dropped down on his knees and started kissing the ends of her fingers, until she made him stand up and do it right.

The Queen of England couldn't of done it with more style, no, nor the Empress Eugénie neither, the little girl from the wagons had them both choking on her dust. She whispered, "Whatever I am, Ownie, you saved my life, and I'm yours to the end, never forget that!" It wasn't quite that simple, a party by the name of Pete Heath had a little to do with saving her life, and so did Charley Polk and a few other people, but when she said it she believed it, and you couldn't hardly call it a lie.

They just forgot about the rest of the show, walking up and down in the dark in front of the church on that old steep brick sidewalk with tree roots sticking up through it. When Abe Whipple come hobbling out, cursing his bad foot, they was standing there looking at each other, him with his hands on her shoulders, Liddie holding onto his wrists. Just looking at each other.

"Well there you are," Abe said. "Here's somebody wants to meet you, Ownie, and then he has to go back and do up the second half of the show. Mr. Ambrose, this is Ownie Cope, Ownie, meet Mr. Madison Monroe Ambrose."

"Howdy," Ownie said, and started to turn his back, because he had more important things to do than talk to some old geezer with one foot in the grave.

"Yes, Mr. Cope, Pete Heath mentioned you. I've been so eager to meet you, I wonder if you're the son of Bessie Cope of St. Louis, I know she left a son by the name of Owen," Ambrose said.

All of the stars went out for Ownie, because he hadn't been long in the habit of forgiving his mother, and it hadn't took root very deep in him. He let go of Liddie and said, "My mother's name was Bessie, yes, what about it?"

"I knew her so well!" Ambrose said. "Your father too. You don't remember him I'm sure, he lost both legs at the knees in the war, and became a Mississippi river steamboat gambler. The most honest gambler on the river, it was universally acknowledged, and the shrewdest. Bessie and my sister were chums, ah yes indeed, I knew her that long ago!"

He said, "I wondered what became of you, Owen. Your mother's family cut her off when she married your father, as I'm sure you know. She went with him on the river boats, up and down, up and down, and took care of him until the end. He died when you were about three, you know. A gallant spirit, a fine gentleman, and he played the best poker in the history of the game."

He said, "It was the only trade your mother knew. She traveled up and down the river, up and down, up and down, playing poker as your father had taught her to play—good poker, almost as good as his! I never heard an oath in her presence, no not so much as a sharp word, Bessie Cope was a real lady in the finest sense of the word and no one failed to appreciate it."

He said, "The packet lines vied to have her aboard, she gave tone to the passage, and kept the crooks out of the games. I was in Inja when she died of typhoid, I was playing to Her Majesty's troops. I always wondered what had become of Owen and Bessie's boy. You look like both of them."

That's how he said it, Inja. He meant India. Old Ownie was reeling on his feet, but he lived up to it, he sure did. He slid his left arm around Liddie and put his right hand out and said, "It's my pleasure, Mr. Ambrose, and I want to thank you for that funeral oration, too. That was just fine, sir!"

"Oh, you liked it?" Ambrose cried. "I remember your mother liked Shakespeare, even as a little girl. So you have her tastes, do you?"

"I sure hope so," Ownie said.

CHAPTER 14

They was married about a week later, with Hoot squeezed into a new black suit for best man, and Rolf kind of uneasy during the service, because Sammie was expecting again, and insisted on coming, and he never knowed when she was going to turn white and start heaving. But she didn't, and he blundered through it somehow, and then they went off on a visit to Jerry Clyde for a honeymoon.

Liz had it in her head they was going to move in with her, and Ownie was going to start a locksmith business, and she'd start him off by having him change the locks on her house. But Ownie wanted to look this proposition in the Rockies over again, and see what Liddie thought of it, before he let Liz start running his life.

They rented a team and buggy from the livery barn to go up to the Q to catch the Denver train. They come past my place on the way, to say good-by and one thing and another, and I reckon Liddie wanted to see Pete Heath's Place again, and make sure she was grateful to God in her heart for all that had happened since she first seen it.

"You know you was who I wanted to be my best man," Ownie said. "You let me down there, Pete."

"I don't see it that way," I said. "When you launch off on something as risky as getting married, you want all the omens you can get. I wouldn't of added nothing to no wedding, believe me."

"You just ducked out of going to church is all," Ownie said. "If Rolf had shut up about it, you'd of been there."

I said well, Rolf did appear a mite too anxious, and sooner or later he'd get me, on my deathbed if not before. But I said the main reason was him and Liddie deserved a whole new deck, with the seal unbroken, and not any old shot-up spooks out of the unhappy past.

He left V.G. with me to take care of until he got back. I had to chain that dog up again, the first time he'd been on a chain since Ownie stole him from me, and then he wouldn't eat until finely I brought him in the house like he was another person. Then he ate.

They was gone until the middle of August. They moved in

with Liz Saymill, who was getting a little feeble and forgetful, and Ownie opened a locksmith shop in the Griffin Block, and repaired guns besides, and sent off for a lathe so he could even turn a barrel for you.

That was another hot August, but they all come to an end, and I remember the date clearly, the fourth of September, because I was in Mooney myself then for one of my rare infrequent visits to get a couple of horses shod. I was in Ownie's shop whiling away a hot day, and watching him file down a piece of brass to make a new part for an old grandfather's clock he was fixing, and wishing I had a good cold bottle of beer.

When Abe Whipple walked in and took off his hat and throwed it down on the counter, and said, "Ownie, guess what."

I didn't like the way he said it, and I reckon neither did Ownie, because he really jerked his head up. "He's here," he said.

"Yes he is," Abe said. "Put his horse up at the barn and arranged for a room over the barn as nervy as you please."

"And there ain't a thing you can do about it," Ownie said.

"Not a thing," Abe said. "That's what gets me, the nerve of the son of a bitch."

"What else can he do?" Ownie said.

"That's right, what else can he do?" said Abe. "But it still takes nerve."

I asked them who they was talking about, and Ownie said, "Doc Harper."

Abe said, "Yes, Doc Harper. How did you find out about it anyway, Ownie?"

"I didn't," Ownie said. "I been expecting him for quite a while, Abe."

"Why?" Abe said. "I want to hear it in your own words."

"Well," said Ownie, "what else can he do? Who could testify against him? Hart Bristol and Capistrano Erland and Jimmy Rackstraw, and they're all dead. Except for one thing, he's free as a bird, not a witness that can pin one single individual thing against him on them blowhole murders."

"You," Abe said. "Well, Ownie, there's many another man

besides you talking about this son of a bitching no-good gunfighting blowholer."

"Yes," Ownie said, "but they never claimed to be gunfighters like me. They never set out on the vengeance trail like me. They never talked to the only eye-witnesses like I talked to Hart Bristol, did they? All this other talk you're talking about, where does it come from? Me!"

He said, "Another thing, Abe, you said it yourself, this fella is a professional. He has went around the country for years and years, gunfighting for a living. He done a stretch in the pen and come right out and what did he do? Went back to gunfighting again."

He said, "Doc Harper's another kind of furry dog from them other three. He's still a blowholer, don't you ever mistake it otherwise. Somewhere in him there's still a streak of yellow. But I done plenty of thinking before I passed up that job with Jerry Clyde. That's where I'd like to be right now, out there raising cows in the mountain meadows, and bringing up a family where kids have got a chance, not here in a crowded stinking town as big as Mooney."

He said, "But it come over me that Doc Harper had to come looking for me, and when he did, by God, I better be where it meant something, where we *settled* it finely, not out there in the mountains where it would be just another gunfight. Make him come here!"

"You made him come here, all right," Abe said.

Owen took the brass out of the vice and put it away in a drawer, and slid his file nice and neat into the sheath on the wall. He smiled and said, "How does it feel to have your tail in the crack finely, Mr. Sheriff?"

Abe just cursed something awful. "I can arrest him," he said. "I can charge him with the murders. I can lock him in jail. But then what? Who can testify against him? Liddie can't. Hoot can't. Miles James can file charges against him, but it's hard enough for Miles to convict somebody with a hundred and fifty witnesses, let alone none. Andy would have to turn him loose, and why he might as well give him a signed endorsement! That's why I ain't going to arrest him, because turning him loose after that is all he needs really."

"He needs more than that," Ownie said, and he opened up the drawer under his workbench and took out his .45 wrapped up in the holster, that he hadn't wore since they come back from the honeymoon in the Rockies. "He needs more than that, a lot more," he said.

"You Goddamn fool bridegroom," Abe said. "You think you're going to outdraw Doc Harper? *Doc Harper?*"

"Like shooting fish in a barrel," Ownie said, and opened up the gun to make sure it was loaded and oiled and working.

Abe just snorted. "You ain't going out of this shop with that gun on," he said. "I won't allow it."

Ownie buckled the gun on. "There's nothing you can do about that either, Abe. Only thing you can do, you can pass the word to Harper that I ain't looking for him but I ain't running from him either. If there's going to be a killing, he has to start it."

"You mean draw first," Abe said.

"Draw first," Ownie said.

"You poor pitiful fool, so now you're going to go out there and give him first draw, and outdraw a *professional,*" Abe said.

"Yes I am," Ownie said, "and beat him, and do you know why? Because I'm a professional too. I'm working as a locksmith, because a man can be professional at more than one thing. But right now I doubt if there's a man in the world that can get a .45 out faster than me, or shoot it straighter as it comes out."

Abe looked at me like he was about ready to bust into tears, and he said, "Oh shit listen to him, now he's the best there is; how about Teddy Schmitz or Lou Kelly or Buster Gutierrez or Brazos Bill Watson, he's better than them too I guess."

Ownie said, "Lou Kelly got killed a couple of months ago in California, shotgunned down by a posse, didn't you hear about that? He wasn't much anyway, mostly blowhard. But today I could kill Teddy Schmitz and then Buster Gutierrez and then Brazos Bill Watson one at a time. I honestly could, Abe."

He said, "I'm fast enough and I shoot straight enough, and the main thing is, Abe, *I ain't afraid of nothing!* No man ever was cooler than me, why a bumblebee could light on me and I wouldn't even twitch my hide like a horse. Why should I? Do you know any man with more to live for, or be proud of, or look forward to, than me?"

"Them's going to make the handsomest last words that ever became a legend by God," Abe said. "You son of a bitch, you're bound and determined to make Liddie a widow, ain't you?"

"No, I'll kill this one," Ownie said. "I couldn't do it in cold blood to them others. But I know what you've got to be to make a gunfighter better than you do, Abe. I always was mean enough, but now I'm proud enough too."

"What about afterward, when somebody else comes after you, as they're bound to," Abe said.

"Oh hell, Abe, you take Doc Harper too serious," Ownie said. "He ain't in a class with Teddy Schmitz and Buster Gutierrez and Brazos Bill Watson. Maybe he thinks he is, but they sure don't."

Abe seen he had his mind made up. He said, "You look just as natural, Ownie! It's hard to believe you're a dead man."

Ownie said, "Oh go on, pass the word to this idiot, he's on the wrong side of the law here and so forth. I'll take all the edge I can get. Nerves is half the battle."

"I already done that," Abe said. "I hunted him up as soon as I heard. I tried to talk to him about them blowhole murders but he stood on his rights and told me to shut up or draw my gun. I had to back off on that, but I told him I wanted him out of here by sundown or I'd run him out feet first if I had to."

"What did he say to that?" Ownie said.

Abe cursed and said, "He said sundown was plenty for no more than he had to do in this farmer town. He said to tell the punkin-rollers and shuck-ears not to worry, he was soon on his way, and they could come out from under the house and slop their pigs in peace."

Ownie laughed right out loud, and said, "He honestly said

that? He had to brag did he. A wild old range rider. Well let's get it over with."

It just took your breath. He put his hat on and fitted it down over his head nice and tight, and strolled out of there into the sunshine, and stood there a minute until his eyes got used to it. That shows you that he was fairly professional at that, to think of his eyes.

He seen Bountiful Meredith across the street, carrying a forty-eight-pound sack of flour home on his shoulder, and he called out, "Howdy, Bountiful, haven't seen you since I got back, how's your missus?"

Bountiful said, "You won't see me now either, what the hell you trying to do to me, leave me out of it." He hurried on down the street, like if Ownie would of said one more word to him, he would of throwed the family flour away and run like an antelope.

"How are you betting, Pete?" Abe said.

I told him I never bet against my own horse or hand, and he said neither could he, although from all he'd heard about Doc Harper, he had a chance to make a little money off'n me. I got up and went to the window to watch, and after a minute Abe did too.

"Someday," he said, "it's going to be possible to make a man take his gun off the minute he comes to town, and an officer of the law will be an officer of the law then, not a sham and a pretense."

"But not yet," I said.

"Look at the son of a bitch," Abe said. "I only hope to God it's over before Liddie hears."

"It will be," I said, because this stranger with the broken nose come out from around the corner across the street, and pushed his hat back on his head, and a couple of boys in front of the blacksmith shop scooted inside like their tails was afire.

Up the street, Ownie was sauntering along with his back to us, just sauntering, kind of looking around on both sides like he was curious but really didn't give much of a damn. You couldn't beat it for nerve. He must of knowed him and Doc Harper was the only two men on that street, he *had* to know it, and yet he just sauntered, there's no other word for it.

"You!" Doc Harper yelled out.

Ownie turned around, about half of the block away, and said, "Who do you mean, me?"

"Yes I mean you, are you Ownie Cope?" Doc said.

"Now you know damn well I'm Ownie Cope, Ownie Cope himself, the one and only," Ownie said.

He turned around and began sauntering towards Doc, kind of grinning, and Doc said, "Then you're who I been looking for. I had to chase you halfway across the state of Colorado to catch up with you and your dirty lies; now say it to my face why don't you, let's get this settled once and for all, you lying son of a bitch."

"It's all right with me that way," Ownie said. "All I ever said about you was that Doc Harper was a dirty filthy cowardly murdering son of a bitch of a blowholer, the lowest of the low, you helped kill John Houten Swiverton and Alice Swiverton, and I talked to the men that was in with you on it. Now does that clear things up for you, you dirty murdering son of a bitch?"

It was all over then, any time a man in Doc's position lets you stand there in the street and make a campaign speech, he hasn't got blood in his veins, he's got you know what. And Doc seen it too late, he didn't have the blood he needed for this one.

"Draw!" he said. "Draw or I'll shoot you down like a dog."

"Draw yourself," Ownie said, and began walking towards him. "The last of the blowholers, that's you. You ain't got long to live you know. Either you draw, or I'll pistol-whip you to death. A little more fight in me than there was in that little girl, ain't there, you son of a bitch! Draw why don't you, draw, draw, draw!"

He wasn't no more than five or six feet away when that famous gunman Doc Harper went for his weapon, and what he looked like when he done it was some old derelict that you might find laying drunk in front of your store some morning when you went to sweep out to open up. Not that he floundered around like no farm boy in getting his gun out, no sir.

But Ownie was just pure rattlesnake, the grin went off'n his face when he went into motion, and here was this .45 in his hand before you really seen him move, and he plugged Doc twice as fast as he could pull the trigger, right in the middle of the chest. You could of put your hand over both holes.

They say a dead man falls forward on his face, and maybe he does usually, but not when he's been slapped by two .45 slugs. Doc leaned backward fast and fell hard, and Abe went sprinting out of the door bellowing for witnesses, and I reckon thirty or forty come leaking out of them buildings as fast as they could come. Anyways, I never did have to testify at the inquest, and a good thing, because I can do without a courthouse as well as I can a church.

I didn't hear the last of it by any means, though, because when Ownie and Liddie had their first baby, it was a boy, a little wrinkled ugly black-headed red-faced thing that hardly ever shut up. If he wasn't squalling about one thing, it was another.

Anyways they named him Peter Heath Cope out of a clear sky, although Pete Heath wasn't my real name and Ownie knowed it. But him and Liddie both wanted to do something for me they said, because where would they of been if I hadn't brought Hoot in out of the storm, and then harnessed up my own four-horse team the next morning. What really gave me a turn was that old Liz Saymill said she thought I was entitled, and it was an attractive name besides, and maybe some of her critics was right when they said the old girl was getting childish in her old age.

I had to go to the son of a bitching babtism and christening, and stand godfather to this ugly little squalling papoose, and hold him while Rolf wet him down as he said the words, not that he needed wetting. He was the pissingest baby you ever seen, Ownie admitted that himself, he said he was just like a funnel, in at one end and out the other.

I got through it all right, you ain't going to throw me by making an exhibition of me, because I've got my own kind of stubborn vain bullheaded pride. I always figger if I'm forced to go somewhere, and I'm out of place there, the hell with it, let others get up and leave if they don't like it.

We got the job done, and Ownie and Liddie loped off with their kid, Peter Heath Cope, because it was fixing to rain and God knew that kid was already soaked from enough causes. Rolf said, "Thanks a lot, Pete, for taking on this chore. I know you hate it, but it meant a lot to Ownie and Liddie, and Hoot too for that matter."

"I notice Hoot ducked it," I said.

"He didn't duck it," he said. "He busted an ankle yesterday, his horse quit on him and let a steer drag it. It's Hoot's own fault, only a three-year-old colt, but you know these smart-aleck kids, they got to prove the colt they broke is as steady as your weary old veteran cow horse."

"That's only the start," I said. "Wait till he's my age, and all stove up and scarred and twisted, he won't think so much of being a cowboy."

Rolf said, "You never worked at cowboying long enough to get saddle sores even! But life has been good to both of us in spite of our natural orneriness, Pete. And look at Ownie and Liddie, and think back to what life had to offer them both, that morning of the blizzard! Ain't you about ready to admit that the good Lord is entitled to some thanks for what He done for all of us, and come be a member of the church where you're always welcome?"

I said, "Well, Rolf, I ain't ready to go that far yet. But I do have to admit, lately it looks like He's got a kind of a streak going for Him."

BOOK III

THE LAND BARON

For Otto and Marylou Erhardt

1

There was this long lean lank Indiana man with a tapeworm by the name of Asa R. St. Sure, that had one of them high loud voices, and he just talked all the time, the windiest man you could imagine. When he commenced to screaming that day, everybody in town could hear him. First this one shotgun shot, and then him screaming, and nobody in any doubt who it was.

Sheriff Abe Whipple was talking to an old white-haired cowboy wearing two guns and a high tall peaked hat. He listened a minute, and it didn't seem to him that anybody could scream like that was in peril of quick death, so he went on and asked this old cowboy what his name was.

"It's Dickerson Royce," the cowboy said, "but I'm mostly called Dick, as you'd guess."

"Well, Dick," Abe said, "I'll tell you something that ain't a guess, one weapon on a man is a weapon of self-defense, but two is just asking for it and someday you'll get it. But not here, not in Mooney, Colorado. So take one off."

Royce said, "That don't seem fair to me, Sheriff. I'll want to think that over first."

"Take all the time you want," Abe said, "so long as it's in jail. A man's entitled to make his own decisions in life, so long as we keep the peace. I can't have any jobless cowboy going around here in the spring of the year wearing two guns."

"I ain't a jobless cowboy," Royce said. "All I do is drink. Now I reckon that sounds curious to you, and most drunks, they'll deny it, they pretend it ain't so. But I'll tell you fair and square,

I've retired from everything but my drinking. I'm a peaceable drinker, I don't make trouble for nobody, but I don't look on myself as jobless. I drink for my living you might say. I used to be a fiend for the women, but that's under control now at seventy-one years of age, and I just drink."

He was a soft slow talker, and he looked Abe in the eye sincerely, like it was the most natural thing in the world to be a career drinker, and he got Abe's goat from the first. This Dick Royce wasn't a tall man, but he had big shoulders and a deep chest, and he hadn't went wrinkled and pot-gutted like your usual old drinking man. He had this red face and blue eyes, and a big white longhorn mustache, and a tangle of white hair under his high Pecos hat with a snakeskin band on it.

Abe listened a minute for that screaming, and it didn't seem to be no more urgent than before. He said, "I'll lay it out for you fair and square too, Dick. I never heard of nobody drinking for a living. It sounds to me like you was just a common illegal vagabond."

Royce said, "Sheriff, I hear somebody screaming his head off, and it sounds to me like you got a breach of the peace on your hands. I ain't critical of you, not at all, and maybe you're one of these men that like to finish one job before you start the next one, so look at this, and then let's see what's making that man scream so hard."

He went to his horse and fished in his soogan roll. Abe kept an eye on him in case he come up with a third gun, but what he come up with was a little canvas bag, with Cheyenne Drovers and Mercantile Bank on it. He handed this to Abe, and Abe opened it and seen a lot of gold coin inside.

"How much is in here and where did it come from, Dick?" he said.

"Around a thousand dollars, last time I counted it," Royce said. "I'm what they call a remittance man, in Texas. I don't know what they call them here."

"I know what a remittance man is," Abe said, but Royce went

right on to explain that his family had run him out of England thirty or forty years ago, and they sent him one hundred and twenty dollars every three months to stay out of England and not disgrace them, and that was called his remittance.

"A new York bank sends it to this here Cheyenne bank," Dick said, "and when I figger my three months is about up, I write to them to send me my draft wherever I am. Once a man gets too old for his vices, his money piles up on him. You can't hardly drink up forty dollars a month. I thought I might buy a little house to live in, and I like the looks of your town, but all my life I've wore two guns. You might as well make me take off my pants."

He never cracked a smile, he just kept staring at Abe stone sober, and scratching his rump as innocent as a child, and Abe tied the bag of gold back up and handed it back to him. It seemed to him that Tapeworm St. Sure had stopped screaming so hard, and was more like weeping and cursing now, so he surely wasn't dying.

Abe said, "You tell me you've put carnality behind you, well I'm sixty-two myself and I wonder what the truth is. You hear some of these old boogers talk in their seventies, and a few in their eighties, and you wonder what the truth is because they say they're just as gamy as ever."

"You're sixty-two are you," Dick said; "well, I'm an important nine years older than you and you come to the right man with that question. You're going into the foolish age, Sheriff, failing in a lot of ways; you can't walk as fur as you used to, or see well enough to shoot as straight, and you don't like a bucking horse no more, and the women start calling you sir and dad and mister. It's a dangerous age, and you've got women on the brain, as I can remember at the same age, and you're going to kill somebody over some woman if you don't take yourself in hand. My advice to you is no woman is worth it. You'll be an old serene peaceful man soon, so prepare for it, and remember the bottle is a young man's poison but an old man's milk. That's my advice to you."

This wasn't what Abe hardly expected, so he said, "My advice to you is hang one of them guns on your saddle horn and try to get used to it, and if you can't, just ride right on out of town."

"Fair enough," Dick said, "and seeing as I'm left-handed, I'll take off the right-hand one."

He done it, and Abe went over across the crick to see why Tapeworm St. Sure was screaming. Tapeworm had been there about three months then, since January. He had run off from his family in Indiana to start life afresh in the West, he said. He stood a humpbacked six foot four, and he didn't weigh no more than one hundred and seventy when he arrived, and he kept getting skinnier and skinnier, and he et more than two average men.

He was going to start a feed lot and slaughterhouse, so he bought this parcel of 3.258 acres more or less, as the deeds say. It used to be the Doll House Hotel, when the swamp across the crick was called Lickety Split, and was a famous well-run red-light district in the old days, until Abe Whipple purged it. Another landmark gone.

He hired a young Georgia boy by the name of Elmo Huger, with a partly paralyzed left arm, to live with him and help him build his feedlot fences. But he couldn't stay interested in working, and would play out in the middle of the day for a nap, and there went another day. Finely Elmo got him to go see Dr. Jerrow.

Once there was two doctors in Mooney, Dr. Nobile across the crick, who was famous for female complaints, and Dr. Tattnal on the town side, who dealt in the usual diseases such as childbirth and gunshots and liver complaints. Doc Nobile left with the painted ladies, and Doc Tattnal turned his buggy over in a blizzard and froze his feet. He was old anyway, and this crippled him up considerable, so he sent off to this Ohio college and got Dr. Milton Jerrow.

Doc Jerrow told Asa R. St. Sure that he had a tapeworm, and Tapeworm said, "Oh God, I'm a doomed man," only he wasn't called Tapeworm yet.

"Nonsense, this isn't the problem it used to be," Doc Jerrow said. "There are numerous poisons that don't affect a human bean, but kill the tapeworm. In a few days you'll have sections of this parasite racing each other to pass out of your body."

"Guess again, young man," Tapeworm said. "You ain't going to give me no poison. You say it won't take on a human bean, take all the chances you like on your own body, but not on mine. Me and this insect has shared the same food and slept in the same bed so long it must have the same constitution I've got, or it wouldn't thrive on my way of life better than I do, why any fool can see that. It's a nuisance, but not as bad as being poisoned, nobody poisons *this* old Hoosier and spades him under in a strange town, so guess again."

He didn't really talk to you, he hollered all the time, with his big blue eyes blazing purple and his big yellow teeth showing, and if you tried to interrupt him he just hollered louder and faster. Doc Jerrow give up and said to go on and live with his tapeworm and keep it for a pet for all of him.

Tapeworm kept getting skinnier and skinnier, and eating more and more, and he got to be kind of proud of his tapeworm, and he talked about it so much that this was how he got his nickname, Tapeworm St. Sure. Elmo stayed on and took care of him for miser's pay, but a boy with a bad arm can't find a job so easy nohow.

Doc Jerrow was with Tapeworm when Abe crossed the crick on the old cottonwood-log footbridge that had felt many a cowboy's boot in its day. Doc was picking birdshot out of Tapeworm's belly, and swabbing it down with an iodine swab, and about every third one he had to cut in. This was when Tapeworm screamed.

"Hello, Sheriff," Doc said. "A little case of attempted assassination that was badly managed, it seems."

"I make them judgments in this town," Abe said. "Who done this to you, Tapeworm?"

Tapeworm groaned and said, "I wish I knowed. I was ambushed. Me and Elmo was scything dead weeds yander, and somebody cut down on me from them trees."

Abe asked where Elmo was, and Doc said he had sent him for more iodine. Tapeworm tried to tell Abe about the attempted assassination. He said, "I seen somebody, that's for sure, not close enough to recognize him, but it was a Marlin single-barrel 12 with silver chasing on the chamber. He shot me down and then run like a dirty cowardly buck deer. Somebody ransacked my house a couple of times lately, too, while me and Elmo was gone. One thing sure, Sheriff, he's a dirty coward."

"Why didn't you tell me somebody ransacked your house?" Abe said. "That's burglary."

"What have I got to steal?" Tapeworm said. "All I've got is this miserable swamp. I've worked like a dog all my life, my family et it up faster than I earned it, and then I get a tapeworm, and now shot at. At least this is the end of this varmint. A tapeworm couldn't hardly live through being peppered with bird shot, could he?"

"Nonsense," Doc Jerrow said. "Your parasite is inside your intestines, and these shots didn't even penetrate your abdominal wall."

Tapeworm rolled his big purple eyes up at Abe and said, "See, I drawed another Goddamn deuce, Sheriff. One shot in the head, that's all he needed, but I get peppered and he gets a clean miss."

Elmo come loping up with another bottle of iodine. Doc painted Tapeworm's belly again and told him to get up and button his pants. He took out a little bottle of black pills and told him to take two of them every three hours until they were all gone sometime tomorrow.

"These are extremely useful for gunshots, especially shotgun," he said. "Time will come when these bird shot I picked out of you will only make a comical story to tell."

"It may be comical to you," Tapeworm said, "but that only shows you never been shot."

He went into his house to lay down, and Abe set down in one of them old red-painted willer chairs, and motioned for Elmo to do the same. "Many's the time I've set in these in happier days," he said, "when this very spot of shade under this very tree shaded some of the prettiest little fallen women you ever imagined. Now an old long-jawed Texas cowpoke says all I've got to look forward to is staying drunk. It's a melancholy thought."

"Yes it is, it sure is," Elmo said. "I never trifled with the fallen women nohow, because I'm a good Babtist and I try to live up to it. But I can see how it would be attractive if you ever got started."

Elmo was kind of a thin good-looking kid that everybody liked, and everybody wished they could think of some way to help him, but nobody could on account of this partly paralyzed left arm. He didn't drink or smoke either, and the only time anybody heard him curse was when he was helping somebody shoe a horse and it stepped on him. He had a nice friendly smile too, and not much to smile about when you think it over.

Abe said, "Elmo, did somebody actually try to ambush this old fraud, or did he trip over his own feet and do it himself?"

Elmo said, "No, he was ambushed, that's the truth, Sheriff."

Abe said, "Did you see who done it?"

"I seen somebody," Elmo said, "but actually it was only a shadder that was gone before I knowed it. I reckon I ort to of paid more attention, but you don't never expect to be a witness in a case like this, and I wasn't prepared."

"What I don't understand," Abe said, "is how he could slip up there and ambush your boss, and you see him, and you didn't even chase the son of a bitch."

Elmo said, "With what, a scythe? Did you ever swing a scythe with a gun on? My gun was in the house. I never seen anybody run faster than that ambusher, and Asa was laying there screaming and thinking he'd had his manly parts shot off, and praise the Lord it turned out to be all higher. The way that shot bunched in such a close pattern, Abe, I bet you find out that gun had a full-choke barrel, if that's any help."

Abe had a lifelong habit of trying to help some raggedy-pants boy to succeed in life. It had turned out well in a few cases, for instance Rolf Ledger, when Rolf was fresh out of the pen, and Abe got him in as minister of the Methodist church. Then there was Thad Rust, when he got throwed out of his own home after selling one of his daddy's calves and keeping the money, and that turned out well too. He made Thad his deputy, and there wasn't nobody else half as reliable would take that job for the twenty dollars a month the county paid.

But there was other boys that had double-crossed Abe and turned out bad, and one that had abused one of Abe's own horses, hitting it over the head until it got so head shy you could hardly bridle it, and one that stole a box of cigars out of the Mooney Hotel, and a couple that killed somebody. Abe felt like helping Elmo as much as anybody else, but he knowed better than to let sentiment creep into a case of attempted assassination.

He said, "Look me in the eye now, boy. Murder from ambush is a serious thing even if it don't come off. It usually means a deep bitter grudge. Murder from ambush is lying in wait, that's premeditation and a hanging matter. Now look me in the eye and tell me who has got that kind of a grudge against old Tapeworm."

Elmo said, "I swear I don't know nobody, Abe! Listen, he took me into this house, and we share our meals together, and he never reproached me with my bad arm, so don't expect me to talk behind his back."

"So you could talk behind his back if you was a mind to," Abe said. "Now we're getting somewhere. Puke it out, boy! Remember, this is a hanging proposition."

Elmo squirmed around considerable, and then he said, "Well there's only one or two things, Abe, you know what a talker Tapeworm is."

"Yes I do, he'll talk your ear off, that man could put his lips over a mule's hind end and blow the bit out of his mouth," Abe said. "What about it?"

Elmo said, "Lately he's been gone a lot from the house, in fact he's got two horses and keeps them both spent, he rides them so hard. And here's a man who hardly ever left his bed after this tapeworm come on him, until just lately. He don't cross the crick, so he'd be seen in town, and where he goes, I don't know. And he never talks to me no more when he gets back, just sets there leaning over and making a little pile of dirt with his hand, and then stomping on it with his boot. Brooding, like."

"Hm," Abe said. "If that's all you can tell me, let's go look over the scene of the ambush."

They done that, and found some tracks showing the ambusher wore boots about the size of Abe's, and a 12-gauge shotgun empty, but the tracks petered out and you could buy shells like that anywhere. Abe gave it up and went home and told his wife, "It's a strange thing, none of this is very serious; when a man uses bird shot from so fur off, it's hard to take him serious. But it seems mighty strange to me that I'm talking to this old busted-down Texas two-gun man when it happened, and I don't know why. But you know how I am, it's the Sephardic Jew in me, I get these feelings. What I feel now is, we ain't heard the last of this by a long shot."

The next morning, Elmo turned Dr. Jerrow out early. He said Tapeworm had slept until almost daylight, and then woke up with agonizing cramps in his belly where he had been shot. "His guts must of been shot up worse than you thought," Elmo said, "because he's passing parts of his own intestines all morning. He's turning inside out, at least sixteen feet so fur, and he can't have much bowel left."

Doc reached for his pants and said, "I'll come with you, but that's not his bowels he's passing, that's his tapeworm. Those pills were tapeworm medicine. There is no specific for gunshot wounds, except shoot first."

Tapeworm was weak as a cat, and mighty put out when he found he had been tricked. "Shotgunned from ambushed and poisoned the same day," he said, "and a lucky near miss both times. Why I'm weak as a cat, and my mouth is so dry I'd have to prime it to spit, and you call yourself a doctor!"

"You're weak from not eating. You'll start getting some good out of your food now, instead of merely fattening your parasite," Doc said.

He charged Tapeworm two dollars, and Elmo fried up some eggs and potatoes, and Tapeworm put them away and was more like his old self. About an hour later, he told Elmo to go up to Frank Mueller's meat market and see what he had that was good today, and Elmo came back with three pounds of round steak. The two of them put that away, and then Edna Whipple sent down some cake and ice cream for the invalid, and Tapeworm cleaned that up.

He got rid of the last of his tapeworm that night, and had his first good night's sleep away from it, and he said he didn't miss it a bit. Abe waited another day, and then went to have a little talk with him. He asked Tapeworm how he was feeling, and Tapeworm said, "Sheriff, I'm just blooming, that's how. Lord knows how long I had this long thin vile insect in me! They change a man. Mine made me walk out on the best wife and children in the world, just when the kids was getting big enough to be a little help. Now I've got rid of it, I'm in the notion to go home again."

"I sure wish I could clear up the mystery of this ambush before you do," Abe said.

"I'm with you on that all the way," Tapeworm said.

Abe retch over and put his hand on Tapeworm's shoulder good and hard and said, "I try to look at both sides of a thing, Tapeworm. I ask myself when I put the chains on a man, what went wrong anyhow? Something sure did, when a happy freckled boy of twelve turns out to be a backshooting bastard at twenty. One of two things, something went wrong during his life, or he was delivered from his mother's womb, doomed to be a criminal."

"After my experience," Tapeworm said, "I'd suspect a tapeworm. Nobody knows how them insects change you."

"So your guess is that the man that ambushed you had a tapeworm, is that it?" Abe said.

Tapeworm said it was possible. He said there was a famous case back in Indiana where a farmer killed his wife and an auctioneer and a justice of the peace with a pitchfork, and then went around pitchforking his own hogs until some neighbor heard them squealing and rode over, and he pitchforked the neighbor and his horse both. He said there was four dead people and fourteen dead hogs before they got the pitchfork away from that old fool, and afterward he had no idee what had come over him, and couldn't remember a thing. He said they put the farmer in the insane asylum, and he was still there the last he heard, after years and years.

"When I get back to Indiana," he said, "I'm going up to that asylum and ask them doctors if they looked for a tapeworm. I don't know what's in them little black pills, but they could change this man's whole life. Then there was another case where a cousin of my wife's, a man dynamited his chimbley," and so on.

Abe seen that Tapeworm was his old self, and had his second wind, and nobody was going to head him after he got his second wind. He gave up for that day.

Then some fool went through Logan County with a flock of sheep on his way south, and some old fool up and poisoned the grass for spite, and some homesteaders' milk cows and a horse or two got poisoned too. Three no-good young jobless cowboys went around saying it served them right, the God-damn Kincaiders was as bad as sheepmen. They tried to burn down some homesteader's house, and the homesteader got killed, and when the cowboys sobered up, they found they was fugitives from justice.

Abe run them down in Mooney County. He left Thad Rust in charge of the office, while he chained these miscreants and took them back to Logan County himself, and collected his mileage there. Any time he could stick some other county the mileage, he done it.

When he got back, the first thing he heard was that Tapeworm St. Sure had sold the Doll House to the two-gun remittance man, Dickerson Royce, and had already left town. Elmo Huger was going to stay with Dick until he could find a job that a practically one-armed man could do, Thad Rust said.

"I could have more cheerful news," Abe said. "I had a feeling we'd hear more of this case, and right now I feel the worst is still to come."

Thad said, "Oh hell, Abe, people come and go when a town gets to be this size, almost five hundred souls now. I'd call Dick Royce and Tapeworm St. Sure about an even swap."

Abe leaned back in his swivel chair and put his boots up on the desk and said, "They'll surely hang them three boys I took back to Logan County. It ain't open season on homesteaders no longer, and I say that's all right with me. But I don't like to see times change too fast. It's sad to think about them boys hanging over what used to be a public benefaction, at least they found it so. They blubbered about their mothers all the way to Logan County. I said to them, 'Boys, what puzzles me is how you never gave a single thought to your mothers while you was liquoring up to the point of trying to burn that man's house down with his kids in it, by God.'"

"I bet that really fetched the tears," Thad said.

Abe said, "Don't be a smart-aleck. I can say things like that at my age, but you sound like just a young smart-aleck. I look at you and see the same age, the same foolish grin, like life is just one great big prank as it was to them cowboys until they learned better."

Thad said, "Oh hell, take off your spurs before you mount me. I've had a bad time too. That Dick Royce, he just sets over there and drinks day and night, and he almost burned his house down today. The most unusual town drunk I ever heard of. Try to reason with him, and he reminds you he's a taxpayer and entitled to courtesy. You go over there and try to talk sense to that son of a bitch of a left-handed one-gunned two-gun man of a Dick Royce, and I gorantee he'll take your mind off your three young doomed cowboys."

"I just wonder about him," Abe said. "One of the things I wonder is, will somebody try to ambush him like they done Tapeworm St. Sure."

"I don't much care if they do," Thad said.

"Don't talk like a young smart-aleck," Abe said. "He's right about one thing. He's a taxpayer now. We've got to care."

2

A few days later, Abe come to see me. I let on it was just a sociable visit, and I had butchered a calf, and my hens was laying good for so early in spring, so I fried up some steak and eggs and made some sody biscuits. Abe had the pleasantest wife in the world, and a good cook, but a man likes to get some good bachelor cooking now and then. He ate hearty.

He finished and pushed his plate back and said, "Pete, do you know what's going to happen one of these days? I'll come out here on a little visit to you, and your dogs will be setting there howling, and your teams will be pounding the ground for feed and water, but you won't hear them because your ears will be full of chicken manure. You know chickens, how when they wake up on the limb at daybreak, they shuffle their feet and let go. I picked up a man that laid dead under a chicken tree for three days. A murder case. He was in bad shape."

I said I hope that never happened to me, and he said he did too, and maybe I ought to move to some other jurisdiction and spare him the worry. He said, "I like to hear of a man making good in life, yes I do, but when I have to hear from my own deputy that a moonshiner like you has turned moneylender, why it makes me wonder."

I had this little place, Pete Heath's Place, eighty acres that wouldn't support a gopher, half a mile off the wagon road between Mooney and the Platte, in a little grove of trashy trees. I traded some horses and raised my own garden, and had a kind of an inn. I didn't have no license but I sold a little whisky to my friends, and a few groceries, and I had two beds to rent, and on weekends I run a nice peaceable poker game.

I wasn't no gambler myself, but I knowed all the tricks and the sharps that plied them, and there couldn't no sharp set down at my tables. And a man running from pursuit, so long as it wasn't Abe pursuing him, could get a meal and a change of clothes, and a few hours of precious rest. But I wasn't no moonshiner.

I'd been on the wrong side of the law in my time, and I carried some metal in my body to prove it, and Abe knowed this. He had never before shoved a moral gun in my back before, and I done some wondering too. I said, "Now I'm a moonshiner and a moneylender, all right, tell me what I've did to earn that kind of talk."

He said, "So you and Tapeworm was friends enough for him to borrow money from you! Thad just happened to tell me this, otherwise I'd never of knowed it. Go on, man, don't be afraid to speak up!"

I said, "Oh that. I didn't loan Tapeworm no money. I loaned it to Mother Morton, when she ran the Doll House, a mere hundred dollars, but she never made no payments, and then you run her out of town, and it was well over two hundred dollars when Tapeworm bought that property."

He asked me if it was a recorded mortgage, and I said, "Do you think I'm that ignorant, letting a madam have a hundred dollars without recording it? Sure it was! Tapeworm run Mother Morton down somewhere, and bought the fee simple from her, but she kindly didn't think to mention the mortgage, and he didn't search title. I didn't hear about it until he was already on the property, but I went to him then and told him if he ever sold it, I got my money first or no abstract would issue."

"First time you ever met him?" Abe said. I said it was, and he wanted to know how Tapeworm acted. I said, "He screamed, yes he did, but I could set there and listen to him scream till the cows come home, before he beats me out of my money."

Abe said, "Hm. I don't reckon it would surprise you none, to hear somebody tried to ambush Tapeworm before he left town."

I said, "Yes, I heard that. I hope you don't think I had anything to do with that, Abe."

He said, "No, but God damn it, Pete, something's going on in that town, and I can't get to the bottom of it. If you're keeping a secret from me and I ever find it out, I'll unhinge your gate for you. Do you know Dick Royce?"

I said, "I met him the day he bought the place from Tapeworm. I quitclaimed in his favor, to save them the two dollars for filing a second document."

He just set there and picked his teeth and rubbed his mustache and looked at me, and he had this way about him, he could make you sweat and swaller your own spit and itch all over. I tried to think how to put it to him. I said finely, "Abe, I could set here and surmise all day, but you want good solid facts, not a lot of my surmises."

"I don't know about that," Abe said. "We'll never know unless you try me, so surmise away, Pete."

I said, "Well, have you heard the C.B.&Q. is going to build a spur into Mooney?"

He said, "*What?*" and almost fell out of his chair. He set there with his mouth open, and I said, "You can surmise anything, and usually it turns out to be just a pack of lies, and maybe I'm bearing false witness against my neighbors when I say that."

Abe catched his breath and said, "True, you could be, but the Bible has another verse, I said in my haste, all men are liars. I never heard anything so fanciful as the railroad coming to Mooney, but you ain't my idea of a fool or a liar either one. I had a feeling I was going to hear more of that ambush, but how does it connect up with the C.B.&Q. railroad?"

I said I didn't know, but that before Dickerson Royce rode into Mooney, him and another man was camped for a couple of weeks on a spring of Cal Venaman's Flying V, only Cal didn't know it or he'd of run them clean out of the country. I said Dick was drinking serious, and never left the camp and never seen nothing to the best of my knowledge, but this other fella, he didn't have nothing to do but set around and wait for Dick to run out of liquor.

He seen this party of surveyors in a rented wagon and team, with the Greeley livery barn name on the wagon, driving stakes in the ground and then pulling most of them up, and leaving a few buried ones. He watched them for a few days, until a Q work train come along and let down a gangplank. They led the horses up one at a time and hoisted the wagon up, and the train took off. As fur as anybody could tell, unless maybe an Indian that could read sign, there hadn't been a surveyor in a thousand miles.

The minute the train was gone, this big tall lank lean man come out of the brush on a horse. The fella that was camped with Dick Royce, he got on his horse and got ready to run, but the other man didn't notice him, only rode up and down where them surveyors had left them stakes buried. He was about six and a half feet tall and humpbacked, and skinny as a bed slat.

"That'd be Tapeworm St. Sure," Abe said.

I said I reckoned so, and he said when was this, and I said, "About a week before he got shot at. After he got shot at, he put the Doll House up for sale, and got some kind of a deal out of Dickerson Royce, and he was so anxious to close the deal, he sent Jimmy Drummond out to see me to get me to come in and quitclaim. Now you put two and two together, Abe, I'd say he ciphered out that the Q is building a spur to Mooney, and I wouldn't be surprised to find out he's optioned some other property around Mooney. As fur as his money would go, anyway."

He wanted to know what property, and I said I didn't know, but if the Q came to Mooney, it wouldn't cross the swamps on the wrong side of the crick. I said my guess was Tapeworm was unloading his 3.258 acres there to buy options nearer the Q.

"It sounds just like him, and you too," Abe said. "I wonder how you'd go about finding this out?"

I said I'd heard there was several parcels of land suddenly optioned to Arthur H. Crawford of Vincennes, Indiana, and I only *heard* that much, but I *knowed* that Tapeworm came from Indiana. I said a man could look first at the registrar's records, and then talk to Alec McMurdoch, president of the Mooney National Bank.

Abe said, "Oh what would he know, he's just an old reformed cowboy that couldn't even read and write until he married a teacher and she learned him."

I said, "No railroad is going to come into a town without coming to terms with the bank. If Alec hasn't got some options himself, he's ignoranter than I thought."

Abe thought it over and then said, "Well you learn a little every day as you go through life, don't you? All you have to do is keep your pores open. I'll look into them two sources you suggested, you bet I will. Only one other thing I wonder about, who it was camped with Dick Royce up there on Cal's property."

"I wonder that too," I said.

He retch over and took hold of my arm and said, "I hate to push a man that's doing his best, boy, but in my mind I keep seeing you laying there under your own chicken-roost tree, shot in the back three days, and all swoll up and plastered with chicken shit. Would that other man be Mike Timpke?"

"I didn't even know you knowed him," I said.

"Startled you a little bit, didn't I?" Abe said. "Well, well, well, I don't reckon you'd care to talk a little bit about Mike Timpke now, would you?"

I said not today if it was all the same to him, and he said he reckoned he'd have to drop in every now and then, and look under the tree where my chickens roosted. He said Mike Timpke hung around Mooney long enough to be offered a job by Charley Parker on the Roofed Lazy 8, and turned it down.

He said, "I take an interest in a man as ragged as him that turns down honest work, you see, and I kind of wondered what become of him. I still do. Thanks for your help, Pete, and stay out from under them chickens." What a way that was to say good-by to a friend.

Sometimes you get to thinking, and you get so discouraged about life you'd complain if they hung you with a new rope. I never was a fiend for the women, like some. Some men have got to have their way with as many as they can, it gets like a gunman carving notches in his .45, they ain't people no more, just marks. Or like them buffalo-killing contests in the old days, any man that kills 340 buffalo in sixteen hours, and wears out two gun barrels and four horses doing it, it's just a madness like the women is with some men.

I was the kind of fool that fell in love, one at a time, and whether I had my way with her or not, she was the only one for me until she throwed me over. It was like that with Retha Timpke. Retha didn't turn me into an outlaw, a man makes that decision himself, but she was my excuse at the time.

Where me and Reverend Rolf Ledger growed up, in Smith County, Kansas, people kept a flinty eye out for the carnal sins, but a lot of it still went on, in haymows and wagon beds, and on the good green sod if it had rained enough to grow grass, and once on top of a threshing machine that I knowed of personally, because the hogs had dirtied the ground everywhere else. I had a worse kind of reputation for carnality than I deserved, because when you're in love and keep hanging around the same woman, there's only one answer to some people.

The Timpkes came from Philadelphia. They wasn't nothing

but trash, but Retha was a beauty, about fifteen, with long black curly hair, and buck teeth that kept you trying to kiss her, and wild black eyes like a gut-shot deer. You take a man who has just lost his one and only beloved, I forget which one, he's defenseless to such a girl.

Their house had started to burn once, and they got the fire out in time, but Retha had to sleep in a room over the cob shed after that. I got well acquainted with the creaky old ladder up the wall of that cob shed. She used to lay there and tell me about Philadelphia, how she'd steal stuff in the stores, and her old man would go around and peddle it in a cart the next day. And so on.

They come to Kansas to look for her brother, and Old Man Timpke was going to catch him and get some money out of him or his heart's blood. Mike was a prizefighter, then twenty-two years old.

He would of been a good fighter except he was too yella and crooked. Retha told me about who he had whipped, this one knocked out in thirty-five rounds, that one in eighteen, and so on. He was going to fight a heavyweight, Porchagee Jack Buckley, although Mike weighed only 161. He had never got knocked out, and Porchagee Jack was going to do it and be famous as the first man to knock out Dynamite Mike Timpke.

Mike was supposed to get knocked out in the twelfth, and Old Man Timpke bet a lot of money he would be knocked out before the fifteenth, and he got seven to one Retha said. "He would of been rich," Retha said, "only this son of a bitching double-crossing Mike bets that *he* wins by a knockout before the twelfth, and cheated his own father."

In the eleventh, when Porchagee Jack Buckley didn't suspect anything, Mike hit him so hard he never was in his right mind afterward, and was always called Poor Old Porchagee Jack. Mike lit out of town with nearly a thousand dollars, and the last they heard, he was on the Kansas-Nebraska border, beating up country boys in small towns for five-dollar side bets.

Retha was always after me for money, so finely I went up to Kearney, Nebraska, and held up a feed store with a gun, and got $32.75 in my first crime, and gave her $20 of it. I got some more for her the same way, maybe three times. Then I found out I wasn't the only man in her life. Some of the best blood in Smith County was sockfooting it up that ladder, boots in hand.

I set fire to the cob house one night in a drunken jealous rage, only Mike had come home with some money, and Old Man Timpke had forgive him, and it was him in the room over the cob house that night, not Retha. He had to jump for it, and just barely made it, because that cob house was a goner that time.

Me and Mike got to be friends, and we stuck up stores all over western Missouri, as fur east as Sedalia and as fur south as Joplin and as fur north as Tarkio, where we finely fell out. Mike was too scared of weapons to make a good outlaw, he was like some men are with snakes, point a gun at him and he might wet his pants. He loved to beat people up with his fists sometimes, instead of minding business, and you've got to mind business if you aim to survive in the outlaw game.

He beat me up in Tarkio for no good reason, so I broke our pardnership by slipping away in the middle of the night, and camping for a week where I could soak in the crick every day until I healed up. I hadn't seen him or heard of him, or even thought of him in years, and that just suited me.

When we settled the Doll House papers, we met in Jimmy Drummond's office, and argued over the debt awhile, and finely I rounded it off at an even two hundred dollars. Tapeworm said, "Fine, Mr. Royce, pay the gentleman and we can proceed with the transfer of papers."

Dick said he wasn't going to pay me a cent, if Tapeworm wanted to sell the property, *he* could pay me off or kiss my foot, whichever he liked. Tapeworm begin to sweat a little, but he seemed mighty anxious to get it sold. He counted out ten double eagles, and I signed the quitclaim for 3.258 acres M/L.

"That means 'more or less,'" Jimmy said. "Now a surveyor will locate the nearest true corner, and run his lines from it, and carry his figgers out three decimals, and tell you flat out that it's 3.258 acres. But this is a computation that you can carry to infinity without reaching a true fixed sum, so we of the profession protect the validity of the title with M/L. Three decimals and that M/L will satisfy any court in the land."

I said, "They ought to raise a marble statue in front of every courthouse in the land, to whoever thought of that M/L, because it's sure a money-maker. You can count on lawyers to get you into the quicksand or keep you out of it for the right price."

Jimmy said, "Yes that's true, but we all run our little private bluffs in life, and I imagine you could tell some tales yourself, Pete." We shook hands all around, and I have to say I never seen more blue eyes at one time in my life. Jimmy's was all right, but I never seen shiftier ones than Tapeworm's, nor colder and meaner ones than Dick Royce's.

I was halfway home with these ten double eagles on me, when I looked back and seen this big flashy pinto about half a mile behind me, a strange horse. When I trotted my little mare, the pinto trotted too. When I pulled my horse in, the pinto slowed down too. I decided I better see who my curious pursuer was, as they say in the story books.

You don't get no warning of my lane until you reach this little grove of runty softwood trees, and unless you look sharp, it could be any old cowpath back into the brush. This was just the way I liked it too, and I was grateful I had it that way when I got there. I pulled off into them trees and waited with my .45 in my hand to see who was riding this strange pinto horse.

I knowed him the minute I seen him.

Mike carried some fat, but he still had the chest and shoulders, and he rode better than when me and him was outlaw pardners. But he had the same white skin and the same black hair and whiskers and the same mean black eyes and mean little mouth.

I kicked my horse out and said, "Hello, Mike, I thought you'd know better than to fool with me."

Mike could just *smell* a gun. He spun the pinto around and let out a scream, "Oh, Jesus, don't aim that gun at me, put it away, put it away please."

I let it hang down and said, "We meet again, do we, what the hell are you up to anyway?"

He couldn't keep his eyes off'n that gun. He said, "I *wish*, Mr. Heath, you'd holster your iron, you *know* how I am about guns, *why* do you do this to me?"

"It's been a long time," I said, "but not so long you've forgot my name."

He kept looking at the gun, and said, "Why I thought you wanted it that way, but however you like it is what suits me, Holbrook."

I was Holbrook Cohelan in the days we knowed each other before, but I said, "My name is Pete Heath, and you know it and don't you ever forget it, Mike. Why are you tagging after me?"

He said just to pass old times, and I knowed that was a lie, and I'd better find out what he was up to. I herded him on down the lane ahead of me, and made the dogs stand back while he got down and tied his horse, and then I had him go ahead of me into the house.

He said, "I sure could use a drink, Mr. Heath. Guns make me so damn nervous."

I said no drinks for him, but I'd make a pot of coffee. I hung the .45 on a nail behind the stove, and he let out a sigh and got some color back, and said that fresh hot coffee was mighty hard to beat.

We talked old times while the coffee boiled. He said Retha married a man by the name of Phil O'Brien in Minnesota, and they had two nice sons and was simply piling up money like wheat. He said, "O'Brien builds harrows to his own patent, the O'Brien Easy Draft, its motto is, It breaks the clods, not your horses."

I said, "It's a good harrow but not worth the cost. The Kincaiders along the Platte buy them and they'll be the rest of their lives paying off the bank."

He said Retha had settled down real good. He said somebody put strychnine in his father's kraut. He said, "The old son of a bitch jounced around for nearly two hours, banging his face on the floor and puking, before he died." I didn't ask where him and his mother was when this was going on.

He said he wasn't hungry, but when I set out the coffee, I got myself a dish of cold boiled potatoes and some butter and salt and pepper and a dull knife, and Mike said, "Say it's years and years since I enjoyed good cold buttered salted potatoes, do you mind if I join you?"

I got him a dull knife, and we set there and et potatoes, and he rambled on about the American River in California, where he'd been the last few years. He must of sweat a quart, trying to think how to come out with whatever was on his mind. And something was, just as I thought from the beginning, knowing Mike.

Finely he had to just blurt it out. He said, "The American River is supposed to be rough country, but it's nothing to Colorado. I had a deal put to me before I was here a week, to kill a couple of men for money. Can you beat that? I never heard of no such thing as putting a price on two men's lives there."

I said, "Well I hope it was a good price, because this sheriff we got here is the hangman's best friend on that kind of a deal."

Mike trembled all over and said, "I wouldn't take such a proposition, what do you think I am, a murderer? But there's three hundred dollars apiece for anybody that wants to drop these two fellas, and I seen the money."

I changed the subject, and we talked about different things, like the swamp fever that was killing horses in Richardson

County, Nebraska, and a fight he seen between a one-legged man and a blind man in Indian Territory, and why it's harder to train a white dog or horse than any other color.

Mike had come out to get a job done, and he wasn't going to leave until it was done. We come to the last cold boiled potato, and I told him to go ahead and help himself. He took it and buttered it and licked the knife, and while he was putting the salt and pepper on, he looked at me. He sure did salt and pepper that last piece of potato.

He said, "It's kind of a shame, that six hundred dollars laying there and no takers. You used to be a handy man with a weapon, Mr. Heath, and I wish to God I was myself."

I said, "I'm no longer on the outlaw side, Mike, that's all in the past with me."

He said, "Well sure, but I heard about your place clear out in California, how a man in a little trouble can find a friend in need here. I didn't have no idee it was my old pardner, just Pete Heath. I thought maybe you might run into somebody passing through in a hurry, that'd take on that job and maybe split with you. At three hundred dollars apiece, that's six hundred dollars and you could handle the money, how is he going to know what the price is?"

That sounded like the old true real Mike, and I knowed he hadn't just made it up on the spur of the moment. I said, "You don't have to set there and sweat that way, Mike, you and me understand each other. This would depend on how hard the job is, maybe. Who are the unlucky parties that have drawed the two black beans?"

He said, "A couple of double-crossing dirty rotten no-good sons of bitches by the name of Dickerson Royce and Tapeworm St. Sure."

3

It set in to rain soon after Abe left, one of them unexpected early warm rains that delude you that we're going to get some crops this year, and some early grass. Abe didn't have no slicker along, and he didn't take pleasure any more in lifting his face to the rain and feeling clean and new and holy and rededicated inside, because by then he knowed better. He was in kind of a tetchy temper when he tied his horse at the courthouse in the rain, and went to the registrar of deeds.

Old fat Minnie Newhouse was deputy there, and deputy in just about every other office. Minnie was as faithful as they come, but she was getting a mite foolish, and she hadn't laid by anything to live on in her old age. Every cent she had went on a worthless son that couldn't do nothing but clean out in the livery barn and borrow ahead on his pay to get drunk.

Minnie dreaded to see Abe. Everytime he come in, it reminded her of when he'd come to tell her that her husband had been gored to death by Carl Pridhof's bull twenty-three years ago. She seen him and said, "Oh God, what now? Oh dear, excuse me, Abe, I'm sorry I said that but you just scare a body to death."

Abe said he wanted a list of title filings lately. Minnie didn't have to look in the book. She fished a pencil out of her hair, and wrote them down backwards, beginning with the last one, as fast as she could write. You could ask her how much taxes you paid year before last and it was the same thing, she'd tell you to a cent.

"Well well, what do you know about this," Abe said, when she give him the list.

"Now what?" Minnie said, and started to cry, and flinch back from Abe, and try to pull her dress together where she always forgot to sew on a front button.

Abe said, "What a hell of a welcome I get here, like I was out drumming up business for the coroner's jury, why God damn it, Minnie, this is an insult."

Abe could steady Minnie when nobody else could. She pulled herself together and said, "I can't help it I reckon, Abe, my brain is getting fuzzy maybe, but you don't have to yell at me. I put in more hours on my job than anybody, even you, and you don't have to yell at me."

"Yes I do," Abe said. "It's like you were a block away. If I don't yell, dear, you don't hear me."

She got an old wadded-up handkerchief out of her apron pocket, and dabbed at her nose, and said, "I guess you do maybe. Seems like I'm two different people, one with a fuzzy brain, and the other'n standing there and thinking what an old fool she is! One of these days, I'll make a terrible mistake and lose my job, and, oh God, how'll I live then? How will Buster live without me? My life ended when you come in that door and said Harold was dead. More than him was gored by Carl's bull, Abe! My first thought was, Well, there ain't no God and there never was, or how could this happen? I still feel that way. I'll tell you something else, I couldn't stand the sight of Carl Pridhof from that day until he died; he cheated it five years and three months and fourteen days after his bull gored Harold, but his time came at last. I'll tell you something else, even today I can't stand the sight of Meade Pridhof, because of his father's bull. There now, that's a confession, old Carl was a founder of the G.A.R. and his son is on the county board with life or death power on my job, and I can't stand the sight of him! Tell him any time you feel like it, I might as well take

Harold's old .30-30 and put Buster out of his misery and then do the same to me. Now what do you think, Abe?"

Abe patted her old fat hand and said, "I think Buster ought to sober up and get out of your house and get a job, if you have to throw him out. And I think you ought to talk to Rolf Ledger."

Minnie said, "The Methodist minister? You wasn't listening to me, Abe. God was gored to death twenty-three years ago! I wouldn't set foot in a church if you dragged me. I see his wife on the street, that Samantha. She was a sweet girl, and talk about smart, she learned to read before she went to school. I used to just idolize that child, but I hate her now. Yes hate her. She's got *her* husband, you bet *he* won't be gored by no bull, you don't hear of preachers dying with their boots on. I wish you hadn't started me, Abe. I'm happier when I'm fuzzy, like."

Abe was just about to remind her that Harold didn't have boots on when he got gored, only moccasins because he was too lazy to earn a pair of boots, and what he was doing in Carl's stud lot was a mystery unless he was going to steal something.

But he didn't. He just said, "There's nothing wrong with your mind, you old fool. You've got a sick soul, that's all. You need healing."

"Like that woman in a convulsion that he healed," Minnie said. "The miracle worker. I don't appreciate this a bit, Abe, I'm not a whore you know."

"You'd be better off if you was," Abe said, and went outside and led his horse up to the bank. They had just run down the shades and locked the door, but he banged on the door and hollered for McMurdoch to let him in.

"Come on, Mac, I'm a law officer, I won't make off with your ill-gotten gains," he said.

Mac was a little short Scotchman that had been nicknamed Banty when he rode for the Flying V in the old days, that nobody ever faulted for nerve. He throwed the door open and said, "Law officer, you're a tumor in the public body politic that's what, don't think you give orders in this bank."

Abe shoved him back so hard he knocked him clear back to the fur wall, and slammed the door behind him, and said, "Let's go back to the board room and bare our souls in privacy, you double-crossing little Scotch son of a bitch." He stuck his belly out and began bumping Mac towards the board room with it, saying, "You little sneaking civet cat you." Bump. "You had the gall to think you could put one over on me." Bump. "You and the C.B.&Q., they've got a few things to learn too."

He bumped Mac into the board room and closed the door, and Mac just wilted down into a chair and covered his eyes with his hand and moaned.

"By God, this is supernatural," he said. "I was sworn to secrecy and so was everybody else, but first Tapeworm St. Sure and now you. How in the name of God did it get out, Abe?"

Abe had just got there but he already knowed one thing, Tapeworm wasn't in on the deal, he had just seen the signs and bet his judgment. Abe leaned his rump against the table and acted like he was about to put his foot up in Mac's lap. He said, "All right, start palavering and don't skip nothing, because if you think I'm bluffing, we lock antlers right now."

"Why it's very simple," Mac said. "I was advised by the Q title agent that they had some old options on rights-of-way and had decided to select a route and build a spur into Mooney. We'll get one train a day, it backs in and then goes right out. I was notified when the route was selected, but the same day, it appears, Tapeworm St. Sure had the same information. I don't know about him, but I was sworn to secrecy."

"How much has he got in your bank?" Abe said.

"Not a cent," Mac said.

"Then, Alec, how the hell did he manage to tie up half of the property in Mooney?" Abe said.

"Coin of the realm, Abe. Gold!" Mac said. "Gold coin to local owners, and by draft on a Vincennes, Indiana, bank to out-of-town owners. Abe, he knowed the route before I did! They told me they *had* a route, but they didn't say where, and I knowed better than to ask. And Tapeworm snaked a piece of property right out from under my own bank on that route!"

"This is so pitiful I feel sorry for you," Abe said. "How much is he in for?"

Mac said Tapeworm had spent at least four thousand dollars on options, and if he picked them all up, it would cost him at least another thirty-six thousand, and while you couldn't find out much from anybody on the Q, from what they *didn't* say, it looked to him like Tapeworm was going to start businesses that would cost him another forty thousand at least.

"And all starting with a little old eight-hundred dollar purchase of that mudhole across the crick," Mac said. "He must have some kind of separate private relationship with some railroad man."

"You go on thinking that," Abe said. "I'd hate to tell you the truth and rupture your heart."

He led his horse through the rain to Rolf's house. Sammie let him in, and then went back to some cookies she was baking. Rolf was in the parlor, rocking the baby's cradle with his toe. It was just not quite a year old then, and cutting teeth. He was trying to figger out a deal the church had been offered.

A man from Denver offered to build a new church building, and sell it to the congregation on a twenty-five-year contract, and pay the fire insurance, and the taxes if any. It would only cost the congregation $680 a year, and they'd still have their old building to sell to raise the mere $1,000 down payment. You could build a new church for around $3,400 cash, but as this man's letter said, few churches had the cash.

It comforted Abe just to step into Rolf's house, not that it was anything fancy, because it was about to fall to pieces when Rolf started fixing it up. But him and Sammie was both strong-minded people, and Abe believed in betting to your strength, and he said if Rolf and Sammie was on the side of frail humanity, all was not lost yet.

"Howdy, Abe, who's in trouble now?" Rolf said. "I never see you unless somebody's in trouble."

Abe said, "I got that same kind of miserable greeting from somebody else. Between you, I'll be despising myself if I keep on meeting my friends."

He throwed his hat over the cat on the carpet, an old trick with this cat, because it would stand for it with Abe's hat, but not with anybody else's. He said, "Look at that varmint, will you? They say they go by smell, so I don't know if it's a compliment or not."

Rolf grinned and said, "It's trying to soak up your brains, and I wish I could too. Here's one preacher of the gospel with a problem he can't take to the Lord, because He'd only tell me to use my head, and I already have."

He told Abe about the offer to build a church, and Abe said, "Tell him to go to hell. A congregation that won't build its own church, it ought to have to hold services under a wet tree. I'll tell you frankly how I feel today about your congregation, Rolf, at least certain important members of it. If you was to throw them another miracle of the loaves and fishes, I'd say charge admission and raffle something off, because they'll leave you with empty baskets and not one word of thanks."

"That's a hard judgment," Rolf said.

"A true one," Abe said. "I knowed these people long before you ever did, boy."

"I go along with you on the church offer, though," Rolf said. "It's bad business and besides, I kind of like that rickety old wooden firetrap we worship in. Now what's on your mind?"

"Guess what's coming to Mooney," Abe said.

"A circus?" Rolf said.

"Just about," Abe said. "The C.B.&Q. is going to build a spur here. Guess what crafty long-headed tightwad cattleman is behind it."

"My father-in-law?" Rolf said instantly.

"Right!" Abe said. "You know, Rolf, we've had cattle barons around here ever since the white man killed off the Indian's buffalo, and nobody can argue with it, Cal's a noble specimen. Now he's going to be a financial baron too. He's been working on the Q for years, collecting figgers on livestock, and the new Kincaiders each year, and the acres put to wheat and barley and sorghum and timothy and them new high-yielding Russian oats. It'd knock your wind out, the tons of stuff going out here every year—and nobody ever added it up before! Now guess whose land the Q will cross to get here."

"This sure is some guessing game," Rolf said. "Cal's again?"

Abe said, "Oh sure, partly, because it's already on his. But then to get out of building a trestle and some deep cuts, it swings to the east across the J Bar B, which you remember well, and guess who owns it now."

Rolf had worked as a cowboy for Jack Butler on the J Bar B when he first come to Mooney, before Jack went to prison in one of the biggest murder cases in Colorado history. He said, "Well, well, Jack had himself a gold mine and never knowed it. Who owns it now?"

Abe said, "There's another kind of baron besides cattle baron and financial baron, the land baron. Some dummy by the name of Arthur H. Crawford of Vincennes, Indiana, optioned that ranch for four thousand dollars, only two hundred and fifty down, before Alec McMurdoch knowed about the new right-of-way. This is our new land baron, Rolf. Guess what same land baron also owns or has options on two-thirds of the land in Mooney alongside the new rail line."

"I wouldn't even try to guess," Rolf said.

"Tapeworm St. Sure," Abe said. "Rolf, Alec McMurdoch is right about one thing, this whole thing is uncanny! Tapeworm is going to have a grain elevator company, and a feed lot company, and a hay and grain company, and a brickyard and building materials company, all on that old rocky flat where we found the man from Alaska with his throat cut, you remember. He was robbed."

"That was before my time," Rolf said.

Abe got up and shifted his hat a little with his toe, and the cat complained some and moved with it, and Abe said, "Look at that critter, will you! Rolf, mark my words, Tapeworm will end up a civic father, and all the old pioneers will be forgotten, and nobody will ever think of what we went through to keep the town alive through drouth and Indians and bandits and evangelists. Mark my words, they'll name a street after him someday! All I can say is, he's welcome to it. I can name you a city with a Griffin Street in it, that had every kind of deadfall knowed to sinful mortal man on it. Why you couldn't walk down that street by daylight or dark, without somebody trying to cave in your head, and when it came to women, I never seen worse culls in my life."

Abe catched his breath and said, "Yet somebody by the name of Griffin, either him in a plug hat or his descendants, they came out for a big dedication when the pine paving blocks was laid. You could smell the hot tar, and they had speeches and a couple of kags of beer, and the mayor was there in a rented barouche behind a good team from the fire barn. What a mockery! Before I was halfway down Griffin Street, I said to myself, well if this is fame, I want none of it! If you ever hear of them naming a Whipple Street after me, you stop it if you have to get up a petition. And I'll tell you something else, Rolf! Alec McMurdoch raised $440 among the merchants for a town carnival. He didn't say why. They think it's just a plain old town carnival, but that's when they're going to break ground for the new depot. How's that for treachery?"

Rolf seen how old Abe had got, not that he was white-headed or drooled tobacco juice, but he seemed to be hearing more hoofbeats behind him than in front. Rolf thought to himself, Look at us two, both started as cowboys, although not together, and the only difference is, Abe took one fork and I took another.

Suddenly it seemed to him that him and Abe had swapped careers without meaning to. He knowed he could of been a good peace officer, if that card had turned up for him. Only he drawed the penitentiary instead, and got converted, and now would spend the rest of his mortal years paying for the indiscretions of his youth. A pretty good peace officer turned into only a middling sort of preacher, was how it looked to him.

Now old Abe was a born preacher, something Rolf had never noticed before. He had the gift of command, and the gift of gab, and the gift of a heart that despised injustice and cruelty and selfishness. All he lacked was the religion, and Rolf had knowed many a preacher that flourished in the trade without that.

The Lord didn't have much to say about who preached His word. You was supposed to feel a call, but the Lord couldn't make you answer His call if you didn't feel like it, and if the wrong man overheard, and took it to be meant for him, why nothing could stop this eavesdropper from brandishing a Bible and forgiving sins and collecting tithes. The older Rolf got, the worse he felt about his own right to preach the Word. You didn't expect every seed to grow when you throwed it among the rocks, as it said in the Bible. But one or two ought to.

He said, "Abe, you can't fight progress."

Abe snorted, "Like the little old lady from Iowa, one of her sons had progress and the other'n a scab on his ass, and neither one passed a comfortable night."

Rolf said, "If the railroad ruins our free decent impoverished life, look what it done to the Indian. He had a nice dirty lazy system, scratching his lice in the sun or shade until he had to go kill or steal something, and he was free to kill and steal all he could get away with. Them days is gone forever, though."

Abe said, "What of it? Nobody envies the Indian. What the

Indian wants is a wooden house with a roof, and sorghum for his mush, and schools for his kids, and whisky in the same proportion as us."

Rolf said, "We get a church paper that makes you wonder if it's the United States Indians they're writing about or what, the way they talk about the free natural life of the noble red man. They never seen even a tame Indian, so they don't mention the lice, and the runty bowlegged babies coughing their lives away, or a buck kicking his squaw into the fire just because she don't get around so fast without enough to eat. You worry me, Abe. What do you aim to do about the railroad?"

"Why nothing," Abe said. "According to law, a railroad corporation is an artificial person, and a person has rights, I don't care how artificial he is. But he obeys the law too, and so long as the Q understands who is running Mooney County, we'll get along fine."

"Is this a secret," Rolf said, "or are you going to spread the news about the railroad?"

Abe grinned and said, "As many people as I can, and you do the same, and we'll learn this artificial person a quick easy first lesson about who they ought to clear things with before they make their move in our town. Look at that cat! I wonder how long he'd stay if I left that hat there. Sometime when we both got the time, if we ever do, let's time him and find out."

After Abe left, Rolf wrote to this fella in Denver and said they'd slouch along with their old wooden church. He knowed he was going to say this, but it was a comfort to have Abe think the same way, and he felt he had comforted Abe some about the railroad, too. You can't ask more of a friendship than that.

He told Samantha about the railroad, and she asked him wasn't it time for him to make a few calls around the congregation, and Rolf grinned and said maybe it was. He went out whistling through the rain, and talked to a few folks, and prayed with a few, and the more he thought about the railroad, the more praying he thought was necessary. Rolf got a lot of grumbling over that whistling of his, people said it wasn't dignified in a preacher and whoever heard of the Disciples whistling? So finely once he put a sign up in the church, ELEVENTH COMMANDMENT, THOU SHALT NOT WHISTLE for a few weeks. It didn't shut nobody up, but he felt better.

It was all over town before the saloon lamps was lit. You couldn't believe so big a secret could keep so long, or spread so fast once it got out. It rained all evening, and you hardly ever seen more than a few horses on the street on a wet night. Tonight every hitch rack in town was tied full.

Cattlemen and homesteaders and Indians and hired riders, they was all there, and Little Dick Silver going around reminding people how he had prophesied someday Mooney would be the Chicago of the east slope of the Rockies, and it was true, he had. Little Dick used to be an army scout in Arizona Territory, and was about eighty-two, and wore his long white hair to his shoulders, and had a mustache and a nice well-trimmed goatee. He was one of them that said the women still bothered him at his age, and it was prob'ly true with him.

"This will bring back the playful ladies too," Little Dick said. "You need a good parlor house or two near a depot, so a man can sacrifice his flesh between trains." Horace Slaughter said if the train was only going to back down from the main line and switch, and then go right out again, a man could hardly get into the spirit of the sacrifice in that length of time. Dave Loomis said yes, he'd be better off to wash his feet in cold water, and they really had Little Dick going.

It had its drawbacks, everybody admitted that, but it was better than teaming freight to Greeley or Fort Morgan. Truth was, them people had kept a light strain on their tugs so long, just to stay alive in that country, they was ready to believe anything. Tell them that the Archangel Gabriel would be conductor on the first train, and they'd believe that, or tell them the government was going to cut a canal through the Rockies so the Pacific packets could dock in Mooney, they'd believe that too.

Nobody took it amiss but Mable McMurdoch, who thought she knowed everything that went on in the bank. Alec hadn't told her, and she never forgave him, nor the Q either. She sent to her sister in Moline for some Rock Island calendars, and she wouldn't let Mac hang a Burlington calendar in the house, and for the Fourth of July program in the church, she wrote a patriotic cantata dedicated to the Union Pacific. Alec had to set there and listen to his wife's own defiant rebellious words to the tune of Columbia the Gem of the Ocean:

Three cheers for the grand old U.P.
That united our far-flung country.
There are numerous cheap imitations.
But only one grand old U.P.

4

That was sure some carnival.

Tapeworm got back in time for it, a changed man that had put on about twenty pounds, and had a new green suit and new boots, and had dyed his hair jet black, but still parted it in the middle. He left his family in Greeley for a few days, and came to Mooney in a rented top buggy behind a good horse. He rented a room at Marcus Sippy's house at first, and took his shirts and underwear to Deeda Meredith to wash, and only washed out his own socks. He opened an account at the bank with a draft for five thousand dollars on a Vincennes bank, and went around hiring men to help build the grain elevator and feedyards and his own new house, and called them all son.

"You won't get anywhere in life, straddling somebody else's horse and chasing somebody else's cows, son," he said. "Building mechanics are the coming thing. Start with the shovel, son, and progress to the hammer and the fascinating steel square."

Elmo Huger was with Dick Royce, painting things up there, and cutting a few weeds, and seeing that Dick didn't lose his money or forget to eat when he was drinking good. He hit Tapeworm up for a job on the new elevator one day. Tapeworm was down there with two men, stringing strings where he wanted trenches dug, and making marks on some plans, and talking all the time like he always did. He had hung his coat over the back of his rented buggy, and was in his vest and shirt sleeves and brocaded necktie, and was smoking a big black crooked cigar.

Elmo started it out by saying, "I didn't have no idee you was a builder, Tapeworm."

"Oh yes, son, many's the house I built and lost my shirt," Tapeworm said, "and do you know why? Because I can't build without quality, and there's no quicker way to go broke than quality. Here's a good rule for you, son. When you're building for yourself, like I am this elevator, slather on the quality all you can, because the main thing is you want it to last. But for somebody else, make sure it stands up long enough to slap on a coat of paint, and the paint will have to hold it together if you aim to come out on the job."

And so on. You give Tapeworm an opening, and you got an answer with an opening proposition, and the contrary theme, and the reasons that demolished your contrary theme, and all the footnotes thereto, and a detailed summation, and a peroration to bring the tears. Then Elmo hit him up for a job.

"Sorry, son," Tapeworm said, "but there ain't no such implement as a one-armed shovel. What I'm looking for ain't the strong back and the weak mind, as the prophet says, but a man with two good arms and a willing heart. You see how it is I'm sure."

"No I don't," Elmo said. "I can dig as much with one arm as them fellas can with both, and lend me one of your shovels and I'll prove it."

Tapeworm said, "No, son, they'll see you hacking away with one good arm, and dangling one, and you know human nature, they'll wonder why they should use both arms when their comrade is getting by with only half that many. No, son, it wouldn't work out."

He said what he had planned for Elmo was to run his son-in-law's cattle property for him. This was the first anybody knowed that Arthur H. Crawford, the dummy on them options, was his son-in-law.

"Art will run the J Bar B," Tapeworm said. "He can't stand it close to cows, they make him sneeze, and Art's city-bred anyhow as the fella says. But I'm turning the J Bar B over to him and my daughter, and with a good manager, that's a snug little property that can pay. I'd go as high as fifteen dollars a month and found."

And so on. When he could slide a word in by its edge, Elmo said, "Tapeworm, listen, them boys digging your trenches get $1.75 a day, and you say you'll pay carpenters $2.25, and an all-around ranch manager is worth $40 of anybody's money. It seems to me you're showing my weak arm a little too much consideration."

Tapeworm said he was sorry Elmo felt that way, the J Bar B was a piddling little property, and it would have to support three people, and he didn't really see how a man could keep himself busy forty dollars' worth. Elmo walked off and left Tapeworm jawing away at the empty air, getting louder and louder the further away Elmo got, until he was finely hollering so you could hear him all over town.

He went over to the old Doll House and found Dick setting in the shade, and rubbing the rust off'n an old rusty double-bitted ax he'd found.

"Look at this here ax," Dick said. "This is a good one, chilled and forged. I found me a piece of good straight-grain second-growth ash, and I'll shape a handle for it myself, and I'll have me a one-dollar ax that only cost me a little old-fashioned careful work."

"I can't wait," Elmo said, and flopped down in one of them old red chairs with his back to Dick. Dick asked him what was wrong, and Elmo told him.

"I could of told you that," Dick said. "I don't know why you bothered with the son of a bitch."

"I worked for him right here on this place," Elmo said. "He knows how much dad-blamed work I do, and he sure never spared me in them days. Now he's a big rich important man, thinking I'll be a flunky for his rich son-in-law Arthur H. Crawford. In a pig's eye."

"Well, Elmo," Dick said, "you got a home here as long as you want it, and let this be a lesson to you, never trust that Hoosier an inch. Take this ax; if Tapeworm knowed I found it here, he'd demand to look at the deed and see if it said anything about an ax, that's the kind of a half-ass Gila monster you've got in the great Tapeworm St. Sure. Elmo, I'd leave you my remittance from England if I could, but it stops when I die, and I got to figger every day I live, I'm beating them limey sons of bitches out of another dollar. I couldn't think more of you if you was my own flesh and blood, Elmo. You're exactly the age my own son would be if I'd had one, bad arm or no. For two cents I'd buckle on a gun and go make two little Tapeworms out of one big one and do the world a favor."

He would of, too, so Elmo had to get him to thinking about something else before he shot Tapeworm and got hung for it. A day or two later, or maybe three, he heard somebody was building a house up on the graveyard hill, and he went up there to see about a job, and sure enough, here was somebody stretching strings to show where the trenches had to be dug. Only it was Tapeworm again, starting to build the biggest house in Mooney, and when it was finished, a store building in the middle of town with his office in it, called the St. Sure Block. He backed Elmo up against a tree before Elmo knowed what was happening, and just talked his leg off. He couldn't talk to his workingmen, because when they stopped work to listen, it was money out of his own pocket. Elmo knowed him well enough to know how he was, and it was his own fault he got stuck that way.

Tapeworm said, "Elmo, opportunity was staring this town in the eye, chin to chin, toe to toe, and who seen it? Your leading citizens? Never, son, never! It was an old sick Hoosier stranger with a parasite in his bowels, a lone bereft friendless man, he was the one who looked opportunity in the eye, chin to chin and toe to toe. This illustrates what I told you many a time when we was holed up in that pigsty across the creek, you remember what it was I used to tell you," and so on.

It seemed to Elmo that the C.B.&Q. had a little to do with looking opportunity in the eye, but it wasn't no use saying something like that to Tapeworm, he'd just jack his voice up another notch and load it with a few more grains of powder, and drownd you out. There went another job that Elmo didn't get.

Tapeworm found out that there was some rooms over the Byron Wescott Mercantile Company, and he rented them and had a privy dug out back by the town wagon lot, and put a padlock on it so nobody could use it but his family, and wired to Omaha to forward his furniture. He had Bill Ahern team it down from Greeley, and him and all them kids moved in above the store, and the first Sunday they was in town, he brought them all to church.

There was ten of them kids, you couldn't hardly blame a man from running away like he'd done, ranging from the oldest one, Virginia Crawford about twenty-seven, down to the youngest one, a little brat boy of six, Felton by name. The son-in-law, Arthur H. Crawford, came to church with the family, and they filled up the whole third pew on the left from the front.

This brat Felton, named after Tapeworm's mother's maiden name, he stood up in the pew with his back to Rolf all during service, and grinned at people like some kind of a baboon, and picked his nose and ate it, and scuffled his feet so hard that Rolf had to holler to be heard. You could see right away that this Felton was the kind of a kid his mother would say, "He's the last one I'll ever cuddle in my arms, he ain't really spoiled and he does love everybody so much." The kind you ache to catch over the ear with a slap with your glove on.

After church, Tapeworm stood there grinning and bowing so everybody else went up the aisle first. Then he marched them out in close-order drill, so you could almost hear the trumpeter blow "At the Trot," and see the squadron pennants flying. They was a real sandy-looking bunch of scrubs, all but the oldest one, Mrs. Arthur H. Crawford. She was kind of brown-haired and slim, while the other'ns favored their mother.

"Reverend," Tapeworm said, "I want to present my family to you."

"My stars and garters, Tapeworm, do you mean these is all your'n?" Rolf said.

Tapeworm's wife r'ared back so hard her corsets squeaked, and she let out a screech, "*What* did he call you?" Tapeworm said it referred to his unfortunate illness. He said, "I hoped that would be forgot by now. It's a bedraggled name for a man in my position."

Rolf said, "You know how it is, once you ford the Missouri. Half the people have already changed their home names, for one reason or another. Names don't really mean too much here, but a nickname sticks."

Tapeworm's wife was just snorting. She was a big strong strawberry blond that sweat a lot, one of them women with such a big bosom, she always seemed to be standing closer to you than you was to her. She said, "I give you my sacred word, I did not move to this hick town to be called Mrs. Tapeworm."

"You should of skipped that," Rolf said. "It'll only give people idees." To jump ahead, Rolf was right, and she got to be knowed far and wide as Mrs. Tapeworm, and she got to where she'd answer to it, but you can't say she ever really got used to it.

Tapeworm lined the kids out, and his wife sang out their names. Rolf shook hands with one and all, even Felton, although most people in Mooney got to where they said they'd rather have a rattlesnake in their lap than Felton St. Sure. Then Rolf called Samantha over, and she had to shake hands with everybody, and welcome them to town.

Rolf took the baby from Sammie, and they started to walk home. "So those are our new Sadducees," Sammie said. Rolf told her not to take so much for granted, and Sammie smiled and said, "No, it's probably not Christian of me, but it's exceedingly realistic. I'll make you a little bet, dear, I'll bet that man is already agitating to be put on the church board."

Rolf said, "I wish you wouldn't always offer to bet me. In this case I'd say you're prob'ly right, but he may also be planning to do the Lord's work if he gets on the board, too. Did he seem nervous to you?"

Sammie said yes he did, very nervous, like he wasn't used to his position in town, and had a secret fear it would all be snatched away from him. Rolf said it kind of hit him that way too.

Sammie said, "Now you be equally honest, and tell me what you think of Arthur and Virginia Crawford."

He said, "I noticed him talking to you, he seems to be quite a talker, or maybe it was just his first chance where Tapeworm couldn't interrupt him." Sammie said was that the only impression, and Rolf said, "I'll tell you the truth, hon, if a man can't grow a real mustache, he shouldn't even try. That little old yellow chicken fuzz of his, why you've got more hair on your legs."

Sammie laughed so hard she had to bend over to get it over with. They walked on, and she said, "He told me a great deal in a few minutes, yet none of it seems very conclusive, or even descriptive. They've been married two years, he went to Princeton two years, he has been to Europe and studied swordsmanship, which is his hobby, both the blade and the point, and he says he has a musical education too."

"He won't find many around here that will fight him with swords," Rolf said.

Sammie said, "I liked Virginia. She may be rattle-brained, but there's a kind heart in her, and I don't think she's happy somehow. And I can't quite see them running the J Bar B. I think perhaps Virginia can rise to any occasion, she gives that impression of strength and courage. But she has led a very sheltered life, and I'm afraid Arthur will be dissatisfied and out of place on a cattle ranch."

Rolf didn't say nothing, but he had learned to listen to Sammie in some things, because she had a lot more sense than he did, and knowed a lot more about people. Not about the kind of people you'd meet in prison, but other people.

He didn't need to tell her the St. Sures could turn out a problem, the kind that pledge big, and then hold back part of it when something don't suit them. But most people was like this. You can't expect people to support something they don't like with their own hard-earned money, and the tighter money is, the more things there are to offend people.

In that way, the St. Sures would be just average Christians, except that Abe had pointed out, this was a case where you had to look at your chips as well as your cards. You take a man that pledges $25 a year, and then holds back $12.50 of it when the preacher takes the wrong stand, you've got to figure from the preacher's point of view it only costs $12.50 to stand on Scripture as he reads it. But if a man pledges $100, and holds back $50—well, Abe said, this is how the Lord separates the men from the boys in the clergy.

"This jaybird has already chunked in the first half of his pledge," Abe said, "so he's entitled to fifty dollars' worth of good intentions. Here's where a preacher needs to fortify himself all he can with prayer and good liquor, and go back to the Scripture for a second reading, and see if it can't be stretched to span that other fifty dollars. Sometimes it can and sometimes it can't, and it's hard lines either way. I reckon this is what the Lord meant when he told that fella to give all he had to the poor and then foller Him. Them unpaid pledges could haunt the Lord Himself, and He didn't have no family to support like most preachers these days. Or that's how it looks to me."

Sammie said Abe was only a realist, but life was one crisis after another, and some could be compromised and some couldn't. And if Tapeworm made too much trouble, she could be perfectly happy as a cowboy's wife.

Tapeworm was too busy with his building jobs to pry into the church much, and he didn't get around to a pledge right away, and Rolf was just as happy. He was pretty busy himself, although not with the carnival.

One thing, he had to start a bucket brigade for Dick Royce, when Elmo Huger got a couple of weeks of work painting the house at Charley Parker's Roofed Lazy 8, the outside only. Charley didn't like paint inside. For a few days while Elmo was gone, Dick would go across the footbridge and buy himself some cheese and stuff, and pick a few things in somebody's garden. But his remittance got in then, and when he went over to eat, he had to get down and crawl across the footbridge a few days.

This got to be too much trouble, and he just stopped eating, and only drank, and slid down in his chair a little more every now and then. A drinker like Dick, he can set for hours, staring at the rat hole in the corner, wrinkling his forehead like he's worrying about something, only he prob'ly ain't, it just itched. He don't want entertainment or company, he don't want charity or understanding, he just wants to set there and drink himself to death without worrying anybody.

Thad Rust found Dick so fur gone he had almost quit breathing. He started after Dr. Jerrow, but he run into Rolf first, and Rolf ran home and got some fresh cream and raw eggs. He had a good bait of grub down Dick by the time Doc got there, and Dick was starting to warm up a little except for his hands and feet.

"He'll just regurgitate it, but that's part of the treatment too," Doc said. "Keep it up."

Rolf slapped Dick every time he tried to puke it up and Dick kept most of it down, and it was an even bet he would live, and he did. Rolf organized a team to take turns going over there and taking Dick something to eat, and said Dick could pay for it when he sobered up. Dick did too.

Rolf didn't have no funerals, but he had a christening and a marriage, two different bunches of people. He had one man dissatisfied with his wife and wanting to leave her, and another family with the woman dissatisfied with the husband, and as fur as Rolf could see, they both had plenty of reason. But he said, "What plans do you have to better yourself? Who's going to support the kids, and who's going to take care of them? If you've got that figgered out, and have got a better life to go to, I won't try to stop you."

They didn't of course. When somebody is dissatisfied, it's eeny, meeny, miney, mo what he's going to light on to say dissatisfied him, and he don't think of bettering himself, only of jumping out of the frying pan. Rolf knitted up them two marriages for better or for worse, and kept the scandal in the family.

He found he was on the carnival tickets committee, and was supposed to sell two hundred tickets at twenty-five cents each to his congregation. He plugged them hard on two straight Sundays, and sold six tickets, leaving only one hundred and ninety-four to go. Blessed Sacrament had a new priest, a young handsome narrow-minded black Irishman by the name of Father Patrick Sandoval, and he sold his two hundred without half trying.

Father Sandoval wasn't above teasing Rolf about it on the street, or anywhere he could, and Rolf seen it was making the Methodists look bad, and the whole Protestant sect from Martin Luther to Brigham Young, who you have to think of as Protestant because he sure wasn't no priest renouncing the flesh. Cal Venaman came to see Rolf one day in the middle of the week, and found him staring at them one hundred and ninety-four tickets like his crown of righteousness in the Hereafter was at stake.

"Bit off more than you can chew?" Cal said, and Rolf said, "Looks like. Cal, I don't see why you can't support your church and send your whole crew to see this carnival."

"I don't want them fighting, is why," Cal said. "Rarely does a gypsy carnival get out of town without trying to steal everything in town on the last day. When the rubes resist, the gypsies take it out on them by beating them with tent stakes. I'm not inexperienced in certain things, and I won't risk my crew."

"I never been to a carnival," Rolf said. He thought he'd try another wild idee on Cal. He said, "Bringing the Q here was your plan, Cal, and now you won't even let your own crew go to the carnival. That's all right if it's your principles, but you ort to do something. Now there's them poor Kincaiders, their kids is just dying to go, and you know none of them can afford two bits a head for the families they have. Why don't you buy some of these tickets, and pass them out compliments of the cattlemen, and charge it off to a moment of unselfish Christian weakness of mind."

Cal got pretty red in the face at first, but he started to nod, and when Rolf got done, he said, "Sometimes you make a remarkable lot of sense, Rolf. Let's see, that's fifty dollars' worth, why I can afford more than that, and surely those prolific Kincaiders have more than two hundred kids. I see thousands of them every time I go down there, literally thousands, like the locusts of old. You go get another three hundred tickets, and bill them to me, and you pass them out with the compliments of the cattlemen."

Rolf just about cried. He said, "I'll really enjoy that. Some of them kids remind me of myself, when my dad was brokering wheat in Kansas. We got left out of everything."

"Many of those French and Bohemian nesters are Catholic, you know," Cal said.

Rolf nodded and said, "I reckon so; well I'll see if Pat Sandoval can pass out a few for us. I think he can be trusted to give credit to the cattlemen."

Cal clapped him on the shoulder and said Rolf was as innocent as a new-hatched bird, but the pope himself can pass out a handful if he'll credit the cattlemen. Another thing occurred to him, and he asked Rolf if he knew Goodwin Bent Tree, and Rolf said he did.

Goodwin Bent Tree was half Cheyenne and half Arapahoe, and had been raised in a mission, and married a German girl. He filed on a half-section Kincaid tract and was working his tail off trying to scratch a living out of that old thin dirt. Rolf said he'd see that Goodwin got some of the free cattlemen's tickets.

"Let's do better than that," Cal said. "Goodwin has a racing pony that has beaten all the Indian horses. Did you know that Alec McMurdoch has bought a quarter horse? So help me, that's how this railroad folly has gone to his head! Let's get up a race between the two horses. Rolf," he said, jumping up to walk up and down, he got so enthusiastic all of a sudden, "let's do better than that! I'll make the carnival board let all Indians in free—they're our responsibility, aren't they? How better to civilize them than let them into a nice noisy dirty unhealthy crooked carnival?"

Rolf began to grin all over. He seen that Cal had struck on a really highlarious plan to make the carnival a success. Them two got real chummy there, and Cal said Rolf had lots of good idees, they only needed mature developing, and they ought to work together more often.

"I'm all for that, Cal," Rolf said. "I know it will make Sammie smile too."

"And don't forget Opal, I wouldn't resent it a bit if she smiled a little more often too," Cal said. "Your sermons for instance, Rolf. Sometimes I think when you read off your text, Oh dear here we go again on that same old shopworn bit of Bible! Then as you begin to speak, your own prison-won wisdom and tolerance and well, vision, seem to give the old words new illumination. The trouble is, you peter out along toward the end most of the time. I'd like to show you how to organize a public address sometime. That's all a sermon is, a public address, and a good public address has tight structure, and I can show you that so yours won't peter out."

Rolf said they'd have to do that someday, although this was further than he really cared to go. But it was a novelty to hear praise from his father-in-law about anything, and he looked forward to seeing all them nester kids and Indians having a good time, and he reckoned he was at least going to learn something about how you run a good successful carnival.

5

Some carnival all right. These two brothers from Missouri, Micah and Arvin Hope, stumbled into my place one day on their way back to Missouri from Arizona. I was took with them completely, they was so innocent; why they might as well not of left home for all they had learned out there. They was mighty happy to lay over a few days, and get good homemade things like fried mush and sorghum, and cow peas with sow bosom, and so forth. They'd found gold in the Superstitions, and was going back to Benton County to start a sawmill, $2,800 worth.

They got to telling me about a man they met going over Wolf Crick Pass, going in opposite directions, and they stopped and talked to him. Both of them thought he was looking them over for weapons, and all they had was .45 revolvers in their packs. All of a sudden, this man jumped onto Arvin and would of beat him to death, only Micah tickled him in the ribs with a knife.

"I think he reely aimed to take our money away from us," Micah said. "He was right peart with his fists, but he sure screamed at the tetch of that knife. He said he was going to California, and I reckon he run all the way without stopping for breath."

I asked what he looked like, and it was Mike Timpke all right. I told them when they went through Mooney to look up Sheriff Abe Whipple and tell him about it, and I give them some tickets Rolf sent out to me so they could see the carnival, and them old boys just had the time of their lives.

There was Wasserman and Kiebold Combined Shows, with an elephant and a lion and some trick monkeys and acrobats, and a six-piece brass band, and this clown that would get astraddle of the lion and stand there and call him names until Micah and Arvin just laughed themselves sick. "You think you're so fierce," this clown said, "why you're nothing but an old pussy cat; I dare you to open your mouth and bite my head off. Why I've got a good notion just to slap your face." They said the lion scowled like he resented it, but he didn't offer to fight back.

There was this woman, the only woman colonel in the Royal Spanish Dragoons, Colonel Dolores Sanchez de Bimini, that done her famous sword dance while riding on a white horse around the ring. She was dark-complected, and the Hope boys thought she was a mite heavier than when she first bought her tights, but she was still a good-looking hairy woman if you like them hairy.

She come out astraddle of her horse, in a red uniform with a split skirt, and her knuckles on her hips, and her back just as straight. Then she up and stood on the horse, and unbuttoned her military split skirt, and there she was revealed in her tights. A man would throw her a sword, and she waved it and danced all over the horse on tiptoe while the band played a tune.

Just when people thought it was over, somebody throwed her another sword, and the band shut up its racket, and she dared anybody to come out and take this other sword and fight her. The first night it was Harold DuSheane, the town half-wit, and they got down there in the sawdust and fought it out, the woman hollering, "Yep! Yep! Ya! Ya! Ho!" while she cut Harold's buttons off. There he stood with his pants down around his ankles and nothing on under them.

Colonel Dolores Sanchez de Bimini made like she was going to nick him in some mighty personal places, and people just screamed. She turned her back and covered her face like she just realized what she was seeing, and old Harold pulled up his pants and loped out of there fast.

The next night there wasn't nobody would fight her, but on the third and last night, the Hope boys said it was a thin young fella with a silky golden mustache. He was half drunk, but the minute he grabbed that sword, Colonel Dolores Sanchez de Bimini had met her match. He let her have first slash, and she took it, and then she started to take another one, and he catched her sword on his and the sparks just flew.

They touched swords so often it sounded like honing a scythe, and that woman began to get madder and madder when she couldn't hit him, and she began to scowl instead of smiling, but the man kept on smiling. Then she jumped at him and nicked him and drawed blood through his shirt, and people just moaned.

"Ah-ha, so blows the wind in that quarter," was all he said, and he really went after her, smiling all the while. He nicked her between the bosoms, and drawed a little blood there, and then around her belly button, and drawed a little there, and then he made his sword whistle around her face awhile.

This colonel, she suddenly let out a yell in a foreign language, and she danced back and pointed her sword at the ground, and bowed her head, and knelt on one knee, admitting plain as anything that she was good and whipped. This man who whipped her, who of course was Tapeworm's son-in-law, Art Crawford, he pointed his sword down too, and stepped back and bowed to her, and then took her hand and helped her up.

"The purtiest thing you ever seed; she was whupped fair and squar', but this man let on like it was just luck," Arvin Hope said. "Half of the people in that crowd was crying, it was so splendid to see."

But this was after the horse race between Goodwin Bent Tree's little Appaloosa mare, five years old, by the name of

Apples, and Alec McMurdoch's chestnut three-year-old stud, Bright Publius, that had cost him five hundred dollars. Mac had an Irishman from Omaha to ride him, Jimmy Dunn, that only weighed 142 pounds. Goodwin Bent Tree was going to ride his own mare at about 165 pounds.

The race almost didn't come off. Goodwin said his horse had to pay its way, everything on his place did, a poor man couldn't afford idle hand or hoof, so what was the prize? There hadn't been no prize put up. "Why this is just to entertain people," Alec said. "There's two thousand of your own people here."

"I don't care if they're entertained or not," Goodwin said.

"Listen, if I'm willing to race my horse in a ridiculous country race, you ought to be," Alec said. "I hear you worked your pony on a lister yesterday, plowing out a row of early potatoes. Why if that's true, I'm racing a blooded horse against a plow horse."

"True it is, everything on my place pays its way, even my wife," Goodwin said. "Gert's a German girl, she don't think nothing of going to the field and doing a man's work, and I reckon you think that suits a buck Indian just fine. Well listen to this, Alec, someday Gert's going to take it as easy as your wife, and then maybe I'll race a horse for just the honor."

"That's neither here nor there," Mac said. "I have only respect for you and Gert, and you damn well know it, and my wife picked up potatoes too in her time. If you've got to have a prize, how about a little side bet between you and me? Say five dollars."

"I haven't got five dollars," Goodwin said, "but how about my horse against yours? You couldn't buy this little mare from me for five hundred dollars, but I'll bet her."

Mac said, "I don't want your pony. That's a ridiculous idee, betting our horses."

"All right," Goodwin said, "I'll put Gert up behind me on Apples and we'll go home and lay out another row of spuds."

"You make me tired," Mac said. "All right, it's a bet, my horse against yours, and by God don't blame me if you turn out to be a dismounted Plains Indian, and there ain't nothing lower than an unhorsed horse Indian, and you know it as well as I do. So don't come to me whining and wanting your horse back."

They laid out the race, and then Jimmy Dunn asked Mac how he wanted him to ride the race, and Mac said, "In a quarter-mile race, you get off to a fast start and keep going faster, that's all."

There was a good two thousand Indians there, loyal to a man, and they went around trying to bet their pocket change on Apples. There was some trouble getting them off'n the course, because an Indian likes to watch his horse races head on, and just step out of the way at the last minute. But finely they got out of the way.

Alec was having prostate trouble, and when it came about time to start the horses, he knowed he'd have to go pretty soon, so he stepped over into the brush that by common consent was where the men went. He done his best all right, but a prostate is no respecter of persons as the fella says, and the harder Mac tried, the less headway he made. Yet he knowed if he give up and buttoned up, here it would come.

He could hear a lot of screaming and yelling, and he kept pushing and grunting and trying, and finely he got the job done. Only by then the race was over, and he didn't have no horse.

Apples beat Bright Publius by one hundred feet, the most fun the Indians had since Little Big Horn. "A short life and a merry one," Mac said to Cal Venaman. "My racing career measured in a few painful drops. That Indian suckered me into that bet."

"Yes he did," Cal said, "but now he tells me he doesn't want your horse, Mac. It was just a sporting proposition to Goodwin."

"What does he think I am, an Indian giver?" Mac said. "I'd never live it down."

"You won't anyway," Cal said. "Have you seen my son-in-law anywhere?"

Mac said no he hadn't, he hardly expected to see a minister at a horse race. Now, where Rolf was, this was another story, and nobody seen Rolf until after the carnival was over. After the horse race, the carnival started to get ready to move out of town, and them people knowed it was their last chance to cash in on these rubes as they called the Mooney people. They raised the prices on everything, and then started to make fun of the boys when they wouldn't spend money on the girls fast enough, and a few people got their pockets picked.

One that got his pocket picked was Bill Ahern, the owner of a freight wagon line, who was already in debt head over heels. He had bid in four big Clydesdale horses seized in the famous Jack Butler murder case, and they was eating him out of house and home, and when he found this woman had lifted his wallet with three dollars in it, he was so disgusted he wanted to whip everybody in sight.

He whipped about five of them carnival men before they got organized when somebody yelled "HEY, RUBE," this being the signal for the carnival men to mobilize as you might say. Goodwin Bent Tree barely had time to put Gert up on Apples, and get up on Bright Publius himself, and it was just one great big fight between everybody except the Indians. They just looked on and enjoyed it, to see the palefaces making war on their own selves.

Cal Venaman was ready to go home, and he had sent his wife home in the buggy, but he had hung around with his boys, thirty-two strong, including his foreman, an old-timer by the name of Shoo Shoo. They was just standing there holding their horses and wondering why they didn't head for home, when they heard this "HEY, RUBE."

Cal said, "Well, boys, this is what happens, and I've always wondered how those carney city toughs would stand against a cavalry charge. Let's keep a cool head and don't kill anyone, because we're going in shooting. Fire slowly, into the air. You'll have no time to reload until we're through them, and we may not have to make a second charge, so make this a good one."

He said, "Now if the elephant gets loose, remember that horses are afraid of elephants, and we'll have bucking horses all over Colorado if you lose control of your mounts. Let's form up now, boys, double file, and follow me shooting."

Somebody said, "You don't want nobody killed, but if somebody gets in front of this iron-mouth bastard I'm riding, I don't promise I can cut around him."

Cal said, "He has no business being in front of you. A reasonable effort is all I ever expect from a man. Ready, boys? CHARGE!"

They went in shooting into the air, and went through that mob like a dose of salts, and there wasn't no more than eight or ten carnival men hurt. The elephant either got loose or was turned loose, and Cal was right again, he just terrified them range ponies. But nobody let his horse get its head down, and nobody got throwed to disgrace the Flying V. The elephant run clear to Cleveland Smith's place near the Platte, taking clotheslines and fences and privies as he went, and was feeding peacefully on Cleve's young fruit trees when the Flying V boys caught up with him.

Cal said, "Boys, we can't hold him if it's a contest of force against force. But this is one of the most intelligent animals alive, and I believe one rope around his forefoot is the ticket. We don't herd him in, we escort him."

That's the way they done it, and it worked out fine. One of Cal's boys said, "Cal, what surprises me, how does a polite gray-haired rich cattle baron know about carnival fighting and elephants and so on?" Cal said, "I wasn't born a polite gray-haired rich cattle baron. Each man reaches his destination in life by his own route; does that answer your question?"

"Not hardly," the cowboy said, "but they say a good storyteller leaves something to the imagination, and by God, Cal, you're one of the best."

Cal unexpectedly took the notion to stand his boys to a drink on him. They tied in front of a saloon and went inside, and then the boys decided to buy a few of their own. Cal had one more with them for manners, but they knowed he was a two-drink man, and wasn't offended when he went outside giving them exactly twenty minutes to liquor up in.

Outside the saloon, he looked across the street and seen his son-in-law, Reverend Rolf Ledger. He hollered and asked Rolf where he'd been, and Rolf said Dad Townsend had been threatening to die, and had sent for him to be converted at the last minute, and Rolf had been there all afternoon and he hadn't died yet.

He said, "He's always been the dirtiest-talking man I ever knowed, there's no shame in him, nor much repentance if you want the truth. Yet except for his filthy talk, he hasn't done nobody any real harm, and I'd like to see the ground-breaking for the depot, and then get back to Dad Townsend's bedside."

"And see if a repentant heart and a dirty mind can inhabit the same body, eh?" Cal said. "The ground-breaking was called off. That's where the fight broke out. The last I saw of Tapeworm and the Q officials, they was fortifying the town pump house. Well it has been a fruitful day, Rolf, and I'm grateful for the idee that you had to stand treat for those range-destroying ingrate Kincaiders."

They parted friends, and Rolf headed back to Dad Townsend, and then this big tall handsome dark-skinned man in a fake Indian outfit came up to Cal and said, "Excuse me, I wonder if I could ask you who that man is you was just talking to."

Cal said, "Why sir, that's my son-in-law, the Reverend Rolf Ledger, do you know him?"

The man said, "I'll be a son of a bitch, well thanks very

much," and went off down the street with the fringes of his store-boughten leggings flying, and Cal said to himself, Well here's another ex-convict Rolf did time in the pen with. I wonder if I should warn him? But the twenty minutes was up, so he stuck his head in the saloon door and hollered, "Time," and his boys come out, and he led them off home rollicking and jolly and at peace with the world.

Thus the carefree life of a cowboy; no more judgment than a half-wit, but nobody on earth faithfuler to a boss that treats him well. They had set a record and knowed it, because how many cowboys can say they catched an elephant in their round-up? It was a cinch to be made into a trail song sooner or later, and it was:

He had no horns and he had no hoofs,
But he had two tails instead,
One growed out of his fat behind,
And one growed out of his head.
I said, "You're the damndest-looking steer
That ever a man did see,
But we'll throw you down and brand your ass
With the mark of the Flying V."

That night Dad Townsend sent for Rolf again, and it wasn't no false alarm, and he slid over the edge with his hand resting in Rolf's, secure in the glory of repentance and forgiveness. It was all over town the next morning, that he went with a prayer on his lips instead of the dirty joke he always promised, leaving eight living children, forty-one grandchildren, and seven great-grandchildren.

When they hauled off and probated his estate, he had left $76,550, too, and a man can't lay up that much and spend every waking hour chasing that good stuff, the way Dad Townsend always claimed he spent his life.

But this news wasn't a caution to what come out before they had even cleaned up the mess of the carnival. Most men would of hid a family shame, but not Tapeworm, no sir, he come riding back from the J Bar B with his horse in a lather, and he started talking before he got down to tie in front of where he was starting to build the St. Sure Block, and he never stopped talking, and he told it over and over again, and if anybody in Mooney missed hearing it from his own lips, it was their own fault. His son-in-law, Arthur H. Crawford, had run off with the woman sword-dancer from the carnival, Colonel Dolores Sanchez de Bimini, leaving behind a spiteful note for his wife Virginia, and another spitefuler one for Tapeworm, and over a hundred dollars in debts in Mooney, mostly two dollars he had borrowed here and five dollars he had borrowed there.

6

There couldn't be no mistake. Colonel Dolores Sanchez de Bimini had her own house wagon, pulled by her white dancing horse and another white extry one, and it had went two hours ahead of the rest of the carnival. Five or six boys, including Felton St. Sure, had seen it leave on a trot, with Art Crawford in it feeling around the front of the colonel's dress while she drove.

Tapeworm asked Felton why he didn't say something about it while there was still time, and Felton said, "I didn't want to, that's why. They wouldn't give us a ride, so we shied some rocks at them."

Tapeworm said, "My children have all been a sore trial to me at times, none more than this wee one, the least and last of my brood," and by then the whole town was ready to agree. There never was no split in public opinion about Felton St. Sure.

Them two old Missouri boys, Micah and Arvin Hope, had remembered to run Abe Whipple down, and told him about meeting Mike Timpke in Wolf Crick Pass, and he said, "This is very interesting." He asked them a lot of other interesting questions, if Mike had talked to them about Mooney, which he hadn't, or if he had mentioned the names of Royce or St. Sure or Heath, which he hadn't. He asked them how they happened to stop at Pete Heath's Place of all places, and they said Arvin's horse had popped its three-quarter girth, and you don't need that girth to hold your saddle on unless you're roping, but the horse had the habit and wouldn't ride with that girth dangling, and Arvin was afoot for a couple of miles, and they just stopped at the first handiest place.

They was such honest old boys they finely made him see it was the truth, and he thanked them kindly. But he had Mike Timpke fresh on his mind when he heard about Arthur H. Crawford running off with the colonel lady, and he knowed what this could mean to the future of Mooney. He run Tapeworm down by following the sound of his voice all over town, and he made Tapeworm go up to the house with him, and set in Abe's own back yard to be questioned.

Tapeworm said Art hadn't wanted to move to Colorado nohow, and the news didn't really surprise him, and it was Virginia's pride that was hurt more than anything, because Art had been a sore trial as a husband from the first, but any child of his had pride enough not to let a piece of bad luck like this whip her. He said, "I've calmed down now, Sheriff. I see this in its true light as an annoyance rather than a tragedy even in the bosom of my own family, so I'll just be running along now, and not take any more of your time up."

Abe said, "You'll set back down on that kag is what you'll do. That little bastard's name is on the paper of a lot of property around this town, some of the most valuable since the Q squatted on us. I can live without a railroad, and the railroad knows it, but I have to consider the people who vote for me. Litigation over land titles that could tie up the railroad plans could break a lot of good decent clean honest hearts here."

Tapeworm looked at Abe like he really pitied him, and said, "My lord, Sheriff, I hope you don't think I'm fool enough to trust a piss-ant son-in-law with my hole card. Art was only a dummy. I got a whole stack of assignments, where he couldn't find them in a lifetime, covering every square foot of that real estate."

"Yes," said Abe, "but are they recorded? Are they on file? It's what's on file that counts."

"Not yet," Tapeworm said, "but they're notarized, and I'm going to file them first thing tomorrow."

"You're going to file them right now," Abe said, "but first I want Jimmy Drummond to look them over for faults or blemishes, and we can't ask Jimmy to work for nothing, so you have a ten-dollar bill ready to hand him."

Tapeworm said, "My own judgment is that Art will get tired of this hairy Spanish colonel woman and come back to his duty, and I don't like to make my family's affairs a matter of public record, and I resent having pressure put on me."

Abe said Tapeworm had a perfect right to resent it, so long as he done it, and Tapeworm knowed Abe well enough by then to know his next job was to file them papers. Abe went with him, and they got the papers out of the stovepipe hole in the rooms where Tapeworm and his family was living, and had Jimmy look them over. Jimmy said they was in one hundred per cent apple-pie order, so they filed them and Tapeworm bellyached about the filing fees, and said he had to be getting back to work.

"No, first let's go back to this little attempted assassination of yours," Abe said. "I've got an office down in the depths of this courthouse, let's go down there and reason together as the Good Book tells us to."

Tapeworm said he had more important things to do, and Abe said he had nothing as important to do as this. Tapeworm said he had put the ambush out of his mind long ago, and Abe said *he* hadn't, not by no means, when one of the town's leading land speculators, somebody tried to shoot him down in cold blood, it was a serious matter.

Tapeworm said, "I wasn't one of the town's leading land speculators then, I was a sick lonely downcast old family man that had abandoned his family, a failure in life, and I had this tapeworm, and I had throwed my whole stake into that little old swamp across the crick, and if that wasn't the judgment of a sick mind, I'd like to know what is. I was living in an old abandoned whorehouse with a one-armed Georgia boy to watch out over me, a derelict from decent society, the flotsam and jetsam of life, and I must say, if you took it such a serious matter when I got shot, you sure as hell took your time getting there."

Abe said, "You was in a mighty pitiful state then, I own that, yet somebody admired you enough to cut loose on you. Let's you and me discuss some long lonely rides you took, and a surveying crew you run into, and similar events."

Tapeworm got a kind of a wild look in his big purple eyes and said he didn't know what rides Abe referred to, or what surveying crews. He said, "I hope you haven't been talking to Elmo Huger, Sheriff. He ain't the most reliable witness. Outside of having only one good arm, Elmo's worst drawback is that he'll tell you anything; you talk about lying, why that boy will look you in the eye and tell you the *God*damnedest lies!"

Abe said, "I've knowed Elmo nigh only three years, and I never knowed him to tell a lie. Now I'm going to deal to the draw, Tapeworm, and here's your first card. I know how you got onto the Q coming here. You hid in the brush and follered their surveyors, you sneaky son of a bitch."

Tapeworm begin to sweat and mop his face, and said, "I did not! I had inside information."

Abe said, "You didn't have no inside information. You got a peek at their hole card and you had the guts to bet it. I give you credit for the guts, but let's see if you have guts enough to reach for this next card I'm going to deal you."

Tapeworm wiped his face with both sleeves, and said, "Sheriff, if such a tale got around it could damage me gravely. You talk about hole cards, why my one and only hole card is my inside information! Even the Q's division superintendent practically licks my hand like a kicked dog, because he thinks one word from me could cost him his job. You're trying to make me look like a jackass, oh I grant you, a lucky jackass, one with guts, but my reputation ain't built on being a lucky jackass with guts to bet, it's built on inside information."

Abe said, "It's up to you, Tapeworm. I don't see no reason to tell everybody what I know, if you and me are going to work together on this case."

Tapeworm moaned, "You call it working together, I say it's like the coyote that trapped the jackrabbit in the fence corner; they worked together too." Abe didn't admit it and he didn't deny it. He just leaned back and crossed his boots and drummed on the table and now and then snuffled through his mustache. For once in his life, Tapeworm run out of words.

There just wasn't no use lying to Abe Whipple sometimes, and he had the judgment to see that. Tapeworm said, "You've got the power of life or death over my reputation. Just when I'm at your mercy, I find you have no mercy in you. What do you want to know?"

Abe said, "Who shot at you?"

"Good God," Tapeworm said, "I ought to be asking you that, you're the sheriff, I was only the victim."

"Well," Abe said, "all cases start with the victim, you know. We get his story straight first, and then we go on from there. Let's make it easy on you. How do you like this next card I'm dealing you, a card by the name of Mike Timpke. Was it him shot at you?"

"Why," Tapeworm said, "I don't believe I know any such party as the one you mention."

"You lie like a dog," Abe said. He leaned over and took Tapeworm by the arm and said, "Why are you afraid of him? Why do you twitch when I only just barely mention his name? Why can't you look me in the eye?"

Tapeworm said, "You're hurting my arm," and Abe said, "I mean to hurt it. Let's bring you to your senses even if it hurts. In all friendliness, you long lean lying Indiana Hoosier son of a bitch, was it or wasn't it Mike Timpke that tried to murder you?"

Tapeworm just caved in like somebody had kicked his props out. He said, "I thought it was him, it sure looked like him, but it couldn't be him because he's the scaredest man about a gun you ever seen! He called out, "Hey," and I looked up and thought sure it was him, and then he just lets go with the shotgun and run, and I knowed right then it was a mistake on my part because Mike wouldn't touch a gun. Like maybe his mother had been frightened by a gun when she was carrying him, and marked him for life. So it couldn't be him, Sheriff."

"Or are you just scared he'll come back and beat up on you this time and beat you to death?" Abe said.

Tapeworm shuddered and sweat some more. He said, "I've got a right to the protection of the law, Sheriff. If that man comes into this town, I want him arrested. That's the most dangerous man I ever seen, but it couldn't of been him that shot at me because he wouldn't touch cold steel in the form of a weapon."

Abe said, "Did he ever beat up on you?"

"Once," Tapeworm said. "Once is enough, with that man. The day the Q loaded up their surveyors, he catched up with me before I got into town, and pulled me off'n my horse, and just beat me awful! There wasn't a mark on me, Sheriff, yet I just ached all over. I had to drag myself every step, yet I knowed I had only so much time before this word got out that the Q was coming. I had to dispose of that swampy 3.258 acres more or less across the crick, and take certain other steps back home in Vincennes before I could profit by the opportunity that had come my way at long last."

He said, "But I tell you this from the bottom of my heart, nothing is going to stop me now! They call me a land baron already, well that's like prime aged whisky to my palate, because all my life I never been called anything but a failure, or at best a schemer. A man comes to a time in life when he wants to hold up his head at last, and if he can't he might as well hang himself to the nearest four-leaf clover, he's so low-down. I give that man all the cash I had on me, over forty dollars, money I could of put in options at the key point in my career. He follered me home and rummidged through my house and helped himself to anything he seen that he wanted, the son of a bitch. Now it looks to me like you're actually taking his part, Sheriff, against a man you admit is the town's leading land speculator."

"What all did he take when he rummidged your house?" Abe said. "A silver-mounted single-barrel Marlin shotgun with silver chasing on the chamber, maybe?"

Tapeworm just folded up. He said, "All right, he took it, a birthday gift from my wife when we happened to be in funds, and my own shells too. Go ahead and try to ruin me, but I tell you right now you can't do it. All my life I been a nobody, poorest of the poor, the humblest of the humble, and meekest of the meek. But when my time come, by God, and I got the Burlington by the balls in an iron grip, give me credit that I didn't let nothing distract me, neither Mike Timpke nor money nor danger nor shame. A man gets a stroke of luck like that only once in his lifetime, and I knowed this was my chance to *have* something and *be* somebody. All I had to do was not make a single mistake, and I didn't. I laid there with thirty-eight bird shot in my belly, and you may of thought I was upset the way I was hollering, but inside I was just cool as a cucumber. I kept telling myself that this little shooting didn't amount to a hill of beans, what mattered was my secret inside knowledge, and I knowed it *couldn't* be Mike Timpke that had shot at me with my own shotgun because he was as scared of guns and knives as some men are of snakes."

"Not quite," Abe said. "I never heard of a man picking up a loaded snake and shooting somebody with it. Tapeworm, any ambush comes from a mighty bitterness of heart; it's first degree murder, lying in wait means hellish and devilish premeditated intent, and under that kind of an emotion, I think even a man that hates snakes could pick one up."

"You may be right, I don't know much about snakes," Tapeworm said. "What's your point?"

"My point," Abe said, "is this; if Mike Timpke hated guns as you say he did, and as other witnesses I can think of also say he did, what did you do that caused him to have such bitterness of heart that he'd pick up a gun and shoot it at you?"

"I have no idee," Tapeworm said.

"You're a liar," Abe said.

Tapeworm said, "All you have to do is prove that, Sheriff. The past is the past with me, and I ain't no improvident cowboy you can whip out of town with the end of a rope with a knot in it. I'm *somebody*. All my life I was nobody, no trade and no education, no chance to get out of the working class, and every time I got a dollar or two ahead, here come another mouth to feed. My muscular strength was my only fortune, and with that loathsome tapeworm eating up my substance as fast as I could spoon it in, even my muscular strength was ebbing. But I took my grip and I swung my whole weight when my chance come, and I made that railroad squeal, and I wasn't distracted from my goal then and I won't be now. You put me on the witness stand about this, and I'll get up there and perjure myself and get away with it, and do you know why, Sheriff?"

"No, why?" Abe said.

"There's times in a man's life when he knows he's suddenly going at a gallop, and nothing can stop him," Tapeworm said. "That's where I am right now, going like hell, and you can't stop me. So don't ask me no more questions about Mike Timpke or anything else, because I ain't going to answer them."

Abe said, "I don't want to stop you, Tapeworm. Danged if I don't kind of admire you, at least you're interesting to talk to. All right, we'll drop it for the time being, but if I ever get my hands on Mike Timpke, we'll take up where we left off."

Tapeworm got tears in his eyes. "Thank you, Sheriff, thank you from the bottom of a full heart. I don't want to swindle anybody. I only want to have a high station in life and live up to it."

"Help yourself," Abe said. "Now what are you going to do about the J Bar B?"

Tapeworm wrung his hands and said, "That's my most immediate urgentest worry. Virginia swears she's going to run it herself. I've got to get her some decent respectable help, but who?"

"How about Elmo Huger?" Abe said.

"I offered him the job once," Tapeworm said, "but he turned me down flat, the ungrateful whelp."

"How much did you offer to pay him?" Abe said. "Why, a measly fifteen dollars a month is what I hear, and I don't blame him. Make it thirty-five dollars a month and I'll deliver him."

Tapeworm said he didn't think he could go that high, Virginia was being stubborn and expensive and he was trying to be patient with her at great cost, but Abe said no real land baron could stand to have the reputation of being low pay. A land baron flung his money around now and then. He picked the time and the place, of course, but the idee was for people to realize he might fling it any old time, and they ought to be ready.

"Why yes, that makes sense, all right, thirty-five dollars," Tapeworm said. "Let's just forget the other."

"You mean Mike Timpke. All right, temporarily let's forget Mike Timpke," Abe said. "I wish you no harm, Tapeworm, but damned if I don't get impatient with you at times! But all right, let's pass over Mike Timpke for the time being, and I'll go get Elmo and ride out with him and have a little talk with your daughter."

"With Virginia?" Tapeworm said.

"Yes, with her," Abe said.

Tapeworm rolled his eyes and said, "I wish you wouldn't do that, Sheriff. But even if you do, I'm *not* going to be whipped, I'm *through* being poor and humble, I've come into my heritage at last, and I'll *never* be poor and humble again."

7

Abe knowed he had quit without getting the whole truth out of Tapeworm, but he was a patient man, and if you talked to Tapeworm long enough, you got a kind of a whistling noise in your ears, and you had to rest them no matter what.

Once Abe fattened some hogs to butcher on the popcorn he raised from a little patch of popcorn that made a good crop but wouldn't pop. It was too hard for them pigs to eat, so he soaked it before he fed it, and that softened it up into a first-class hog mash. Only down in the bottom of the barrel, it started to work on him before he knowed it, and for a while, them hogs was eating forty-proof mash. Afterwards, Abe found a few ears he had missed, and they popped just fine. He seen he had wasted a whole crop of popcorn on his hogs by not letting it dry out, but he made light of his loss by saying at least he had the happiest hogs in town for a while.

"After I talk to Tapeworm St. Sure awhile," Abe said, "I remember how them hogs looked, all leaning against the breeze kind of, and shaking their heads to get rid of that whistling noise in their ears, and if you want to see something silly, look at the expression of a drunk hog. I hate to look in a looking glass after I talk to Tapeworm, because that's how I think I'll look, just like a hog full of forty-proof mash."

But he didn't drop it. He went across the crick and found Dick Royce with his shirt off digging his own new privy hole. He said, "Dick, you're a well-muscled man with your shirt off. I've an idee that in your time, you've been a hard cat to skin barehanded."

Dick stabbed his spade into the ground, and leaned his arms on top of it, and said, "Thanks for the compliment, Sheriff, but I've went to seed a lot in the last few years. I was always strong, but I have to say in all good conscience that I lost more fights than I won. I very early became dependent on the gun, you see, and then on two guns, and being armed changes your nature. I don't recall I ever shrank from a trial of the manly art, but you've got to get a man's guns off before it can come to that, and sometimes it's easier just to shoot it out. I'm ashamed to tell you some of the men that whipped me with their fists."

"You're a pretty good talker, too," Abe said.

"You talk about talkers, Tapeworm St. Sure is the talkingest man I ever seen in my life," Dick said.

Abe said, "Yes, he just drills right on, and your weakness is, you come to a natural stopping place now and then, and a man can bust in on you."

"Are you funning at me?" Dick said.

"No I ain't," Abe said. "I'm only trying to get a word in edgewise, to ask you if it came to blows between you and Mike Timpke, what would happen. Because I *know* what would happen in a trial of guns between a two-gun man like yourself, and that coward about guns."

A sort of light-colored shadder slid over Dick's light blue eyes, but he didn't shy back, he just nodded and scratched his belly and said, "Well I never wondered about that. There's some men you naturally ask yourself, who is the best man? But not him. I seen him hit a few men, and you can't see his fists move, he hits so fast. I'd ruther be kicked in the mouth by a mule. I'd sooner hand you a bobwire and tell you to take a few free cuts at my face, and you wouldn't cut me up half as much as that son of a bitch with his fists. You've got to admire a good fighter that only defends himself, but Mike

Timpke has got a mean streak too, he loves to hurt people. My advice to you is to pick up the axle of a buggy and brain him before you close with him with the fists."

"I size him up that way myself," Abe said. "Why did you and him fall out?"

"What makes you think we fell out?" Dick said.

"Why you camped as pardners up on the Flying V," Abe said, "and now here's plenty of room in the good old Doll House for both of you, but I look in vain for your former camping pardner."

That light-colored shadder slid over Dick's eyes again, like he wondered where in the world Abe picked up all his information, and he said, "We wasn't pardners, he worked for me is all. There ain't room enough in this town for him and me no more, let alone in my own house. Supposed to take care of the horses and rustle firewood, and feed us when I drank too much, although I done the cooking when I was able. What you'd call an orderly in the Cavalry, that about describes Mike. Pardners my foot. I met very few men I'd go pardners with, and that snake in the grass wasn't one."

Abe said, "Oh? Well I heard he was heading West anyway, last seen in Wolf Crick Pass."

"I ain't surprised," Dick said. "I hope the 'Paches get him on the other slope. They brag that them 'Paches is whipped, but that's just government lies, you never whip them people, no more than you could Yaquis. I can take you down in Sonora and show you the Yaqui Nation stronger than ever, no matter what you heard about them. It's a piss-poor country that will lie to its own people, like the United States did about whipping the Yaquis and the 'Paches, but I'm just as glad there's a few of them still around, when you tell me Mike Timpke is heading west through Wolf Crick Pass. I hope they nail him and turn the squaws loose on him. I'd love to see that."

Abe was getting a kind of a whistling noise in his ears again, so he said he wanted Elmo Huger. Dick said Elmo was around somewhere, but had lost his money at a new-fangled game of roulette at the carnival, a dime a spin for a doll with a china head.

Dick started to tell about the game, a dime at a time, but Abe advanced his skirmish line quick, and said, "I have to take him away from you, Dick. I've got a good job for him, thirty-five dollars a month."

"What will become of me?" Dick said. "I've got to where I depend on Elmo. He's a good kind faithful modest boy."

"We have to pass him around to where the greatest need is," Abe said. "I'll tell Rolf Ledger to get his bucket brigade going on you again, and you tell Elmo to tie his clothes in a bundle and come helling after me towards the J Bar B."

He led his horse to Rolf's door, and Sammie answered his knock, and said that somebody had come to fetch Rolf, she didn't know who, and she had no idee when he'd be back.

"Well, just tell him he'll have to keep an eye on Dick Royce for a while," Abe said, "because I'm taking away Dick's prop and mainstay, Elmo Huger."

Sammie said all right, and she said, "I wish I could feel better about Rolf's caller today. He was dressed like an Indian, but I know an Indian when I see one, Abe. This was only someone Rolf knew in the pen, I'm sure. This happens all the time! We're the first depot west of the Kansas prison. Rolf says prisoners learn about these things by a kind of silent drumbeat, and it's all over that prison that a man just released can stop here and get a meal, perhaps a dollar or two, but most importantly, a kind word and understanding when he's frightened and lonely and bitter."

"It must be a sore trial to you, after the easy carefree life of a cattle baron's daughter," Abe said.

"It's more than that," Sammie said. "It's a cross I'll bear the rest of my life—and do you know, Abe, I wouldn't have it any other way! This is my life, my man and my God, and every moment is splendor to me."

"You're a better Christian than I could be, Sam," Abe said.

She leaned crosswise of the door and kind of shook her head and said, "Oh no, doctrinally I'm a poor specimen. The more I study Christianity, the less I know what a good Christian is. But, Abe, I am learning a little about the man Jesus. I don't know if He was a holy man, or the Son of God, or what. I don't know if He really died for me, or if believing can save me, or what it is to be saved."

She said, "But when I get mixed up in the whys and the wherefores, I only need to look at this humble, silent, stubborn man I married, with his kindness, with his bravery, with his generosity, with his patience and meekness and love and humbleness—and Abe, then I know how it was that Jesus served God. People double-crossed Jesus too. People tried to wear Him down. People hurt Him. People lied to Him, and lied about Him, just as they do to Rolf."

She said, "But they couldn't conquer Him. They couldn't make Him lose faith in people or God, and they can't make Rolf lose it either. I can't quite understand how it is that Rolf saves people in Christ's name, but I know he saves them. People would follow him as they followed Jesus, if he let them. But he sends them home and tells them to love one another."

She said, "Oh, I'm still a Venaman, Cal's daughter, headstrong and proud and selfish! But I'm learning, and I know I've married a great man, lowly and humble and ignorant in everything except the love of God, and this is my daily glory, to help my man serve God as Jesus served God. This is what Daddy can never understand, how I glory in being a minister's wife—me, of all people! And every day I see new proof that my faith in Rolf is right. Why even today, that fake Indian—Abe, do you have any idea of the nickname he had in prison? I never did, yet this fake Indian called him Preach, and I'm sure Rolf will tell me this was just some kind of an old nickname he had in prison."

Abe said, "Do you tell me!" and he thought, well this was

sure his day to get snagged by talkers. He looked up and seen an expression on Sammie's face, like she felt she had run on at the mouth too much, and only made a fool of herself. He took her hand and said, "Well, little lady, it all turned out for the best, didn't it? I'll whisper a little secret. I'd be one of Rolf's followers too, if he wanted any."

She leaned over and kissed Abe on his bald head, and said, "Oh you do understand, don't you? Then I can tell you something else I wouldn't tell anyone, even Mama. Sometimes when I see Rolf coming home, so tired he almost has to hold onto the saddle horn from the way people have been imposing on him, do you know what my first thought is? I say to myself, Here he comes, Jesus on horseback! God bless you, Abe."

Abe didn't really get rid of the whistling in his ears until he found himself leading his horse down the trail nearly a mile away, when Elmo Huger come pounding up on the trail behind him. Abe put his foot in the stirrup and swung up, and said to himself before Elmo got there, "Jesus on horseback. Well, horse, if you and me have patience, we'll hear everything before we go galloping out of this vale of tears together."

It was Chief Buffalo Runs, that had brought a medicine show to Mooney, only to find out that he was preempted by the carnival, that had come to see Rolf. He seen he didn't have a chance against the carnival, so he just camped out on the prairie until the carnival left, and then he moved in and started his squaw to setting up the show where the carnival had been, and he rode in and had a little private talk with Rolf.

Rolf saddled up a horse after they had their little talk, and rode out to where this medicine show was going to be held, if anybody came to it after the carnival. Most of the oilcloth signs was up, and as this Chief Buffalo Runs said, "I rely on the three familiar favorites, the oil, an unguent, and a tonic.

This is what people want, Preach. I've got the best set of billboards carried by any wagon, too. Look!"

His billboard was big oilcloth signs that he hung up to make a kind of a wall, or you might say a box canyon, to corner people near his wagon. He had Genuine Titus County Rock Oil, refined or natural according to your infirmity. He had the Winnebago Unguent Balm, composed of extracts of roots, barks, herbs, and berries, for itching, bleeding, or protruding piles, for saddle sores, wens, cysts, pimples, pustulations, eruptions, or any sore or festering place that wouldn't heal.

"But the tonic is still what people look for most," Chief Buffalo Runs said. "I use Wah-Bon-See's Natural Elixir. He was a chief of one of the horse tribes. Three ounces of a mixture of sassafrass, essence of juniper, syrup of figs, and soluble magnesite chalk. The secret is in the proportions. Add an ounce and a half of paregoric. Fill your eight-ounce bottle up with 190-proof grain alcohol, shake well before using, and take an ounce three times a day for agues, fevers, grippe, malaria, or run-down debility. For loss of male vigor or female fluidity, or sterility in both sexes. It can't hurt anybody, even if taken in slight excess, and it must be good for people because they come back and ask me for it every time I make a mistake and hit a town again."

"Sure some handsome signs," Rolf said. "I remember you trustied in the sign shop. It sounds better to me than burglarizing banks."

"It don't pay as well," Chief Buffalo Runs said.

"I remember you was an artist on the piano, too," Rolf said. "I suppose that's part of your show."

"Not a piano," Chief Buffalo Runs said. "I haul an organ around with me, and I learned sleight-of-hand from Harley Weber, who you recall I'm sure, and I recite some poetry. "The Doctor A-Weeping at the Bedside," "I Know My Mother Misses Me," "Will This Sailor See the Dawn," "O Whither Wafts Yon Bit of Thistle Down," and so forth. Me and Bernadette do a mind-reading act. She's deef and dumb, you know, and we talk sign language and that's a hair-raiser. Well she ain't really deef and dumb, Rolf. But she don't talk American and I don't even know what her language is. She's some kind of a Greek or Turk or Bulgarian I met in New Orleans, right after I got out. Some of them river roughs was getting gay with this poor woman. I learned them a lesson they'll never forget. You know how it was in the granite dormitory when a clash come on."

"I remember," Rolf said. "You got a real nice outfit here, Harry."

There was two wagons and two real good teams, and two extra horses broke to saddle and harness both. There was just this fake Indian and the woman, that went by the name of Princess Moon Ring. They tied their horses and set down in the shade on a wagon tongue, and Chief Buffalo Runs called the woman out and made her shake hands with Rolf. She bowed all over the place, and then kind of slid back of the house wagon, where she had her camp stove. In a minute she popped out with two big mugs of coffee and some kind of twisted hot syrupy buns, different than Rolf had ever et before, and they just hit the spot.

"You've got a nice wife, Harry," he said.

"Wife, ha," Chief Buffalo Runs said. "I s'pose you'll have to expose me for a fake and a burglar, Rolf, but damned if it ain't hard lines! You always was a slave to your conscience, but you treated me fair and square, or a little more, and I can't forget it."

He said, "But here's what tears my heart out. I could go up there and open this town's bank with a dime's worth of black powder, and clean out four or five houses in the same night. Before anybody was wiser, I'd be long gone on the fastest horses in town. It don't pay, you'll tell me. I know that as well as you, but I'll tell you this, Preach, that woman deserves more than I can ever give her in these wagons. If I was half a man,

I'd clean out a nice fat country bank, and leave her the teams and wagons and the organ to sell, and all the money I got from the bank, and get out of her life. Why don't I, you'll ask."

"Yes, that was going to be my very next question," Rolf said.

"Mainly," Chief Buffalo Runs said, "it's because she'd just pine away and die. I know what your next question is, for me for God's sake? And my answer is yes, for me. She's some kind of a foreigner that believes if a man rescues a woman, she belongs to him from then on, and she's got to love him and serve him and always be true to him, and don't ask me how she got this over to me, but *I know it's true*! Reason two, if I have to take care of her, this is the only trade I know except burglary, and I can't get along without her, she's the heart of the show as well as the business. Reason three, one of these days, somebody's going to catch up to me, and they'll hang me and set fire to the tree, and maybe her with me. But so help me God, Preach, I can-*not* go away and leave her, because what I feel for her is a pure strong love. Now laugh at that if you like, but it's the truth."

"I don't see nothing to laugh at," Rolf said. "You got a good outfit, and a good-looking faithful hard-working wife, what's your problem, Harry?"

"Wife, ha," Chief Buffalo Runs said.

"You ain't married to her?" Rolf said.

"Oh listen to this fool talk," Chief Buffalo Runs said. "You know why we ain't married, for the same reason I was always in so much trouble in our favorite clammy stone summer resort. My grandfather was a slave and my mother was a slave and the only reason I ain't one, I was born too late. I'm a quarter nigger and the rest of me is Seminole and Irish and German, but the world calls me a nigger, and by God I'm just as proud of that as I am the Seminole and Irish and German. That's what used to get me into so much trouble back there, Preach, I not only admitted it, by God I said I was proud of it."

"I never seen what anybody had to be proud of in that place," Rolf said. "A proud convict just has to be the vainest dreamer in the world. But you didn't bring me out here just to hear the story of your life. What do you want from me?"

Chief Buffalo Runs got kind of a hangdog look on his face, and said, "Preach, I ain't going to do much business right after the carnival, but I'm broke, I laid in a stock of constituent drugs last week, and besides the horses need a rest. I could pick up a few dollars here, if you could bend your conscience enough so you wouldn't have to tell your town constable I'm not an Indian, only a fake nigger ex-convict running around with a white woman. But no, I can't ask you to do that, Preach. You was too level with everybody, I can't ask that."

The woman was hanging up some clothes she'd just washed, but she kept looking over their way, like she knowed something was bothering her man, and the look on her face was really something to see. Like he was both her sunrise and her sunset.

"You really ought to get married," Rolf said. "You owe it to her and you owe it to yourself and you owe it to your self-respect."

"Oh hell, Preach, have you lost your mind?" Chief Buffalo Runs said. "You know what would happen if we got married and it came out I was a nigger! Why do you think I didn't do it long ago, you fool you?"

Rolf said, "I don't understand what you're trying to get at. All I see is an old Indian by the name of Chief Buffalo Runs, and another Indian by the name of Moon Ring. Nobody really expects Indians to get married by the white man's law, but they respect them when they do. What I see is a man making a good living for the woman he loves, working hard at a trade when he could be robbing banks and houses like a thief in the night, the best burglar west of the Ohio River living the hard life of a fake Indian medicine man."

He said, "Harry, or I ort to say Chief Buffalo Runs, if I went to the courthouse with you, and said that here's a heathen couple that has seen the light and want to make it white-man legal, they'd issue you a license, and I could marry you free gratis without charge. I'd issue a certificate, and if you took it and went on West, it seems to me it could carry you through any bad times that turned up. Say if somebody we both knowed in the clammy stone summer resort, if he lets on you're a nigger instead of being a true friend as ex-convicts ort to be to each other, why the way I see it, if the state of Colorado says you're Indians, any state in the Union has to own up that's what you are."

Chief Buffalo Runs just flopped down on his knees in the dust, and laid his head in his arms on the wagon tongue, bawling like a baby. Rolf knelt down and took advantage of their position to say a prayer, and then the woman seen them on their knees and started wailing and weeping, and finely she got down on her knees too, and yanked some beads out of her pocket, and was twice around the Rosary and starting the third lap before Chief Buffalo Runs got control of himself.

Rolf took them to the courthouse and got them their license. He married them in the church, with Alec and Mable McMurdoch for witnesses. Mable was there to practice next Sunday's hymns on the organ and Alec to find out what she done with the key to the smokehouse.

It was all over town before night, how Rolf had committed another miracle, and converted a couple of Indians, and them people of Mooney wouldn't of been normal if they hadn't had the curiosity to go to the medicine show that night. Nobody planned to buy any medicine, and they was all a little jaded after the carnival, and as Tapeworm said, really too sophisticated now for a medicine show. They just wanted to see the new red Christian brethren.

But old Chief Buffalo Runs, he had him a streak going, and he rode it the way Tapeworm had rode his. He just brought tears to their eyes, talking about their cysts and wens and issues of blood and pus, and him and his bride left town thirty-two dollars richer than when they come in, and no harm to anybody.

"It ain't that I don't appreciate what you done, Preach," Chief Buffalo Runs said when him and Rolf shook hands good-by, "but I want you to know I'm just as proud of the black slave quarter of me as I am of the free white three-quarters."

"I know, but you've got a wife to support," Rolf said. "It seems to me a man ought to be able to be proud and sensible both."

8

When Abe and Elmo got to the J Bar B, Virginia was in an old pair of farmer's overhalls, and she was barefoot, with her hair tied up in a rag, and she was giving that cabin what-for. Her and Art had moved in just before the carnival, and this was her chance to sail in with soap and water and elbow grease, and she sure was.

She'd cried some, and her eyes showed it, and her nose was stuffed up, but she was one of them women that figured work was a cure for most things. They seen her shaking out blankets in time to get a good look at her, and then she went inside and give Abe his chance to speak to Elmo.

"Jack Butler built a good tight barn here," Abe said, "and you've slept in many a worse place in your time. Take your duffle out there and make yourself a bed. I reckon you'll eat with Tapeworm's daughter, however she wants it. But there's only one bed in that cabin and there's only going to be one person in it, her."

"That settles one of my worries about taking this job," Elmo said. "I come from a good Babtist family, and I won't stand for nobody getting no idees about me and a woman I only happen to be working for."

"You got your guts with you today to mention such a thing," Abe said. "Make your toss in the barn and then come in and meet Mrs. Arthur H. Crawford, the woman you only happen to be working for."

Virginia was a kind of a pretty woman with a nice shape, and darker hair than any other St. Sure including Tapeworm, and an intense expression like she'd been born with a tack under her crupper. Abe tied his horse to a post and knocked at the door, and she come to it with her elbows on her hips and just glared at him.

"You're wasting your time, Sheriff," she said. "I defied my father and I defy you. I'll not be evicted from my own property, and I will not go back into Mooney and be a laughingstock, the abandoned wife."

"At least let an old man come in and rest his tired feet, Virginia," Abe said.

She didn't say yes or no, either one, so he went on in and set down and said, "Whatever you and your pa decide, that's all right with me, and I'll put the shelter of my office over you and nobody will molest you."

"Whatever I decide, you mean," Virginia said. "This was bought with my own money. Art was only a dummy. Papa has assignments from him on everything."

"I know that," Abe said, "but now you tell me it was your money he was spending, and that's news to me."

"Oh, Papa didn't have a cent of his own except a little he brought from California," Virginia said. "I'm not Adelaide's daughter. My mother was a rich widow, a lot older than Papa; it was a terrible scandal when they got married. I might as well out with it, they *had* to, I was about to be born. Mama was at a flighty age, and you know Papa, when he gets wound up, he could talk a coon out of a hole in a holler tree."

"Yes he could," Abe said, but he surely did set up and take notice when she mentioned California. He hadn't never heard California mentioned in connection with Tapeworm before, only Mike Timpke and Dickerson Royce.

"Mama left her money in trust," Virginia said. "I came into it when I was twenty-five, and just then Papa came home with this crazy idee about cashing in on the Q coming to Mooney."

She stopped and laughed and thought it over kind of dreamy.

She said, "I don't think I would of let him have it, except Adelaide kept telling him it was another of his hare-brained idees, and so forth. Papa had holes in his pants when he got back to Vincennes from here, and he hadn't shaved. Yet he didn't look pitiful somehow, not to me. I know what a fool he is in some ways, and what a windbag, but I still admire Papa."

"And you don't admire Mrs. Tapeworm," Abe said.

"Yes I do," she said, "but in a different way. She follered Papa all over the country, putting up with some of the craziest schemes he had, and somehow she fed us and sewed for us, so you've got to admire her. But I felt Papa deserved just one more chance, even if it was going to cost me every cent my own mother had left me."

She got wound up, so it was easy to see she had her father's gift of gab in her, and Elmo come in from the barn and leaned against the wall, and Abe just listened and learned things about Tapeworm he never could of found out any other way.

All his life, Tapeworm hated being poor and humble, hated it worse than anybody in the world, and he had this passion for women too. "But when things were going good for Papa," Virginia said, "he never looked at another woman. Only when things were bad. So I'm sure he'll never be a menace to any woman in Mooney, but I'll bet he could if he tried. Papa has winning ways about him."

She said Tapeworm moved them all to Dakota when he got a windmill franchise, and there he became knowed as Windmill St. Sure. He had them farmers sign orders for windmills, only they was really worded like promissory notes. He discounted the notes at the bank, but he done his sincerest best to get them windmills delivered, too, and a few of them was. Then the windmill company went broke, and they barely got across the river into Sioux City ahead of a mob that was going to tar and feather the whole family.

"There was only six kids of us then," Virginia said, just as happy as if she was telling about going to grandfather's farm for the holidays. "Then we went to Sarpy County, Nebraska, and Papa was agent for the O'Brien Easy Draft Harrow, but an Easy Draft man had already been through there, and it was slim pickings. Papa didn't want to go to Omaha. There was a man there that had been his partner in a town-lot company in Dodge City, and it went broke, and this man was going to kill Papa. We had to wait about a year, until this man got killed in a dynamite blast in a quarry."

"I reckon there's no use asking if your daddy had anything to do with that blast," Abe said.

Virginia said no, Papa was shucking corn for one-half cent a bushel and they was living in a dugout on the banks of the Platte in a town called Cedar Creek. Tapeworm heard about his old enemy being dead, and he borrowed an old broken-down horse and shaft wagon, and they set out on the long trip to Omaha, about forty miles. They was so hungry when they got to Omaha early in the morning, they was too weak to cry, and Tapeworm had only three nickels in his pocket to make his start on.

"I bet he come home that night with a ham and a jug of wine and a turkey gobbler," Abe said.

Virginia said, "Wrong, he came back in a rented buggy with a trotting horse, and two big gunny sacks full of groceries, and warm coats for the littlest kids, and a set of combs with brilliants in them for Adelaide, and fifteen dollars in cash in his pockets."

Abe said he could of predicted it but he'd be interested to know how he done it, he always had admired Tapeworm's fertile mind, everybody else's scourge would be his opportunity. Virginia said that was exactly the way it was; it was a bad year for flies that year, and they gave her papa this idee and he cashed it in.

Tapeworm went to a printer and gave him the fifteen cents down on a two-dollar-and-fifty-cent order for some wrappers and some pink instruction sheets, and he wrote out what he wanted printed up on each. Then he went around wherever gangs of men was working, and offered them the Gold Medal Double Your Money Back Guaranteed Fly Killer, It Kills Them Without Fail Every Time, or Double Your Money Back. They sold for twenty-five cents each, and all he had to do was get one man in a gang to buy one, just one was all it took.

This lucky purchaser would open his package, and inside was two blocks of wood, also the pink instruction sheet that said, *Place fly carefully between blocks of wood and press firmly together. Double your money back if fly does not die instantly!* Well you can imagine, twenty-five cents gone and he's about ready to throttle Tapeworm, only Tapeworm tells him, "My friend, here's an opportunity to exercise your sense of humor and make some money on your friends. These sell for twenty-five cents retail, and you can sure testify to this can't you, but I can let you have them for a dollar twenty-five a dozen in quantities. That's a clear profit of a dollar seventy-five a dozen, and look at the fun, and I happen to have several dozen with me, how many dozen can you use?"

Abe was a law and order man, and this was a sure-enough swindle, yet it would prob'ly pass a lawyer's test for legitimacy. He couldn't condemn it and he couldn't endorse it, all he could do was admire old Tapeworm's nerve, and his fertile mind as Virginia said. Them's the hardest kind of hornswoggles to deal with, when they've got one foot on the legal side of the law.

He said, "Virginia, how much of your money has Tapeworm got tied up in this railroad proposition? This ain't no two-bit fly trap. You've been skinned out of your inheritance, I'm afeared, and your pa has set up a dirty sinful monopoly no better than the beef trust or the Bank of England."

Virginia said that when her ma died, it was about thirteen thousand dollars left in trust, but when she became twenty-five, it was up to twenty-four thousand. Abe said, "Oh, Good God, no!"

Virginia said, "It's only money, and life with Papa has taught me that money is important only twice in your life, when you've got too much of it, and when you haven't got a cent. Papa loves all of us kids even if he can't keep us straight sometimes; he abandoned us a few times it's true, but any man would with hungry mouths to feed in disappointment after disappointment, and the house full of wet didies on every chair, and Adelaide screeching at him for grocery money. Papa's the gamest man I ever seen. He can take blow after blow and his fertile mind keeps working."

She said, "Papa learned us all one thing, Sheriff, *you can't set still in life*! It's better to fall backwards than to stand still, at least you learn something. Standing still is how you start to die, Papa says. You can't settle for what life is willing to give you. You've got to keep moving until you can get it by the throat."

Abe said, "Yes, that's about how he put it to me, only he didn't say throat. But, honey, it looks like he has swindled his own daughter."

She said, "No, Mr. Whipple, I was of age, and I handed over the money willingly because I love him and he taught me not to be afraid of anything. And I hand it to him on one thing, he warned me about Arthur."

"I was going to get around to him," Abe said. "If it ain't too tender a subject, little lady, he seems to complicate things. There's no assignment you can file to dispose of a husband, and this little son of a bitch can cloud your title from now on."

"Not him," Virginia said, "because when we had this quarrel the other night, about him sword-fighting with that fake Spanish woman, he told me I didn't have no claim on him because he was already married to a woman in Fort Wayne, and had two children ten and eight years old. He said I could prove that by writing to her, Mrs. Fidelia Crawford. I can tell when he's telling the truth, too, because he didn't often enough for it to get tiresome."

"That's something anyway," Abe said. "You'll let him get away with everything else, and you'll try to make this old two-bit cow ranch pay off? Excuse me, but you haven't got a critter on it, not one."

"I told Papa he had to pay off the option and give me the ranch free and clear, and I want four thousand dollars in cash," Virginia said. "He owned up that I had a right to most of the land in Mooney, all but twenty-five hundred dollars' worth of it, and he didn't even reproach me about Artie. But I said no, just the ranch and four thousand in cash, and he could have everything else."

"I see," Abe said, "but I don't see how a jaybird like Crawford managed to talk you into marriage, and I'm confused too about this other twenty-five hundred dollars that your pa had."

"I don't know about it, except that he said he had it buried over there where he lived when he had the tapeworm, and they could torture him to death and he'd never tell where," Virginia said. "He must of brought it from California with him."

"At some risk, surely," Abe said, remembering about Mike Timpke.

"Everything Papa done was risky," she said. "About Artie, he was a musician and instrument salesman. He sold Papa a harp for me, and had to give me lessons on it. I reckon what made him lose his head and marry me when he already had a wife, Papa paid him five hundred dollars in advance for the lessons. Nothing's too good for his family when Papa's in funds, and Artie thought he was a millionaire."

"Artie had larceny in him somewhere," Abe said, "because a four-horse wagon couldn't haul five hundred dollars' worth of harps."

"Oh no, the instrument costs two hundred dollars, on top of the lessons, and Artie was a very talented instructor," Virginia said. "I became quite good, and I love it. Nothing is really lost if, deep in your heart, you learn something that enriches your life. Papa taught us that. Look, I'll show you."

She opened the bedroom door, and Abe said, "Honey, you been swindled again, a harp is a little bit of a thing that you blow on. That looks to me like the insides of a piano that somebody slathered a lot of gold and white paint on it."

She said no, what Abe called a harp wasn't a harp at all, a mouth harp was really a little bitty organ with reeds, and hers was the only piece of machinery legally entitled to call itself a harp. She said it was one of the oldest instruments ever invented, there was ancient Italian paintings showing angels playing them, and this was how well her kind of a harp was thought of among cultured people.

"So that's the kind of harp the angels play," Abe said. "I've always had a picture of them in my mind, setting around blowing on their harps, and there's no finer music than a good harp around a campfire, with some lonely boy blowing his heart out for his mother back home. Do you really mean you can flog music out of that stretch of odds and ends of wire?"

She set down on the edge of the bed in her old overhalls, and made sure her hair was all behind her and wouldn't get tangled rag and all in the wires, and she nuzzled that contraption to her shoulder, and began to claw at them wires for all she was worth with both hands. It was kind of a skim-milk music to Abe, no weight or bottom to it, like chewing beeswax instead of tobacco, the harder you chew, the weaker it gets. But when she come to the end of it, old Elmo Huger said, "Say that sounds to me like 'Blow Bugle Blow.'"

"Oh do you know that too?" Virginia said. "I can sing alto if you know the melody."

Elmo said he didn't know the melody, just the tune and the words, and go ahead and start if she wanted to, because his mammy back home had learned it to him. She took some long loose swipes over the wires with both hands, and she give him a nod, and you'd think Elmo had been singing to a harp all the way from Georgia, the way he cut loose with them words:

The shadow falls on castle walls,
And snowy summits old in story.
The long light shakes across the lakes,
Where the wild cataract leaps in glory.
Blow bugle blow, set the wild echoes flying,
And answer, echo answer, dying . . .
dying . . .
dying.

It kind of tailed off to a mere whine that way at the end, and she didn't really sing the same tune he did, she just sort of loped around after him without ever catching him until the end, but it made Abe's backbone shiver like touching the blade of a razor when they both suddenly stopped at the same time.

"Did you know Lord Tennyson wrote those words?" Virginia said when they finished, and Elmo said no, he got them from his mammy, and she got them from her pappy, and he brought them when he come from England, and he wasn't likely to know any lords.

He said, "Grandpappy and his brother stole some meat, and they got caught with the bones, and got the choice of emigrating or getting their fingers cut off at the roots. Well you can guess which they chose. No, I think it's some other tune Lord Tennyson wrote, ma'am, it just don't stand to reason a British lord would share his tune with a convicted hungry half-starved meat stealer."

Abe said, "Enough of music; my advice to you, Virginia, is let this boy scout around and buy you some good young cow stock and a couple of likely young crossbred bulls. Start with the best you can get, because you haven't got range enough you can afford to feed culls, and Elmo may have a bad arm, but he knows a critter as well as any man I ever met, and I'd trust him with my last cent."

He looked at Elmo and said, "My advice to you is sleep in

the barn, you little son of a bitch, no more duetting to the harp or any other way."

So saying he was off to town, but he didn't have a whole lot of faith Elmo was going to stay in the barn. He could only hope for the best, but he didn't put much faith in Elmo's Babtist upbringing on the hot nights that was coming, a Babtist is a normal man like every other one where women is concerned.

He said, "Horse, I'm glad I'm past that age of foolishness, or soon will be if Dick Royce has got the right of things. I wouldn't sleep in no barn myself, even at my age, horse, and Elmo's just at the age where the sap is bulging his every vein. But I done the best I could."

He went home and thought over his situation, and done what he knowed he ort to of done long ago, only he hated to stir up old stinks. He set down and wrote a letter to the Cheyenne Drovers and Mercantile Bank, and then took a walk around his realm to make sure all was at peace, and went to bed with a clean conscience and a serene heart.

Only to wake up the next day to find out that Tapeworm St. Sure's youngest kid, Felton, had gone and got himself either lost or kidnaped. It was cause enough for celebration to the town that had endured Felton lo these many weeks, but for some reason his parents had a weakness for this little brat.

"Find my baby, Sheriff," Tapeworm said, with tears in his eyes. "It happened in your jurisdiction. I'm at the end of my rope. What good is fame and money without my little boy Felton?"

9

How this happened, I'd had a real busy summer, with lots of emigrants coming through, and I made a little money but I had to let my garden go at times. There was this one bunch of emigrants had an old harness-cut sorrel mare, with a suppurating fisslo on her shoulder, and they had her for swap. I knowed a Kincaider would take her and work her, poor old thing, so I swapped them for her, and let her stand in my lot until her shoulder got well.

Then I give her to this Indian that had went to missionary school, and had been in the infantry, and voted, and had took up land. When he was a kid, he'd go around with his shirt and pants open like a wild Indian will, and them missionaries would scold him, and he'd say, "Oh them pesky buttons." So that got to be his voting name, Pesky Buttons.

This sorrel mare's name was Mamie, and one day Pesky Buttons rode her into Mooney, with just an old ear bridle. Felton St. Sure seen her standing in the shade, and he was just at the age to want to be a train robber, so he untied her and managed to get up on her bareback. Old Mamie started to my place, the only home she really knowed, and when Felton hauled on the rope reins, he only broke this old ear bridle. She throwed the bridle and there he was on her naked, ascared to stay on and ascared to jump off.

He come into my place in the afternoon, bawling like a cut ram, old Mamie trotting right along and punishing a rump already red and bleeding on him. I said, "What have we here, what's your name, son?"

He kept on bawling and said, "None of your Goddamn business, help me down." I hadn't even heard of the famous Felton St. Sure then, and I knowed Pesky wouldn't sell Mamie, so I said to myself, here's some trifling emigrant kid that stole her, and I'll see how much I can do for his manners with a strap before I find time to turn boy and horse over to Abe Whipple.

I catched him by the suspenders and grounded him and told him to go into the house. He said, "You go to hell, you son of a bitch." I just said to myself, No time like the present, and went into the barn and got myself a well-oiled hitch rein about six feet long. I snapped it at his sore rump and stung him so hard he jumped a foot into the air and come down screaming.

I said, "Into the house now," and he went, and I follered him in. I said, "You'll have to stay around here a while, and that means earn your keep and keep a civil tongue in your head. Once again, what's your name?"

He said he'd die first, and I said all right, his name was Percy to me. He said he'd cut my heart out if I tried to call him Percy, and by God if he didn't try a couple of days later when I was taking a nap, but I came awake and retch for my strap in time. Before many days passed, he was answering to Percy like he was born to it.

I had this brat on my hand two weeks. Them fake Indians, Chief Buffalo Runs and Princess Moon Ring, had stayed with me a few days to breed one of their mares to a stud I had, and they sawed me some winter wood, and I helped them stock up their supply of Wah-Bon-See's Natural Elixir at my pump.

Chief Buffalo Runs felt so good at being married and notarized as an Indian that he was of a mind to go to California and settle there. I warned him about Wolf Crick Pass and Mike Timpke, but he said since Preach throwed the sacrament over them, nothing was going to spoil life for him and his bride.

This about them fake Indians didn't have nothing to do with Felton except that while they was there, I had these two white geese, an old six-year-old gander and a hen goose, and these two gray hen geese, and this woman of his trained them for watchdogs. I didn't know it could be done, but it sure worked out that way.

Them geese wanted to whip everything that come on my place. I never thought how they'd take to Felton, or Percy as I called him, but a goose will mother anything, and they took to him like he was some kind of a gosling, and they dedicated their lives to keeping him close to the place.

I called this gander Sam Bass, and he was a quiet modest old fool most of the time, you never knowed they was around usually. But you let that kid try to sneak off somewhere, and here old Sam Bass come after him at the charge, leading his hen geese and screaming at the top of his voice. If Percy didn't turn around and leg it for the house, they was on top of him like a tornado, flogging him with their big strong wings and rapping him with their big strong beaks, until that kid was just a mass of welts everywhere.

All I had to do when he cursed or talk dirty was to say, "Time for another lesson, Sam Bass," and these geese would come hissing and flapping, and Percy would try to shinny up my leg, screaming his head off. Thus little by little, him and me became friends, maybe not exactly friends, but one night he said, "Pete, I'd ruther live with you than anyplace in the world, even with your dad-blamed old geese. Someday I'll be big enough to whup them anyway."

I said, "Listen, Percy, someday I'll get it out of you who you are and where you live, and I'll wire your hands behind you and wire a rock to your ankle, and ship you home."

He said, "You do and I'll come right back. You're an outlaw, ain't you, Pete? I can tell by the shifty look in your eye."

He kept after me about that, until I finely said no I was just an old busted-down cowboy, but I had been an outlaw in my time, and gave it up as a losing game. Percy said, "See there, I knowed. I was just funning you about looking shifty, Pete. Know how I knowed? Because you won't let nobody get behind you, even me. You're worse than them Goddamn geese about letting somebody get behind you."

I slapped him until his ears rang for cursing, and I have to say this, the little bastard could take it like a man by then. He wanted me to tell him stories of my outlaw life, and I picked out the worst ones I could think of, to discourage him with the whole proposition. All he'd say was, "Criminy, tough luck, but the kind of pardners you picked, what else could you expect? If I was your pardner, that wouldn't of happened."

I just worked that kid's tail off, and he throve on it, and kind of got used to it, and didn't bellyache as much as your average kid about work. He begged me to learn him to shoot, and he admitted to being almost seven years old, high time to learn and no credit to his folks they'd neglected his shooting. I got out an old single-shot .30-caliber rifle I had, and I never seen anybody pick it up so quick. I used to reward him for doing his chores by letting him shoot the rifle. You'd think he would shoot me once he got his hands on a gun, after the way I cracked him with my strap, but he never did. I expected him to shoot the geese too, but he never had the courage. I seen him point the rifle at them twice, but I just yelled, "Get him, Sam Bass," and they sailed after him flapping their wings and hissing, and Percy throwed the gun away and skinned up the windmill.

One night some boys dropped in to play poker, and one was a kind of a jokey old cowboy that had to say everything different. Like when it was time to ante, he'd say, "Decorate the mahogany, boys," and when he had three queens, they was three sluts, and two pairs was both beds full, and a full house was both beds full and the baby sleeping crosswise.

This kid that I called Percy wouldn't go to bed, he loved to watch that poker game, and he picked it up as fast as the shooting. He asked me a lot of questions about it the next day, and a man has to be honest with a growing boy over the facts of life, and I told him what I could.

Never play in a game with wild cards. Never play with a stranger with long sleeves, one of them has your aces in it and the other one a little sleeve gun. Never play against women if you can get out of it. Never play against two troopers from the same regiment. Watch out when a man starts easing down lower in his chair, because it means he helped in the draw. These are things every growing boy ought to learn.

The next night, a couple of boys dropped in and wanted a game, and we waited awhile but nobody else showed up, and Percy said, "Pete, you set in for a change, and I'll play a hand." I thought to myself, Here's a chance to learn this whelp more facts of life.

I loaned him a stack of fifty one-cent chips, and we cut for deal, and I won, and Percy said, "Decorate the mahogany." Them two cowboys just laughed their heads off. One of them opened, and we all stayed, and everybody drawed three cards. The cowboy that opened it, he checked it to Percy, and Percy said, "Let's all decorate the mahogany, she's tilted edgewise," another of that old fella's comical sayings.

I dropped out because I didn't help, and I wanted to lay back and learn this whelp a good lesson, and Percy had to call on table stakes, and the others just seen him, and one of them had three nines and one had three jacks. Percy laid his hand down and said, "Four sluts," and raked in the pot.

It was that way all evening, beginner's luck, and what a lesson, because that little brat win more than eleven dollars. I didn't have any way of knowing that he had Tapeworm's fertile mind, all I seen was that here was a born poker player, and he done it so natural, like there wasn't nothing fantastical about a mere boy playing that kind of bloodcurdling poker.

I let him sleep late the next morning while I tried to figger out how you teach a kid like that a lesson. It was kind of mizzling outside, and just started to rain good and hard when here come Virginia Crawford and Elmo Huger to look at a young bull I had for sale. They didn't have no buggy or wagon, so they had rode over on a pair of horses Elmo had bought for her.

Virginia didn't have on overhalls this time, not by any means. She had on an old slicker, and under it a pair of skin-tight velvert pants she had made, and a man's shirt she had made only a man would choke to death if his was so tight. You never seen a woman got up the way she was.

Percy slept on an old buffalo hide in the common room. I skinned in there quick, because I didn't want him to see a woman got up like that, why she might as well of been naked. He was gone, but the winder was open, so I knowed he had already skinned out. So I let the geese worry about Percy.

We went out and looked this bull over, and Elmo said he was a nice enough bull but not worth what I was asking. I said why not, and he said, "Why he's no more than two, not a proved sire, he's a nice blocky bull but how do you know how much service he's got in him?" I said this was a chance you took with any two-year-old, I knowed for sure he'd made his leap already, but how much service in a season he was good for, of course that was part of the gamble.

Virginia said, "What's service?" Elmo got all choked up for a minute, and then he said just as sassy, "Ma'am, you're a cattleman now, service is what you buy a herd bull for."

She got a little pink, was all. She asked how old they had to be, and Elmo said they wasn't ready for a full season until they was three or four, and I was just as embarrassed as I could be. Elmo said, "Pete, we have wasted your time and ours. I don't see no gold plating on his horns, so you keep him for somebody greener than me."

I said come in the house and have a cup of coffee and let's think it over. We went in, and Virginia took off her slicker, and I tell you I had to look the other way. Them two set down at the table, and she kind of leaned up against Elmo and hiked an arm up on his shoulder so she could ruffle his hair.

She said, "I hope you're not old-fashioned, Mr. Heath. I'm sure you know me and Elmo are living together in free union." I said I didn't get around much and I hadn't heard nothing, but I sure wondered what had happened to Elmo's Babtist inclinations.

She said, "What can the clergy do for you? I tried marriage once, and find a preacher let me in for bigamy. Now I have waked up. The world is chuck-full of hypocrites, but I'm not one of them. Have you got any corn shucks? I like a smoke now and then, and that's one more thing I won't be sneaky about any longer."

She was beginning to get Elmo's goat, but what could I do but get her some corn shucks. She rolled a cigarette as slick as you please, and lit it up and blowed smoke through her nose, just like a man.

"I learned to do this once when Papa broke his thumb and couldn't roll one," she said. "Why shouldn't a woman smoke too? Why should a man have all the fun out of life?"

Elmo said, "Oh for heck's sake, Virginia," but she just blowed smoke in his face and then leaned over and kissed him.

I said, "You look here now, in this country only hillbilly women and squaws smoke," and Virginia kissed Elmo again and touched the tip of her tongue to the lobe of his ear, and said, "Now that's not true. I smoke and I'm neither hillbilly nor squaw."

Elmo buried his face in his hands up to his wrists and said, "For heck's sake, Virginia," again. She said, "Don't hide your face. There's nothing to be ashamed of, as I've told you again and again. There's nothing to be ashamed of, ever, except cowardice."

He said, "For heck's sake, will you." Virginia looked at me, and she said, "Elmo had a Babtist upbringing, he was very narrow; but I love him and he loves me, and what business is it of anybody how we sleep on my own property? What do you think, Mr. Heath?"

I said, "Well, I'm the worst moral authority in the world, and the only thing occurs to me, you and Elmo ought to be real sure of each other before you get yourselves into any such Indian marriage. That's all it is, an Indian marriage."

She said, "Were you sure every time you got in bed with a girl? I'm sure and Elmo is sure. Elmo's sweet and shy and kind and thoughtful, and that's enough for me."

Elmo hauled off and groaned and covered his face again, and she touched her tongue to his ear again and said, "Well not quite enough. You have to think of service, don't you? Elmo's in his prime that way."

That was as fur as she got. *Whack*, Elmo took her across the mouth with the back of his hand. He was just about to cry, but he said, "I can't keep you from shaming yourself, but by God you will *not* shame me. If your price is only a heifer in heat, why I say God damn you, that ain't what I let myself in for."

A slap can stun you if you ain't braced for it, and he didn't spare the weight of his good arm. She set there bleeding where her own teeth had cut her lip, a headstrong unhappy bull-headed woman that had been hurt by one man and tried to take it out on the world with another'n, and didn't know what had went wrong.

"Get up," Elmo said, and she got up and he put her slicker around her. He said, "Go outside. I'll be right out."

She kind of staggered out, and Elmo looked at me like a poisoned dog and said, "Pete, she didn't have no idee how it sounded, that's all I can say."

I said, "That's plain enough to be seen. It won't go beyond here."

He didn't answer me. He just went out, and there was Virginia standing in the rain beside the horses. He said, "Up with you," and she put her foot in his hand and he mounted her on her horse, and he got on his, and off they went into the rain.

I just thought to myself, Well you old mushmouth Georgia boy, that's a ramrod and not a shoelace you got for a backbone, in case anybody wondered. But if you can give that up, with a shape like hers, you're a stronger man than I was at the same age.

This little uninvited guest I had come slipping out of the brush and said, "What did he belt her for, anyway? How come she's dressed like that, showing her butt? No corset or anything."

Well, this proved it had got beyond me, I couldn't be responsible for this little bastard no more. I told him to put a bridle on his horse, and a saddle this time, and I went in and shaved off a week's growth of whiskers to give Elmo and Virginia time to get a good head start. A real good one, because if I could remember back to that age, and I thought I could, they was a cinch to pull up under a dry tree somewhere and try to talk it out, and only make each other madder and heartsicker.

Then me and Percy set out for town, and we hadn't went more than a couple of miles than we run into Thad Rust and his posse, and Abe had another one over north of town, everybody looking for this little lost or kidnaped snipe of Tapeworm St. Sure's.

Thad just went wild. He said, "This could go hard with you, Pete, and I hope it does; seventy-five men out night and day scouring the country and running up a big county bill. And all the time you've had this little lost bastard in that gambling hell of yours."

I said, "Oh sure, I tolled him in and hogtied him. If Tapeworm can't keep track of his get, and if this is how you police the county, I say give it all back to the Indians. Go hard with me, your foot; I figger Tapeworm owes me a board bill like impounding an estray horse."

Thad yawned and said, "Send him a bill. I bet he'll pay it, he's that fond of this little scorpion. I rue the day that tribe ever came to town."

Him and the posse rode back to town, and I didn't shed no tears at the parting believe me. It turned out to be a Saturday afternoon, and the town was full when Thad and his command come riding down the street with the missing brat up on Pesky Buttons's horse. Tapeworm seen it from his upstairs window and came whooping down the steps like a rutting elk, with Adelaide behind him in her corset and wrapper. They was uncommon fond of that brat for some reason.

They had a good crowd at church the next day, with Tapeworm and his entire family, including Virginia, although Elmo didn't come. He just stood outside the church and sneered. Rolf come up with a good sermon, the Prodigal Son. No references to Felton, in fact he rode around Felton without leaving a track, but they all got the point, and half the crowd was weeping their fool heads off. They had the collection and some hymns, and then Rolf got set to haul off and give the benediction, when all of a sudden, Tapeworm sang out, "Brother Ledger!"

Rolf stood there with his arms up in benediction position and said, "What is it, Brother Tapeworm?"

Tapeworm said, "I been a guest in your town and your church for some time now, partaking of the love and fellowship and so forth, basking like a man who wandered long on a cheerless trail and at last found a place he felt he could call home."

He was just about to let go all holts and soar off into one of them whooping tirades of his, when he recollected he was trespassing on Rolf's range. It was a real agony, but he fetched himself up short long shy of his natural range, and swallered a couple of times.

He said, "My family and I was never babtized, though we profess ourselves Christians. So now on this day of great rejoicing for us, I ask the privilege of joining the blessed circle of the Methodist elect, confessing our sins, mine especially, and accepting the sacrament of babtism and the grace and glory that go with it. And as a pledge of our love and dedication, I want to pledge a pledge of three hundred dollars to your church fund, one hundred of it in cash this very minute."

Them people just about clapped. It was wholesale for sure, considering how many Tapeworm was bringing in under one pledge, but an even dozen is a landmark in any preacher's life. Rolf got a mite swoony for a minute, because here came that unpaid pledge, and this outfit wasn't going to be easygoing Christians in any sense. But he faced it like a man, and asked them to step forward and be babtized, and they filed out of the pew and done it.

Old Tapeworm flopped down on his knees, although it ain't required in the Methodist style, and Adelaide sweat and grunted a little, but she made it to her knees too. One by one the kids got down, looking sheepish and grinning the way kids will, all but Virginia, *she* wasn't going to bow to no public opinion by kneeling.

Then she suddenly busted out weeping, and down she went on her knees, and I forgot to say she had on a real modest dress this time. Rolf went down the line and called their names, and shook the water over them, and touched their foreheads with it, and called them his brothers in Christ. It even seemed to get through to Tapeworm when Rolf called him that, because he covered his eyes with his knuckles for a minute, and gulped that he wished he was worthy to be that.

When Rolf and Sammie was walking home after church, here come old Elmo sauntering up to them with a sneer on, and he said, "You know what, Reverend?"

Rolf said, "No, what? I kind of looked for you in there with the St. Sures, Elmo."

"Not me," Elmo said. "That babtism won't take. If sprinkling and anointing could wash away your sins, why did John the Babtist lead Jesus Christ into the river and dip him?"

Rolf said, "I thought Jesus was sinless already. What did He have to wash away?"

Elmo said, "It's the principle of the thing. You wasn't getting them people ready to iron, you was giving them the way, the the truth and the life through the blood and body of Christ Jesus. Us Babtists sprinkle clothes before we iron them, but we immerse people in the waters of life."

Rolf said, "Jesus was babtized in the River Jordan, and if I had it handy, I might lead a parade into it myself. But nothing's handier than the Platte here, and this time of year, it's a mile wide and an inch deep."

"Make fun if you like," Elmo said, "but mind my words, it ain't going to take."

Elmo was going to walk off, but Rolf had been wondering about them sleeping arrangements out at the J Bar B himself, and he could see there was sure something wrong with Elmo. He said, "What's the matter with you today, Elmo, did one of them frisky J Bar B horses toss you this morning? Shame on you."

Elmo said, "I quit that job. I'm living with Dickerson Royce again until I make up my mind. I'm thinking of going to be a house painter."

Well there was Rolf's answer; he had himself a scandal in his congregation unless Virginia included Elmo in it when she confessed her sins before babtism. Sammie said, "It's too bad. I never thought of Virginia and Elmo, yet they'd be a good match, it's so sad they got started off wrong."

Rolf said, "There's your answer on immersion. Elmo don't swear and he keeps the Sabbath and so forth, but immersion failed him on Number Seven."

"Do you know anything that will get a lonely young man and woman past the Seventh?" Sammie said.

Rolf shook his head. "It takes faith, fear, and luck, and usually that ain't enough unless somebody blunders along at the right moment," he said. "The carnal sins come so easy to the young, they surely can't be as bad as the old folks say."

10

By the dog days, you wouldn't of knowed that town. The C.B.&Q. was slow getting started, but once it did, things just flew. The worst problem was finding men for the jobs. The Q started building road bed from both ends, laying rail as they went from the other end, and they sent a bridge and building crew in to put up a depot in Mooney, and the crew strang the telegraph wires long before the rails got there. Everybody in Mooney got to be a railroader. You didn't hear nobody talk about the bridge and building crew, no indeedy, it was, "How is the B&B coming with the depot?" Everybody knowed the difference between a passing track and a side track and a rip track, and you heard them talking about spring frogs and angle bars and eighty-five-pound steel and so on, until every night in the saloons it was like a board of directors meeting of the Railroad Trust.

Abe tried to get Elmo to go back to work for Virginia, but Elmo wouldn't; he had opened up to be a house painter, and next thing you knowed, he had to hire a couple of men and buy brushes for them, and he went around complaining about high wages until he sounded just like Cal Venaman. Abe told him, "Elmo, you little Georgia runt, you ain't going to be happy as no house painter, you can't ride a horse painting a house; take an old man's advice and don't fight the best instincts that make you a born horseman and cattleman." Elmo said he reckoned he'd blunder along the way he was, and when he got too low-spirited for prayer to help, he'd get his money out and count it.

Abe got Goodwin Bent Tree and his wife Gert to come over and stay with Virginia and work for her, and run their place by horseback. Virginia learned Gert how to talk English, and Gert learned Virginia how to cook German food, and Goodwin was at it from before daylight until after dark, taking care of two places. He said he prob'ly would be the richest Indian in the happy hunting ground.

They finished the telegraph before the rails got to Mooney, and sent a station agent by the name of Chauncey Gilliam there to take and send messages and hurry along the depot. He was a big fat man that went around with his cap on with Station Master on it, and a pencil stuck under it, and he wouldn't answer if you called him Chauncey, he said he represented the entire C.B.&Q. and owed it to them to be called Mr. Gilliam.

He said there ort to be a solemn dedication when the wires opened, and they tried to get hold of Abe Whipple to send the first message, but Abe was out of town on one of them long mysterious trips of his'n, and they didn't want to use Thad Rust and give him biggety idees, so they decided on Meade Pridhof. He was chairman of the county board, and was named after General George Gordon Meade, and was what you'd call a cattle baron.

They had this celebration, and got Rolf there to say a prayer, and Father Sandoval to bless the wires, and then they asked Meade what he wanted to send to the division superintendent of the Q. Meade printed something out and handed it to Mr. Chauncey Gilliam, and he was about to put on his spectacles and set down to his key and send it, only Tapeworm asked if he could see it first.

Tapeworm said, "Meade, this is a very strange kind of a message to send over the wires, don't you think? WHAT HATH GOD ROTTED, what does it mean?" Meade said he didn't have no idee, but it was the first message ever sent over any telegraph in history. Tapeworm offered to write a new one, and Meade said go ahead, and Tapeworm done it, and Mr. Gilliam set down and sent it. The telegraph office was in a little old tool shed until the depot was built, and you should of heard people cheer when all that clicking started to come out of that shed. It meant a new era for Mooney.

Abe was gone about three days, arriving back on a Sunday afternoon. The reason was, I had got a letter from them fake Indians, and I didn't get more than two or three letters a year, and Abe had brung this one out to me. He didn't come right out and *say* he wanted to read it, but he said it was addressed in a mighty scholarly hand, and it had come all the way from California, and paper as thick as that must be real dear, so finely I let him read it. All it said was:

> *Dear Mr. Heath: A hasty line to warn you that I took pains to inquire about the party we discussed. As you may imagine, I have sources of information of my own. He was in Santa Maria awhile, working on a cow outfit, but got too free with his fists as usual. Last seen in San Bernardino, last heard of saying he was returning to Colorado to get what's coming to him or have somebody's heart's blood. I would take this seriously. Resp. yours, Buffalo Runs.*

"Yes sir, a mighty scholarly Indian," Abe said when he finished reading. "So he's going to get what is coming to him. That could be true at that. I wonder if you take this seriously, Pete."

I said I did, and I said there was a fella in about a week ago that let on that he was just a cowboy out of a job, and he might of fooled some people but he sure didn't fool me, because he looked to me like a railroad detective. I said, "I can't say for sure of course, Abe, but he just looked to me a whole lot like a man I heard of by the name of Perry Brokenauer, who I bet you have heard of too."

Abe said, "You'd lose that bet, who is this Perry Brokenauer?"

I said he was a U.P. detective widely knowed as One Shot Perry, or the terror of train robbers and wreckers and depot-burners. He said what in the hell was the U.P. doing, taking a hand in some other railroad's territory. I said, "Well you know how it is, Abe, the U.P. just about runs Cheyenne, and if anybody with influence in Cheyenne wanted a good detective, why I reckon his first thought would be to ask the U.P."

Abe said, "Well you learn a little every day if you keep your eyes and ears open," and that same day he set out on this long mysterious trip, leaving Thad Rust in charge of law and order meanwhile.

When he got back in the middle of this Sunday afternoon, pretty tired and not in a very good mood, the first thing he heard was that there was a delegation across the crick looking over the old abandoned run-down red-light district, and his old friend Lieutenant Governor C. Julian Wheeler was among them. He went over to see what this delegation was about.

This C. Julian Wheeler was an old-timer who had been a famous pack-train operator and before that a hard-rock driller. He had got into the town-lot business some years ago, and had to run for office to protect his titles, and there wasn't nothing open but the lieutenant governor, so he run for it. He said it was a puny kind of a public office, all you had to do was ask every morning if the governor had woke up alive, and if he had, you could go back to sleep. But he won it and it kind of satisfied him, so he had been lieutenant governor for many a long year.

He was a big man of better than six foot four, about seventy years old, but still a mighty tough old man. He shook hands with Abe and said, "Howdy there, Abe; no use asking you where you been I reckon, we almost had to decide this without you."

Abe said, "It was official business, Goosy, you can bet on that. Decide on what?"

This Goosy nickname went clear back to C. Julian Wheeler's days as a hard-rock driller, when somebody discovered how goosy he was. The goosiest man in the history of Colorado. You could go up behind him and whisper in his ear and then goose him, and he'd yell out whatever you had whispered to him, and jump about a foot, and fling his arms out like a semaphore. The best show in town, only you wanted a fast horse handy when he got control of himself, because he resented being goosed.

Most hard-rock drilling then was by two-men teams taking turns, one holding the star-drill and giving it a quarter-turn after every lick, and the other one swinging the hammer. Goosy was so big he done it all himself, and was paid by the foot, and was making them other teams of two men look bad. So one man by the name of Buck Wycliff, he offered to talk to Goosy about it, and he did.

Goosy said, "The trouble is, there's no hard-rock drillers among you. You want me to slow down, well all I can do is tie one hand behind me, how's that?"

Buck said however he wanted, that was all right with them. Then he happened to think it over, and he said, "Oh hell, how can you hold the drill and swing the hammer both, with one hand tied behind you?"

Goosy said, "Why I hold the drill in my teeth and hit myself on the head with a hammer, that's how you tell a real hard-rock driller," and he pulled Buck's hat down over his eyes and laughed at him. Buck said, "You have a sense of humor I see; well fine, let's keep it all in fun."

The next payday they was all lined up to pick up their pay, and Buck got behind Goosy, and just as Goosy was reaching to pick up his handful of money, Buck goosed him and whispered in his ear, "These sons of bitches are stealing us blind."

Goosy lept a foot in the air, and he throwed his money all over that office, and yelled out, "THESE SONS OF BITCHES ARE STEALING US BLIND." That ended his career as a one-man drilling team.

Buck Wycliff later went to Phoenix and changed his name to Tom Grant, and married the daughter of an Irish cavalryman, and left her quite a bit of money when he was killed in a mine he owned. He let a charge of dynamite go off too soon, and it set off eleven other charges, and about 150 tons of quartz come down on him, and Buck was only about two inches thick in places when they dug him out.

Goosy always give Buck Wycliff credit for him being elected lieutenant governor. He couldn't of made a speech to save his soul, and the first time he got up to try, he just stood there like a deef and dummy. There was one old-time hard-rock driller in the crowd though, and he yelled out, "Hey, Goosy, these sons of bitches are just stealing us blind."

Everybody laughed, but when they was through, old Goosy just said, "Yes they are, they are indeed, that's why I'm running for lieutenant governor. The little man hasn't got a chance, he's stole blind by the banks and trusts and the railroads, and the cattlemen too are stealing him blind, and the mine owners, yes sir, and the horse brokers and wholesale grocers, and I'm against every one of them and for the common man." This was how he came to be called Goosy by his friends.

When Abe asked him, decide what?, Goosy told him that Tapeworm St. Sure had went around and bought up the tax titles to all of the property across the crick except Dick Royce's, and offered to donate it to the state for a normal school, to educate teachers in.

Tapeworm had it all figured out. Where Huey Haffener's old Jackrabbit Club used to stand, there would be an Arts Building with an office for the president and one the teachers could use when they wasn't teaching. Then there would be a patch of pasture he called a Common, and then a Science and Philosophy Building, with a room for a library, and one to store the janitor's tools in, and an auditorium to be called St. Sure Hall, and if there was room, a laboratory. Then another little patch of pasture, and a girls' dormitory with a ten-foot brick fence around it, the Millicent Felton St. Sure Hall, after Tapeworm's late mother.

Tapeworm was stumbling around in the mud with the delegation, chewing on one of them big black crooked cigars. He tucked his thumbs in the pockets of his green vest and said, "How do you like that for push, Abe? I guess somebody here is on his toes, eh? We'll put this town on the map yet."

Abe was just sick at heart about this happening while his back was turned, and it took him a minute or two to get warmed up. He said, "Where was you going to sleep the boy pupils, on pool tables in the back of the saloons, I reckon." Tapeworm said why no, they'd board with the various families around town, so everybody would have a chance to prosper. Well that warmed Abe up fast.

He said, "You mean turn them loose on our own girls, and then pen the girl pupils up so any drunken cowboy don't even have to bother to run them into a corner, all he has to do is climb the wall. Why there'll be so many cowboys going over that brick wall you'll have to put signs on top, In and Out. And what do you plan to use, steamboats or a dam? I been here more years than I care to count, and I never seen a year the crick didn't flood this two or three times a year. You see how the crick fishhooks around this property, why when it rains this is just one huge big vast muddy ocean! We used to keep a raft tied upstream, and let it down slow and careful to pick them poor little scared whores out of the upstairs winders, and now you want to do this to girl college pupils. If you put up a dam, them flood waters have to go somewhere; what are you going to do, steer them down the street and flood the town out? Or maybe it's a steamboat. I'm asking you a practical question, Tapeworm, which will it be, a dam or a steamboat?"

Goosy said, "Nobody told us this Goddamn property floods."

Abe said, "Nobody put blindfolds on you either, any fool could see it floods. This is what you get, Goosy, for not checking with me on a proposition in my jurisdiction. It's damn unfair and I resent it."

Goosy said to Tapeworm, "All right, what's your solution to the flooding question?"

Tapeworm hauled in a deep breath, and he said, "That's a good question, Governor, and I'm glad you brung it up; let's lay our cards on the table, let's have it all out in the open, clear and aboveboard, fair and square, that's how I do business every time, just ask anybody. The reason this property won't flood, by the time the railroad and me get done excavating our various projects, we'll have four thousand cubic yards of good rock and clay fill to dispose of at a fair and reasonable and economical price. I say let the state of Colorado buy that cheap and very high-grade fill and haul it over here and spread it around over this tract. Then I say let her rain, we got this crick whipped, there's no place it can go except where it already is, in its channel. That was a good question, and it shows that Sheriff Abe Whipple is thinking of our civic welfare as usual, and I say in tribute to him, nobody guards our civic welfare like Sheriff Abe Whipple."

Goosy Wheeler got a kind of a glitter in his eye when Tapeworm started talking about them four thousand yards of economical rock and dirt fill that had to be bought, and Abe knowed he was whipped if the court had to rule on that kind of evidence, but it wasn't in that man to quit, he had to give it one more try if it killed him.

He said, "Well, by God, the poor man hasn't got a chance any more. Is this why I cleaned out the den of iniquity that used to be here? We was far better off with a well-run red-light district. You plan to turn a lot of college pupils loose on us, why if they was worth a good Goddamn for anything, their folks would keep them to home to help around the place, instead of exiling them off to some college. Bonfires and weenie roasts and whooping in the streets at all hours, why you're deliberately daring us to pull another Boston tea party here, and throw the whole bunch of them in the crick. College pupils is no earthly use to anybody. They can't carry their liquor, just wipe their nose on the bar towel and they're drunk, and they'll mark a deck of cards on you, and abuse your livery teams, and they don't know the meaning of the word respect for a woman. Goosy, have you ever been around a college? You take your life in your hands."

Goosy said, "I ain't sure, Abe. It seems to me there's one in Denver, I heard of it I think, but I never had no occasion to track it down. There's two new brick buildings going up there. I heard one of them is the John Deere Plow Company, but you can hear anything, people just put out them lies so they can borry money for their building. Maybe one of them is a college."

Abe said, "Goosy, why couldn't we have a state insane asylum, or what's wrong with a good home for the feeble-minded? I tell you this, if you put a college in here, somebody else can have my badge, and I'll organize a band of vigilantes. I'll have Edna sew the armbands tonight; by God, either morality means something or it don't."

Goosy said, "Well damn it all I don't know, it seems to me you people would get together on these things."

"You can't fight progress, Abe," Tapeworm said.

That was about the worst thing he could of said. You mention progress to Abe, and it inspired him as nothing else could, and it sure did then. He said, "You can if you try. What about Dickerson Royce and his property? You've got him right smack in the middle of the pasture next to the girls' dormitory. Now there's a hell of a view for a bunch of college girls, or for Dick either."

"No problem," Tapeworm said. "The state can condemn his property, it's a routine procedure and he'll be paid the fair market price."

"After paying your price to buy it, I see," Abe said. "So you'd take an old retired cowboy's home in his twilight years. This is rich, throwing an old two-gun man out to make room for lawless inconsiderate college kids. Let's go see what Dick has got to say about it."

They slopped through the mud to the old Doll House. Dick was setting on an empty whisky crate, scraping away at a piece of wood with a piece of glass. He wasn't dead drunk by no means, but he was tilting a little. Elmo Huger was laying in a hammock, resting up after a hard week of house painting.

Abe asked him what he was scraping that piece of wood for, and Dick said he was smoothing down a piece of nice second-growth ash for an ax he had found, and Abe said it was too short for an ax handle.

"Not if you like a short one," Dick said, "and I always favor a short ax handle. A short handle and a sharp bit; I could show you some real artistry with an ax if I had this finished, or if you could wait."

Abe said they couldn't wait. He explained this college proposition to Dick, and Dick said, "I've got nothing personal against a college myself. I went to one for a while, when I worked for a bricklayer by the name of Raymond A. Shafer. We built a cow barn so they could raise their own milk. It was a college run by the Seven Day Advents, and they wouldn't let us smoke or even drink coffee, and I found out I could do it if I had to, and I sure did then because there wasn't no other jobs anywhere. Now to choose between a college and an insane asylum, my experience is this, if you've got somebody insane in your family, it's handy to have the asylum in your home town, it saves shipping the body home when they die. I seen that happen to a friend of mine, his wife went insane and it cost him eleven dollars to ship her remains home. I never knowed they had homes for the feeble-minded. I knowed a feeble-minded girl once and she lived in a shack under a railroad bridge, with a purple birthmark on her left tit, the shape of a purple bat with one crippled wing. Jesus, what a girl; I'm glad that's all behind me, they don't have no judgment at all when they're feeble-minded. If you force me to a quick decision, I can only say let's toss a coin. Elmo, have you got a two-bit piece? I say if it's a serious matter, it's too serious for a penny, let's toss a quarter."

"I've got a silver dollar," Elmo said.

"Throw her up," Dick said. "Heads for college, tails against it. I'll go along with the way she falls."

"Fair enough," Goosy Wheeler said. "Let's get her settled."

Tapeworm said, "For God's sake, you can't make such a decision on the flip of a coin. Governor, I appeal to you to stop this farcical outrageous ridiculous farce."

Goosy took off his hat and mopped it out and said why didn't they table it for thirty days while the town got together and decided one way or another. Abe knowed he had this college proposition whipped if they done it that way, and so did Tapeworm, and they argued over that for a while.

Dick Royce said, "It seems to me you're all making up my mind for me, and that won't do. You came here for my decision and by God that's what you're going to get. The way I am, nobody bullies me, old as I am. I live up to what I said and I defy anybody to prove different. Elmo, throw your silver dollar, let's see her spin and twinkle, it's fair to everybody that way."

Elmo throwed it, and it come up tails against a college. Tapeworm said he wouldn't abide by any such farcical decision, and Dick said, "By God, you will, you're on my property, you can send the militia to put me out; why I stood off a squadron of Texas Rangers for thirty hours with only two guns, and the Colorado militia sure don't spook me none."

No question about it, the college question was dead, and it

learned Tapeworm a lesson, just how much power Abe Whipple had in this town. He would have to think of something else to do with his four thousand yards of fill. He said to Abe, he never would of started this if he'd knowed how Abe felt about colleges, he respected Abe's leadership as much as any man in town, only Abe wasn't in town then, and so forth.

"Let this be a lesson to you, Tapeworm," Abe said. "You can buck public opinion only so fur, and a college is a mighty daring proposition for a good steady old-fashioned decent town like Mooney."

They filed across the crick to have a drink together, and some old broken-down cowboy recognized Goosy Wheeler and hollered to him, "Hey, Goosy, these sons of bitches are stealing us blind!" Tapeworm got real upset, not knowing that famous old story, and he hollered out, "Don't pay no attention to that drunkard."

"I ain't a drunkard," the cowboy said, and Goosy hollered out, "Well if you ain't a drunkard by age sixty, you ain't going to make it." Which was another one of his famous philosophies that made him one of the original pioneer politicians of the West.

11

The first blizzard and the first train reached Mooney at the same time that fall, and there they both stood for three days, until the Q had to send a snowplow down the new spur to get the train. It only snowed about six inches, but it blowed so hard there was drifts fifteen feet deep in some places. One of them was right across the front door of Tapeworm's new yella house up on top of the hill, and there was another'n across the back, so he didn't get out for three days neither. He said being penned in the house with them kids give him a new view of the woman's world, and a new respect for Adelaide, and a conviction it was time to start learning Felton to mind before some penitentiary done it for him.

It cleared off then, and was pleasant all through Christmas and the New Year. The train came in regular and went out regular, and when the roads opened up, the Kincaiders began to haul their grain to Tapeworm's elevator so they could get some cash to pay their bills with, and I had this little old patch of barley I'd threshed out, and I thought I'd sell some of it too.

The big surprise was when I teamed in about sixty bushels one day in January, and here Dick Royce was working in the elevator. That's how hard it was to hire men, even Dick could get a job. I told him I wanted him to take his sample from all over the wagon, not just in the worst-looking barley, and he said, "Nobody has to tell me how to take a sample, go on and drive up and let's unload it, keep the procession marching."

A lot of people don't understand how a grain elevator works, but I did and he did. There's pits under the driveway, and you dump your load in them pits. When the elevator gets ready to ship out a carload, you have to remember it's almost always usually the tallest building in town, and the reason for this is, they have to elevate that grain up and fan it and clean it before they let it go down into the railroad car. That's why they have to be so high, to make room for all the machinery it takes to move different kinds of grain, and fan it and sift it and load it.

I drove my wagon up the ramp, and Dick showed me which pit, and I stopped in the right place. He took the tailgate out of the wagon and tripped the lever, and the weight of the wagon let the back end go down and the front end come up, to dump it quick. Your team has to get used to it, but your doubletrees go up with the wagon, so dumping is no strain on them.

When you've dumped your load, they weigh your wagon empty, and then you can go get another load or go put your team up, whichever it is. I went and got another load on that evening yet, but I didn't haul it in until the next day.

It was just colder than the dickens, but the elevator was wide open, so I drove in and stopped on the scales and waited to be weighed and sampled, but Dick didn't come out and neither did anybody else. My team was a little spooky after their experience here yesterday, when the wagon dumped, and I was afraid to just get down and let them stand.

Finely I had to, because nobody came, and I didn't want to just set there and I didn't want to go home. My horses kept shooting their ears forward, and snorting, and kind of stomping their feet, and when I got down off'n the wagon beside them, I thought I could hear somebody yelling.

It seemed to be coming from underneath somewhere, so I lifted up first one hatch door and then the other, and looked down in the pits. There he was at last, clear down in the bottom of the emptiest grain pit, Tapeworm St. Sure himself. He was so cold he could barely croak, and when I throwed him a rope he couldn't hold onto it; I had to pull it back and tie a loop in the end and throw it down again.

He throwed the loop around him and I hauled him up. I had to just let him lay there while I led my team over to where I could tie them up. I toted him into his office where the scale beam was. The fire was out in the stove, but I got it going, and I catched a boy that was going past and sent him for Doc Jerrow and a pint of quickstep, which is what they called rock and rye around there. It was used to bind you up whenever you had the quickstep diarrhea.

We got Tapeworm warmed up between the fire and the rock and rye, and he began to weep and tell us about how he had scolded Dick Royce a little this morning because he was drinking on the job. Dick said, "All right, I quit then."

Tapeworm said, "You can't quit without giving notice." Dick said the hell he couldn't. They argued around about that for a while, and then Tapeworm made the mistake of walking across the ramp next to an open hatch, and Dick hit the trip that dumped the wagons, and Tapeworm was standing at the moment right on the part where the hind wheel sets. It dumped him into the pit about nine in the morning, and here it was one-thirty in the afternoon. That was how Dick quit his job at the elevator.

I helped Tapeworm to his office in the St. Sure Block, or the Tapeworm Building as most people called it, and he sent out for another bottle of quickstep, a quart this time. He got to telling me about his long tiresome experience being snowed in, and he said, "I don't see how you stood it with Felton all the time he was out there with you, that child has got beyond his mother and me; you have to watch him every minute or off he goes, and he'll get lost in a blizzard yet, mark my words. I simply don't see how only eighty acres could contain him."

I told him about old Sam Bass and his hen geese, and I said,

"You get me a good young gander and you can have Sam Bass and a hen goose. They'll remember Felton and he'll sure remember them; if he don't, they'll remind him."

Tapeworm said Mrs. Constable raised geese, and he'd see if he could get a gander from her, and he did that very day. He sent one of his men from the feed yards out in a rig to my place, and I catched old Sam Bass and a gray hen goose, and they was in their new home by evening. Tapeworm had it fenced, and it didn't take them no time at all to learn their new beat.

They remembered Felton too, and he remembered them. I didn't run into Tapeworm for about a month, and when I asked him about the geese, he said it worked out just fine. For a while, they couldn't even send Felton to the store for groceries, the geese wouldn't let him leave.

"I had to walk him to the store myself, and let the geese foller," Tapeworm said, "but after I done that a couple of times, they had the idee. They run him all the way to the store and all the way back. They go to school with him too, and come home and wait until it's time to go after him when school is out. They go to church with us, and wait on the steps until church is over, a mighty fantastical thing. I didn't know geese could be trained."

I said I hadn't either until this woman trained mine, although they'd mother anything when they was in the mood. Tapeworm said, "The only thing, I'd like to change that gander's name, Mr. Heath. Sam Bass don't seem right to me, after all he *is* a goose and he's doing his best within his lights. I'd like to call him Goosy."

I said it was his goose, if it gave him any satisfaction, go ahead. He said, "It does indeed, it gives me a great deal of satisfaction, enormous satisfaction I might say. I try not to harbor a spiteful spirit. I live up to my position in the town as a man should, why I just been elected to the church board, and I donated ten dollars to help buy a new public horse tank. I'm reconciled to the unfortunate nickname I bear. I wish it could be otherwise, but after all it commemorates an important time in my life, a period of agonizing decision so to speak, and I don't mind now that my wife has got used to it, I really don't. But it relieves the tedium to be able to look at that fool gander now, and recall a certain man with a foolisher nickname than mine, yes and by God deserves it too."

He never did forgive the lieutenant governor, and he had to dump all that fill on that swamp free of charge, and finely donate it to Mooney County as a public park, and put up a marble bird bath in the middle of it, the Millicent Felton St. Sure Memorial. But this is jumping several years ahead.

Going back to this blizzard, when it cleared up, Sammie Ledger told Rolf they ought to go out and see how Virginia and Gert got through it. They left the baby with the neighbors and saddled up a couple of horses, and Sammie put on a pair of men's pants and some gloves, and they set out. They found Virginia all alone in the house, not really scared, but getting mighty lonesome.

She burst into tears the minute she seen them. "It's so good to see a human bean again!" she said. "I've got potatoes and beans and bacon, and Goodwin saw to it that there's plenty of firewood. But oh how lonely it can get here!"

She said Gert had went home before the storm to do some things, and would prob'ly be back any day now, but they had their own problems out on their claim. In fact she was sure she was better off than they was, only they had each other and she didn't have nobody.

Sammie throwed Rolf a signal with her eyebrows, and he went out and made himself useful in the barn. Virginia had took good care of things there, the way Goodwin had learned her. She had seven horses in the barn and fifty-five young heifers in a corral where they could get at a haystack feeder, and she'd built a fire in the tank heater every day, to melt the ice so the stock could drink. She had the makings of a cattleman's wife all right.

The minute Rolf was outside, Sammie said, "Virginia, I've got a reputation around here for speaking my mind, not always to advantage either. I'm going to take a chance and do it again. What happened between you and Elmo Huger."

Virginia began to bawl again, and she said, "It was my own fault, I spoiled it all; I'm like my father, I spring back after adversity but sometimes I spring back too fur. I was so bitter when Artie left me, I was so down on marriage and respectability and so on, but I can't tell a minister's wife about it, it's so awful."

"You wouldn't believe some of the things a minister's wife learns against her will," Sammie said.

"Nothing this awful," Virginia said.

"I suppose you mean he was in your bed," Sammie said.

Virginia liked to jump out of her chair. "Well yes, he was, if you put it that way," she said. "But that's not the worst. I made myself a kind of a men's suit, only a man wouldn't wear pants as tight as them, why I could hardly get into them myself."

She told Sammie about making a fool out of herself out at my place. She said, "I don't care, I *do* like a smoke now and then, but I needn't of created such a Paris exhibition out of it. Even today I roll myself a cigarette every now and then, isn't that awful?"

Sammie said she liked to puff a smoke now and then herself, and had only give it up because it didn't become a clergyman's wife, not because it was sinful. She said she didn't think surely Elmo would object if she rolled a smoke in private now and then.

"Maybe not," Virginia said. "Maybe not, but I don't see how I can just throw myself at him. He's too shy to try to make up to me." She blowed her nose a couple of times, and cried some more, and said, "Yes I could throw myself at him, only shy as he is, it'd only scare him off forever."

Sammie said, "He wasn't too shy to get into your bed, and he shan't be too shy to make an honest woman of you. Let Rolf handle it. He knows how to handle these things. Get some clothing together, and I'll have Rolf saddle a horse for you. You're coming into town and stay a few days with us. Rolf will quickly bring that narrow-minded cracker boy to march time."

She left Virginia packing, and went out to the barn to break the news to Rolf, and he said he wasn't going to have nothing to do with it. He said a preacher could barely keep up with the problems people unloaded on him, and the quickest way to get into trouble was volunteer himself before his help was asked, and Sammie might as well learn right now that being the pastor's wife didn't make her the assistant pastor.

When he got the horse saddled, they started out for town, the three of them. It was getting along toward dark, so Rolf took a short-cut he knowed about that didn't drift.

They was about halfway to town when they seen this human body in a snowbank, a big fat man with kind of red whiskers that hadn't been cut in a month, laying on his back. Rolf jumped down and felt of him, and said, "It's unbelievable but he's breathing a little, he's even warm yet. A good strong spark of life in him."

"Who is he?" Sammie said. "I've seen him around town, I think."

"So have I," Rolf said, "but the town is so full of riffraff since the railroad came in, who knows?"

He said they could help him gather a little brush for a fire, and then they better whip it to town and send somebody out to help him, and bring a team and wagon. They raked up enough brush to start a fire, and off they went. Rolf scrounged around for more brush and more brush, to keep the fire going.

Darkness came, and he only hoped the rig would get there pretty soon, because he was out of brush just about.

It didn't come, because when Sammie and Virginia got to town, they didn't know how to describe the short-cut they had took. Thad Rust grumbled some, but he got a wagon out with a four-horse team, and he found some volunteers that didn't realize what they was getting into, and he done the best he could. But he never did get closer than two miles to where Rolf and this big half-froze drunk was.

When Rolf seen the fire was going out, he tried to get this big drunk up on his feet, but it was no good, he couldn't make it. Rolf knowed he had to do something before it got too dark to do anything, so he started dragging this fella around by his feet, letting his head bump over the ground, to start the blood to flowing.

In a little while, this fella began to moan and grumble, and then he wanted to fight, and finely Rolf got him to stand up, and then he wanted to set right down again. "You tarnation fool, you'll only freeze to death," Rolf said.

"I'm so sleepy, so tired, I feel so bad," this drunk said.

"You'll feel a sight worse if you freeze," Rolf said, and so forth, but there's no use talking sense to a drunk, it's water off'n a duck's back. Rolf knowed he had to get under this big fool's hide somehow.

"Aha, so that's it," he said. "I see now, and I'm sure glad to find out the truth about you in time."

The drunk looked up and smiled at him through his whiskers and said, "What *ever* are you talking about? Why I never even *seen* you before."

"No," Rolf said, "but I seen you, and I thought all the time you was a decent upright person, but now the truth comes out; what about your poor mother?"

"What about her?" the drunk said.

"So this is the way you abuse her, is it?" Rolf said. "Well I'm sure glad to find this out. A man that would treat his mother the way you've treated yours, he's too low to hang. He ought to be shot like a chicken-killing dog. No, even that's too good for him. The mother that bore you in pain and blood and suffering, that fed you from her own tender breasts, or maybe you know more about her than I do. Maybe she's not the mother I think she is. Maybe she's just some old rip."

"You dirty son of a bitch," this big drunk said.

Well Rolf seen he had found a way to get to him, so he said, "I apologize. I should of seen that you wouldn't treat a *decent* mother this way. I misjudged you. How did I know what a dirty old sow of a mother you had?"

"You son of a bitch, wait till I get my hands on you," this big drunk said.

He tried to get up, and the first time he didn't make it, but Rolf kept telling him what an old rip and sow and so forth his mother was, and the drunk got up and come at him and chased him until he fell down. He would of went to sleep again where he fell, only Rolf leaned over and slapped him right across the mouth.

"That shows you what I think of your mother," he said. "I'd slap her too if she was here, the old sow. I don't blame you for the disgrace you are to humanity, what can you expect, brought up by an old rip like that?"

The drunk floundered around in the snow and promised to break Rolf's back if it was the last thing he done on earth. He got up and took out after Rolf in the dark, and this time he kept his feet quite a while, but down he went again, out like a light.

Rolf knowed it was going to be tougher this time, and it was. He hauled the drunk up to where he was setting up, and said, "You can't blame your father for doing what he did, how was he to know he wasn't your real father? I guess he was like you, he couldn't stand the sight of the old rip that bore you and didn't even know herself who your father was. So this is why you act like you do, at last I understand, it's your disgraceful old chippy of a mother."

On and on like that all night, because this drunk had been sopping it up for nearly a week, and had stumbled around in the blizzard with a jug getting drunker and drunker, a perfect example of the danger of drinking in a storm. You can't trust your own judgment just when you need it the most.

By daylight he had this drunk pretty well sobered up, and then a couple of Cal Venaman's riders seen them and helped them get back to the J Bar B. This drunk was so mad he wanted to fight all three of them, and all he wanted was to get into town and get his hands on a gun and come back and blow Rolf full of holes.

Only going into town he sobered up the rest of the way, and the Flying V rider that rode in with him kind of helped him along by finishing the job Rolf had started, and this poor big fool was just blubbering when they reached home. Rolf didn't get home until the next day, the day the snowplow reached Mooney, and he stopped to watch it before he went home.

When he got home, here was Minnie Newhouse waiting for him in the parlor, with a cake she'd baked up and some mittens she'd knitted and an old brass and opal ring she said had belonged to her husband and was the only thing of value she owned.

She said, "I can't bake very good or knit very good, Reverend, but I never was a Mary, I ain't even a very good Martha, but Sammie says it's the spirit that counts. All the years I've been full of hate! Now show me how I can serve the Lord to praise Him for this healing."

Rolf shook her hand and throwed himself down in a chair with his feet sprawled, he was so tired. He said, "What got into you all of a sudden, Minnie? I'd be glad to see you in church sometime, but this kind of a fit of conversion, I just wonder what brung it on."

She said, "Oh, Reverend, if you could of seen Buster this

morning, a whole day without a drink and he's still confident, and so am I, he'll never drink again as long as he lives. And all because you showed him the way, the truth and the life. He never was that wicked to me, Reverend, not as bad as you said. He just never did realize, until you showed him how it made his mother look to act the way he did."

Rolf said, "Oh, was that Buster? I sure didn't know it, Minnie, or I never would of talked about you thataway."

"No, I am a sow and a rip, I've been so bitter and full of hate," she said. "Will you try on the mittens and just eat a bite of the cake? I'd feel better. It's the only offering I know how to make."

The mittens fit all right, and he said he always did like a nice heavy cake that stuck to your ribs. He wouldn't of took the ring, only he seen how much it meant to the poor simple woman. He said to Sammie afterward, "I've got to be careful about everything I say. I keep forgetting it ain't just me talking. I wish I hadn't never of took this job. They expect too much."

12

Rolf took down sick that night, a cold that settled into his chest, and by morning he was plumb out of his head. Sammie catched some kid going past the parsonage and sent him at a trot for Dr. Jerrow, and he come to the house and said it was lung fever, and it was up to Rolf to whip it himself since there wasn't no medicine that would touch it.

He set there listening to Rolf rave and yell and holler for a while, and it just made his hair stand on end. He said, "Mrs. Ledger, I've heard some raving in my time, but nothing like this. Ripping people's eyes out with a spoon handle, and live worms crawling out of pork, and something about a young boy, why I hesitate to say what it sounded like to me."

Sammie said, "You needn't hesitate. I've heard it all last night. It's his life in prison coming back to him. I thought he was healed of those memories, and I'm sure he thought so too. But he'll carry it in him forever, I'm afraid."

"I'm afraid so," Doc said. "I'll stop in every now and then, but all you can do is keep him warm and make him drink all the water you can. It won't help if you get sick yourself, you know."

"If I get sick," Sammie said, "it'll be because it's necessary to God's plan for Rolf."

Doc said, "You may be right, but He's prob'ly got a plan for me too, and I have a deep, deep feeling that part of it is to keep you and your husband alive if possible. I'll get someone else to sit with him."

He passed the word, and there wasn't no lack of people to set with Rolf. That's how I come to be in town; I thought to myself, Well me and old Rolf come from the same old lean acres, and I can stand my sentry-go at his bedside too. Me and Thad Rust and Elmo Huger and Buster Newhouse mostly took turns for a few days; in fact if it hadn't been for this emergency, old Buster would prob'ly have fell off'n the wagon. But by the time the strain was over and he could let down and get drunk again, he had lost most of his thirst. That can happen.

Rolf was twelve days in bed, and he missed a Sunday on the job, and Tapeworm volunteered to get up there and lead a sort of a round-robin prayer service. Everybody thought, Well, here we go, another long-winded oration on humility, with lessons from his own life.

But old Tapeworm surprised them. He picked out some hymns he liked himself, "Shall We Gather by the River," "God Will Take Care of You," and "Sweet Bye and Bye." Mable played them without much enthusiasm, she hadn't forgive him for sneaking the C.B.&Q. into town like he done, but he was in one of them moods where he carried all before him. Then he called on Chauncey Gilliam, the new station agent, to lead in prayer, and Mr. Gilliam hauled off and done himself proud, and then Tapeworm read a little three-page lesson he'd wrote up entitled, "Our Duties As Members of a Christian Congregation."

Everything was so well received he mellowed up enough to throw a three hundred-dollar check into the pot, two hundred dollars to pay off the rest of his pledge and one hundred on general principles. There was a meeting of the church board afterward, and it was so worried about Rolf that it raised his salary ten dollars a month if they could raise the extra money. Then Tapeworm made them a proposition he said he'd been working up for quite some time.

He volunteered to build them a new church with his own

money, and when it was finished, they could move into it by only turning the old church over to him, and then pay $710 a year for twenty years and he'd pay the fire insurance. He said, "I'm kind of an expert on building finance, and I've got the crew of skilled expert workmen, and I don't mind raising the capital to do this with. As I said in the little lesson I read this morning, our money works as well as our muscle, and I feel this is my duty to the Christian congregation whose fellowship I share."

He was a hard man to stand against, but they done it; they voted to hold off a decision until they could at least talk it over with Rolf. Tapeworm was disappointed, but he didn't ask for his check back.

But that evening about dark, when Marcus Sippy and his wife went up to pay Tapeworm and his family a social call, they found every door and window barred, and all the lamps blowed out, and Tapeworm standing behind the front door with a double-barreled shotgun on the safety half-cock. He was so scared he was just pale blue in the face.

"Come in quick, Blanche, and you, Marcus, go down and tell Abe Whipple I need protection quick," he said with his teeth just chattering. "I been waiting all day for somebody that could do this for me, but nobody ever comes up here on the hill. I was safer down there in them old rooms in town."

Marcus seen he was really in bad shape, so he said he'd go get Abe. Blanche went in, and seen they was all huddled in the parlor, with Mrs. Tapeworm and the girls crying, and Tapeworm was prowling from winder to winder, peeking out from behind the blinds with that shotgun at the ready. Couple of times, he thought he heard somebody, but it was only them geese patrolling the house and looking for Felton.

Abe had his boots off and his feet to the stove, and he wasn't too happy about a duty call in this weather, but he went. He made Tapeworm go into the kitchen with him to talk. It was pretty cold in there, and Tapeworm's teeth was already clicking, but Abe didn't want to scare the womenfolk any more than they already was.

"Mike Timpke," he said.

"I think so," Tapeworm said. "I didn't get a good look, but it was the right size, and who else would be sneaking around my house like that?"

"Why would he?" Abe said.

Tapeworm got that bullheaded look, and said, "I don't owe him nothing, I never done anything I'm ashamed of or against the law, he is only an extortioner and I'm a taxpayer, entitled to protection of the law."

"Tapeworm, there ain't men enough in Mooney to guard this house if a man wanted to get through bad enough," Abe said. Tapeworm just looked stubborner and chattered his teeth harder. Abe said, "It was something out in California, wasn't it?"

Tapeworm said it wasn't nothing he ever did anywhere, he wasn't ashamed of his record, and so forth. Abe said, "I ain't going to lie to you, Tapeworm, there's real danger to you I'm afeared. When a man as scared of guns as he is will haul off and fire your own silver-mounted shotgun at you, I take it for granted he means business. I wish you'd tell me the whole story."

Tapeworm looked like he was thinking it over, but he shook his head and said, "Sheriff, the past is the past. I'm through scrounging and I'm through being poor and humble, and roving the country looking for a place to bring up my kids. Here I've took root, I'm a changed man, born anew as the Good Book says. I ain't guilty of a thing, not a particle of guilt, and I *will not* supplicate what I'm entitled to by God as a taxpayer!"

"Have it your own way," Abe said. "I'll do the best I can for you. I can't ask Thad to sleep away from his wife another night. I had him out all last night, trying to pot a damn coyote or coon or something that has been in my hen house. I'll spend the night with you."

"I thank you, Sheriff," Tapeworm said. "From the bottom of my heart, I thank you gratefully."

"Now why don't you all go upstairs and build a fire in the stove up there?" Abe said. "You've got a stove up there, haven't you? This misbegotten son of a bitch maybe can blaze away on impulse with a shotgun, but he won't be no dead-eye marksman that could pick you off in the second story. There's your safety, Tapeworm."

"I never thought of that," Tapeworm said.

He took his family upstairs and built a fire in the stove, and pretty soon he tiptoed down and took up an armload of food. "We're having a kind of a picnic," he whispered. "Can I bring you a sandwich? I butchered a hog last week you know, and Adelaide made head cheese. She makes the best head cheese I ever et."

"Well that would be real sociable," Abe said. "You know, Tapeworm, sometimes you're almost human. I'll boil up a pot of coffee, if you want."

"Just don't get shot," Tapeworm said.

"Oh hell, I defy him to shoot me!" Abe said. "Or whip me with his fists. He may be tough, but this is a job with me, I do it for a living."

He banged around among Mrs. Tapeworm's pots until he found the big coffee pot, and he went out on the back porch and found the milk crocks and skimmed off some heavy cream for it. Tapeworm kept a Jersey cow, he said he wouldn't have nothing but a Jersey, or at least a half Jersey and half Shorthorn.

Them geese came running to the door the minute they heard Abe on the dark porch, but he spoke to them and they went away. He had his picnic downstairs, and they had theirs upstairs. Abe's feet hurt, but he kept his boots on because he didn't want to be in his sock feet if he had to run out and take a shot at Mike Timpke.

Along about eleven, Tapeworm and Felton tiptoed down the stairs, and Tapeworm whispered, "Felton has to go to the privy. Will you let him out, and stand guard until he comes back?" Abe said he didn't like this, why didn't the kid use the pot? Tapeworm said, "He's just at that age, he won't use it after the girls have, you know how boys is. Nothing's going to happen to him long as them geese is out there."

Abe took this little varmint by the arm and steered him to the back door. The geese came running, and he said it was almost like human talk, the way they chirruped how glad they was to see Felton. Felton though was pretty tired of them, he just said, "Get out of my way you crazy worthless bastardly fools, oh I'll be glad when I'm big enough to kick the hell out of you!"

Abe heard the door of the privy slam shut after Felton when the cold wind catched it, and after a while, it seemed to him he heard the hinges screek. But Felton didn't come back, and quite a while later he still hadn't come back, and pretty soon Abe realized it was way too long for him to be out there in the privy.

He called out, "Tapeworm!" and Tapeworm answered from the foot of the stairs, "Yes, what's keeping him?" Abe said he didn't know but he meant to find out. He put on his coat and slipped outside. Tapeworm had really put the quality in his new house, a sidewalk all the way to the privy, so Abe didn't have to stumble around none to find his way.

But he did stumble anyway in a few steps, and he knowed what it was the minute his foot hit it, and when he squatted down to feel it in the dark, sure enough it was a goose. He didn't wait to find the other'n. He turned and loped back into the house, yelling, "Tapeworm, Tapeworm, get me a lantern, I think the son of a bitch has got your kid."

That's just what had happened. Tapeworm forgot all about

how scared he was, and charged out with a lantern and a shotgun, and here was both of the geese deader than Emperor Tiberius. Abe took the lantern and picked up sign enough to see what happened.

"He was hiding in the privy himself, Tapeworm," he said, "I reckon just to keep out of the wind. That California weather thins your blood. I reckon he grabbed your little varmint the minute he stepped into the privy, and either tied him up or knocked him out until he could slip outside and take care of the geese. Knocked him out, prob'ly. That fits this skunk, from what we know of him."

"Oh dear God," Adelaide said.

"Then all he had to do was leave Felton in the privy, and go out and deal with them geese one at a time," Abe said. "They wouldn't squawk or honk. They'd only hiss, and stick their necks out, and I can just imagine his strength and quickness, how he'd grab them. He wrung their necks like spring chickens, and I swear I'd of bet that couldn't be done."

He said, "He had a horse well tied over in the corner of the graveyard, and believe me it had to be tied good and hard in weather like this, or it'd pull the bridle and go where it's warm. God knows where they are now. I'll stir out a posse, but only to search the town. I don't want to get on his trail yet. I don't want to crowd him, not when he's got that boy along. The way he seems to hate you, Tapeworm, well I hate to think."

"Oh the monster, the monster," Tapeworm said.

He did get up a posse, but he let Thad ride around and waste time with it in the dark, while he came to stir me out of a nice warm bed in the hay at the livery barn. He told me what had happened, and he said, "It's close to two-thirty in the morning by now. He ain't going to tote this little wildcat boy very far. He can't tame him that long, and it wouldn't suit his plans nohow. He aims to sell this boy back to Tapeworm for cash money, and somehow the sum of twenty-five hundred dollars sticks in my mind. This is the money Virginia couldn't account for, when we was talking about her father's finances. Now I wonder where he'd hide out nearby, while he works out his scheme to deal this kid back for twenty-five hundred dollars?"

I said, "I think you've about got it figgered right, Abe, that's about what he'd do."

Abe said, "Yes, Pete, I reckon I'd of made a good outlaw myself."

I said, "Well you know enough about it now, but it's a young man's game, Abe, and at your age, I just doubt if you've got the desire. It takes desire."

I was going to go on and explain what I meant by desire, but Abe said, "Well one desire I do have is to know where this son of a bitch is, and I just wonder if you're not the man that can tell me. I didn't stir you out of the hay in any such weather to swap philosophy of life with. I'll lay my cards on the table, this man has got a kind of a crooked outlaw mind, and if anybody knows that kind of a mind, it's somebody else with the same crooked outlaw mind. Now you start letting down your milk, before I have to start pulling hard."

I said, "I knowed this was what you was going to expect of me, and I can't help you. Nobody knows how Mike Timpke's crooked outlaw mind works! You might as well ask a mink why it does the things it does, or a civet cat, or a barn owl, or a prairie dog. That's more what he is, a kind of an animal. There's one other man that I think could come closer to guessing him than me."

He said, "Rolf Ledger," and I said yes, his time in the pen and his friendship with all them felons had give him a point of view even I didn't have. Abe said, "Yes, but Rolf's not to be trusted. He'd just pile out of bed and go after this man himself, and either get his neck broke or have a relapse of the lung fever. I guess all we can do is wait."

I said that was how it hit me, and he asked me if Virginia Crawford was still at Rolf's place, and I said I reckoned she was, somebody was taking care of the baby for Sammie, but she sure kept herself out of sight. He said he would have to go over there and break the news to her about her little brother being stole, before she blurted it out to Rolf.

That's what he done, and she seemed to have an uncommon fondness for that little varmint. She cried and everything. She said she'd go over and try to comfort Adelaide, but then she'd come back and help Sammie with the housework as soon as she could be sure she wouldn't give it away about her poor little brother being stole.

That's what she meant to do, poor girl, but on the way up the hill to Tapeworm's place she blundered into Elmo Huger, and all Elmo meant to do was tip his hat down politely and walk on, but he had on this winter cap instead with ear muffs, and he blundered all over the place before he got it off. Then he dropped it in his flustration, and had to stoop and pick it up like a jackass.

"Oh well, I can't do anything right, I always was a fool I reckon," he said.

"Not as big as me," Virginia said, and took out to cry, and he took a step closer to her and said, "No, I'm the biggest fool in the world," and so on, and pretty soon they was hugging and kissing right there in the street, and it was an hour before she remembered about her brother being stole.

After Abe left off pestering me, he went over to see Dick Royce, but Dick was still drunk. He was Abe's first thought, but he knowed Dick had just got his remittance last week and this was his week for good hard serious drinking.

Tapeworm got his letter in the mail that day. Mike had just slipped it under the door of the post office, and at first Thea Bloodgood the postmaster just throwed it away because it didn't have no stamp on it. Then when she heard about Felton being kidnaped, she scrounged around and found it and took it to Tapeworm, and made him pay the postage due, and he opened it and this is what it said:

> *i have got your kid Asa he costs you $2,500 you have Long owed me, wait till i ciper This out how to handle it. My Turn now dont you think.*

No signature. He didn't need to sign it. Tapeworm didn't know Mike Timpke's hand but I did, and it hadn't changed. Tapeworm just cried like a baby and said he'd gladly pay the money if only he could have his youngest little buck lamb back. Abe asked him if he didn't think it was about time for him to start dealing a new hand, and Tapeworm only said it was too late for that, for God's sake not to bother him about anything except getting his baby back.

Abe didn't have the heart to push him. There was them in town like Frank Mueller the butcher, who was a socialist and atheist, who said they bet you could raise a purse to outbid Tapeworm, if this kidnaper would only keep Felton forever.

It come on to snow again a little, and one of the longest weeks in the history of Mooney went past. Then there come this other letter for Tapeworm, mailed from Greeley:

> *Trust the precher rev. Lejer, nobody else. He take $2,500 gold egles and dubble egles and goes NORTH on FLYING V trail to three conttonwoods, a cowpath northwest from there until he sees This Boys cap in the grass. thare will Be a letter under it for him, more orders.*

"But he don't say when to do this," Abe said when Tapeworm showed him the letter. "I reckon he means right away, but Rolf's still pretty weak and it's kind of late in the day. We'll let him start tomorrow."

Tapeworm just looked at him with tears running down his big long lean ugly Indiana face, gulping, "Please? Please? Please?" Abe let out a big long sigh and said, "All right, Rolf wouldn't refuse you and I can't either. I guess this checks the bet to him."

13

Abe went up to break the news to Rolf, and Tapeworm went to break out twenty-five hundred dollars in eagles and double eagles, money he had to kiss good-by forever and not much real hope he'd ever get his kid back either, from the looks of things then.

When Abe got to the parsonage, Rolf had just finished marrying Elmo to Virginia. He grinned all over at Abe and said, "I'm still kind of weak, and this took all the starch out of me. And I don't think Elmo is very sure a Methodist marriage has any holiness in it."

"I'll bet on the marriage," Elmo said. "It's only the babtism that worries me, Reverend. I'm weakening maybe, but I still favor the full drench."

"What is it for heaven's sake?" Virginia said. She could see by Abe's face that this wasn't no offhand social visit.

Abe showed Rolf and them the note, and they read it over Rolf's shoulder. He had to break down and tell Rolf about the kidnaping they had kept from him all this time. Sammie said, "Well, he shan't go, of course. This would mean his death. Why that's a long ride for a well man in this weather."

Rolf said, "Oh pshaw, Sammie, don't take on so, a short day out and a short day back, where do you think this fella is, Cheyenne or someplace? If somebody will saddle me a horse, and you make me some grub to take along, Sammie, why I'll go put on some warmer socks, two pairs."

"You will *not* go out of this house!" Sammie said, and began to cry. "Yesterday was the first day you've been dressed, why it's idiotic!"

Abe said, "Sammie," and when she didn't pay no attention to him he said it again, louder, "Sammie!" Rolf was already trying to get to the bedroom to put them socks on, and she was trying to hold him back, and it was just a regular old chicken fight in that little old parsonage.

Sammie turned around and catched a look in Abe's eye, and she just lost all of her strength, and she let go of Rolf, and he went into the bedroom and put on his socks and an extra wool shirt too. Abe went up to Sammie and took hold of her arm and said, "Sammie, remember what you used to call him when you saw him riding in so tired? Jesus on horseback."

"Well what's that got to do with it, this is crazy, he's a sick man, you fool!" she said.

"Sammie," Abe said, "what does a savior do with his time if he ain't saving somebody? He drawed the duty, that's all; I couldn't stop him and you couldn't stop him, nobody could, it's meant to be this way that's all. So buck up and stop this crying and be of some help to him when he needs the support of a wife."

"Be of some help, I like that," Sammie said. She fished around in her apron until she come up with a handkerchief to wipe her eyes and nose on, and she said, "I'll tell you this, Abe, if Jesus had been a married man there wouldn't be a Christian religion because there wouldn't have been a crucifixion, or a confrontation in the garden with Peter cutting off the soldier's ear—none of that! Only men get into those messes. A wife would have kept Him at home."

"She might of tried," Abe said. "I don't think she'd of had very much luck either."

Rolf kind of flopped around getting up onto his horse, but he handled himself all right after that. He dropped the bag of gold pieces in his pocket and grinned at them kind of peakedly, and said, "It feels like I'm back in the working world again. It's sure different from the usual run of preaching jobs anyhow."

He didn't even kiss Sammie good-by. He just winked at her and turned the horse around and let it break into a nice easy-riding singlefoot. There's no easier gait than a good smooth singlefoot, and this horse could keep it up all day, a big black five-year-old gelding weighing almost 1,050 in working flesh.

"You know we don't even dare foller him, Sammie," Abe said. "It would just mean the death of the kid."

Tapeworm let out a squall at that, but Sammie turned around and looked at him, and she was smiling then, and she said, "Don't lose your courage, for pity's sake! Maybe Abe can't follow him, but Someone will. He'll be back and so will Felton."

"Oh for your faith, oh for your faith," Tapeworm said. "It has been an eternity for Adelaide and me, I've aged a thousand years, I only wish I had your faith."

"You might wish you had her clean conscience too while you're at it," Abe said.

The hardest thing in the world is to wait, and Abe liked to be busy anyway. He went back to have another try at Dick Royce, but Buster Newhouse was down there doing his work of repentance on him, taking care of Dick and trying to wean him from the bottle. He said that Dick had staggered off somewhere carrying that ax he was so fond of with the short handle.

What happened, Dick come to enough to want a drink, and that's just barely coming to, for a man in his condition, and he found out that Buster had poured out all this iniquitous expensive whisky of his, and he was going to take his ax to Buster. Buster told him not to make a lot of scandalous racket, Tapeworm's boy had been kidnaped and this vile evil outlaw kidnaper, Mike Timpke, had said he would only deliver the boy to Rev. Ledger for twenty-five hundred dollars, nobody else.

Dick kind of hauled himself to his feet by holding onto the

wall, and he said, "Why that's the limit, what that Mike Timpke will do, that son of a bitch is just the limit. If he came around here with any of his bold idees, but he knows better; he tried to come at me a few times with them fists of his, but put a gun in his guts or tickle his throat with a knife, and you've got yourself just a whining puppy. Do you know what that whisky cost me, Newhouse? That wasn't cheap whisky. I've seen the stuff you drink, and look at the shape you're in, it's making an old man of you before your time," and so on.

He started out to cut some wood, and that was the last Buster seen of him. They looked around for him some, and at least they didn't find his body, and Abe said he had enough to worry about without trying to find some old drunk like Dickerson Royce.

The train came in late that day, and these two men got off in their nice warm coats and caps and boots, and I happened to be down to the depot because I hadn't seen a train come in yet, not to Mooney anyways, and the minute I seen them I said to myself, Railroad detectives. You get to where you can tell. They went gumshoeing around awhile before they signed into the hotel, but when Abe heard about them and went looking for them, they wasn't in their rooms. Nothing made him as mad as some other kind of a policeman fringing over into his personal jurisdiction, and he was about fit to be tied when they finely come to see him at his house.

They showed him documents to prove they was Perry Brokenauer of the U.P. and Howard C. Kupper of the C.B.&Q. Abe said, "Well, gentlemen, you took your time coming to pay me a little courtesy call, but I reckon you have your reasons. I haven't got a whole hell of a lot of time, because we've got a one-man crime outburst right here in Mooney County, but I'll give you all I've got."

They was both average-size men but a little on the chunky side, maybe forty-five or fifty years old, not the kind you'd want to meet on a dark street either if they happened to be broke. That's where railroad detectives come from, the other side of the law.

Brokenauer did the talking. He said, "I work for the U.P. but I'm here as a courtesy to the Cheyenne Drovers and Mercantile Bank, and Mr. Kupper is here only because his railroad may be involved in a kind of a slanting way. What we're here on of course is the Dickerson Royce mystery."

Abe said, "You're welcome I'm sure, but I don't understand what the mystery is."

Brokenauer said, "Why Royce has been dead for three years, and somebody has been collecting the money he, and only he, was entitled to get from his family in England."

Abe said, "*What?* If he's dead, then who is this marble-headed old raunchy Texas jaybird that has been misappropriating his rightful entitlements? Are you pretty sure of your facts?"

Brokenauer said, "Quite sure. The man who has apparently been collecting Royce's checks is George Hyde Pertwee, also known as Tex Perkins, also known as the Matamoros Kid. Strongly built man, heavy drinker but quite healthy, about seventy years old, usually favors a big steerhorn mustache."

Abe rubbed his face first with one hand and then another, and finely said, "I'll be a son of a bitch, that's the son of a bitch all right. Let me get this straight, if I can get rid of this whistling noise in my ears. First, is this old Texas coot supposed to of murdered this real flesh-and-blood Dickerson Royce?"

Brokenauer said, "No, Royce was murdered all right, but by a vicious wanted criminal by the name of Mike Timpke." Abe kind of grunted and said he'd heard of that one, all right, go on. Brokenauer said, "Royce had accumulated quite a little money, due to the fact that he had been serving a term in prison and couldn't spend his remittance. He talked too much about it, and Timpke, who was in prison at the same time, was waiting for him when he got out. Unfortunately, for Timpke that is, in his last month in prison, Royce had been in correspondence with a mining-stock brokerage house, Horace O. P. Edgeware and Company. I defy you to improve on that name, Sheriff, if you're going to start a nice fat little stock-brokerage swindle. Look at the initials; they spell Hope, how can you beat that?"

Abe's voice was a little thick and trembly when he got it out. He said, "Let's pass over Mr. Horace O. P. Edgeware for the moment, since I reckon you want him for fraud and I may have some idees on that, and go back to—"

Brokenauer cut in, "No, strangely enough he's not wanted for fraud. To everyone's surprise, the mining stock Mr. Edgeware sold to Royce while the latter was in prison has turned out to be worth the price. We have no reason to believe Edgeware believed it was worth anything when he sold it, but once in a million times, these things happen, they hit good ore and the stock is now worth what Royce paid for it."

"I know, twenty-five hundred dollars," Abe said. Brokenauer said that was the exact amount and how did Abe know it? Abe said he'd like to go into that later if they didn't mind.

Brokenauer said, "We haven't had any trace of Edgeware and really aren't interested in him. What happened, it seems, is that Timpke tried to torture Royce by beating him, to make him pay over the twenty-five hundred dollars. Since Royce no longer had it and couldn't persuade Timpke that he didn't, the beating went on and on until Royce was dead."

He said, "At this point, Tex Perkins, as I choose to call him, entered the picture. He found out somehow that Timpke had killed Royce. He decided to assume Royce's identity and go on collecting the remittance. The bank is responsible for having made thirteen quarterly payments of a hundred and twenty dollars each to the wrong man, and the signature does not even match; it was an obvious and embarrassing fraud, the bank slipped up, that's all you can say. They want that money back, but it's quite plain this old two-gun drunkard can never raise it, so they'll want to extradite him to Wyoming and try him."

He said, "In a way, it's a harsh form of justice. Timpke did the killing, but Horace O. P. Edgeware got the twenty-five hundred dollars and Tex Perkins has got the remittance all this time. The one thing that puzzles me is why Timpke never tried to levy on either of the others. He's a brutal, dangerous man. Taking either of those sums of money out from under his nose would be like snatching raw bleeding meat away from a tiger. I would expect him to try, at least."

Abe kind of choked, "He did, on both. Well well, we have certainly got us a situation here—"

Just then he could hear people starting to yell and holler and scream out in the street, and he grabbed up a lantern and went out, and I was there in the crowd, I seen it too, it was really a spectacle to behold.

There was a little moonlight, and first you could see Rolf Ledger coming down the street on his black gelding, just about all in but still able to stay in the saddle by hanging on now and then. A dead game boy. Behind him came Dickerson Royce as we knowed him, or in reality Tex Perkins as he really was, and on behind his saddle was this little varmint of a Felton St. Sure.

I was one of them that got to old Rolf just as he kind of give a little sigh and started to dive out of the saddle onto the frozen ground. We toted him into Abe's house, with him kicking and fighting every step of the way, and hollering, "Oh let me up, I'm all right, I just played out is all, I feel fine except I haven't got my strength back yet."

This so-called Dick Royce come into the house with Felton ahead of him, Dick kicking him in the hind end every other step, and saying, "Go on there, you little hyena, you ungrateful scorpion," and so on, and Felton screaming back, "You son of a bitch, you can't kick me, my papa will have you run out of town, you old sot you." This so-called Dick give him one last kick clear into Abe's living room and halfway across it, and then looked around for some place to put an old dirty frozen gunny sack he was carrying.

He said, "I could sure do with a little snort," and then Brokenauer came up to him and said, "George Hyde Pertwee, alias Tex Perkins, alias the Matamoros Kid, I arrest you on the charge of fraud against the Drovers and Mercantile Bank of Cheyenne, Wyoming, and I warn you that anything you say may be used against you."

This old so-called Dick drawed himself up and said, "What do you mean fraud, what kind of a sandy are you trying to run on a simple innocent Englishman, son of a bitch if this ain't American hospitality for you."

Brokenauer looked at Abe kind of hopeless, and Abe said, "Dick or Tex or whatever your name is, I admire your gall more than your judgment and God knows I'm grateful you brought Rolf and this little hyena in, more grateful for Rolf than for the hyena. But the jig is up, and damned if I for one ain't kind of sorry, except that when I think of you and Mike Timpke working together, why I say anything that happens, you've got it coming."

Dick or whatever his name was said, "Oh what the hell do you mean, working together; I told you before I wouldn't go pardners with that dirty yella cowardly snipe for anything, he only worked for me. If this ain't gratitude for you, what is. I find this poor boy of a preacher on his ass in the snow, and I bring the poor well-meaning boy back to his church and his family and his God, and you ask him yourself if he wouldn't be one dead son of a bitching preacher if I didn't come along then. And I bring back Tapeworm's cub because that's part of the deal, the preacher wouldn't come back without him, and this brat was *more* trouble, he didn't want to leave Mike, and he just about had Mike drove completely crazy with wanting to be his pardner in a train robbing venture. That shows you the kind of a brat he is, he'd go pardners with Mike Timpke.

Well *he's* another one that can kiss my foot too, nobody's going to go pardners with Mike, he tried that famous double-uppercut knockout punch of his on the wrong man this time, yes he did, a left-handed expert with a good sharp short-handled double-bitted ax."

All this time he was shaking that old frozen dirty filthy gunny sack upside down. It let go, and Rolf's eyes bugged out and he puked clear across the room from a setting position. Brokenauer let out a howl like a wolf, and Kupper jumped back against the wall. Abe lept back too, like it was a bushel of rattlesnakes Dick had fetched in, and let out this kind of a womanish screech, "Good God, get that thing out of here!"

It was Mike Timpke's head.

This is the kind of thing you're going to run into every time your town gets too big, and starts attracting all kinds of undesirable people, and Mooney, Colorado, was up to 606 and still growing, so anybody was justified in calling it the coming Chicago of the east slope of the Rockies. The only difference between Chicago, or Denver for that matter, and some crossroads store in Indian Territory is that there's more people, and more of them is bound to be undesirable.

They never did find out exactly what happened. Rolf said he played out and fell off'n his horse and was a good bet to finish his priestly career out of sheer plain ordinary weakness less than five miles from home. Pretty soon though along come Dick Royce, reeling along swinging this ax, and he scolded Rolf for setting there in the snow, a grown man his age, and he asked him if he'd seen a man riding a paint horse and carrying a nasty miserable little kidnaped kid.

Rolf couldn't get through to him, but Dick made him fairly comfortable by chopping some wood and starting a fire for him, and he sure could handle that ax one-handed. Then he went off like he knowed where he was going, and I reckon he did all right.

There was this old shanty that was first a sheep-shearing shed in the long gone forgotten days when there was quite a few sheep here before the Cavalry came and stirred up all this trouble with the Indians, and then Cal Venaman used it for a line camp until he got his cross fences up, and then it kind of went to nothing. According to what they could get out of Felton, this was where him and Mike was denned up, and he was trying to get Mike to play him some two-handed poker instead of the solitaire Mike was playing, and Mike said there wasn't no such thing as two-handed poker, and Felton said let's invent it.

They heard this commotion outside; Dick had tripped over the wire Mike had rigged in the snow to trip anybody that tried to sneak up, and Mike run outside, and Dick said, "You Goddamn ignorant fool, you could trip somebody leaving a wire like that."

Mike let him get to his feet. He seen that Dick didn't have no gun on him, so at last here was his chance to square accounts, or so he thought. He seen the ax, but it didn't rate as a weapon to him, all he had to do was keep an eye on it. He said, "Put up your hands, you old son of a bitch, it's just between you and me and here's where we settle accounts."

Where he made his mistake was in forgetting that Dick was left-handed, and with an ax that sharp it was a fatal one all right. He hit once and catched Dick on the side of his stomach, to double him up and turn him away so he couldn't lean over and get hold of the ax with his right hand. But he could with his left, and with that short true well-balanced second-growth ash handle it whistled through the air and cut Mike's head off.

Felton could just make you sick, telling how Mike stood there with his hands hanging down and the blood squirting out of the top of his neck, and his head laying there licking its lips in the snow, and then he fell over and Dick told Felton to find a gunny sack while he saddled that no-good raw-boned rough-riding camel of a paint horse that Mike favored so much.

"You go plumb to hell, I ain't going back to school," Felton said, and Dick started after him with the ax and chased him around awhile, and Felton seen it wasn't no use, it was go to school or end up in two pieces like Mike, so he screamed out, "I'll quit, lay off, I'll do as you say."

They couldn't shame Dick a bit about cutting that man's head off, nor about misappropriating the money that belonged to the true real Dickerson Royce, in fact he kept on insisting that *he* was Dickerson Royce and he didn't intend to discuss it another minute. Just to mention it to him started him off on one of them long loud indignant tirades of his'n, and he wouldn't stand for being arrested, he'd put on his guns and die with his boots on first, and if this was American hospitality to hell with it, and so on.

The only man that finely could do anything with him was Tapeworm St. Sure. He told Dick he could have the twenty-five hundred in gold he was going to pay the kidnaper, and he could pay off the Drovers and Mercantile Bank of Cheyenne with that, and be a free man. Dick said he didn't give a damn what the bank done, they could cut off his remittance if they liked, he always knowed he could get a job at the elevator here, and an old man didn't need much money.

"I didn't aim to go quite that far, because damn you, you dumped me in my own pit and just about froze me to death. But you did save our darling's life, and I'm a man that pays his debts whether of cash or honor; ask anybody about me and they'll tell you Asa R. St. Sure's word is as good as his bond, so the job is yours."

"Your bond ain't no good either," Dick said, "but just keep that brat kid of yours away from the elevator, and you and me will get along all right."

Perry Brokenauer and Howard C. Kupper got in some rabbit hunting while they was on an expense account, and then they went home, and the town settled down as much as it could with a railroad in it, until the crisis that Abe had always feared. Tapeworm brought up this plan of his to build a new church for the Methodists for only $710 a year for twenty years, and Rolf closed his eyes and prayed in silence a minute and then came out against it.

He knowed his career was in this stack of chips, especially when Tapeworm got wound up and began laying out the entire plan. He said, "Me and Adelaide mean to leave money in our wills when we finely die for a memorial winder, and the kind I've got in mind would look out of place in that old shacky church. It would cost as much as six hundred dollars, maybe more by the time we die."

He said, "What it will be, there'll be the Holy Family when Jesus is a little tad of about eight, not as a babe as He's usually shown, but walking along carrying his top or a dead frog or something beloved of boys, just a typical American boy except for this halo around His head. In the background you'll have Pike's Peak, with the angels playing their harps in clouds over it, and behind the Holy Family there'll be the serpent that tempted Eve, and the four horses of the Apocalypse, and a herd of friendly saved Christian Indians with their hands out for a mission handout. The Savior's life you might say translated to our own familiar Colorado, and underneath that a colored glass sign saying Sacred to the Memory of Asa and Adelaide St. Sure, died secure in the faith, and then the dates."

That purely charmed the board, but Rolf stood up just fine, as polite as could be, never calling Tapeworm anything but Brother Tapeworm, and the madder Tapeworm got, the kinder Rolf was. Tapeworm swore he'd bring in the Episcopals or the Lutherans, or even join up with the Catholics. Rolf said, "Well now, Brother Tapeworm, we'll welcome another house of worship here, indeed we will, and when I think of the expense another church is going to be to you, why I feel like moving that this board rise in a moment of silent tribute. With property so high now, and building costs up, I don't see how you can do it on less than two thousand dollars, and I may say, Brother Tapeworm, that's a mighty handsome donation to some lucky denomination."

That cooled Tapeworm off fast, and he backed up his wheelers and swang his leaders around so to speak, and off he went in the other direction. Like it was him that wanted to preserve that old shacky wooden church all the time. The board hated to miss out on that glass winder, but Rolf led them in prayer and got them safely past it, and called for a motion to adjourn, and Tapeworm himself made it, and got out of there fast.

The way we heard about it, I'd been staying in town and sleeping in the hay at the livery barn ever since Rolf first got sick, and had this tame Indian by the name of Charley Polk taking care of my place. Your house was always a mess after Charley stayed in it awhile, but he took good care of the stock, and he kept the barns clean. We had a checker game going in the harness room of the livery barn when Tapeworm and Alf Constable came in, and they stood around to watch us awhile.

"Maybe the rest of you has got time to spare for the intellectual pursuits of checkers," Tapeworm said, "but time is a specie that depreciates rapidly for me, so I'll bid you all good night and God bless you." He went out, and somebody asked who had raked *him* with the spurs, and Alf told us what a narrow escape Tapeworm had had from talking himself into financing a new church.

I win that game and the next one, making seven games straight, playing the best checkers I'd played since me and Rolf Ledger was kids together working on Everett Beech's Three Dot X in Red Willow County, Nebraska. But that's another story. Anyway I got up from the kag where I was setting, to let somebody else play, and here was Abe Whipple standing there by the door watching us.

Abe throwed me a sign to see him outside, and I went out,

and he asked me if I knowed where Rolf was. I said I didn't, but I heard he'd just rassled with the angel in the form and shape of Tapeworm St. Sure, and he was prob'ly in his church restoring his spirit. I told him about the stained glass winder and so forth, and Abe said, "Well, that's where they separate the men from the boys in the clergy. You got to admit, Pete, that Mammon took a hell of a whipping this night. You come with me, let's go find him."

I said no sir, I wasn't going to no church at this time of night; they was spooky enough by day, but you take a church at night without no lamps lit, and they can just scare the hell out of you. Abe said, "That's what you get by having your conscience so overloaded its wheels are bent." I said my conscience didn't have nothing to do with it, but I went with him anyway, because that's what you generally do when Sheriff Abe Whipple suggests it.

Here was Rolf setting in this rickety old sacred edifice of his that he had just saved by resolute Christian courage and Swede bullheadedness. He was in one of the middle pews on the left, slumped down with his cold hands locked together between his knees and his hat on the pew beside him. He said hidy to us, and Abe moved in and set down beside him and said, "Soaking up a little of the Lord's spirit, are you? At least you saved it, if what I hear is true."

I waited in the aisle, because I didn't want Rolf to get no ideas about me feeling any spiritual need in the middle of the night. Rolf didn't pay no attention to me. He said, "Well I tried, but I come out of it dry this time. Maybe it's too cold in here, or something. I wonder now if I done the right thing. The new church would have a stove in each end."

"And you'd have to cut the firewood for it," Abe said. "You didn't make no mistake, boy. Where did you go when you left the graveyard this afternoon?"

"For a long walk, is all," Rolf said.

"You got a sorely troubled spirit, is that what ails you?" Abe said.

"Just a tired one," Rolf said.

I listened to them jaw back and forth for a while, and this was how I found out they had buried Mike Timpke that afternoon, all by themselves. Abe mostly felt somebody had to dispose of the remains before they got to be a problem, but Rolf done it with all the fixings of the church, including a prayer for mercy for the soul of the departed. Abe said a prayer for Mike Timpke was a pure waste of Rolf's time and the Lord's besides, because if Mike had one single solitary redeeming feature, he had kept it well hid for his whole mortal life.

Rolf said, "I reckon you're right, Abe. Instead of bringing grace to Mike, why the feeling I've got, I just feel unworthier than ever. Not one of them so-called Christians in the congregation turned out to help bury that man, no sir, but you show them a stained-glass winder and a new church, and dad-blamed if they wasn't all on hand for board meeting tonight."

Abe asked him what his point was, and Rolf said, "Why, suppose the Lord Himself had turned up in Mooney today, and had time for only one event, which would He have picked, burying Mike Timpke or arguing in that dad-blamed board meeting about Tapeworm's colored glass winder? You know as well as I do. Inasmuch as ye do to the least of these My brethren, so do ye likewise unto Me."

"Well, Mike was the least all right, no argument about that," Abe said. "You had a full day, Rolf, no argument there either, you buried the one that went astray this afternoon, and ministered to the ninety-and-nine at the board meeting tonight. Well now we're up against another little problem somewhere in between. You're going to have to go out and get a .32 gun away from Delia Woodley some way or other. Ralph came home and started slamming her and the kids around this evening again, and she outs with this little gun and shot him in the arm, and it's only a flesh wound and Ralph won't sign no complaint. Now I know they ain't practicing Methodists, but there ain't a thing a law officer can do about it, so it's up to you to get that gun away from her, nobody but you."

"No," Rolf said. "I'm giving up the ministry, Abe. I can't stand no more of it. Abe, when I looked at Mike Timpke laying dead in his coffin there, I knowed that I came *that* close to ending the same way, why only the luck of the draw kept it from being *him* praying over *me*, and if you don't believe me, ask Pete Heath there."

I said, "Don't drag me into your arguments, Rolf. The way you feel now, I feel all the time. This may be a holy place to you, but it's just plain spooky to me."

Rolf got a kind of a gleam in his eye, like here came another tussle with Pete Heath's rebellious spirit, but he looked over at Abe and said, "Nothing doing. I knowed I was ready to chuck in my hand at the board meeting tonight, and the only reason I never done it, I hadn't talked to my wife yet. But I'm through with the ministry. Through!"

Abe yawned and belched and said, "Well all right, if you're that dead sure, only put it off until tomorrow, and go out and get that gun away from Delia tonight. You know what's going to happen if you don't."

"No," Rolf said.

Abe acted like he hadn't even heard him. He said, "Delia never has stood up to Ralph before. If she'd only quit on this one pot, she's got him good and scared. But she's such a mousy little thing, and she's got five bullets left, and I figger in an hour or two she's going to start brooding over all the times Ralph slammed her around before, and her moment of victory is going to get out of hand."

"Yes," Rolf said, "that's about how it'll work out, I reckon. You can tromp on a woman like Delia only so long, and then watch out."

"That's right," Abe said, and yawned again. "Watch out."

He didn't say no more, and Rolf set there a minute and then

started arguing with him. He said, "Why should it be my put-in? Go down there in the middle of the night and wake them up, a perfect stranger butting into a private family quarrel, just tell me this, why should I?"

"Then who should?" Abe said. "Not me! I went as fur as I could, or even further. Tell me who else I can go to. Tell me! Or let her go ahead and shoot him through the heart, that's what she'll do next time, is that what you want? S'pose she does that, who's going to bury Ralph tomorrow? And who's going to comfort the widow in jail when she realizes what she's done, she's orphaned her own kids is what, and who's going to cherish the orphans and shelter them from the storm? Not you, you say. Maybe so, but I tell you this, Rolf, when a woman shoots her own husband, that marriage is in clear and present danger as Jimmy Drummond says. Tomorrow will be too late. Who else but you has got a license to butt in? That's my whole point, do it before you quit ministering, Rolf!"

Rolf kind of whimpered, "It's rough country and no water, coming between a husband and a wife, and you tell me yourself it was only a flesh wound. I never had no such miserable chores when I rode for a living!"

"You're still riding for a living," Abe said. He put his hand on Rolf's arm. "Figger it this way, your flock ain't sheep so you ain't really a shepherd. Your flock is wild untamed longhorns, and you ride for a living same as usual."

He didn't crowd Rolf no more, just set there and snuffled through his mustache, and shivered now and then, and finely Rolf stood up and picked up his hat and said, "All right, one last time, and if Delia shoots me instead of her no-account husband, who comforts *my* widow and orphan?"

"It's the luck of the draw, you said so yourself," Abe said. "I'm just as sorry as I can be, Rolf, but you see, life has checked the bet to you again."

"For the last time," Rolf said.

He got up and went out, not even looking at me, and we

walked over to his house, and he went in and told Sammie he had one more parish call to make before bedtime. Abe saddled up a horse for him, that same nice big strong black singlefooter, but Rolf still had all his good habits, and he checked the cinches and the bridle himself before he clumb up into the saddle.

"Still riding for a living," he said, "only not my own. For somebody else's every time, and I'm plumb tired of it. So put that in your pipe and smoke it, Abe!"

He rode off without looking at me, and I was past the crisis again, and wouldn't have him pushing me to join his damn church. Abe and me stood there and watched him plod off into the darkness, kind of slouched over in the saddle like a tired old cowboy, steering his horse by weight and by jawing at it, instead of using the reins.

"Where do you think you're going, you hammer-headed old fool horse," he said. "Get over there, you old fool, watch where you put your feet, you're clumsy as a cow."

And so on. I said, "I reckon he means it this time, Abe, and I don't blame him. There can't be no harder horribler job in the world than his."

"Sure he means it," Abe said, "but wait until tomorrow. There—there—do you see that, Pete—do you see that?"

Rolf had rode out from under the shadder of the trees. There wasn't no moon, but the sky was just frosted over with stars, so many it was like they was stuck on top of each other. Old Rolf kind of checked that big black horse of his in for a second or two, and looked up. He kind of shook himself, like a man will, to loosen up his muscles before he picks up a load that's all he can tote. Or more than he can, unless he gets help from somewhere.

Rolf squared his shoulders and stopped slounching, and just as he went out of sight, Abe said, "Jesus on horseback. The heavens declare the glory of God, and the firmament showeth His handiwork," and before I knowed what I was doing, I had said, "Amen!" It sure was a spooky feeling.